KU-054-598

PENGUIN MODERN CLASSICS

VOSS

Patrick White's great-grandfather went from England to
Australia in 1826, and the family has remained there. Mr
White was born in England in 1912, when his parents
were in Europe for two years; at six months he was taken
back to Australia, where his father owned a sheep station.
When he was thirteen he was sent to school in England,
to Cheltenham, 'where, it was understood, the climate
would be temperate and a colonial acceptable'. Neither
proved true, and after four rather miserable years there
he went to King's College, Cambridge, where he special-
ized in languages. After leaving the university he settled
in London, determined to become a writer. His novel
Happy Valley was published in 1939; *The Living and the
Dead* in 1941. Then, during the war, he was an R.A.F.
Intelligence officer in the Midddle East and Greece.

His other books are *The Aunt's Story* (1948), *The Tree
of Man* (1955), *Riders in the Chariot* (1961), *The Burnt
Ones* (1964), *The Solid Mandala* (1966), *The Vivisector*
(1970), and *The Eye of the Storm* (1973). Many of these
have been published in Penguins. Since 1948 Patrick
White has lived in Australia. He was awarded the 1973
Nobel Prize for Literature. His latest book is *The Cockatoos* (1974), a collection of short stories.

PATRICK WHITE

VOSS

PENGUIN BOOKS

Penguin Books Ltd, Harmondsworth, Middlesex, England
Penguin Books, 625 Madison Avenue, New York, New York 10022, U.S.A.
Penguin Books Australia Ltd, Ringwood, Victoria, Australia
Penguin Books Canada Ltd, 2801 John Street, Markham, Ontario, Canada L3R 1B4
Penguin Books (N.Z.) Ltd, 182–190 Wairau Road, Auckland 10, New Zealand

—

First published by Eyre & Spottiswoode 1957
Published in Penguin Books 1960
Reprinted 1962, 1966, 1968, 1970, 1971, 1972, 1973, 1975, 1976, 1977, 1979, 1980

—

Copyright © Patrick White, 1957
All rights reserved

—

Made and printed in Great Britain by
Hazell Watson & Viney Ltd, Aylesbury, Bucks
Set in Linotype Granjon

Except in the United States of America,
this book is sold subject to the condition
that it shall not, by way of trade or otherwise,
be lent, re-sold, hired out, or otherwise circulated
without the publisher's prior consent in any form of
binding or cover other than that in which it is
published and without a similar condition
including this condition being imposed
on the subsequent purchaser

FOR
MARIE D'ESTOURNELLES
DE CONSTANT

1

'THERE is a man here, miss, asking for your uncle,' said Rose. And stood breathing.

'What man?' asked the young woman, who was engaged upon some embroidery of a difficult nature, at which she was now forced to look more closely, holding the little frame to the light. 'Or is it perhaps a gentleman?'

'I do not know,' said the servant. 'It is a kind of foreign man.'

Something had made this woman monotonous. Her big breasts moved dully as she spoke, or she would stand, and the weight of her silences impressed itself on strangers. If the more sensitive amongst those she served or addressed failed to look at Rose, it was because her manner seemed to accuse the conscience, or it could have been, more simply, that they were embarrassed by her harelip.

'A foreigner?' said her mistress, and her Sunday dress sighed. 'It can only be the German.'

It was now the young woman's duty to give some order. In the end she would perform that duty with authority and distinction, but she did always hesitate at first. She would seldom have come out of herself for choice, for she was happiest shut with her own thoughts, and such was the texture of her marble, few people ever guessed at these.

'What will I do with this German gentleman?' asked the hare-lip, which moved most fearfully.

The flawless girl did not notice, however. She had been brought up with care, and preferred, also, to avoid an expression of longing in her servant's eyes. She frowned rather formally.

'We cannot expect Uncle for at least another hour,' she said. 'I doubt whether they have reached the sermon.'

That strange, foreign men should come on a Sunday when she herself had ventured on a headache was quite exasperating.

'I can put the gentleman in your uncle's study room. No one ever goes in there,' said the servant. 'Except, there is no knowing, he could lay his hands on something.'

7

The squat woman's flat face suggested it had experienced, and understood, all manner of dishonesty, but was in the habit of contemplating such behaviour from a dull distance since she had become the slave of virtue.

'No, Rose,' said the girl, her mistress, so firmly at last that the toe of her shoe thumped against her petticoats, set them sawing at one another, and the stiff skirt, of a deep, lustrous blue, added several syllables to her decision. 'There is no avoiding it, I can see. It would not be civil. You will show the gentleman in here.'

'If it is right,' her thoughtful servant dared to suggest.

The young woman, who was most conscientious in her needle-work, noticed how she had overstitched. Oh, dear.

'And, Rose,' she added, by now completely her own mistress, 'after we have talked for a little, neither too long, nor too short, but decently, you will bring in the port wine, and some of my aunt's biscuits that she made yesterday, which are on the top shelf. Not the best port, but the second best. It is said to be quite nice. But make sure, Rose, that you do not wait too long, or the refreshment will arrive with my uncle and aunt, and it would be too confusing to have so much happen at once.'

'Yes, miss,' said Rose, whose business it was not. 'Will you be taking a glass yourself?'

'You may bring one,' said the young woman. 'I shall try a biscuit, but whether I shall join him in the wine I cannot yet say.'

The servant's skirts were already in motion. She wore a dress of brown stuff, that was most marvellously suited to her squat body.

'Oh, and Rose,' called the young woman, 'do not forget to announce Mr Voss on showing him into the room.'

'Mr Voss? That is the gentleman's name?'

'If it is the German,' replied the girl, who was left to consider her embroidery frame.

The room in which she sat was rather large, darkened by the furniture, of which the masses of mellow wood tended to daunt intruding light, although here and there, the surface of a striped mirror, or beaded stool, or some object in cut glass bred triumphantly with the lustier of those beams which entered through the half-closed shutters. It was one of the first sultry days of spring, and the young woman was dabbing at her upper lip with a handkerchief as she waited. Her dress, of that very deep blue, was almost swallowed up, all but a smoulder, and where the neat cuffs divided it from her wrists, and at the collar, which gave freedom to her handsome throat. Her face, it had been said, was long-shaped. Whether she was beautiful it was not at first possible to tell, although she should, and could have been.

The young woman, whose name was Laura Trevelyan, began to feel very hot as she listened for sounds of approach. She did not appear to listen, however, just as she did not appear nervous; she never did.

The keenest torment or exhilaration was, in fact, the most private. Like her recent decision that she could not remain a convinced believer in that God in whose benevolence and power she had received most earnest instruction from a succession of governesses and her good aunt. How her defection had come about was problematic, unless it was by some obscure action of antennae, for she spoke to nobody who was not ignorant, and innocent, and kind. Yet, here she was become what, she suspected, might be called a rationalist. If she had been less proud, she might have been more afraid. Certainly she had not slept for several nights before accepting that decision which had been in the making, she realized, several years. Already as a little girl she had been softly sceptical, perhaps out of boredom; she was suffocated by the fuzz of faith. She did believe, however, most palpably, in wood, with the reflections in it, and in clear daylight, and in water. She would work fanatically at some mathematical problem, even now, just for the excitement of it, to solve and know. She had read a great deal out of such books as had come her way in that remote colony, until her mind seemed to be complete. There was in consequence no necessity to duplicate her own image, unless in glass, as now, in the blurry mirror of the big, darkish room. Yet, in spite of this admirable self-sufficiency, she might have elected to share her experience with some similar mind, if such a mind had offered. But there was no evidence of intellectual kinship in any of her small circle of acquaintance, certainly not in her own family, neither in her uncle, a merchant of great material kindness, but above all a man, nor her Aunt Emmy, who had upholstered all hardnesses till she could sit on them in comfort, nor her Cousin Belle, with whom she did share some secrets, but of a hilarious nature, for Belle was still young. So really there was nobody, and in the absence of a rescue party she had to be strong.

Absorbed in the depths of the mirror and her own predicament, Laura Trevelyan forgot for these few flashing instants her uncle's caller, and was at once embarrassed when Rose Portion, the emancipist servant, stood inside the room, and said:

'Mr Voss, miss.'

And closed the door.

Sometimes, stranded with strangers, the composed young woman's lovely throat would contract. Overcome by breathlessness, she would suspect her own words of preparing to lurch out and surprise, if not actually alarm. Then they would not. To strangers she was equable, sometimes even awful.

'You must excuse my uncle,' Laura Trevelyan said. 'He is still at Church.'

Her full skirt was moving across the carpet, sounding with petticoats, and she gave her cool hand, which he had to take, but did so hotly, rather roughly.

'I will come later. In perhaps one hour,' said the thick voice of the thin man, who was distressed by the furniture.

'It will not be so long,' answered the young woman, 'and I know my aunt would expect me to make you comfortable during that short time.'

She was the expert mistress of trivialities.

The distressed German was rubbing the pocket of his jacket with one hand. It made a noisy, rough sound.

He began to mumble.

'Thank you,' he said.

But grumblingly. It was that blundering, thick accent, at which she had to smile, as superior, though kind, beings did.

'And after the journey in the heat,' she said with that same ease, 'you will want to rest. And your horse. I must send the man round.'

'I came on foot,' replied the German, who was now caught.

'From Sydney!' she said.

'It is four kilometres, at most, and perhaps one quarter.'

'But monotonous.'

'I am at home,' he said. 'It is like the poor parts of Germany. Sandy. It could be the Mark Brandenburg.'

'I was never in Germany,' said the firm young woman. 'But I find the road to Sydney monotonous, even from a carriage.'

'Do you go much into your country?' asked Voss, who had found some conviction to lean upon.

'Not really. Not often,' said Laura Trevelyan. 'We drive out sometimes, for picnics, you know. Or we ride out on horseback. We will spend a few days with friends, on a property. A week in the country makes a change, but I am always happy to return to this house.'

'A pity that you huddle,' said the German. 'Your country is of great subtlety.'

With rough persistence he accused her of the superficiality which she herself suspected. At times she could hear her own voice. She was also afraid of the country which, for lack of any other, she supposed was hers. But this fear, like certain dreams, was something to which she would never have admitted.

'Oh, I know I am ignorant,' Laura Trevelyan laughed. 'Women are, and men invariably make it clear to them.'

She was giving him an opportunity.

But the German did not take it. Unlike other men, English officers stationed there, or young landowners coming coltish from the country for the practical purpose of finding a wife, he did not consider himself under obligation to laugh. Or perhaps it was not funny.

Laura Trevelyan was sorry for the German's ragged beard, but it was of a good black colour, rather coarse.

'I do not always understand very well,' he said. 'Not all things.'

He was either tired, or continued to be angry over some experience, or phrase, or perhaps only the room, which certainly gave no quarter to strangers; it was one of the rich, relentless rooms, although it had never been intended so.

'Is it long since you arrived in the Colony?' asked Laura Trevelyan, in a flat, established voice.

'Two years and four months,' said Voss.

He had followed suit when she sat down. They were in almost identical positions, on similar chairs, on either side of the generous window. They were now what is called *comfortable*. Only the cloth was taut on the man's bony knees. The young woman noticed thoughtfully that his heels had frayed the ends of his trousers by walking on them.

'I have now been here so long,' she said almost dreamily, 'I do not attempt to count the years. Certainly not the months.'

'You were not born here, Miss Bonner?' asked the German. It had begun to come more easily to him.

'Trevelyan,' she said. 'My mother was Mrs Bonner's sister.'

'So!' he said. 'The niece.'

Unlocking his bony hands, because the niece was also, then, something of a stranger.

'My mother and father are dead. I was born in England. I came here when' – she coughed – 'when I was so young I cannot remember. Oh, I am able to remember some things, of course, but childish ones.'

This weakness in the young woman gave the man back his strength. He settled deeper in his chair.

So the light began to flow into the high room, and the sound of doves, and the intimate hum of insects. Then, too, the squat maid had returned, bearing a tray of wine and biscuits; the noise itself was a distraction, the breathing of a third person, before the trembling wine subsided in its decanter into a steady jewel.

Order does prevail.

Not even the presence of the shabby stranger, with his noticeable cheekbones and over-large finger-joints, could destroy the impression of tranquillity, though of course, the young woman realized, it is always like this in houses on Sunday mornings while others are at Church. It was therefore but a transitory comfort. Voices, if only in whispers, must break in. Already she herself was threatening to disintegrate into the voices of the past. The rather thin, grey voice of the mother, to which she had never succeeded in attaching a body. She is going, they said, the kind voices that close the lid and arrange the future. Going, but where? It was cold upon the stairs, going down, down, and glittering with beeswax, until the door opened on the morning, and steps that Kate had scoured with holystone. Poor, poor little girl. She warmed at pity, and on other voices, other kisses, some of the latter of the moist kind. Often the Captain would lock her in his greatcoat, so that she was almost part of him – was it his heart or his supper? – as he gave orders and told tales by turns; all smelled of salt and men. The little girl was falling in love with an immensity of stars, or the warmth of his rough coat, or sleep. How the rigging rocked, and furry stars. Sleeping and waking, opening and closing, suns and moons, so it goes. I am your Aunt Emmy, and this is your new home, poor dear, in New South Wales, I trust that you will be happy, Laura, in this room, we chose the curtains of a lighter stuff thinking it might brighten, said the comfortable voice, which smelled beneath the bonnet of a nice carnation soap. It did appear momentarily that permanence can be achieved.

'I beg your pardon,' said Laura Trevelyan, bending forward and twisting the stopper in the long neck of the decanter, glass or words grated. 'I am forgetting to offer you wine.'

Then the visitor moved protestingly in his chair, as if he should refuse what he would have liked to accept, but said:

'*Danke*. No. A little, perhaps. Yes, a half.'

Sitting forward to receive the full, shining glass, from which he slopped a drop, that Miss Trevelyan did not, of course, notice.

His throat was suddenly swelling with wine and distance, for he was rather given to melancholy at the highest pitch of pleasure, and would at times even encourage a struggle, so that he might watch. So the past now swelled in distorting bubbles, like the windows of the warehouse in which his father, an old man, gave orders to apprentices and clerks, and the sweet smell of blond timber suggested all safety and virtue. Nothing could be safer than that gabled town, from which he would escape in all weathers, at night also, to tramp across the heath, running almost, bursting his lungs, while deformed trees in places snatched at his clothes, the low, wind-combed trees, almost invariably under a thin moon, and other traps, in the shape of stretches of unsuspected bog, drew black, sucking sounds from his boots. During the *Semester*, however, he had a reputation for bristling correctness, as befitted the great surgeon it was intended he should become, until suddenly revolted by the palpitating bodies of men. Then it was learnt he would become a great botanist instead. He did study inordinately, and was fascinated in particular by a species of lily which swallows flies. With such instinctive neatness and cleanliness to dispose of those detestable pests. Amongst the few friends he had, his obsession became a joke. He was annoyed at first, but decided to take it in good part; to be misunderstood can be desirable. There were certain books, for instance. He would interrupt his study of which, and sit in the silence of his square room, biting his nails by candle-light. The still white world was flat as a handkerchief at that hour, and almost as manageable. Finally, he knew he must tread with his boot upon the trusting face of the old man, his father. He was forced to many measures of brutality in defence of himself. And his mother crying beside the stove, of which the green tiles were decorated with lions in relief. Then, when he had wrung freedom out of his protesting parents, and the old people were giving him little parcels for the journey, not so much as presents as in reproach, and the green forests of Germany had begun to flow, and yellow plains unroll, he did wonder at the purpose and nature of that freedom. Such neat trees lined the roads. He was wondering still when he stood on the underside of the world, and his boots sank into the same, gritty, sterile sand to which he used to escape across the *Heide*. But the purpose and nature are never clearly revealed. Human behaviour is a series of lunges, of which, it is sometimes sensed, the direction is inevitable.

Fetched up at this point, Voss made a polite gesture that he had learnt somewhere, cleared his throat, and said gravely to Miss Trevelyan:

'Your health.'

She drew down her mouth then, with some almost bitter pleasure, again twisted the stopper in the neck of the decanter, and drank to him, for formality's sake, a sip of shining wine.

Remembering her aunt, she laughed.

'For my aunt,' she said, 'all things that *should* be done, *must* be done. Even so, she does not approve of wine for girls.'

He did not understand. But she was beautiful, he saw.

She knew she was beautiful, but fleetingly, in certain lights, at certain moments; at other times she had a long, unyielding face.

'It is fine here,' said Voss at last, turning in his chair with the greater ease that wine gives, looking about, through the half-open shutters, beyond which leaves played, and birds, and light, but always returning to the predominant room.

Here, much was unnecessary. Such beautiful women were in no way necessary to him, he considered, watching her neck. He saw his own room, himself lying on the iron bed. Sometimes he would be visited by a sense of almost intolerable beauty, but never did such experience crystallize in objective visions. Nor did he regret it, as he lay beneath his pale eyelids, reserved for a peculiar destiny. He was sufficient in himself.

'You must see the garden,' Miss Trevelyan was saying. 'Uncle has made it his hobby. Even at the Botanic Gardens I doubt there is such a collection of shrubs.'

They will come, she told herself, soon, but not soon enough. Oh dear, she was tired of this enclosed man.

The young woman began to wriggle her ankle. The light was ironical in her silk dress. Her small waist was perfect. Yet, she resented the attitude she had begun to assume, and liked to think it had been forced upon her. He is to blame, she said, he is one of the superior ones, even though pitiable, those trousers that he has trodden on. And for her entertainment, she began to compose phrases, between kind and cold, with which she would meet a proposal from the German. Laura Trevelyan had received two proposals, one from a merchant before he sailed for Home, and one from a grazier of some substance – that is to say, she had *almost* received, for neither of those gentlemen had quite dared. So she was contemptuous of men, and her Aunt Emmy feared that she was cold.

Just then there was a crunching of soft stones, and a sound of leather and a smell of hot horse, followed by the terrible, distant voices of people who have not yet made their entrance.

'There they are,' said Laura Trevelyan, holding up her hand. At that moment she was really very pretty.

'*Ach,*' protested Voss. '*Wirklich?*'

He was again distressed.

'You do not attend Church?' he asked.

'I have been suffering from a slight headache,' she replied, looking down at some crumbs clinging to her skirt, from a biscuit at which she had nibbled, in deference to a guest.

Why should he ask this? She disliked the scraggy man.

15

But the others were all crowding in, resuming possession. Such solid stone houses, which seem to encourage brooding, through which thoughts slip with the ease of a shadow, yet in which silence assumes a sculptural shape, will rally surprisingly, even cruelly to the owner-voices, making it clear that all the time their rooms have belonged not to the dreamers, but to the children of light, who march in, and throw the shutters right back.

'Mr Voss, is it? I am truly most interested to make your acquaintance.'

It was Aunt Emmy, in rather a nice grey pelisse from the last consignment.

'Voss, eh? High time,' Uncle said, who was jingling his money and his keys. 'We had all but given you up.'

'Voss! Well, I am blowed! When did you return to town, you disreputable object?' asked Lieutenant Radclyffe, who was 'Tom' to Belle Bonner.

Belle herself, on account of her youth, had not yet been encouraged to take much part in conversation when company was present, but could smile most beautifully and candidly, which she now did.

They were all a little out of breath from precipitate arrival, the women untying their bonnet strings and looking for reflections of themselves, the men aware of some joke that only the established, the sleek, or the ordinary may enjoy.

And Voss was a bit of a scarecrow.

He stood there moving woodenly at the hips, Laura Trevelyan noticed. She personally could not assist. She had withdrawn. But nobody can help, she already knew.

'I came here unfortunately some considerable time in advance,' the German began in a reckless lather of words, 'not taking into account your natural Sunday habits, Mr Bonner, with the result that I have spent the patience of poor Miss Trevelyan for the last three-quarters of an hour, who has been so good as to entertain me during that period.'

'That would have been a pleasure for her,' said Aunt Emmy, frowning and kissing her niece on the brow. 'My poor Laura, how is the head?'

But the young woman brushed aside all questions with her hand, and went and stood where she might be forgotten.

Aunt Emmy's thoughts would swim close to the surface, for which reason they were almost always visible. Now it was obvious that pity for one who had been born a foreigner did not exceed concern at her niece's indiscretion in offering, perhaps, the best port wine.

So Mrs Bonner was moved to tidy up the tray, although decanters will not tell.

'Now that you have come, Voss,' said her husband, who was inclined to jingle his money, for fear that he might find himself still apprenticed to the past; 'now that you are here, we shall be able to put our heads together over many little details. It goes without saying I will fit you out with any goods in my own particular line, but shall also be pleased to advise you on the purchase of other commodities – victuals, for instance, Voss – do not attempt to patronize any but the houses I recommend. I do not suggest that dishonesty is rife; rather, you will understand, that business is keen. Then, I have already approached the owners of a vessel that might carry your party as far, at least, as Newcastle. Yes. You will gather from all this that the subject of your welfare is never far distant from my mind. No doubt you will have been giving your own earnest consideration to many of these matters, although you have not seen fit to inform me. Last Friday, by the way, I received a letter from Mr Sanderson, who is preparing to entertain you on the first stage of your journey. Oh, there are many things. We must, indeed, tear ourselves away from these ladies, and,' said the draper, dreadfully clearing his throat, 'talk.'

But not yet. The two men implored not to be surrendered so mercilessly to the judgement of each other's eyes. They were two blue-eyed men, of a different blue. Voss would frequently be lost to sight in his, as birds are in sky. But Mr Bonner would never stray far beyond familiar objects. His feet were on the earth.

'I must say I am glad to see you again, old Voss,' said Lieutenant Radclyffe, with no evident signs of pleasure.

He was a third blue, of a rudimentary handsomeness. He would thicken later into more or less the same shape as the man who was to become his father-in-law, which perhaps was the reason why Belle Bonner loved her Tom.

'Where have you been?' the Lieutenant pursued his unimportant acquaintance. 'Lost in the bush?' He did not expect, nor listen to answers. 'Are you back with poor Topp? I hear that all his thoughts are for a certain young lady who is taking lessons in the flute.'

'A peculiar, and not very suitable instrument for a young girl,' Mrs Bonner was compelled to observe. 'If difference is desired – and there are some who are averse to the piano – there is always the harp.'

'Yes, I am again lodging in the house of poor Topp,' said Voss, who was by this time almost crazed by people. 'I was not lost. Although I have been in the bush; that is, in the more populous part of it. I have lately made a journey to the North Coast, gathering some interesting plant and insect specimens, and to Moreton Bay, where I have spent a few weeks with the Moravian Brothers.'

All this time Voss was standing his ground. He was, indeed, swaying a little, but the frayed ends of his trouser legs were momentarily lost in the carpet. How much less destructive of the personality are thirst, fever, physical exhaustion, he thought, much less destructive than people. He remembered how, in a mountain gorge, a sandstone boulder had crashed, aiming at him, grazing his hand, then bounding away, to the mutilation of trees and death of a young wallaby. Deadly rocks, through some perversity, inspired him with fresh life. He went on with the breath of life in his lungs. But words, even of benevolence and patronage, even when they fell wide, would leave him half-dead.

'We must make that journey some day, Belle,' said Tom Radclyffe, who had already set forth with his desirable bride. 'To Moreton Bay, I mean.'

Although indifferent to travel, he was not blind to the advantages of their being lost together in some remote place.

'Yes, Tom,' Belle agreed, idly, quietly, with golden down upon her upper lip.

These young people had a habit of looking at each other as if they might discover an entrance into some yet more intimate chamber of the mind. She was still quite unformed and breathless. She was honey-coloured, but rather thick about the throat. These characteristics, together with an excellent constitution, Belle Bonner would pass on to her many descendants, for the creation of whom she had been purposely designed.

'You will have everyone in a fever of exploration, Voss,' laughed Mr Bonner, the man who unlocked situations, who led people by the arm. 'Come on in here now,' he said, 'while the ladies are getting themselves up for dinner.'

Then they are committed to each other, Laura Trevelyan saw. Uncle is so good, she yawned. But the German was antipathetic, while offering prospects to be explored. He had a strong back, sinewy rather, that began to obliterate the general seediness. Now that she could no longer observe his face, she remembered it, and might have sunk deeper than she had at first allowed herself into the peculiarly pale eyes.

The two men had gone, however. It was a deliberate, men's departure once they had begun. They went into a smaller room that was sometimes referred to as Mr Bonner's Study, and in which certainly there stood a desk, but bare, except of useless presents from his wife, and several pieces of engraved silver, arranged at equal distances on the rich, red, tooled leather. Gazetteers, almanacs, books of sermons and of etiquette, and a complete Shakespeare, smelling of damp, splashed the pleasing shadow with discreet colours. All was disposed for study in this room, except its owner, though he might consider the prospects of trade drowsily after Sunday's beef, or, if the rheumatics were troubling him, ruffle up the sheets of invoices or leaves of a ledger that Mr Palethorpe had brought out from town. The study had flowered with Mrs Bonner's ambition. Its immaculacy was a source of pride, but it did make some people afraid, and the merchant himself was more at ease in his hugger-mugger sanctum at the store.

'Now we can discuss,' suggested Mr Bonner, and thought to add: 'Privately.'

He had a certain love of conspiracy, which makes Freemasons of grown men, and little boys write their names in blood. Moreover, in the company of the shabby German, he began to enjoy the power of patron over protégé. Wealthy by colonial standards, the merchant had made his money in a solid business, out of Irish linens and Swiss muslins, damask, and huckaback, and flannel, green baize, and India twills. The best-quality gold leaf was used to celebrate the name of EDMUND BONNER — ENGLISH DRAPER, and ladies driving down George Street, the wives of officers and graziers, in barouche and brougham, would bow to that respectable man. Why, on several occasions, he had even been consulted in confidence, he told, by Lady G—, who was so kind as to accept a tablecloth and several pair of linen sheets.

So Edmund Bonner could afford to sit with his legs stuck out, in the formidable study of his stone house.

'You are quite certain you are ready to undertake such a great expedition?' he now dared to ask.

'Naturally,' the German replied.

He had his vocation, it was obvious, and equally obvious that his patron would not understand.

'You are aware, I should say, what it could mean?'

'If we would compare meanings, Mr Bonner,' said the German, looking at each word as if it were a round pebble of mystical perfection, 'we would arrive perhaps at different conclusions.'

The thick man laughed the other side of the red desk. It pleased him to have bought something he did not altogether understand. Refinements are acquired in this way, and eventually clothe the purchaser like skins, which he will take for granted, and other people admire. Mr Bonner longed to experience the envy of others. So his nostrils now grew keener.

'I am compelled into this country,' continued the oblivious Voss.

'That is all very well,' said the merchant, easing his thighs forward, 'that is enthusiasm, I suppose, and it is as well that you should have it. I can attend to a number of the practical details myself. Stores, up to a point. The master of the *Osprey* will carry you to Newcastle, provided you are ready to embark by the date of his intended departure. There is Sanderson at Rhine Towers, to see you on your way, and Boyle at Jildra, which will be your last outpost, as we have decided. Each of these gentlemen has generously volunteered to contribute a mob of cattle, and Boyle, in addition, he tells me, will provide sheep, as well as a considerable herd of goats. But any scientific equipment, that is your province, Voss. And have you recruited suitable companions to accompany you in this great enterprise?'

The German sucked in the fringes of his moustache. He could have been suffering from indigestion, if it was not contempt.

'I will be ready,' he said. 'All arrangements are in hand. I have engaged already four men.'

'Who?' asked the man whose money was involved, together with that of several other daring citizens.

'You are not acquainted,' said Voss.

'But who?' persisted the draper; his vanity would not allow him to think there might be anyone he did not know.

Voss shrugged. He was indifferent to other men. On the several short expeditions he had made, he had gone accompanied by the sound of silence, the chafing of leather, and sighing of his own solitary horse.

'There is Robarts,' he began, and it was unnecessary. 'He is an English lad. We are met on board. He is good, simple.' But superfluous.

'There is Le Mesurier,' he said. 'We have also travelled together. Frank has great qualities, if he does not cut his throat.'

'Promising!' laughed Edmund Bonner.

'And Palfreyman. You will approve of Palfreyman, Mr Bonner. He is an exceptional man. He is the ornithologist. Of great principles. Also a Christian.'

'I do believe,' said the draper, a little comforted, 'I believe that Palfreyman is known to my friend Pringle. Yes, I have heard of him.'

'And Turner.'

'Who is Turner?'

'Well,' said Voss. 'Turner is a labourer. Who asks to be taken.'

'And you are confident that he is a suitable associate?'

'I am of every assurance that I can lead an expedition across this continent,' Voss replied.

Now he was a crag of a man. He beetled above the merchant, who wondered more than ever with what he had become involved, but was stimulated by it.

Still, it was in his nature to play with caution.

'Sanderson has two men he will recommend to you,' he said.

So that Voss became cautious in turn. Anonymous individuals were watching him from behind trees as well as from the corners of the rich room. He suspected their blank faces. All that was external to himself he mistrusted, and was happiest in silence, which is immeasurable, like distance, and the potentialities of self. He did not altogether trust those he had chosen for his patron's comfort, but at least they were weak men, he considered, all but one, who had surrendered his strength conveniently to selflessness.

'I would like to avoid the conflict of opinion that a large party will certainly involve.'

'You will be gone a year, two years, nobody knows; in any event, a long time. During that period you will profit by being able to draw upon a diversity of opinion. Great distances will tax physical strength. Some of your party may be forced to fall out; others, one must face the melancholy fact, may pass on. You appreciate my point of view? It is also Mr Sanderson's. He is convinced that these men will be of value to the expedition.'

'Who are they?' asked the cloudy German.

The merchant at once mistook indifference for submission. The expression on his face had clarified as he sat forward to continue in full pride of superior strength.

'There is young Angus. You will like Angus. He is the owner of a valuable property in the neighbourhood of Rhine Towers. A young fellow of spirit — I will not say hot-headed of anyone so amiable — who visited the Downs several years ago, and was at that time anxious to pursue fortune farther to the west, though just then conditions happened to be unfavourable.

'Then,' said Edmund Bonner, to his ivory paper-knife, that his wife had put on his desk one birthday, but which he had never used, 'there is also Judd. I have not met Judd, but Mr Sanderson swears by him as a man of physical strength and moral integrity. An improviser, besides, which is of the greatest importance in a country where necessities are not always to hand. Judd, I understand, has shown himself to be most commendably adaptable. Because he came out here against his will. In other words, was a convict. Free now, naturally. The circumstances of his transportation were quite ridiculous, I am led to believe.'

'They always are,' interrupted Voss.

The merchant suspected that he might have been caught in some way. He was suspended.

'Most of us have committed murders,' the German said, 'but would it not be ridiculous, Mr Bonner, if, for that murder which

22

you have committed, you have been transported to New South Wales?'

Mr Bonner, who was left with no alternative, laughed at this joke, and decided to withdraw from deep water. With the elegant but strong paper-knife he began to tap a strip of canvas he had unfolded on the scented leather of his desk.

'I expect you will consider it imprudent, Mr Voss, if I ask whether you have studied the map?'

Here, indeed, was a map of a kind, presumptuous where it was not a blank.

'The map?' said Voss.

It was certainly a vast dream from which he had wakened. Even the draper suspected its immensity as he prodded at the coast with his ivory pointer.

'The map?' repeated the German. 'I will first make it.'

At times his arrogance did resolve itself into simplicity and sincerity, though it was usually difficult, especially for strangers, to distinguish those occasions.

'It is good to have a good opinion,' laughed the merchant.

His honest flesh heaved, and himself rather drunken, began to read off his document, to chant almost, to invoke the first recorded names, the fly-spots of human settlement, the legend of rivers.

Mr Bonner read the words, but Voss saw the rivers. He followed them in their fretful course. He flowed in cold glass, or dried up in little yellow pot-holes, festering with green scum.

'So you realize how much must be taken into account' – the merchant had recovered himself. 'And *tempus fugit, tempus fugit!* Why, I am blessed if it is not already time for dinner, which provides us with an excellent illustration of what I have been trying to convey.'

Thereupon, he slapped his strange, but really rather pleasing, because flattering protégé on the knee. *Flattering* was the word. Edmund Bonner, once a hollow, hungry lad, was flattered by someone whose whole appearance suggested that he was hungry in his turn.

Now the whole stone house was booming with bronze, for Jack Slipper had come in from the yard and struck the great gong, his naked arms tensed and wiry, as Rose Portion went

23

backwards and forwards, with dishes or without, ignoring all else but her own activity.

'You must be feeling peckish,' the expectant Mr Bonner remarked.

'Please?' asked Voss, perhaps to avoid making a decision.

'I dare say' – the merchant gave it extra weight – 'you could put away your share of dinner.'

'I am not prepared,' replied the German, who was again unhappy.

'Who ever had to prepare for a plate of prime beef and pudding!' said the merchant, already surging forth. 'Mrs Bonner,' he called, 'our friend will stay for dinner.'

'So I anticipated,' said Mrs Bonner, 'and Rose has laid a place.'

The men had come out to her and, in fact, to all the company, who were now assembled in a cool hall, shifting their feet upon the yellow stone. Cool stone drank the laughter of the young people, and their conversation, which they made purely for the pleasure of speaking. Tom and Belle would sometimes play for hours at this kind of bat and ball. And there were the Palethorpes, who had arrived since. Mr P., as Mrs Bonner would refer to him, was her husband's right hand, and indispensable as such, if also conveniently a Sunday joke. Mr P. was bald, with a moustache that somewhat resembled a pair of dead birds. And there was his wife – she had been a governess – a most discreet person, whether in her choice of shawls, or behaviour in the houses of the rich. The P.s were waiting there, self-effacing, yet both at home, superior in the long practice of discretion.

'Thank you, I will not stay,' Voss said, now in anger.

A rude man, saw Mrs Bonner.

A foreigner, saw the P.s.

Someone to whom, after all, I am completely indifferent, saw Laura Trevelyan, although he is not here, to be sure, for my benefit. What is? she was compelled to add.

Laughter and the society of others would sometimes drive this young woman to the verge of self-pity; yet she had never asked for rescue from her isolation, and now averted her eyes from Mr Voss in particular.

'You will not stay?' blustered the host, as if already potato-in-mouth.

'If that is the intention of Mr Voss,' said Mrs Bonner, 'then we shall sustain a loss.'

'You have made a bad poem!' laughed Belle, kissing at her mother's neck.

The young girl was inclined to ignore visitors when any of her family was present.

'The more beef for Mr P.!' cried Lieutenant Radclyffe, who was chafing even in his humour.

'Why, pray, for Mr. P.?' exclaimed the gentleman's wife in discreet protest, but giggled to please her patrons. 'Is he a lion, then?'

Everybody laughed. Even Mr P. showed his teeth beneath his dead birds. He was a man of all purposes.

Consequently Voss was almost forgotten.

'I am already bidden,' he said.

Although it was really unnecessary to assure those who were so little anxious for assurance.

Expectation was goaded by smells that drifted past the cedar doors, with the consequence that the yellow flags were becoming intolerable to most feet.

'Then, if Mr Voss is already engaged,' said Mrs Bonner, to release someone who was unacquainted with the convolutions of polite behaviour.

'Too bad, old Voss!' said the brisk Lieutenant, who would cheerfully have abandoned this unnecessary acquaintance, to rush in himself, slash with a sword at the sirloin, and watch the red juices run.

But the owner of the house continued to feel the weight of his responsibilities. He was compelled to offer parting advice, even if imperiously:

'We must keep in touch, Voss. Daily communication, you know. There will be many things to decide. You will find me at my business premises any morning. Or afternoon, for that matter. But keep in touch.'

'Naturally,' replied the German.

Sooner or later he was leaving, through the laughter and conversation of ladies, who had entered the dining-room, and were recalling the sermon and bonnets, as they seated themselves upon the chairs to which gentlemen blindly assisted them. However high his vision had soared, the now leaden German trod in thick boots along the gravel. The indifference of voices in a room, even of the indistinct voices, becomes a criticism. So that he went faster, and grew clumsier, and leaner.

He was an uncouth, to some he was a nasty man.

All the way along the gritty road this nastiness was apparent to Voss himself. At such times he was the victim of his body, to which other people had returned him. So he walked furiously. He was not lame, but could have been. On that side of the Point there were several great houses similar to the Bonners', from which human eye could have been taking aim through slits of shutters. Barricades of laurels blinded with insolent mirrors. Rooted in that sandy soil, in the straggling, struggling native scrub, the laurels had taken possession; strengthened by their own prevalence, the houses of the rich dared the intruder, whether dubious man, or tattered native tree.

So Voss turned the corner and went from that locality. Gritty winds tended to free him. A wind off the sea, even off becalmed baywater and sea-lettuce, was stirring his beard as he descended the hill. Through the window of a slab cottage on the left, that sold little bits of pickled pork, and withered apples, and liquorice, an old woman was staring. But Voss did not look. There were other random cottages, or shops, and a drinking-house, with horses tied outside to a ring. But Voss did not look. He followed the ruts, raging at those flies which the wind did not seem to deter. His beard flew. He was very sinewy, a man of obvious strength when observed in the open, yet who could have been trailing some humiliation, and as he walked, really at an inordinate pace, from time to time he would glance anxiously through the trees upon his right, at nothing substantial, it appeared. There the bay flickered through the scrub that still stood along the road before the town. Glittering feverishly as the whites of certain eyes, its waters did not soothe, at least, in those circumstances, and in that light.

So the foreigner came on into the town, past the Cathedral and the barracks, and went and sat in the Gardens beneath a dark tree, hoping soon to enter his own world, of desert and dreams. But he was restless. He began to graze his hands, upon twigs, and stubble of grass, and the stones of his humiliation. His face had dwindled to the bone.

An old, grey-headed fellow who happened to approach, in fustian and battered beaver, chewing slowly from a small, stale loaf, looked at the stranger, and held out a handful of bread.

'Here,' invited the oldish man, himself chewing and quite contented, 'stick this inside of you; then you will feel better.'

'But I have eaten,' said the German, turning on the man his interrupted eyes. 'Only recently I have eaten.'

So that the man in the beaver went away, trailing crumbs for the little birds.

At once the German, beneath his tree, was racked by the fresh mortification to which he had submitted himself. But it was a discipline for the great trials and achievements in store for him in this country of which he had become possessed by implicit right. Unseeing people walked the sandy earth, eating bread, or sat at meat in their houses of frail stone foundations, while the lean man, beneath his twisted tree, became familiar with each blade of withered grass at which he stared, even the joints in the body of the ant.

Knowing so much, I shall know everything, he assured himself, and lay down in time, and was asleep, slowly breathing the sultry air of the new country that was being revealed to him.

*

'Well, what do you think of him?' asked Mr Bonner, wiping the fat from his mouth with a fine napkin.

'Today confirmed the impression I received at our meeting a few months ago,' said Lieutenant Radclyffe. 'A madman. But harmless mad.'

'Oh, Tom, what an accusation to make,' said Mrs Bonner, who was in a mood for kindness, 'and with no grounds, at least that we can see – yet.'

But Tom was not concerned. Such an individual could not further his own career.

'And do you really intend to send the creature on an expedition into this miserable country?' asked Mrs Bonner of her husband. 'He is so thin. And,' she said, 'he is already lost.'

'How do you mean *lost*, Mamma?' asked Belle, taking her mother's hand, because she liked to feel the rings.

'Well, he is,' said Mrs Bonner. 'He is simply lost. His eyes,' she said, 'cannot find their way.'

She herself was groping after what her instinct knew.

But Rose Portion had brought in a big apple-pie that was more important to some of those present.

'Do not worry,' said the merchant, as he watched his wife release the greeny, steamy apples from the pie. 'There will be others with him,' he said, 'to hack a way.'

'Of course,' said Mrs Bonner, who loved all golden pastry-work, and especially when a scent of cloves was rising from it. 'Nor did we really have time to understand Mr Voss.'

'Laura did,' said Belle. 'Tell us about him, Lolly. What is he like?'

'I do not know,' said Laura Trevelyan.

I do not know Laura, Mrs Bonner realized.

The Palethorpes coughed, and rearranged the goblets out of which they had gratefully sipped their wine. Then a silence fell amongst the flakes of pastry, and lay. Till Laura Trevelyan said:

'He does not intend to make a fortune out of this country, like other men. He is not all money talk.'

'Other men are human,' said her uncle, 'and this is the country of the future. Who will not snap at an opportunity when he sees one? And get rich,' he added, with sudden brutality of mouth. 'This country,' protested his full mouth.

'Ah, this country!' sighed his wife, who remembered others, and feared for her complexion.

'He is obsessed by this country,' said Laura Trevelyan. 'That was at once obvious.'

'He is a bit mad,' pursued the Lieutenant monotonously.

'But he is not afraid,' said Laura.

'Who is afraid?' asked Tom Radclyffe.

'Everyone is still afraid, or most of us, of this country, and will not say it. We are not yet possessed of understanding.'

The Lieutenant snorted, to whom there was nothing to understand.

'I would not like to ride very far into it,' admitted Belle, 'and meet a lot of blacks, and deserts, and rocks, and skeletons, they say, of men that have died.'

'But Laura, together with the obsessed Herr Voss, is unafraid. Is that it?' asked Lieutenant Radclyffe.

'I have been afraid,' said Laura Trevelyan. 'And it will be some time, I expect, before I am able to grasp anything so foreign and incomprehensible. It is not my country, although I have lived in it.'

Tom Radclyffe laughed.

'It is not that German's.'

'It is his by right of vision,' answered the young woman.

'What is that?'

She was trembling. She could not say.

It is unlike Laura, felt her Aunt Emmy.

'Here we are talking about our Colony as if it did not exist until now,' Mr Bonner was forced to remark, 'Or as if it has now begun to exist as something quite different. I do not understand what all this talk is about. We are not children. We have only to consider the progress we have made. Look at our homes and public edifices. Look at the devotion of our administrators, and the solid achievement of those men who are settling the land. Why, in this very room, look at the remains of the good dinner we have just eaten. I do not see what there is to be afraid of.'

'Do not worry, Laura,' said Aunt Emmy. 'Is your head not better, dear?'

'Why my head?' asked Laura.

People were looking questions at her. The glances of some of them even implied that she was of the same base metal as the German.

'Oh, my head,' she remembered. 'Yes. No, it is better, I think.'

Though presently, when they had got up from the table, she went away to her room.

2

SUSSEX STREET was not yet set so rigid that a cock might not shatter its importance, or blunt-nosed bullock, toiling over ruts, snuff at the dusty urban air, or piano scatter its distracted notes, from the house of Tópp, Professor of Music, which was situated halfway down. The house itself was rather solemn, awkwardly conceived and executed, lacking in the grandeur which stone should create, for stone it was, honestly revealing how painfully it had been hewn. There in its almost weathered sides were the scars where the iron had entered in, like livid ribs, and in certain lights the dumpy house suggested all suffering. The rooms were agreeable enough, although centipedes would invade in the course of a humid summer, and green mould grow upon the boards, to the extent that Mrs Thompson, the old woman who attended to the needs of Topp, the proprietor, and any lodger, would begin to complain about her bones. How she would complain; but Topp was fortunate, his friends ventured to suggest, to have secured the services of a decent widow, without encumbrances, as it is said. Certainly there were sons, but distributed, and at a distance, where they were engaged in clearing and populating their adopted land. Primitive in appearance and of classic behaviour, her employer suspected the old woman of being the original Thompson. Often at evening, after tidying her excellent person, she would declaim the Thompson narrative for poor Topp, who had listened so often he had learnt to prompt the voice of legend. But they were both, perhaps, comforted.

Topp, the music master, and a single gentleman, was comparatively silent and unprolific. He was a small, white, worried man, with small, moist, white hands, shameful in that country of dry, yellow callouses. All he made was music, for which he was continually apologizing, and hoping he might not be called upon to explain what useful purpose his passion served. So he would hurry past the doorways of hotels, from which laughter came, and dream of an ideal state in which the official tongue was music. Although he taught the pianoforte, visiting select homes during the morning hours, Topp played the flute for pleasure. Exquisite, pearly, translucent notes would flower on that unpromising wood, and fall from the windows as they faded, causing bullock teams to flick their tails, or some drunkard to invoke Jesus Christ. On days when Topp played his flute the dumpy house was garlanded with music, and it did sometimes happen that people passing in the street, through dust or mud, would grow gladder without thinking to discover why.

To Johann Ulrich Voss, lying on the iron bed in one of the two upper rooms for which he paid the music master, the music was also homage of a kind. At intervals he might lift a hand, graciously acknowledging a phrase, but out of that great distance to which he was so often withdrawn. Men came to see him now, going straightway up the narrow stairs, or waiting in the street, on step or mounting-block, if the German happened to be from home. He is about the business of this great expedition, the old woman Mrs Thompson would explain on such occasions, and did also let it be understood that she could have revealed the nature of that business, only discretion would not allow. Go up, though, my dear, and make yourself comfortable, we are long enough on earth, she advised those she favoured. Or: Wait, she would command of those she suspected; this is a gentleman's rooms, let me remind you, not a cockpit; if you will rest a while upon the step, you will find it clean, God knows, scrubbed down every day, and the weather permittin.

In the absence of the German, Harry Robarts was always forced to wait upon the steps. It was not that she disliked the lad, just that she could not take to him, poor fellow, with his wide mouth and reddish cheeks. Christian though she was, or hoped, she could not let her health suffer by sympathizing unduly with every simple boy; there were limits to what a widow might be expected to bear.

One evening that spring, when the street was already dissolving, and amiable pedestrians were calling to one another in friendship, and Topp's pupil had caught the brilliance of the sunset if only for a few bars, Harry Robarts came to Voss, and ran up the stairs unimpeded by Mrs Thompson, because her gentleman was there. The boy went in and found his friend examining a list, of ropes, and waterbags, and other tackle, as well as an increased quantity of flour, for which the German had yet to contract with recommended firms.

'It is me, sir,' panted the lad, twirling a cap of kangaroo skin that he had bought from a hawker on landing in the Colony.

'What is it, then?' asked the German, and continued to suck the end of a beautifully sharpened lead pencil.

'Nothing,' said the boy. 'I came. That is all.'

The German did not frown, as he might have in other circumstances, at other people. Poor Harry Robarts was an easy shadow to wear. His wide eyes reflected the primary thoughts. Voss could sit with him as he would with still water, allowing his own thoughts to widen on it.

So that, if he was weak in wit, Harry did enjoy certain other advantages. And muscular strength too. He was white-skinned, but heavy-shouldered. For one instance, there was the mahogany box, the corners bound in brass, the hasps brass, and handles jangling with the same metal, in which the German kept his things. At the shipside on London River, in the stench of green water and rotting fruit, Voss had stood looking at his box. He would, in fact, often experience fits of humiliating helplessness in the face of practical obstacles. In the night, and light off green, lisping water, it seemed that he would never free himself from his inherent helplessness, when Harry came, uninvited, out of the darkness, asked what it was, swung the box — it could have been a canvas thing — upon his shoulder, glad to offer his services to someone who might think for him. He was all breathless, not from the weight, but from enthusiasm; was he not embarked for new worlds in that same vessel as the gentleman? All that night in the black ship, beneath the swinging lanterns, Voss felt weak with knowledge, and the boy beside him strong with innocence.

Harry stuck to Voss. The German explained to him the anatomy of the flying fish, and named the stars. Or Harry would perform feats of strength, without his shirt, his white skin now ablaze with the tropics; he would stand on his hands, or break the links of a chain, not through vanity, but in an exchange of gifts.

Harry was always present, until Voss accepted it, and afterwards at Sydney, when he was not at work — he had been taken on as a carrier's lad — would run up the stairs, when the German was at his lodging, and say in one breath, as on the present occasion:

'It is me, sir. Harry. I have come.'

That same evening Le Mesurier came up. Voss always knew when it would be Frank. The latter's steps were thoughtful. He was somewhat moody. He would be looking at a spider, or into the grain of the balusters, or out of a little, deep-set window that opened upon a yard at the back, in which were kegs, and iron, and long ropes of ivy, and a grey coat with a yellow eye. Frank Le Mesurier could not look too much, though what he did with what he saw was not always evident. He did not communicate at once. His skin was yellowish. His thin lips were dark in that livery skin, his hollow eyes had dark lids, his nose, less fleshy than most, was rather proud.

'Can you tell me,' Le Mesurier had asked as they were standing on the white planks of the same ship, 'if you are coming to this damned country for any particular purpose?'

'Yes,' answered Voss, without hesitation. 'I will cross the continent from one end to the other. I have every intention to know it with my heart. Why I am pursued by this necessity, it is no more possible for me to tell than it is for you, who have made my acquaintance only before yesterday.'

They continued to look at the enormous sea.

'And what, may I ask in return, is your purpose? Mr Le Mesurier, is it?'

Some sense of kinship with the young man had made the German's accent kind.

'Purpose? So far, no purpose,' Le Mesurier said. 'But time will show, perhaps.'

It was clear that the vast glass of ocean would not.

The German felt himself drawn even closer to the young man, as they steadied themselves against the swell. If I were not obsessed, Voss reflected, I would be purposeless in this same sea.

The dark, young, rather exquisite, but insolent fellow did not cling like Harry Robarts; he would reappear at intervals. Frank would stick at nothing long. Since his arrival at Sydney he had been employed by several business houses, had worked for a settler in the Hunter Valley, even as a groom at a livery stable, but at all times was careful to polish his boots. His waistcoats were still presentable, and would rouse comment in hotels from those who bored him. He did not listen long to the conversation of others, having thoughts of his own of greater importance, and would sometimes slip away with no warning at all, with the result that he soon became detested by those talkers who had their professional pride. He was a snob, too. He would go so far as to suggest that he had more education than others, which, of course, was true. Somebody soon discovered that he had written a poem on a metaphysical theme, for details of which nobody dared ask. It was known, however, that he liked to discuss God, after he was drunk, on rum for choice, ploughing through the dark treacle of seductive words and getting nowhere at two o'clock in the morning. Getting nowhere. If he had become coolly cynical rather than embittered, it was because he still entertained a hope that it might be revealed which part he was to play in the general scheme.

Voss had encountered Le Mesurier one evening at dusk amongst the scrub and rocks gathered together above the water on the northern side of the Domain, and asked, as it seemed the time and place:

'Have you discovered that purpose, Frank, that we have discussed already on board the ship?'

'Why, no, I have not, Mr Voss,' said the elusive Frank, and the goose-flesh overcame him.

He began to pitch stones.

'I rather suspect,' he added, 'it is something I shall not discover till I am at my last gasp.'

Then Voss, who had sat down in a clearing in the scrub and larger, ragged trees, warmed more than ever to the young man, knowing what it was to wrestle with his own daemon. In the darkening, yellow light, the German's arms around his knees were spare as willow switches. He could dispense with flesh.

Le Mesurier continued to throw stones, that made a savage sound upon the rocks.

Then Voss had said:

'I have a proposition to make. My plans are forming. It is intended that I will lead an expedition into the interior, westward from the Darling Downs. Several gentlemen of this town are interested in the undertaking, and will provide me with the necessary backing. Do you care to come, Frank?'

'I?' exclaimed Le Mesurier.

And he pitched a particularly savage stone.

'No,' he said, lingeringly. 'I am not sure that I want to cut my throat just yet.'

'To make yourself, it is also necessary to destroy yourself,' said Voss.

He knew this young man as he knew his own blacker thoughts.

'I am aware of that,' laughed Frank. 'But I can do it in Sydney a damn sight more comfortably. You see, sir,' he added longingly, 'I am not intended for such heights as you. I shall wallow a little in the gutter, I expect, look at the stars from a distance, then turn over.'

'And your genius?' said the German.

'What genius?' asked Le Mesurier, and let fall the last of his ammunition.

'That remains to be seen. Every man has a genius, though it is not always discoverable. Least of all when choked by the trivialities of daily existence. But in this disturbing country, so far as I have become acquainted with it already, it is possible more easily to discard the inessential and to attempt the infinite. You will be burnt up most likely, you will have the flesh torn from your bones, you will be tortured probably in many horrible and primitive ways, but you will realize that genius of which you sometimes suspect you are possessed, and of which you will not tell me you are afraid.'

It was dark now. Tempted, the young man was, in fact, more than a little afraid – his throbbing body was deafening him – but as he was a vain young man, he was also flattered.

'That is so much, well, just so much,' protested Le Mesurier. 'You *are* mad,' he said.

'If you like,' said Voss.

'And when does this here expedition of yours intend to leave?'

It was too ridiculous, and he made it sound so.

'One month. Two months. It is not yet decided,' said the voice of Voss through the darkness.

He was no longer interested. He was even bored by what he had probably achieved.

'All right then,' said Le Mesurier. 'What if I come along? At least I shall think it over. What have I got to lose?'

'You can answer that better than I,' Voss replied.

Though he did, he suspected, know the young man pretty well.

As the moment of reality had receded, they now began to walk away, in soothing sounds of dark grass. Both men were somewhat tired. The German began to think of the material world which his egoism had made him reject. In that world men and women sat at a round table and broke bread together. At times, he admitted, his hunger was almost unbearable. But young Frank Le Mesurier was now thrilled by the immensity of darkness, and resented the approach of those lights which would reveal human substance, his own in particular.

Later, of course, he was able to recover the disguise of his cynicism, and was clothed with it the evening he reached the top of the stairs, and discovered Voss at home in his room, with that miserable boy Harry Robarts, who was killing flies on the window sill.

Harry looked up. Because he did not always understand his speech, as well as for other reasons, he suspected Mr Le Mesurier.

'Ah, Frank,' said Voss, who dared at once to test his power while remaining occupied at his desk; 'since you made up your mind, I believe you are afraid that I will give you the slip.'

'I could not hope to be so happy,' said Le Mesurier, and did in a sense mean it.

For he was always halfway between wanting and not.

Voss laughed.

'You must speak with Harry for a little,' he said.

And began with some ostentation choosing a pen and a large sheet of very clean paper to compose a letter to a tradesman. He liked to feel that, just beyond his occupations, other people were waiting on him.

'Well, Harry, what shall we discuss?'

In addressing Harry, or any young person, or puppy, Le Mesurier would compose his dark mouth with conscious irony. For protection. Young things read the thoughts more clearly, he sensed. And this idiot.

'Eh?' he asked of the boy, holding his neck in a certain manner.

'I dunno,' said Harry, gloomily, and crushed a fly with his forefinger.

'You were never helpful, Harry,' Le Mesurier sighed, seating himself, and stretching out his rather elegant legs; 'when we should stick together. Hopeful flotsam in the antipodes.'

'You were never nothun to me,' said Harry.

'That is candid, at least.'

'And I am no flotsam, whatever that be.'

'What are you, then?' asked Le Mesurier, though he had tired.

'I dunno what I am,' said Harry, and looked for help.

But Voss was reading through his letter. Whether he had heard, it was not possible to tell.

Doubting that he could count upon his patron's protection, Harry Robarts grew more miserable. Many disturbing and opaque thoughts began to move in his clear mind. What am I? What is it necessary to be? His thick boots had become a weight of desolation, and his rough jacket suddenly smelled of animals. He was nothing except when near to Mr Voss, but this nearness was being denied him. Once he had opened his protector's cupboard and touched the clothes hanging there, even stuck his nose into the dark folds, and been assured. But this was of the past. He was now faced with the terrifying problem of his own category propounded by Mr Le Mesurier.

'You are perhaps subtler than you know,' the enemy sighed, and felt his own cheek.

There were several nicks where the razor had sought out stubble in the early furrows of his face, which was almost the colour of a citron on that afternoon. Oh, Lord, why had he come? His own skin was repulsive to him. The young man remembered a haycock on which he had lain as a little boy, and the smell of milk, or innocence. Recognizing something of that same innocence in Harry Robarts' harmless eyes, he resented it, as a refuge to which he might never again retreat.

Now he too must rely upon the German. But the latter was reading and reading his wretched letter, and biting his nails, not badly, it must be said, perhaps one especial nail. Frank Le Mesurier, who was fastidious in some respects, loathed this habit, but continued to watch and wait because he was in no position to protest.

'I will ask you to deliver this letter, Harry – not now, it will keep till morning – to Mr O'Halloran, the saddler, in George Street,' Voss said.

What did he know? It was not, however, his policy to expose the weaknesses of others unless some particular advantage could be gained.

'You will be pleased to hear that I have received favourable news,' he announced.

He was speaking rather brightly, in a manner that he might have learnt, in a foreign tongue, from some brisk, elderly lady talking men's talk to men. The fact that it was not his own manner did add somewhat to the strain.

Harry Robarts pursued the situation desperately with his eyes in search of something he could understand. He would have liked to touch his saviour's skin. Once or twice he had touched Voss, and it had gone unnoticed.

'I cannot believe that this infernal expedition is really about to materialize,' grumbled Le Mesurier.

Risen to the surface again, he was indifferent to everything. His long legs, disposed in front of him, were downright insolent.

'In less than two weeks we shall board the *Osprey*,' said Voss. 'The five of us. And set sail for Newcastle, with our fundamental stores. From there we shall proceed to Rhine Towers, the property of Mr Sanderson.'

For reading and writing the German wore a pair of neat spectacles.

'The five of us?' said Le Mesurier, smouldering a little. 'There is Palfreyman, of course. Oh, yes, one forgets Turner.'

'Turner will be here presently, I expect.'

'And we will be ridin' horses as you said?' asked Harry Robarts.

'Or mules,' said Voss.

'Or mules.'

'Though I expect it will be one horse to a man, and mules as pack animals. That will rest with Mr Sanderson, however, and Mr Boyle of Jildra.'

So much did rest with other people, but these were the immaterial, material things. So he frequently deceived his friends. So also in the darkening room a man and a boy continued to wait for moral sustenance. Instead he chose cheerful phrases which were not his own. His sallow cheeks had even grown pink, as a disguise. But I shall lead them eventually, he considered, because it is intended I shall justify myself in this way. If *justify* was a plain word, it was but a flat occasion. Inspiration descends only in flashes, to clothe circumstances; it is not stored

38

up in a barrel, like salt herrings, to be doled out. In the confused mirror of the darkening room, he was not astonished that his face should have gained in importance over all other reflected details. Cheerfully he could have forgotten his two dissimilar disciples. They were, indeed, an ill-assorted pair, alike only in their desperate need of him.

Presently Topp's old housekeeper sighed her way to the upper landing with a nice sweetbread for their lodger's supper, and a glass of wine that the latter knew would taste of cork.

'Sitting in the dark, almost,' said Mrs Thompson, in the tone she kept for children and the opposite sex.

Then she lighted a pair of candles, and set them on the little, rickety cedar table to which the German had taken his tray. Soon the room was swimming with light.

Voss was eating. There was no question of his offering anything to his two dependants. They were so far distant from him now in the fanciful light that they gloated over him without shame, and the crumbs that fell from his mouth.

'Is it nice, then?' asked Mrs Thompson, who throve on the compliments of her gentlemen.

'Excellent,' said the German, as a matter of course.

Actually, he did not stop to think. The quicker done, the better. But he won her with his answers.

He is a greedy-looking pig, really, thought Frank Le Mesurier. A German swine. And was surprised at himself.

'You should eat slower,' said the old woman. 'A lady told me you should chew your food thirty-seven times.'

He was a handsome-looking man.

'And build yourself up.'

Thin about the face, with veins in the forehead. She recalled all the sick people she had ever nursed, especially her husband, who had been carried off by a consumption shortly after arrival on those shores.

She sighed.

Topp came in, bringing with him a bottle and glasses, knowing that Voss would not have offered anything, for that was his way. The music master did not blame him. Great men were exempt from trivial duties, and if the German was not great, his landlord would have liked him to be. Once Topp himself had composed a sonata for piano and flute. He had never dared own it, however, and would introduce it to his pupils as: 'A little piece that we might run through.'

Usually modest, tonight he was also melancholy.

'It is the southerly winds that get into one's bones,' he said, 'after the heat of the day.'

Mrs Thompson was prepared to enlarge upon the climatic disadvantages of the Colony, but heard a lady of her acquaintance calling her from the street.

'If it is not one wind, it is another. Ah, dear, it is terrible! Though on days when there is none, a person soon wishes there would be. This is the most contrariest place,' was all she had time to say.

Voss had sat back and was picking his teeth of the sweetbread. He also belched once, as if he had been alone with his thoughts.

'I do meet scarcely a man here,' he said, 'who does not suspect he will be unmade by his country. Instead of knowing that he will make it into what he wishes.'

'It is no country of mine,' declared Topp, who had poured the wine, 'except by the unfortunate accident of my being here.'

Such was his emotion, he slopped the wine.

'Nor mine, frankly,' said Le Mesurier. 'I cannot think of it except as a bad joke.'

'I came here through idealism,' said Topp, feverish with his own situation, 'and a mistaken belief that I could bring nicety to barbarian minds. Here, even the gentry, or what passes for it, has eaten itself into a stupor of mutton.'

'I see nothing wrong with this country,' dared Harry Robarts, 'nor with havin' your belly full. Mine has been full since the day I landed, and I am glad.'

Then his courage failed, and he drank his wine down, right down, in a purple gurgle.

'So all is well with Harry,' said Le Mesurier, 'who sees with his belly's eyes.'

'It will do me,' said the sullen boy.

One day he would find the courage to kill this man.

'And me, Harry,' said Voss. 'I will venture to call it my country, although I am a foreigner,' he added for the company, since human beings have a habit of rising up in defence of what they repudiate. 'And although so little of my country is known to me as yet.'

Much as he despised humility, other people expected it.

'You are welcome,' sighed Topp, although already the wine had made him happy.

'So you see, Harry,' said Le Mesurier, 'you have a fellow-countryman, who will share your patriotism in embracing the last iguana.'

'Do not torment him, Frank,' said Voss, not because it was cruel to bait dumb animals, but because he wished to enjoy the private spectacle of himself.

Harry Robarts went so far as to wipe his grateful eyes. Like all those in love, he would misinterpret lovingly.

As for Voss, he had gone on to grapple with the future, in which undertaking he did not expect much of love, for all that is soft and yielding is easily hurt. He suspected it, but the mineral forms were an everlasting source of wonder; feldspar, for instance, was admirable, and his own name a crystal in his mouth. If he were to leave that name on the land, irrevocably, his material body swallowed by what it had named, it would be rather on some desert place, a perfect abstraction, that would rouse no feeling of tenderness in posterity. He had no more need for sentimental admiration than he had for love. He was complete.

The leader looked at his subordinates, and wondered whether they knew.

But an unidentified body was falling up the steep stairs of the house. It thumped, drawing all attention, then burst through the doorway of the upper room. Candles guttered.

'It is Turner,' said Voss, 'and drunk.'

'I am not what you would call sober,' admitted the person in question, 'nor yet drunk. It is the stringybark that has shook me up a bit. The stuff would rot your guts.'

'I would not let it,' replied the German.

'A man's nature will get the better of him,' said Turner gloomily, and sat down.

He was a long, thin individual, whose mind had gone sour. He was rather squint-eyed, moreover, from examining the affairs

41

of others while appearing not to do so, but wiry too, for all the miserable impression he made. He had been employed those two months at the brickfields, and there was almost always some of the dust from the bricks visible in the cracks of his skin and creases of his clothes.

'I had news,' Voss said to him, 'but have almost decided it will not interest you.'

When Turner cried:

'You do not intend to drop me on account of me nature, for which a man is not responsible! Anyone will tell yer that.'

'If I take you, it will be because your nature will not receive much encouragement in those parts.'

And because of a morbid interest in derelict souls, Voss suspected. Still there was in Turner sober a certain native cunning that put him on his mettle. A cunning man can be used if he does not first use.

'Mr Voss, sir,' pleaded Turner, drunk, 'I will strain every muscle in me back. I will do the dirty work. I will eat grass.'

'Only too obviously another convert,' said Frank Le Mesurier, and got up.

Anything that was physically repulsive to him, he would have trodden under foot. He would not have cared to brush against Turner, yet it was probable, riding through the long, yellow grass, their stirrup-irons would catch at each other in overtures of intimacy, or lying in the dust and stench of ants, wrestling with similar dreams under the stars, their bodies would roll over and touch.

If this German is really philanthropist enough to take the man, he reflected. Or is he a fool?

But Voss would not help him to distinguish.

'Mr Topp,' the German was saying, 'if I had mastered the art of music, I would set myself the task of creating a composition by which the various instruments would represent the moral characteristics of human beings in conflict with one another.'

'I would rather suggest the sublimity of perfection,' said the innocent music master, 'in great sweeps of pure sound.'

'But in order to understand it, you must first find perfection, and that you will never do. Besides, it would be monotonous, not to say monstrous, if you did.'

Turner, who was holding his perplexed head in a kind of basket of fingers, exclaimed:

'Oh, oh! Gawd save us!'

Then he remembered, and turned on Le Mesurier, who was ready to retire, a look of deliberate malice.

'Converts, eh?' Because it rankled. 'You, with all your talk, are not such a saint, if gutters could tell. I seen you, in not such a Sunday wescoat, and mud on it, too. And whorin' after women under the trees. And holdin' forth to the public. Contracted with a practisin' madman, you was, accordin' to your own admission, for a journey to hell an' back.'

Then Turner began to laugh, and to wink great face-consuming winks at the listening boy.

'If it was I, and I was drunk, then I cannot remember. Except that I have been drunk,' said Le Mesurier, and they could see the gristle of his nose.

'We are not the only sinners, eh, sonny?' golloped the winking Turner.

He felt the necessity of drawing in the boy. It was always better two to one.

'I am willing to admit I have been drunk,' said Le Mesurier.

'It is true,' said the sullen boy, who would enjoy the luxury of taking sides once he had learnt the game.

'It is sometimes necessary,' frowned Le Mesurier.

'Ho-ho!' exploded Turner. 'Tell the worms! As if they will not know about the moist.'

'But there are droughts, Turner, that no worm will experience in his blunt head as he burrows in the earth. His life is blissfully blindly physical. The worst that can happen to your worm is that he may come up and be trodden on.'

'You are a gentleman,' said Turner, whose lips had been dogging every word, 'and I do not follow all of that. But I have me suspicions.'

Le Mesurier would sometimes laugh in his nose.

'And I will take your face off for it,' Turner said.

He did get up, together with Harry Robarts, who was his friend of a few moments. The breathing was enormous. It seemed that the passion which had swelled and was filling the room was the all-important one.

Until Voss pricked it.

'I am not interested in personal disagreements,' he said; 'who is drunk, who is a madman, who is disloyal. These are, in any event, of minor consideration. What distresses me more is my own great folly in continuing, like a worm, Frank, butting my head at whatsoever darkness of earth, once I have conceived an idea. You, Turner, Frank, are part of this strange, seemingly inconceivable idea. It distresses me that I cannot lay it aside, with all its component and dependent difficulties. But I cannot. Now you will go, please, out of this room, which is mine, you have forgotten. And you will remember also that the street is the property of all the citizens of this town. When we meet again, I trust you will have accepted one another's faults, because we must be together for a long time.'

Afterwards, nobody remembered having seen his face. His words, though, they recalled, were cast in metal, and one of his feet had kicked a little lump of hard mud that had been lying on the carpet, and which had struck the wainscot rather loud.

When they had all gone, even poor Topp, who would have liked to stay and let the wine conduct some discussion of a philosophic nature, Voss went into the back room, took off his clothes quickly, and without thought, lay rather stiffly on the bed, as was his habit, and slept. He fell, straight, deeply into himself. It was not possible really, that anyone could damage the Idea, however much they scratched it. Some vomited words. Some coughed up their dry souls in rebounding pea-pellets. To no earthly avail. Out of that sand, through which his own feet, with reverence for velvet, had begun to pay homage, rose the Idea, its granite monolith untouched. Except by Palfreyman – was it? He could not distinguish the face, but the presence was pervading the whole dream. And now Voss was stirring on his straight bed. It was a humid night. His hands were attempting to free his body from the sweat with which it had been fastened.

On the following, and several successive mornings, which were all bright and shadowless, made keener by the red dust that would fill the street in sallies of grit, Voss went here and there in his tall, black, town hat. He decided on the pack-saddles of Mr O'Halloran. He negotiated with a Mr Pierce for an eight-inch sextant, prismatic compasses, barometers, thermometers, and sundry other instruments. Enough flour for two years was to be delivered direct to the vessel from Barden's mill.

On the Thursday, as he noted briefly in his journal, he 'met Palfreyman', who arrived in town from Parramatta, where he had been recuperating from an illness at the property of a friend.

Palfreyman and Voss spent some time together, in fact, walking in the Botanic Gardens, talking, or in silence, accustoming themselves warily to each other, and considering some of those questions that would arise out of a partnership of many months.

Palfreyman was a shorter man than Voss, but the honest simplicity of his expression seemed to raise him to the height of most others. His face, of which the skin normally was burnt to the yellow-brown that colourless faces acquire in the sun, had been drained by his recent illness to a greenish white, the outline somewhat blurred. His eyes, of a light grey, were very straight-looking in their deep sockets, under the dark lids. Although his upper lip was exposed, whiskers of a good brown covered the lower parts of his face. He was dressed carefully, though without vanity, in several greys, with the result that the German's hot coat and black sculptural trousers had an air of monumental slovenliness. Voss was, in fact, shamed into dusting spasmodically at his own sleeves as they walked, and once or twice twitched slightly at his cravat.

'You will be strong enough already to undertake this journey, Mr Palfreyman?' he asked, and frowned, at some thought, or wrinkle.

'I am perfectly strong.'

Staring at bright sunlight the Englishman would often wear an amazed look, as if the light were too illuminating.

'I have been fed on eggs and cream by the wife and daughters of my friend Strang for I don't know how many weeks. It was an unfortunate business, though really no more than a slight twist to my back when the horse fell. I confess I was shaken at first. To be incapacitated permanently by some accident to my back is a fear under which I have always laboured. But here I am, perfectly recovered.'

Voss, who was also staring at the bright light, had been forced by it to smile. That is to say, the skin was tight against his teeth.

45

He made quick, sucking noises to give Palfreyman the impression he was listening.

'Besides,' continued the ornithologist in his rather gentle voice, 'it might be some time before I should receive an invitation to join another such expedition. It is an opportunity in which His Grace would, I feel, be personally interested.'

Mr Palfreyman had been commissioned by an English peer, a petulant one left over from a previous reign, who collected all manner of things, from precious stones and musical instruments, to stuffed birds and tigers. In his Palladian house, His Grace seldom looked at his possessions, except on sudden impulse, to tear out a drawer for an instant on a nest of poor eggshells, or to delight a mistress with a branch of wired humming-birds. But to collect, to possess, this was his passion. Until he was tired of all those lifeless objects. Then they were quickly swathed and handed to the nation.

In the service of this peer Mr Palfreyman had made the voyage to New South Wales. If the motive of his commission was largely whimsical, his professional integrity did not allow him to recognize it. He was a scientist. Dedication to science might have been his consolation, if it had not been for his religious faith. As it was, his trusting nature built a bridge in the form of a cult of usefulness, so that the two banks of his life were reconciled despite many an incongruous geographical feature, and it was seldom noticed that a strong current flowed between.

Now Mr Voss and Mr Palfreyman, who had been led here and there by conversation, were standing on a little, actual, rustic bridge in the Botanic Gardens. Circumstance was joining them, whether comfortably or not.

Mr Voss was saying, 'I do not doubt you will have every opportunity, Mr Palfreyman, to further your patron's interests, in virgin country, west of the Darling Downs. I was merely considering the question of your health.'

They were standing rather grotesquely on the ugly ornamental bridge. They were looking down, but without observing what it was that lay beneath them. (It was, in fact, a mess of dead water-lily leaves.)

'My health,' said Palfreyman, 'has always been tolerably good.'

'You are strong-willed, I see,' laughed Voss.

For some reason, the latter knew, he would have liked to dispose of Palfreyman, who answered:

'It is not a question of *my* will, Mr Voss. It is rather the will of God that I should carry out certain chosen undertakings.'

Voss drew up his shoulder to protect himself from some unpleasantness. Then he was again normally tall, beside the smaller, but convinced Palfreyman, whose grey eyes were still engrossed beyond the withered lily leaves.

'Your sentiments will recommend themselves to Mr Bonner,' said Voss, 'who is of the opinion that the rascals I have got together do not give a sufficiently moral tone to the expedition. Like most gentlemen well established in their materialism, Mr Bonner invokes moral approval.'

The German would have liked to make some further witticism, but it did not come naturally to him. Even his laughter sounded convulsive, against an agitation of banana palms, two or three of which were standing there behind them.

'Look,' said Palfreyman, pointing at a species of diaphanous fly that had alighted on the rail of the bridge.

It appeared that he was fascinated by the insect, glittering in its life with all the colours of decomposition, and that he had barely attended to the words of Voss.

The latter was glad, but not glad enough. He would have liked to be quite certain, not from any weakness in his own armour, but from his apparent inability to undermine his companion's strength. Naturally it was unpleasant to realize this.

But it was only a matter of seconds. And there was the oblivious Palfreyman pointing with taut finger at the insect, which obviously was all that existed.

Immediately the fly had flown, the two men embarked on some further conversation of a practical nature, and Voss agreed to take Palfreyman to Mr Bonner the very next day.

'He is an excellent man, you know,' said Voss. 'Generous, and trusting. The patron *par excellence*.'

Palfreyman merely smiled, almost as if it had been the shadow of his illness on his greenish, full, contemplative face.

'Now, look after yourself, my dear fellow, in this city of unexpected dangers,' said Voss nicely, as they were taking leave of each other in the sun at the gates.

He could be very nice, and wanted badly to be nicer. He smiled with a genuine charm, although his teeth were inclined to be pointed. He put his hand on his colleague's arm, which was an unusual gesture for him.

Then they parted. Palfreyman, who was frequently very happy in this insubstantial world, walked with the slowness of leisure. But Voss hurried about some business, the wind whipping his trouser legs.

During the days that followed, the German thought somewhat surreptitiously about the will of God. The nurture of faith, on the whole, he felt, was an occupation for women, between the preserving-pan and the linen-press. There was that niece of the Bonners', he remembered, a formal, and probably snobbish girl, who would wear her faith cut to the usual feminine pattern. Perhaps with a colder elegance than most. Then, there were the few men who assumed humility without shame. It could well be that, in the surrender to selflessness, such individuals enjoyed a kind of voluptuous transport. Voss would sometimes feel embittered at what he had not experienced, even though he was proud not to have done so. How they merge themselves with the concept of their God, he considered almost with disgust. These were the feminine men. Yet he remembered with longing the eyes of Palfreyman, and that old Müller, from both of whom he must always hold himself aloof, to whom he would remain coldly unwedded.

So he went about, and the day was drawing close.

Again on several occasions he recalled that old Brother Müller. Earlier in the year Voss had spent several days as a guest of the Moravian Mission near Moreton Bay. It was the harvest, then. The colours of peace, however transitory, drenched the stubbled fields. The scene was carved: the low whitewashed cottages of the lay brothers, the slim, but strong forms of the greyish trees, the little wooden figures of the sunburnt children. They were all in the fields, harvesting. Several women had taken rakes and forks, and were raking the hay, or pitching it up to their husbands upon the drays. Even the two old ministers had come, exchanging black for a kind of smock, of very placid grey. So all were working.

It was the form of Brother Müller, who had founded their

settlement, that seemed to predominate over all others. Such peace and goodness as was apparent in the earthly scene, in the light and shadow, and the abundance of fragrant, wilting hay, might indeed have emanated from the soul of the old quietist.

'I will come and work with you,' called Voss, who, up till then, in fact, all the days of his visit, had been walking about restlessly, chewing at a straw, plucking at leaves, carrying a book which conveyed nothing to him.

Nobody had questioned his aloofness from the work, but now the guest began to tear off his awkward clothes – that is, he flung aside his rusty coat, loosened the neck of his pricking shirt, rolled up the sleeves on his wiry arms, and was soon raking with frenzied movements beside Brother Müller. One of the women who was pitching the fodder up to the drays went so far as to laugh at their guest's particular zeal, but everyone else present accepted it placidly enough, taking it for granted that even the apparently misguided acts obey some necessity in the divine scheme.

Then Voss, who had spent several nights in speculative argument with the old minister over glasses of goats' milk sweetened with honey, called out in the lust of his activity:

'I begin to receive proof of existence, Brother Müller. I can feel the shape of the earth.'

And he stood there panting, with his legs apart, so that the earth did seem to take on something of its true shape, and to reel beneath him.

But the old man continued to rake the hay, blinking at it, as if he had got something in his eye, or were stupid.

Then Voss said, generously:

'Do not think, Brother, because we have argued all these nights, and I have sometimes caught you out in a friendly way, that I want to detract at all from God.'

He was laughing good-naturedly, and looked handsome and kind in his burnt skin, and besides, was straddling the world.

'*Ach*,' sighed the old man; haymaking could have been his vocation.

Then he leaned upon his rake. There was behind him a golden aureole of sun.

'Mr Voss,' he said, with no suggestion of criticism, 'you have a contempt for God, because He is not in your own image.'

So Voss walked quicker through the streets of Sydney all those days preceding the departure of the great expedition, of which that world was already talking. Men of business took him by the shoulder as if they would have had some part of him, or intended to share a most earnest piece of information. Young girls, walking with servants or aunts, looked at the hems of their skirts as they passed, but identified him to their less observant companions immediately afterwards. That was Mr Voss, the explorer.

So that, for the explorer himself, the whole town of Sydney wore a splendid and sufficient glaze.

3

Soon after this it happened that Rose Portion, the Bonners' servant, was taken suddenly sick. One afternoon, just after Mrs Bonner and the young ladies had finished a luncheon of cold ham, with pickles, and white bread, and a little quince jelly, nothing heavy like, because of the Pringles' picnic party that afternoon, Rose simply fell down. In her brown gown she looked a full sack, except that she was stirring and moaning, even retching. Dry, however. Mrs Bonner, who was a Norfolk girl, remembered how cows used to fall into the dikes during the long winter nights, and moan there, so far off, and so monotonously; nothing, it seemed, would ever be done.

Yet here was Rose upon the floor, half in the dining-room, half in the passage to the pantry, and for Rose something must be done at once.

'Rose, dear! Rose!' called the young ladies, leaping, and kneeling, and slapping the backs of her hands.

'We must burn a feather,' decided Mrs Bonner.

But Miss Laura ran and fetched her dark green smelling-bottle, which was a present from a girl called Chattie Wilson, with whom they were in the habit of exchanging visits and presents.

Then, when Rose's head had been split almost in two by that long, cold smell, she got up rather suddenly, moaning and crying. She was holding her fists together at the brown knuckles, and shaking.

'Rose, dear, please do tell us you are recovered,' implored Belle, who was herself frightened and tearful; she would cry for people in the street who appeared in any way distressed. 'Do stop, Rose!'

But Rose was not crying, not exactly; it was an animal mumbling, and biting of her harelip.

'Rose,' said Aunt Emmy at last, quite dryly, and unlike her, 'Edith will give you a hand to clear the rest of the things. Then you must lie down and rest.'

Aunt Emmy sounded and looked drained, although perhaps it was the salt-cellar, one of the good Waterford pair, that should never have been used, and of which she was now picking up the fragments; it could have been this that had caused her some pain.

Then Laura Trevelyan, her niece, who was still kneeling, understood otherwise. It was awful. And soon even Belle knew, who was young, but not too young. The instincts of all three women were embracing the same secret.

They knew that Rose Portion, the emancipist servant, was with child.

Rose had come to work at Bonners' only after she was freed. The merchant would not have employed a convict, as a matter of conscience, and on account of petty thefts. If they are free, he used to say, there is a chance that they are innocent; if they are not free, it is taken for granted that the assigned servant is to blame.

Free or restrained, it was the same to Rose. Fate, her person seemed to suggest, had imposed far heavier, far more dreadful, because invisible, chains. This did not affect her constitution, however. Though shackled, she would work like an ox. When Mr Bonner was laying out the rockeries that afterwards became so nice, she was carrying baskets of earth and stone, and leaving her heavy imprint on the original sand, while Jack Slipper and the lad were grumbling, and dragging and leaning, and even disappearing. Rose was not compelled to lend herself to heavy labour. Nor to sit up. Yet, there she was, when the young ladies went to balls, or lectures, or musical evenings, as they frequently did, she would be sitting up, her heavy chin sunk in her bosom, with her hands pressed together, almond-shape, in her great lap. Then she would jump up, still glittery from sleep, without smiling, but pleased, and help the young ladies out of their dresses. She would brush Miss Laura's hair, even when the latter did not wish it.

'Go now, Rose,' Miss Trevelyan would say. 'That is enough.'

But Rose would brush, as if it were her sacred duty, while her mistress remained a prisoner by her hair.

Because she was ugly and unloved, Rose Portion would attempt to bind people to her in this way. Yet Laura Trevelyan could not begin to like her maid. She was kind to her, of course. She gave her presents of cast-off garments and was careful to think about her physical well-being. She would make a special effort to smile at the woman, who was immediately grateful. Kindness made her whole body express her gratitude, but it was her body that repelled.

So it was, too, in the case of Jack Slipper, that other *individual*, as Mr Bonner almost always referred to him after the man had been sent away. Of undisclosed origin, the latter had performed odd jobs, scoured the pans and beat the carpets, worked in the garden although it was distasteful to him, and even driven the carriage at a pinch, in improvised livery, when Jim Prentice was down with the bronchitis. But whatever duties were allotted to him, Jack Slipper had always found time to loiter in the yard, under the lazy pepper trees, scratching his armpits, and chewing a quid of tobacco on the quiet. So Laura would remember, and again see him spit a shiny stream into the molten laurels. He used to wear his sleeves cut back for greater freedom, right to the shoulder, so that in his thin but sinewy arms the swollen veins were visible. He was all stains, and patches of shade, and spots of sunlight, if ever Laura was compelled to cross the yard, as, indeed, sometimes she was. It must be admitted he had always acknowledged her presence, though in such an insolent and familiar manner that invariably she would turn the other way on confirming that the man was there. Jack Slipper ended in the watch-house. The rum was his downfall. The night they took

52

him up, you could have lit the breath upon him, they said. So he received a sentence. Mr Bonner went down and spoke to him, telling him it was his habit to stand by those he employed, but seeing as he did not care for Jack's behaviour, he would have dismissed him, even without sentence being passed. The fellow only laughed. He wiped his hairy nose with his wrist, and said he would have gone, anyway.

So that was the end of Jack.

But Rose remained, her breasts moving in her brown dress. Laura Trevelyan had continued to feel repelled. It was the source of great unhappiness, because frequently she was also touched. She would try to keep her eyes averted, as she had from Jack Slipper. It is the bodies of these servants, she told herself in some hopelessness and disgust, while wondering how her aunt would have received her thoughts, if spoken. Similar obsessions could not have haunted other people. I will put all such things out of my mind, she decided; or am I a prig? So she wondered unhappily, and how she might correct her nature.

Now, when this calamity had felled the unfortunate Rose, Laura Trevelyan was more than ever unhappy. As life settled back, and the things were removed from the dining-table, and the smallest pieces of the Waterford salt-cellar had been recovered, she held herself rigid. Nobody noticed, however. Because she was practised in disguising her emotions, only someone with more than eyes in their head would have seen.

Aunt Emmy did not, who was holding a pretty but useless little handkerchief to her troubled lips. Aunt Emmy said:

'Now, girls, this is something between ourselves, most emphatically. It is providential that the dining-room does not communicate directly with the kitchen, so that Cassie and Edith need not suspect. Mr Bonner must be told, of course, and will perhaps offer a helpful suggestion. Until then – nothing.'

'We have forgotten the Pringles' picnic, Mamma,' said Belle, who was hearing the grandfather clock strike.

No event was so disastrous that Belle could not recover from it. She was still at that age.

Her mother began to suck her teeth.

'Dear, yes,' she said. 'Mrs Pringle will be provoked. And the carriage is for half past, if Mr Prentice can rouse himself. Rose,' she called, 'ask Edith to run across to Jim, and remind him to bring the carriage round. Dear, we shall be late.'

Going at once to change her dress, Laura Trevelyan regretted all picnics. A strong day was bending the trees. The garden was a muddle of tossed green, at which she frowned, patting a sleeve, or smoothing hair. Most days she walked in the garden, amongst the camellia bushes, which were already quite advanced, and the many amorphous, dark bushes of all big hospitable gardens, and the scurfy native paperbarks. At one end of the garden were some bamboos, which a sea-captain had brought to Mr Bonner from India. Originally a few roots, the bamboos had grown into a thicket, which filled the surrounding air with overwhelming featheriness. Even on still evenings, a feathery colloquy of the bamboos was clearly audible, with sometimes a collision of the stiff masts, and human voices, those of passers-by who had climbed the wall, and lay there eating pigs' trotters, and making love. Once Laura had found a woman's bonnet at the foot of the bamboos. A tawdry thing. Once she had found Rose Portion. It is me, miss, said her servant's form; it was that airless in the house. Then Rose was pressing through the thicket of bamboos. On occasions the night would be full of voices, and unexplained lights. The moist earth was pressed at the roots of the bamboos. There were the lazy, confident voices of men, and the more breathless, women's ones. I have give you a fright, miss, Jack Slipper once said, and got up, from where he had been propped upon his elbow beside the darkness. He was smoking. Laura had felt quite choked.

Now this young woman was holding her hands to her head in the mirror. She was pale, but handsome, in moss green. If Laura had more colour, she would be a beauty, Aunt Emmy considered, and advised her niece always to drop her handkerchief before entering a room, so that the blood would rush to her cheeks as she stooped to pick it up.

'Laura!' called Belle. 'The carriage is here. Mamma is waiting. You know what Mrs Pringle is.'

Then Laura Trevelyan shook her shawl. She was really handsome in her way, and now flushed by some thought, or by the wind which was assaulting the trees of the garden with greater force. There were the needles from trees falling through the window upon the carpet. There was the dry sighing of the bamboos.

When the party had disposed itself in the carriage, and Mrs Bonner had felt for her lozenges and tried to remember whether she had closed the window on the landing, when they had gone a little way down the drive, as far as the elbow and the bunya bunya, there, if you please, was the figure of that tiresome Mr Voss, walking up springily, carrying his hat, his head wet with perspiration.

Oh dear, everybody said, and even held hands.

But they pulled up. They had to.

'Good afternoon, Mr Voss,' said Mrs Bonner, putting out her head. 'This is a surprise. You are quite wicked, you know, with your surprises. When a little note. And Mr Bonner not here.'

Mr Voss was opening his mouth. His lips were pale from walking. His expression suggested that he had not yet returned from thought.

'But Mr Bonner,' he was forming words, 'is not at the store no more than here. He is gone away, they say. He is gone home.'

He resented bitterly the foreign language into which he had been thrown back thus precipitately.

'He is gone away, certainly,' said Mrs Bonner gaily, 'but is not gone home.'

Occasions could make her mischievous.

Belle giggled, and turned her face towards the hot upholstery of the dark carriage. They were beautifully protected in that padded box.

'I regret that they should have misinformed you so sadly,' Mrs Bonner pursued. 'Mr Bonner has gone to a picnic party at Point Piper with our friends the Pringles, where we will join him shortly.'

'It is not important,' Voss said.

He was glad, even. The niece sat in the carriage examining his face as if it had been wood.

She sat, and was examining the roots of his hair, the pores of his skin, but quite objectively, from beneath her leaden lids.

'How tiresome for you,' said Mrs Bonner.

'It is not, it is not of actual importance.'

Voss had put his hat back.

'Unless you get in. That is it,' Mrs Bonner said, who furiously loved her own solutions. 'You must get in with us. Then you can give Mr Bonner such information as you have. He would be provoked.'

So the step was let down.

Now it was Voss who was provoked, who had come that day, less for a purpose, than from a vague desire for his patron's company, but had not bargained for all these women.

He bumped his head.

Then he was swallowed by the close carriage with its scents and sounds of ladies. It was an obscure and wretched situation, in which his knees were pressed together to avoid skirts, but of which, soft suggestions were overflowing.

He found himself beside the pretty girl, Miss Belle, who had remained giggly, as she sat holding her hands in a ball. Opposite were the mother and her niece, rocking politely. Although he recognized the features of the niece, her name had escaped him. However, that was unimportant. As they rocked. In one place a stench of putrid sea-stuff came in at the window and filled the carriage. Miss Belle bit her lip, and turned her head, and blushed, while the two ladies seemed oblivious.

'Fancy,' said Mrs Bonner with sudden animation, 'a short time ago a gentleman and his wife, I forget the name, were driving in their brougham on the South Head Road, when some man, a kind of *bushranger*, I suppose one would call him, rode up to their vehicle, and appropriated every single valuable the unfortunate couple had upon them.'

Everybody listened to conversation as if it were not addressed to them personally. They rocked, and took it for granted that someone would assume responsibility. Mrs Bonner, at least, had done her duty. She looked out with that brightness of expression she had learnt to wear for drives in the days when they first owned a carriage. As for the bushrangers, she personally had never encountered such individuals, and could not believe in a future in which her agreeable life might be so rudely shaken. Bushrangers were but the material of narrative.

Presently they turned off along the sandy track that led down through Point Piper. The wheels of the carriage fell, as it were, from shelf to shelf of sandstone. Immediately the bones of the well-conducted passengers appeared to have melted, and the soft bodies were thrown against one another in ignominious confusion. In some circumstances this could have been comical, but something had made it serious. So the face of the grave young woman showed, and somehow impressed that gravity on the faces of the others. She withdrew her skirt ever so carefully from the rough black cloth that covered the German's protuberant knees.

Some of the Pringle children came bursting through the scrub to show the way, and ran alongside, laughing, and calling up at the windows of the newly arrived carriage, and even directing rather impudent glances at a stranger who might not have had the Bonners' full protection. The Pringles always arrived first at places. In spite of, or because of her fortune, for she was rich in her own right as well as through her husband, Mrs Pringle could have felt the need to mortify herself. She would march up and down with a watch in her hand, and shout at people quite coarsely, Mrs Bonner considered, shout at them desperately to assemble for departure, but it was all well intended. Irritation was a mark of her affection. She was most exacting of her husband, would raise her voice at him in company, and continually demand evidence of that superiority which he did not possess. These displays she met with a patient love, and had recently given her an eleventh child, which did mollify her for a little.

'Ah, there you are,' exclaimed Mrs Pringle, who with her assistants had been unpacking food behind the bushes in a circle of carriages and gigs.

The tone of her words expressed as much censure as politeness would allow. At her side, as almost always, was her eldest daughter, Una.

'Yes, my dear,' said Mrs Bonner, whom events had made mysteriously innocent. 'If we are late, it is due to some little domestic upheaval. I fear you may have been anxious for us.'

When the Bonners were descended, the girls kissed most affectionately, although Una Pringle had always been of the opinion that Laura was a stick, worse still, possessed of *brains*, and in consequence not to be trusted. In general, Una preferred the other sex, though she was far too nice a girl to admit it to a diary, let alone a *friend*. Now, using the glare as an excuse, she

57

was pretending not to examine the gentleman, or man, who had accompanied the Bonners, and who, it seemed, was also the most terrible *stick*. True to her nature, Una Pringle immediately solved a simple mathematical problem involving two sticks.

Mrs Bonner saw that she could no longer defer the moment of explaining the presence of the German, so she said:

'This is Mr Voss, the explorer. Who is soon to leave for the bush.'

Formal in its inception, it sounded somehow funny at its end, for neither Mrs Bonner nor Mrs Pringle could be expected to take seriously a move so remotely connected with their own lives.

'The gentlemen are down there,' said Mrs Pringle, hoping to dispose of an embarrassment. 'They are discussing something. Mr Pitt has also come, and Woburn McAllister, and a nephew or two.'

Many children were running about, in clothes that caught on twigs. Brightly coloured laughter hung from the undergrowth.

Voss would have liked to retire into his own thoughts, and did to a certain extent. He loked rather furry in his self-absorption. The nap of his hat had been roughed up, and he was cheaply dressed, and angular, and black. Nobody would know what to do with him, unless he did himself.

So Mrs Pringle and Mrs Bonner looked hopefully in that direction in which the gentlemen were said to be.

'You girls go down with Mr Voss,' insisted Mrs Pringle, conscripting an impregnable army, 'while Mrs Bonner and I have a little chat.'

'Shall we?' asked Una, though there was no alternative.

They all walked decently off. Their long skirts made paths along the sand, dragged fallen twigs into upright positions, and swept ants for ever off their courses.

'Do you like picnics?' asked Una Pringle.

'Sometimes,' Belle replied. 'It depends.'

'Where is Lieutenant Radclyffe?' Una asked.

'It is his afternoon for duty,' answered Belle, importantly.

'Oh,' said Una.

She was a tall girl, who would be married off quite easily, though for no immediately obvious reason.

'Have you met Captain Norton of the *Valiant*?' Una asked.

'Not yet,' yawned Belle, who aspired to no further conquests.

Belle Bonner had adopted a flat, yet superior expression, because Una Pringle was one of those girls for whom she did not care, while forced by circumstance to know. Force of circumstance, indeed,. had begun to inform the whole picnic. Till several children came, pulling, and jumping, shouting through shiny lips, inspiring Belle, whom they sensed to be an initiate, with a nostalgia for those games which she had scarcely left off playing. The boisterous wind soon flung her and several bouncing children amongst the fixed trees. Her blood was at the tips of her fingers. Her rather thick but healthy throat was distended. She herself was shouting.

'Such vitality Belle has,' sighed Una, who was left with that Laura and the foreigner.

'Do you run and jump, Mr Voss?' she inquired with an insipid malice.

'Please?' asked the German.

'I expect he does,' said Laura Trevelyan, 'if the occasion demands it. His own very private occasion. All kinds of invisible running and jumping. I do.'

Voss, who was brought back too abruptly to extract the full meaning from her words, was led to understand that this handsome girl was his ally. Though she did not look at him. But described some figure on the air with a muff of sealskin that she was carrying for the uncertain weather, and as a protection against more abstract dangers.

Trevelyan was her name, he remembered. Laura, the niece.

The gay day of wind and sharp sunlight had pierced the surface of her sombre green. It had begun to glow. She was for ever flickering, and escaping from a cage of black twigs, but unconscious of any transformation that might have taken place. This ignorance of her riches gave to her face a tenderness that it did not normally possess. Many tender waves did, besides, leap round the rocky promontory along which they were stumbling. There was now distinctly the sound of sea. As they trod out from the trees and were blinded, Laura Trevelyan was smiling.

'There are the men,' said Una rather gloomily, and did not bother to refrain from squinting, for all those gentlemen to whom she had pointed were already known to her.

The other members of her party held their hands above their eyes, and then distinguished, through the sea glaze, the elderly gentlemen perched on golden rocks, and younger men who had taken off their hats, and boys wrestling or throwing stones. The drama of that male black was too sudden against the peacock afternoon.

'We had better go down,' said Laura, 'and deliver Mr Voss.'

'But I would interrupt,' protested the German. 'What are they talking about?'

'Whatever men do talk about,' said Laura.

'Business,' suggested Una.

Some situations were definitely not his.

'And the English packet. And the weather.'

'And vegetables. And sheep.'

As they descended relentlessly towards that male gathering, the girls' fears for their ankles would sometimes crack the enamelled confidence of their voices. In the circumstances they would accept a hand or two. And Mr Voss had a strong wrist. He flung himself into this activity less in the cause of chivalry than in an endeavour to remain occupied.

They did arrive, however, and there were many eyes, looking up, showing their whites, because it was not yet evident what defences would have to be erected.

Only Mr Bonner leaped all incipient barricades, clapped his protégé on the shoulder, and cried in a very red voice:

'Welcome, Voss. If I did not suggest you take the steps you have clearly taken of your own accord, it is because I was under the impression it might not be in your line. That is, you are of rather a deep dye. Although, I am of the opinion nevertheless, that every man has something for his fellow, and it is only a matter of hitting on it. In any event, here you are.'

Mr Bonner bristled with apologies for anyone who needed them.

Some of the younger men, with leathery skins and isolated eyes, braced their calves, and shook hands most powerfully with the stranger. But two elderly and more important gentlemen, who would be Mr Pringle and the unexplained Mr Pitt, and whose stomachs were too heavy, and whose joints less active, merely cleared their throats and shifted on their rocks.

Then it was told how Voss had come. He smiled a great deal. Anxious to convey goodwill, he succeeded only in looking hungry.

'He was a godsend,' said Laura, hearing the unnatural tones the situation was forcing her to adopt. 'We used him as a protection against bushrangers.'

The younger men laughed immoderately. Those of them with whom she was acquainted did not care for Laura Trevelyan, who was given to reading books.

Mr Pringle and Mr Pitt were slower in their mirth, more sceptical, for it was they who had been conducting that dialogue of almost mystical banality which had suffered interruption.

Mr Bonner continued to look red. His pride in his German could not rise above his shame. So men will sweat for some secret gift they have failed to reveal to others, and will make subtle attempts openly to condemn what is precious to them.

'Voss, you know, is to lead this expedition we are organizing. Sanderson is behind it, and Boyle of Jildra, and one or two others. Young Angus of Dulverton is to be a member,' he added for those of his audience who were of the same age and temper as the young landowner.

The younger men looked smilingly incredulous in a solid majority of tight, best cloth. They had folded their arms. Their seams and their muscles cracked.

'It is a great event,' said the congested Mr Bonner, 'and may well prove historical. If they bring back their own bones. Eh, Voss?'

Everybody laughed, and Mr Bonner was relieved to have made his sacrifice with an almost imperceptible movement of the knife.

Voss could always, if necessary, fail to understand. But wounds will wince, especially in the salt air. He was smiling and screwing up his eyes at the great theatre of light and water. Some pitied him. Some despised him for his funny appearance of a foreigner. None, he realized with a tremor of anger, was conscious of his strength. Mediocre, animal men never do guess at the power of rock or fire, until the last moment before those elements reduce them to – nothing. This, the palest, the most transparent of words, yet comes closest to being complete.

Mr Pringle cleared his throat. Because his material status

entitled him to attention before anyone else present, he would speak slowly, and take a long time.

'It seems to me, though, from such evidence as we have collected – which is inconsiderable, mark you – as the result of mere foraying expeditions from the fringes, so to speak, it seems that this country will prove most hostile to anything in the nature of planned development. It has been shown that deserts prefer to resist history and develop along their own lines. As I have remarked, we do not *know*. There may, in fact, be a veritable paradise adorning the interior. Nobody can say. But I am inclined to believe, Mr Voss, that you will discover a few blackfellers, and a few flies, and something resembling the bottom of the sea. That is my humble opinion.'

Mr Pringle's stomach, which was less humble, rumbled.

'Have you walked upon the bottom of the sea, Mr Pringle?' the German asked.

'Eh?' said Mr Pringle. 'No.'

His eyes, however, had swum into unaccustomed depths.

'I have not,' said Voss. 'Except in dreams, of course. That is why I am fascinated by the prospect before me. Even if the future of great areas of sand is a purely metaphysical one.'

Then he threw up a little pebble, which had been changing colour in his hand, turning from pale lavender to purple, and caught it before it reached the sun.

The audience of healthy young men laughed at this German cove, their folded arms stretching the cloth still tighter on their backs.

Poor Mr Bonner was desperately ashamed. He would have liked to push the fellow off somewhere, and intended in future to reserve the luxury of their association for private occasions, although the present one was certainly no fault of his.

He thought of his wife. And frowned at his niece.

Laura Trevelyan was at that moment tracing with her toe the long, ribbony track of some sea-worm, as if it had been important. In the rapt afternoon all things were all-important, the inquiring mouths of blunt anemones, the twisted roots of driftwood returning and departing in the shallows, mauve scum of little bubbles the sand was sucking down, and the sun, the sun that was hitting them over the heads. She was too hot, of course, in the thick dress that she had put on for a colder day, with the result that all words became great round weights. She did not raise her head for those the German spoke, but heard them fall, and loved their shape. So far departed from that rational level to which she had determined to adhere, her own thoughts were grown obscure, even natural. She did not care. It was lovely. She would have liked to sit upon a rock and listen to words, not of any man, but detached, mysterious, poetic words that she alone would interpret through some sense inherited from sleep. Herself disembodied. Air joining air experiences a voluptuousness no less intense because imperceptible.

She smiled a little at this solution of sea and glare. It was the sun that was reddening her face. The hem of her skirt had become quite irregular, she saw, with black scallops of heavy water.

'I say, Laura,' said Willie Pringle, coming up, 'we have had no races this picnic, and a picnic is not a picnic without races, do you think?'

Willie Pringle was a boy, or youth, or young man by courtesy, who was rather loosely made, or had not hardened yet, with a rather loose, wet, though obviously good-natured mouth, and eyes that so far nobody had suspected of understanding. He had but recently joined the firm of his father and uncles, the solicitors, as office boy or very junior clerk, and was still feeling important.

'Do you really think races are necessary?' asked Laura, who had raced in the past, but who was now tracing through some slow necessity of her own the path of the sea-worm with her toe.

'Well, no, races are not necessary. But are they not the sort of thing that people do at a picnic?' Willie said, who wanted very badly to do those things which people did.

'Silly Willie!' Laura laughed, lazily but lovingly.

Willie laughed too.

He would have liked to share with Laura esoteric jokes and tastes. Once he had done a drawing of her, not because he was in love, he had not thought about that, but because her image had invaded his mind with immense power and brooding grief. Then, because his drawing was an empty, aching thing, his recurring failure, he had quickly torn it up.

63

'No,' his voice shouted, at a picnic. 'It is not NECESSARY. But everyone is waiting. All these children. Let us do something.'

But Laura would not join in.

Mrs Bonner wished that Willie Pringle had been a few years older, which perhaps would have simplified matters; things do arrange themselves by propinquity, and Willie was an eldest son, of prospects, if not physical charms. Mrs Pringle, however, did not share Mrs Bonner's wish. Herself more than rich, she did naturally aspire to consort with money. Moreover, she held a private opinion, very private indeed, that Laura Trevelyan was sly.

One young man, in bone and orange skin, had begun to tell of the prevalence of worms in his merino flock at Camden. His elders followed his account with appeased eyes. Everyone was glad after the rankling experience of demoniac words to which they had been subjected by the German, who still stood there, though reduced, picking at his finger-nails.

For two pins I would run him down the beach by his coat collar, said Mr Bonner, who had sided finally with the sheep.

'But we must *do* something,' protested Willie Pringle. 'If not races, then I must think of some idea. You, Laura, if only you would help. Some game, or something. Or they might collect driftwood, and pile it into a heap, and light a bonfire.'

'Are you so desperate?' asked Laura Trevelyan.

He was, but did not know it yet.

'They are wasting the afternoon!'

His mouth worked, upon the beginnings of words, or laughter, and gave up.

Even as a little boy Willie Pringle had a suspicion that a great deal depended on him, but what it was he had not found out. So far his efforts had been confined to desperate attempts to copy the behaviour, to interpret the symbols of his class, and thus solve the mystery of himself. But all truths were locked. So he would look at the heartbreaking beauty and simplicity of a common table or kitchen chair, and realize that in some most important sense their entities would continue to elude him unless he could escape from the prison of his own skull. Sometimes he would struggle like an epileptic of the spirit to break out. The situation had made his hands moist and his limbs more rubbery and ineffectual than they should have been. People laughed at him a good deal. They had not yet made up their minds whether he was a monster, or a sleepwalker, or what. Later, when they found out, they would probably shun him.

Belle solved Willie's immediate problem by an inspiration of her own. She came running, together with two Pringles, two little girls, who had to hold on, either to her flying skirt, or preferably to some part of her inspired form. They would manacle her wrists with hot hands whenever she stopped short. Belle had taken her bonnet off. Her hair fell gold. Her skin, too, was golden, beneath the surface of which the blood was clearly rioting, and as she breathed, it did seem almost as though she was no longer the victim of her clothes.

'Wait, Belle! Wait!' cried the little girls.

'Wait for us,' called several others.

Ah, Belle is released, Laura Trevelyan saw, and was herself closer to taking wing.

Belle had a spray of the crimson bottlebrush that she had torn off recklessly. It was quite a torch flaming in her hand. She had in her skirt several smooth pebbles, in dove colours, and a little, flat, red tile, and a lump of green glass, which the bubbles made most desirable.

'Where are we going?'

The little girls' voices were imperious, if frail.

Several boys left off torturing one another and ran in the wake of the girls, demanding a *dénouement*.

'We are going to build a temple,' Belle called.

Blood will veil blushes. Besides, she was very young herself.

'Anyone would think that Belle was twelve,' complained Una Pringle, who arranged the flowers most mornings for her mother.

'What temple?' some screamed.

Boys were pressing.

'Of a goddess.'

'What goddess?'

Sand flew.

'We shall have to decide,' Belle called over her shoulder.

A great train of worshippers was now ploughing the sand, making it spurt up, and sigh. Some of the boys tossed their caps in the air as they ran, and allowed them to plump gaily upon the golden mattress of the beach.

'Belle has gone mad,' said Willie Pringle, with dubious approval.

Matters had been taken out of his hands. This was usually the case. Trailing after Belle's votaries, he stopped to touch periwinkles and taste the shining scales of salt, and although he had not yet learnt to resign himself to his nature and his lot, his senses did atone in very considerable measure for his temporary discontent.

At least, the men talking upon the rocks were no longer paramount. This was clear. Something had been cut, Una and Laura both knew, whether the German did or not; in any event, the latter was himself a man.

Men are certainly necessary, but are they not also, perhaps, tedious? Una Pringle debated.

Una and Laura began to extricate themselves.

'Woburn McAllister, the one who has been telling about the worms, is the owner of a property that many people consider the most valuable in New South Wales,' Una remembered, and cheered up. 'He must, by all accounts, be exceedingly rich.'

'Oh,' said Laura.

Sometimes her chin would take refuge in her neck; it could not sink low enough, or so it felt.

'In addition to his property, Woburn Park, he has an interest in a place in New England. His parents, poor boy,' continued Una, as she had been taught, 'both died while he was a baby, so that his expectations were exchanged for a considerable fortune right at the beginning. And there are still several uncles, either childless or bachelors. With all of whom, Woburn is on excellent terms.'

Laura listened to Voss's feet following her shame in soft, sighing sand. Una did look round once, but only saw that German, who was of no consequence.

'And such a fine fellow. Quite unspoilt,' said Una, who had listened a lot. 'Of excellent disposition.'

'I cannot bear so much excellence,' Laura begged.

'Why, Laura, how funny you are,' said Una.

But she did blush a little, before remembering that Laura was peculiar. There is nothing more odious than reserve, and Una knew very little of her friend. But for the fact that they were both girls, they would have been in every way dissimilar. Una realized that she always had disliked Laura, and would, she did not doubt, persist in that dislike, although there was every reason to believe they would remain friends.

'You take it upon yourself to despise what is praiseworthy in order to appear different,' protested the nettled Una. 'I have noticed this before in people who are clever.'

'Oh dear, you have humbled me,' Laura Trevelyan answered simply.

'But Miss Pringle is right to admire such an excellent marriage party as Mr McAllister,' contributed Voss, drawing level.

Shock caused the two girls to drop their personal difference.

'I was not thinking of him as exactly that,' Una declared.

Although, in fact, she had been. Lies were not lies, however, if told in the defence of honour.

'Still,' she added, 'one cannot help but wonder who will get him.'

'Quite right,' agreed Voss. 'Mr McAllister is obviously one of the corner-stones.'

He was kicking the sand as he walked, so that it flew in spurts of blue-whiteness before becoming wind.

'I have passed through that property,' he said. 'I have seen his house. It will resist time indefinitely, as well as many of the insect pests.'

Una had begun to glow.

'Have you been inside?' she asked. 'Have you seen the furniture? It is said to be magnificent.'

Laura could not determine the exact reason for her own sadness. She was consumed by the intense longing of the waves. The forms of burnt rock and scraggy pine were sharpening unbearably. Her shoulders felt narrow.

'I would not want,' she began.

The disappearing sand that spurted up from Voss's feet did fascinate.

'What?' Una asked severely.

'I would not want marriage with stone.'

Una's laugh was thin.

Though what she did want, Laura did not know, only that she did. She was pursued by a most lamentable, because so unreasonable, discontent.

'You would prefer sand?' Voss asked.

He stooped and picked up a handful, which he threw, so that it glittered, and some of it stung their faces.

Voss, too, was laughing.

'Almost,' said Laura, bitterly now.

She was the third to laugh, and it seemed with such freedom that she was no longer attached to anyone.

'You will regret it,' laughed Voss, 'when it has all blown.'

Una Pringle began to feel that the conversation was eluding her, so that she was quite glad when the solid form of her mother appeared on the edge of the scrub, ostensibly calling for added assistance with cups and things.

This left Voss and Laura to follow vaguely. It was not exactly clear what they should do, only that they were suddenly faced with a great gap to fill, of space, and time. Peculiarly enough, neither of them was appalled by the prospect, as both might have been earlier that afternoon. Words, silences, and sea air had worked upon them subtly, until they had undergone a change.

Walking with their heads agreeably bowed beneath the sunlight, they listened to each other's presence, and became aware that they were possibly more alike than any other two people at the Pringles' picnic.

'Happy is the assured Miss Pringle,' Voss was then saying, 'in her material future, in her stone house.'

'*I* am not *un*happy,' Laura Trevelyan replied, 'at least, never for long, although it is far from clear what my future is to be.'

'Your future is what you will make it. Future,' said Voss, 'is will.'

'Oh, I have the will,' said Laura quickly. 'But I have not yet grasped in what way I am to use it.'

'This is something which perhaps comes later to a woman,' said Voss.

Of course, he could be quite insufferable, she saw, but she could put up with it. The light was gilding them.

'Possibly,' she said.

Actually, Laura Trevelyan believed distinction between the

68

sexes to be less than was usually made, but as she had remained in complete isolation of ideas, she had never dared speak her thoughts.

It was so calm now that they had rounded a buttress of rock. The trees were leaning out towards them with slender needles of dead green. Both the man and the woman were lulled into living inwardly, without shame, or need for protection.

'This expedition, Mr Voss,' said Laura Trevelyan suddenly, 'this expedition of yours is pure will.'

She turned upon him an expression of such limpid earnestness that, in any other circumstances, he would have been surprised.

'Not entirely,' he said. 'I will be under restraint by several human beings, to say nothing of the animals and practical impedimenta my patrons consider necessary.'

'It would be better,' he added abruptly, 'that I should go barefoot, and alone. I *know*. But it is useless to try to convey to others the extent of that knowledge.'

He was grinning in a way which made his face most irregular, leaner. His lips were thin and cracked before the season of thirst had set in, and there was a tooth missing at one side. Altogether, he was unconvincing.

'You are not going to allow your will to destroy you,' she said rather than asked.

Now she was very strong. For a moment he was grateful, though he would not have thanked. He sensed how she would have taken his head, and laid it against her breast, and held it with firm hands. But he had never allowed himself the luxury of other people's strength, preferring the illusion of his own.

'Your interest is touching, Miss Trevelyan,' he laughed. 'I shall appreciate it in many desert places.'

He was trying to bring her down.

But she had crossed her fingers against the Devil.

'I do not believe in your gratitude,' she said wryly; 'just as I do not believe that I fully understand you. But I will.'

As they continued to walk beneath the black branches of the trees, the man and woman were of equal stature, it seemed, and on approaching the spot at which the most solemn rites of the picnic were in the course of being celebrated, in the little clearing, with its smell of boiling water and burnt sticks, its jolly faces and acceptable opinions, the expression of the two late arrivals suggested that they shared some guilty secret of personality. Only, nobody noticed.

The men, who had climbed up from the rocks by a less circuitous way, were herding together. Pressed by Mrs Pringle herself, a governess, and two children's nurses, everybody was busy eating. Little boys were holding chops over the coals on sticks specially sharpened by the coachmen, so that an incense of green bark mingled with the odour of sacrificial fat. Girls blew on hot tea, and dreamily watched circles widen. Ladies, suffering the occasion on carpet stools that had been brought out and set amongst the tussocks, were nibbling at thin sandwiches and controlling their shawls.

Now it could have been noticed that the German fellow was still standing at the side of Laura Trevelyan, no longer for protection, rather, one would have said, in possession. He was lording it, and it was by no means disagreeable to the girl, who accepted food without, however, looking up.

Only once she did look down, upon his wrist, where the cuff cut into it, pressing the little dark hairs.

'As I was saying, a slight domestic upheaval,' confided Mrs Bonner, made more mysterious by the passes of her recalcitrant shawl. 'More than slight, perhaps. Time will decide. Rose Portion has given us cause for anxiety.'

'Oh, dear,' groaned Mrs Pringle, as if she were suffering internally.

And waited.

Mrs Bonner caught the shawl.

'I am in honour bound, Mrs Pringle, not to go into details.'

But she would, of course.

Both ladies nursed this prospect deliciously on their unreliable stools.

Then Laura Trevelyan saw Rose standing in her brown dress, her knuckles pressed tight together. The harelip was fearful.

'No, thank you, Mr Voss,' Laura said. 'Not another crumb.'

And with that decision, she moved, so that she was standing somewhere else, protected by smeary children.

'Look, Laura,' said Jessie Pringle, 'how I have polished the bone of my chop.'

'She is a dog,' said Ernest.

Then there were blows.

Laura was glad of the opportunity to act, and was at once separating, admonishing, soothing, with the tact and firmness expected of her. She was saying:

'Now, Jessie, there is no need to cry. Look. Wash your fingers in this tin of warm water, and dry them on your handkerchief. There. Everybody knew you to be a sensible girl.'

But Rose Portion was bringing hot water in the little brass can, which she wrapped in a towel, as if it had been precious, and left in the basin of the washing-stand. Rose Portion took the brush and brushed Laura's hair, holding it in one long switch, brushing it out and down, in long sweeps. Sometimes the back of the brush thumped on Rose's big breasts, as she brushed monotonously on.

Laura Trevelyan looked. It was impossible not to see the German where he was standing in the grey scrub, his dry lips the moister for butter, fuller in that light. The light was tangling with his coarse beard.

Ah, miss, said Jack Slipper, you have come out for a breather, well, the breeze has got up, can you hear it in the leaves? Whatever the source of the friction of the bamboos, it usually sounded cooler in their thicket. But in summer there were also the murmurous voices of insects, and often of men and women, which would create a breathlessness in that corner of the garden. Full moonlight failed to illuminate its secrets. There was a hot, black smell of rotting. The silver flags, breaking, and flying on high, almost escaping from their lacquered masts, were brought back continually by the mysterious ganglion of dark roots.

'Come now, Laura,' said Mrs Pringle, 'many hands make light work. There are all these things to collect. We shall be late, as it is, for the children's baths,' she added, consulting a small watch in blue enamel suspended from her person by a little chain.

Laura Trevelyan had held back, dreaming, in her moss-green jacket. She was rather pale. Little points of perspiration glittered on her forehead, at the roots of her hair. In less oblivious company, her shame might have become exposed. As it was, she received Mrs Pringle's suggestion with relief. She began to help

71

Miss Abbey, the governess, to gather forks into bundles, scrape plates, wrap remainders. In this way she was able to avoid actual sight of the German, even if her mind's eye dwelt on the masculine shape of his lips, and his wiry wrist with the little hairs. By moving still faster, she could perhaps destroy these impressions. So she did, in a fury of competence. He was terribly repulsive to her.

And the journey home was even more oppressive than the journey out, for Uncle had been added to those already in the enclosed carriage. He was all jokes, now that he need not be ashamed of Voss. He loved the German when he could openly admire the purpose for which the latter had been bought. He would tap his protégé on the knee, both to emphasize ownership, and to assist language.

But Voss grunted, and looked sideways out of the window. They were all tired of one another, all except Mr Bonner, one of those fleshy men who never for a moment suffer the loss of a dimension.

When they reached that place where the road turned into Potts Point, Voss at once edged forward, and said:

'I will alight here, if you please.'

'No, no, Voss,' Mr Bonner protested, with that congestion of enthusiasm which suggests a throttling. 'Stay with us till we reach the house. Then Jim will drive you to your lodgings.'

Regrettably, his kind offer sounded something like a command.

'It is unnecessary,' said Voss, wrestling with the wretched carriage door.

The sash was against him. He was tearing his nails.

Mrs Bonner began to make some sound that vaguely signified distress.

'If you halt the carriage, I will descend here,' repeated Voss, from the region of his knotted throat.

He was desperate to escape from that carriage.

Then Mr Bonner, by shouting, perhaps even by oaths, did attract the attention of Jim Prentice on the box, and as the vehicle stopped, himself leaned forward to touch with a finger the door that delayed the German's freedom.

The trapped crow stalked out. Although rusty and crumpled,

72

he had triumphed, and the last blaze of evening light will help enlarge most objects to heroic proportions. The man would be ludicrous, Laura saw, if it were not for his arrogance; this just saves him, terrible though it is. His eyes were glittering with it in the mineral light of evening.

'I thank you for the pleasant *Ausflug,*' he began, but struck his hands together in frustration; 'for the pleasant day, Mrs Bonner,' he added.

He had not quite escaped. Round him, words continued to writhe.

Aunt Emmy was, of course, charmed, and formed her mouth into several appropriate shapes.

Uncle, who was under the impression that foreigners understood only what was shouted at them, proceeded to mutter his views on a certain individual.

'I will communicate with you, Mr Bonner,' said Voss, looking in all other directions, 'on any matter of importance. The time is now so short for me to impose upon your goodness.'

He was smiling slightly.

'If I have been a burden.'

Everybody was astounded but Voss, who seemed to be enjoying himself. He was drinking down the evening air, as if no one could appreciate what he had suffered. Even his nostrils despised.

'I thank you again,' he said, completing some pattern of formality significant only to himself.

And did bow.

To himself, Laura saw.

All this queerness was naturally discussed as the carriage crunched onward, and the German, walking into the sunset, was burnt up. In the carriage three people were talking. Three held innocent opinions. The fourth was silent.

Laura did not speak, because she was ashamed. It was as if she had become personally involved. So the sensitive witness of some unfortunate incident will take the guilt upon himself, and feel the need to expiate it. So the young woman was stirring miserably in her stuffy corner, and would have choked, she felt, if they had not arrived, driving in sudden relief under the hollow-sounding portico. It was necessary, she knew, to humiliate herself in some way for the German's arrogance. She could feel her nails biting her own pride.

Then Rose Portion, who had been waiting for them in the dusk, came out and opened the carriage door, and let down the little step for the masters' feet.

4

FEW people of attainments take easily to a plan of self-improvement. Some discover very early their perfection cannot endure the insult. Others find their intellectual pleasure lies in the theory, not the practice. Only a few stubborn ones will blunder on, painfully, out of the luxuriant world of their pretensions into the desert of mortification and reward.

To this third category belonged Laura Trevelyan. She had been kept very carefully, put away like some object of which the precious nature is taken for granted. She had a clear skin, distinction, if unreliable beauty. Her clothes were soothing, rather moody, exactly suited to her person. No one in that household could write a more appropriate note on occasions of mourning, or others calling for tact, in that version of the Italian hand which courts the elegant while eschewing the showy. She was the literate member of the family, even frighteningly so, it seemed to the others, and more by instinct than from concentrated study. Not that the merchant had denied his girls the number of governesses requisite to their social position, and the French Mademoiselle, and the music master, it need not be added. The niece's knowledge of the French tongue, modest, though sufficient, was terribly impressive to some, and on evenings when her aunt entertained, she would be persuaded to perform, with admirably light touch, one of the piano pieces of Mendelssohn or Field.

If she was a prig, she was not so far gone that she did not sometimes recognize it, and smart behind the eyes accordingly. But to know is not to cure. She was beset by all kinds of dark helplessnesses that might become obsessions. If I am lost, then who can be saved; she was egotist enough to ask. She wanted very badly to make amends for the sins of others. So that in the face of desperate needs, and having rejected prayer as a rationally indefensible solution, she could not surrender her self-opinion, at least, not altogether. Searching the mirror, biting her fine lips, she said: I have strength, certainly, of a kind, if it is not arrogance. Or, she added, is it not perhaps – will?

One morning, while the curtains were still keeping the sun at bay, Laura Trevelyan set her mouth, and resolved to exercise that will in accepting the first stages of self-humiliation. As she had been giving the matter thought since quite an early hour, all the young woman's pulses were beating and her wrists were weak by the time Rose arrived to admit the light.

The girl watched the thick arms reach up and jerk in that abrupt manner at the curtains. Then, when the room had received back its shape, and the can of water was standing in the basin, and one or two things that had fallen had been picked up and set to rights, the woman said:

'You have not slept, miss.'

'I would not say that I had not slept,' Laura replied. 'How can you tell, Rose?'

'Oh, I know. There are things you can tell by knowing.'

'You are determined to mystify me,' laughed the girl, and immediately frowned to think how she must run the gauntlet of her servant's intuition.

'I am a simple woman,' Rose said.

Laura held her face away. The yellow light was blinding her.

'I do not know what you are, Rose. You have never shown me.'

'Ah, now, miss, you are playing on my ignorance.'

'In what way?'

'How am I to show you what I am? I am not an educated person. I am just a woman.'

Laura Trevelyan got up quickly. She would have liked to open a cupboard, and to look inside. Her feelings would not have been disturbed by such a reasonable act and sight of inanimate objects. However, nothing important is easy. So she looked instead at Rose, and saw her struggling lip. In moments of distress, or even simple bewilderment, this would open like a live wound.

75

They were both exposed now in the centre of the thick carpet. They could have been trembling for a common nakedness. In the girl's case, of course, her nightgown was rather fine.

'There, miss,' said Rose, covering her mistress with usual skill. 'The mornings are still fresh.'

The two women were touching each other, briefly.

'They are not really,' shivered Laura Trevelyan, for whom all intimacies, whether of mind or body, were still a plunge.

Then she walked across the room, combing out her hair that the night had thickened.

'Rose,' she said, 'you must see that you take care now. That you do nothing unnecessarily strenuous. That you do not lift weights, for instance, nor run downstairs.'

She was ashamed of the clumsiness, the ugliness of her own words, then, of their coldness, but she had not learnt to use them otherwise. She was, in final appraisal, without accomplishment.

'You must not hurt yourself,' she said ridiculously.

Rose was breathing. She was arranging things.

'I'll not harm,' she said at last. 'I have come through worse. I have been laid right open in my time.'

She did not expect exemption.

'I shall resist all attempts to make me suffer, or to bring suffering to others,' said the younger woman, to whom it was still a matter of will and theory.

The rather strange situation made her speak almost to herself, or to an impersonal companion. Since she had begun to prise the other's close soul, she herself was opening stiffly.

'I did not expect to suffer,' Rose Portion was telling. 'I was a young girl, in service in a big house. I was in the stillroom, I remember, under as decent a woman as ever you would be likely to find. It was a happy place, and in spring, when the blossom was out, you should have seen it, miss. It was the picture of perfection. That was it, perhaps. I did trust, and expect over much. Well, it is all past. I loved my little boy that was given me, but I would not have had him suffer. That was what they did not understand. They said it was a thing only a monster could have done, and all considered, I was getting off light with a sentence of transportation for life. But they had not carried my little boy, nor lain with all those thoughts, all those nights. Well, there it is. I was not meant to suffer, not then, or now – you would have said. But sufferin' creeps up. And in different disguises. You do not recognize it, miss. You will see.'

Soon after this, as she had done what she had to do, the squat woman went out of Laura Trevelyan's room. The girl remained agitated, moved certainly by Rose's story, but disturbed rather by dangers she had now committed herself to share.

So that when Aunt Emmy, in the days that followed, was going about the house, wondering what should be done about Rose, her niece did not know.

'You are no help at all, Laura,' Mrs Bonner complained, 'when you are usually so bright, and full of clever ideas. Nor can I expect help from Mr Bonner, who is too upset by that German. If it is not one thing, it is another. I must admit I am quite distracted.'

'We shall think, Aunt,' said Laura, who was rather pale.

But thought, which should be an inspiration, was clogging her.

Laura is becoming heavy, Aunt Emmy said, and would add this worry to her collection.

Then, she hit upon a cure, so simple, but infallible, at least to Mrs Bonner, for to cure herself was to cure her patients. She would give a party. It would revive all spirits, soothe all nerves, even the frayed German ones. For Mrs Bonner loved conviviality. She loved the way the mood would convey itself even to the candle-flames. She loved all pretty, coloured things; even the melancholy rinds of fruit, the slops of wine, the fragments of a party, recalled some past magic. Whether as a prospect or a memory, a party made her quite tipsy – figuratively speaking, that is – for Mrs Bonner did not touch strong drink, unless on a very special occasion, a sip of champagne, or on hot evenings, a glass of delicious brandy punch, or sometimes of a morning, for the visitor's sake a really *good* madeira, or thimbleful of dandelion wine.

'Mr Bonner,' she now said, seriously, though holding her head upon one side in case she might not be taken so, 'it is but a week, do you realize, to the departure of Mr Voss and his friends. It is only right that you, in your position, and we, naturally, as your family, should celebrate in some way. I have been thinking,' she said.

'Eh?' said her husband. 'I am not interested in that German except in so far as I am already committed. Let the relationship remain plain; it is so distasteful to me. It would be hypocritical to add trimmings, not to mention the expense.'

'I understand,' said Mrs Bonner, 'that he is something of a disappointment. But let us leave aside the character of Mr Voss. I would like to see you do justice to yourself, and to this – I cannot very well refer to it as anything but an event of national significance.'

She did not know she had achieved that, until she had, and then was very pleased.

Her husband was surprised. He shifted.

After coughing a confident though genteel cough, Mrs Bonner produced the flag she intended to plant upon the summit of her argument.

'An historical occasion,' she pursued, 'made possible by the generosity of several, but which you, originally – do not deny it, my dear – which you, and only you, inspired!'

'It remains to be seen,' said Mr Bonner, more kindly because it concerned himself, 'whether it was an inspiration or calamity.'

'I thought now,' said his judicious wife, 'that we might give a little party, or not a party, something simple, a pair of birds and a round of beef, with a few nice side dishes. And a good wine. Or two. And as for the friends of Mr Voss, I do not intend to invite all and sundry, for some, I understand, are just common men, but one or two who are *comme il foh*, and used to mix with ladies and young girls. Belle has a new dress that nobody has seen, and Laura, of course, can look charming in anything.'

So Mr Bonner was gently pressed, and finally kissed upon the forehead.

Mrs Bonner conceived her plan upon the Friday, exactly one week before the projected departure of the expedition by sea to Newcastle. On Friday afternoon, Jim Prentice, after saddling Hamlet, took the cards, that were in Miss Trevelyan's fine Italian hand, to drop at the lodgings of Mr Voss and Mr Topp, and those of Mr Palfreyman, who, it had been decided, might be considered *comme il foh*. And there was a Miss Hollier, whom people invited when they were in a scrape for an extra lady. Miss Hollier was a person of modest income and middle age, but of really excellent spirits. Well trained in listening to others, she would sometimes pop such good ideas into their heads they would immediately adopt her suggestions as their own. Moreover, and appropriate to the occasion, the lady was a distant connexion of Mr Sanderson of Rhine Towers, one of the patrons of the expedition. Lastly, there was Tom Radclyffe. If the Lieutenant had been omitted from Mrs Bonner's list of those who were to receive cards, it was because he remained in a state of almost constant communication with a certain person. It was taken for granted Tom would come.

These, then, were the guests who were bidden for the following Wednesday.

It proved to be a night of drifting airs. Belle Bonner had come, or floated into her cousin's room to show her dress of light. It was a dress of pure, whitest light, streaming and flashing from her. Her hands and arms would pass through those shafts of light to smooth out any encroaching shadow. Her hair, too, shone – her rather streaky, but touching hair, still drenched with sunlight, and smelling of it.

'Oh, Belle!' said Laura, when she saw.

The girls kissed with some tenderness, though not enough to disarrange.

'But it does not fit,' said Belle, becoming desperately herself. 'I shall split open. You will see.'

'And ruin us!' Laura cried.

They were both laughing, unreasonably, dreadfully, deliriously. They could well die of it.

'At least Miss Hollier will not see,' Laura burst out, too loud, through her laughter; 'not if you were standing in your worst chemise and petticoat. She is far too well brought up.'

'Stop, Laura!' Belle begged.

She was mopping herself.

'I insist, Laura. You really must. Perhaps not Miss Hollier, but somebody else. I do believe Mr Voss notices everything.'

Almost immediately it was felt they must remember their age, and they set to work, sighingly, to repair themselves.

If Laura would be noticed less than Belle, it was because she was beautiful on that night. This became slowly clear. Belle ravished, like any sudden spring flower, but Laura would require her own climate in which to open. She wore a dress of peacock colours that did not take to full light, but brooded and smouldered in subtle retirement, which did, in fact, invite her arms and shoulders to emerge more mysteriously. Her head was a jewel, but of some dark colour, and of a variety such as people overlook because they have not been taught to admire.

'Let us go down,' Belle suggested, 'before Mamma is there, and have a quiet sip of something to give us courage.'

So the two girls, smelling of French chalk and lavender water, were winding down. It was a heady staircase. They had pinned clusters of camellias at their breasts, and were holding themselves rather erect, lest some too sudden gesture or burst of emotion should turn the petals brown.

That night anything could happen. Two big lamps had transformed the drawing-room into a perfect, luminous egg, which soon contained all the guests. These were waiting to be hatched by some communication with one another. Or would it not occur? The eyes appeared hopeful, if the lids were more experienced, themselves enclosed egg-shapes with uncommunicative veins. All the while the white threads of voices tangled and caught. Men's voices that had come in, toughened the fibre. But nobody said what they intended to say. This was sidetracked, while the speakers stood smiling at what had happened, and adopted, even with traces of sincerity, the words which had been put into their mouths. It was still rather a merciless dream at that early hour.

Until Tom Radclyffe, who was blazing with scarlet, and whose substantial good-fortune was the best reason for self-confidence, burst out of the awkward dream and took reality by the hand. The stuff of her surprising dress caused him little shivers of devotion as it brushed along his skin. Everyone else, sharing his devotion, was agreed that Belle was the belle.

Even Mr Voss suffered a pang for cornfields and ripe apples.

'Seldom have I regrets for the Germany I have left,' he remarked to Miss Hollier, 'although I will suddenly realize I have a yearning to experience another German summer. The fields are sloping as in no other land, with such slow sweeps. The trees are too green, even under dust. And the rivers, ah, how the rivers flow!'

So that the excellent Miss Hollier felt quite melancholy.

Then Mrs Bonner, who had a surprise for Mr Voss, brought a book she had remembered, that some governess had left, it could have been, of German verses, evidently.

'There,' she said, with an amusing laugh, as if patting bubbles upward.

'*Ach*,' breathed Voss, down his nose.

But he seemed pleased.

He began to read. It was again a dream, Laura sensed, but of a different kind, in the solid egg of lamplight, from which they had not yet been born.

Voss read, or dreamed aloud:

> '*Am blassen Meeresstrande*
> *Sass ich gedankenbekümmert und einsam.*
> *Die Sonne neigte sich tiefer, and warf*
> *Glührote Streifen auf das Wasser,*
> *Und die weissen, weiten Wellen,*
> *Von der Flut gedrängt,*
> *Schäumten und rauschten näher und näher. . . .*'

He closed up the book rather abruptly.

'What is it, Mr Voss?' Mrs Bonner asked. 'You *must* tell,' she protested.

'Ah, yes,' begged Miss Hollier. 'Do translate for us.'

'Poetry will not bear translation. It is too personal.'

'That is most unkind,' said Mrs Bonner, who would pursue almost morbidly anything she did not understand.

Laura now turned her back. She had touched hands with the German, and exchanged smiles, but not those of recognition. She did not wish for this. He was rather sickly when moved by recollection of the past, as he was, in fact, when collected and in the present. She was glad when the dinner was served and they could give their attention to practical acts.

All went well, although Cassie had overdone the beef. Mr Bonner frowned. Dishes were in profusion, and handed with unexpected skill, by Rose Portion, whose condition was not yet obvious beneath her best apron, and an elderly man, lent by Archdeacon Endicott who lived in the same road. The Archdeacon's man was of awful respectability, in a kind of livery and cotton gloves, and only once put his cotton thumb in the soup. In addition to these, there was the invisible Edith, whose *oo-errr* was heard once from behind doors, and who would gollop the remainders of puddings before walking home.

Voss ate with appetite, taking everything for granted. That is how it ought to be, Laura had to tell herself. She was annoyed to find that she was fascinated by his method of using a knife and fork, and determined to make some effort to ignore.

'I would be curious to read little Laura's thoughts,' remarked Tom Radclyffe, with the pomposity of one who was about to become her cousin.

It did amuse him to be hated, at least by those who could be of no possible use.

Laura, however, would not hate just then.

'If I take you at your word, you may regret it,' she replied, 'because I have been thinking of nothing in particular. Which is another way of saying: almost everything. I was thinking how happy one can be sitting inside a conversation in which one is not compelled to take part. Words are only sympathetic when they are detached from their obligations. Under those conditions I am never able to resist adding yet another to my collection, just as some people are moved to make collections of curious stones. Then, there was the pretty dish of jellied quinces that I saw in the kitchen this evening as I passed through. Then, if you still wish to hear, Miss Hollier's garnet brooch, which I understand she inherited from an aunt, and which I would like to think edible, like the quinces. And there was the poem read by Mr Voss, which I did understand in a sense, if not the sense of words. Just now, it was the drumstick on Mr Palfreyman's plate. I was thinking of the bones of a dead man, uncovered by a fox, it was believed, that I once saw in Penrith churchyard as I walked there with Lucy Cox, and how I was not upset, as Lucy was. It is the thought of death that frightens me. Not its bones.'

Mrs Bonner, who feared that the limits of convention had been exceeded, was making little signs to her niece, using her mouth and the corner of a discreet napkin. But Laura herself had no wish to continue. It was obvious that her last remark must be the final one.

'Dear me, if these educated young ladies are not the deuce,' said Tom Radclyffe, whose turn it was to hate.

Ideas disturbed his manliness.

'I am sorry, Tom, to have given you literally what you asked for,' Laura said. 'You must take care not to run the risk in future.'

'*I* am sorry that you should have such horrid thoughts on a jolly occasion. The bones of a dead man in a grave!' Miss Hollier said. 'Mr Palfreyman has been telling me such delightful, really interesting and instructive things about birds.'

Mr Palfreyman appeared sad.

He was, in fact, happiest with birds, and realized this as he watched Miss Hollier's shining teeth. But he was wrong, he knew, unreasonably so. Some people cannot bear to touch the folded body of a dead bird. He, on the other hand, must learn to overcome his impulse to retreat from kind hands.

Puddings had by this time been brought: brittlest baskets of caramel, great gobbets of meringue. When the big, thick, but somehow thoughtful woman who was waiting at table set down among them the jellied quinces, Voss saw that it was indeed a pretty dish, of garnet colour, with pale jade lozenges, and a somewhat clumsy star in that same stone, or angelica.

Then the German looked across at the niece, who had been avoiding him all the evening, it seemed, though until that moment he had not felt the need for her attention. Without intending it sardonically, he smiled and asked:

'If you have not understood the poem by the words, how would you interpret it?'

Laura Trevelyan frowned slightly.

'You yourself have made the excuse that must always be made for poetry,' she replied.

Just at that moment, under the influence of discussion, everyone else at the table was deaf to the German and the young woman, who were brought together for the first time since the Pringles' picnic, rather more closely than Laura would have wished.

However, she now returned his smile, and said:

'You must allow me my secrets.'

He wondered whether she was being sincere, or just womanly,

83

but as he had drunk several glasses of wine, he did not really care. Her head, he noticed, was glittering in its setting of candlelight, either with the hysteria of a young girl, or that sensibility at which she hinted, and which he rather despised unless he could learn its secrets.

He kept looking at her on and off, while she bent her head and knew that some kind of revelation must eventually take place, terrible though the prospect was.

In the course of ritual, after the ladies had abandoned the gentlemen to the port and everyone had been bored for a little, Mrs Bonner pounced on Mr Topp and smiled and asked: Would he? It was obvious that he had been invited only for this moment. As it was invariably the case, he was neither surprised nor offended, but addressed himself to the pianoforte with such relief that the susceptibilities of his hosts would have been hurt if they had but considered. Mrs Bonner, however, was creating groups of statuary. This was her strength, to coax out of flesh the marble that is hidden in it. So her guests became transfixed upon the furniture. Then Mrs Bonner, having control, was almost happy. Only, thought and music eluded her. Now she was, in fact, standing in her own drawing-room with this suspicion on her face, of something that had strayed. If she could have put her finger on it, if she could have turned infinity to stone, then she would have sunk down in her favourite chair, with all disposed around her, and rested her feet upon a little beaded stool.

Mr Topp played and played. He would have continued all night, as he had developed the vice of playing for himself, but Miss Hollier had to be pressed, and was eventually persuaded to execute that piece in which she crossed her wrists several times, ever so gracefully, above the keys.

Then Tom Radclyffe must stand up to sing *Love's Witchcraft*. He had a high bass. Real fervour filled his scarlet coat, and caused some vibration amongst the objects in glass and china on the shelves of cabinets. Belle Bonner's skin had turned a cloudy white.

'Maiden look me in the face,'

the Lieutenant sang;

'Steadfast, serious, no grimace!
Maiden, mark me, now I task thee
Answer quickly, what I ask thee!
Steadfast look me in the face.
Little vixen, no grimace!'

Now Belle was neither flesh nor marble. She was enveloped in, and had herself become, a cloud of the most assiduous tenderness. To have remained in such a trance, of cloud wrapping cloud, would have been perpetual bliss, but her practical nature led her out and away, and she was walking along the gravel paths surrounding a house in which she was established, with every sign of prosperity and elegance – and Love; Love, of course. Love approached along that same gravel, smelling familiarly of macassar, or, assuming another of his forms, stroked with the skins of seven babies. Until Belle blushed, and those who had been looking for it, saw.

By that hour, before the tea-things were brought in, the lamplight, which in the beginning had been a solid, engrossed yellow, was suffused with the palpitating rose colours. The petals that had fallen on mahogany were reflected upward. The big, no longer perfect roses were bursting with scent and sticky stamens. And it was rather warm.

Partly for that reason Laura Trevelyan had gone out through the moths to the terrace where the stone urns were, and where somebody had been crushing geranium, but the heavy air of darkness was, if anything, more distasteful to her than that of the rapt, cloying room. As she strolled she was still attended by the light from lamps. This, however, could not be stretched much farther, and she did hesitate. It was now possible that the usually solid house, and all that it contained, that the whole civil history of those parts was presumptuous, and that the night, close and sultry as savage flesh, distant and dilating as stars, would prevail by natural law.

Drifting in that nihilistic darkness with agreeable resignation, the young woman bumped against some hard body and immediately recovered her own.

'I beg your pardon, Miss Trevelyan,' said Voss. 'You also have come out in search of refreshment.'

'I?' said Laura. 'Yes, it was stuffy. The first hot nights of the season are difficult. But so deceptive. Dangerous, even. A wind may spring up in half an hour from now, and we shall be shivering.'

She was already, despite the fact that they were swathed in a woollen darkness. Down there, round the bay, there was still a rushy marsh, from which a young man who had recently gone in search of mussels had contracted a fever, it was told, and died.

But Voss was not at that moment interested in climatic peculiarities.

To what extent is this girl dishonest? he wondered.

Unaccustomed to recognize his own dishonesties, he was rather sensitive to them in others.

It is disgraceful, of course, Laura realized; I have come out here for no convincing reason. She was defenceless. Perhaps even guilty.

'I try to visualize your life in this house,' said Voss, facing the honeycomb of windows, in some of which dark figures burrowed for a moment before drowning in the honey-coloured light. 'Do you count the linen?'

He was truly interested, now that it did seem to affect him in some way not yet accounted for.

'Do you make pastry? Hem sheets? Or are you reading novels in these rooms, and receiving morning calls from acquaintances, ladies with small waists and affectations?'

'We indulge in a little of each,' Laura admitted, 'but in no event are we insects, Mr Voss.'

'I have not intended to suggest,' he laughed. 'It is my habit of approach.'

'Is it so difficult then, for a man, to imagine the lives of poor domesticated women? How very extraordinary! Or is it that you are an extraordinary man?'

'I have not entered into the minds of other men, so that I cannot honestly say with any degree of accuracy.'

But he would keep his private conviction.

'I think that I can enter into the minds of most men,' said the young woman, softly. 'At times. An advantage we insect-women enjoy is that we have endless opportunity to indulge the imagination as we go backwards and forwards in the hive.'

'And in my instance, what does your imagination find?'

He was laughing, of course, at the absurdity of that which he expected to be told. But he would have liked to hear practically anything.

'Shall we go a little?' he invited.

'Walking in this darkness is full of dangers.'

'It is not really dark. When you are accustomed to it.'

Which was true. The thick night was growing luminous. At least, it was possible almost to see, while remaining almost hidden.

The man and woman were walking over grass that was still kindly beneath their feet. Smooth, almost cold leaves soothed their faces and the backs of their hands.

'These are the camellia bushes Uncle planted when he first came here as a young man,' Laura Trevelyan said. 'There are fifteen varieties, as well as sports. This one here is the largest,' she said, shaking it as if it had been an inanimate object; it was so familiar to her, and now so necessary. 'It is a white, but there is one branch that bears those marbled flowers, you know, like the edges of a ledger.'

'Interesting,' he said.

But it was an obscure reply, of a piece with the spongy darkness that surrounded them.

'Then you are not going to answer my question?' he asked.

'Oh,' she said, 'that silly claim I made! Although, to a certain extent, it is true.'

'Tell me, then.'

'Everyone is offended by the truth, and you will not be an exception.'

That it would take place, they both knew now.

Consequently, when she did speak, the sense of inevitability that they shared made her sound as if she were reading from a notebook, only this one was her head, in which her memorandum had been written, in invisible ink, that the night had breathed upon; and as she read, or spoke, it became obvious to both that she had begun to compile her record from the first moment of their becoming acquainted.

'You are so vast and ugly,' Laura Trevelyan was repeating the words; 'I can imagine some desert, with rocks, rocks of prejudice, and, yes, even hatred. You are so isolated. That is why

87

you are fascinated by the prospect of desert places, in which you will find your own situation taken for granted, or more than that, exalted. You sometimes scatter kind words or bits of poetry to people, who soon realize the extent of their illusion. Everything is for yourself. Human emotions, when you have them, are quite flattering to you. If those emotions strike sparks from others, that also is flattering. But most flattering, I think, when you experience it, is the hatred, or even the mere irritation of weaker characters.'

'Do you hate me, perhaps?' asked Voss, in darkness.

'I am fascinated by you,' laughed Laura Trevelyan, with such candour that her admission did not seem immodest. '*You* are *my* desert!'

Once or twice their arms brushed, and he was conscious of some extreme agitation or exhilaration in her.

'I am glad that I do not need your good opinion,' he said.

'No,' she said. 'Nobody's opinion!'

He was surprised at the vehemence of feeling in this young girl. In such circumstances, repentance, he felt, might have been a luxury. But he did not propose to enjoy any such softness. Besides, faith in his own stature had not been destroyed.

He began to bite his nails in the darkness.

'You are upset,' he said, 'because you would like to pity me, and you cannot.'

'If that were the case, I would certainly have cause to be upset,' she blurted most wildly.

'You would like to mention me in your prayers.'

By this time Laura Trevelyan had become lost somewhere in the dark of the garden. But I, too, am self-sufficient, she remembered, with some lingering repugnance for her dead prayers.

'I do not pray,' she answered, miserably.

'*Ach*,' he pounced, 'you are not *atheistisch*?'

'I do not know,' she said.

She had begun to tear a cluster of the white camellias from that biggest bush. In passing, she had snapped the hot flowers, which were now poor lumps of things. She was tearing them across, as if they had not been flesh, but some passive stuff, like blotting-paper.

'Atheists are atheists usually for mean reasons,' Voss was say-

88

ing. 'The meanest of these is that they themselves are so lacking in magnificence they cannot conceive the idea of a Divine Power.'

He was glittering coldly. The wind that the young woman had promised had sprung up, she realized dully. The stars were trembling. Leaves were slashing at one another.

'Their reasons,' said Laura, 'are simple, honest, personal ones. As far as I can tell. For such steps are usually taken in privacy. Certainly after considerable anguish of thought.'

The darkness was becoming furious.

'But the God they have abandoned is of mean conception,' Voss pursued. 'Easily destroyed, because in their own image. Pitiful because such destruction does not prove the destroyer's power. *Atheismus* is self-murder. Do you not understand?'

'I am to understand that I have destroyed myself. But you, Mr Voss,' Laura cried, 'it is for you I am concerned. To watch the same fate approaching someone else is far, far worse.'

In the passion of their relationship, she had encountered his wrist. She held his bones. All their gestures had ugliness, convulsiveness in common. They stood with their legs apart inside their innocent clothes, the better to grip the reeling earth.

'I am aware of no similarity between us,' Voss replied.

He was again cold, but still arrested. Her hands had eaten into his wrist.

'It is for our pride that each of us is probably damned,' Laura said.

Then he shook her off, and the whole situation of an hysterical young woman. He was wiping his lips, which had begun to twitch, though in anger, certainly, not from weakness. He breathed deeply. He drank from the great arid skies of fluctuating stars. The woman beside him had begun to suggest the presence of something soft and defenceless.

Indeed, Laura Trevelyan did not feel she would attempt anything further, whatever might be revealed to her.

'For some reason of intellectual vanity, you decided to do away with God,' Voss was saying; she knew he would be smiling. 'But the consequences are yours alone. I assure you.'

It was true; he made her know.

'I feel you may still suspect me,' he continued. 'But I do believe, you must realize. Even though I worship with pride. Ah,

89

the humility, the humility! This is what I find so particularly loathsome. My God, besides, is above humility.'

'Ah,' she said. 'Now I understand.'

It was clear. She saw him standing in the glare of his own brilliant desert. Of course, He was Himself indestructible.

And she did then begin to pity him. She no longer pitied herself, as she had for many weeks in the house of her uncle, whose unfailingly benevolent materialism encouraged the practice of self-pity. Love seemed to return to her with humility. Her weakness was delectable.

'I shall think of you with alarm,' she said. 'To maintain such standards of pride, in the face of what you must experience on this journey, is truly alarming.'

'I am not in the habit of setting myself limits.'

'Then I will learn to pray for you.'

'Oh dear, I have caught you out doubly,' he laughed. 'You are an Apostle of Love masquerading as an atheist for some inquisitorial purpose of your own. My poor Miss Trevelyan! I shall be followed through the continent of Australia by your prayers, like little pieces of white paper. I can see them, torn-up paper, fluttering, now that I know for certain you are one of those who pray.'

'I have failed to be. But I will learn.'

These simple ideas were surrounded with such difficulties they would scarcely issue out of her inadequate mind.

Then he was touching her, his hand was upon her shoulderblades, and they realized they had returned into their bodies.

'Is it not really very cold?' she said at once, shivering.

'People will come to look for you. You are lost in the garden.'

'They are too agreeably occupied.'

'I have been hateful to you this evening,' confessed the German, as if it had just occured to him, but she did not resent it; in her state of recovered conviction his defects were even welcome.

'We were unwise,' he said, 'to flounder into each other's private beings.'

She smiled.

'I know you are smiling,' he said. 'Why?' he asked, and laughed.

'It is our *beings* that pleases me,' she replied.

'Is it not expressive, then?'

'Oh, it is expressive, I dare say, in its clumsiness.'

The beautiful, but rather tentative young girl of that evening, in her smouldering, peacock dress, and the passionate but bewildered soul of the woman that had flapped and struggled in the dark garden in its attempt to rescue (let us not say: subdue) were being dispossessed by a clumsy contentment of the flesh.

'I have long given up trying to express myself,' she sighed warmly.

The man yawned.

He knew that he did enjoy the company of this young woman, who was exhausted, and standing as naturally in her shoes as her careful upbringing would allow.

'When I was younger,' said this girl, as if it had been a long time ago, 'I kept a diary. Oh, I wrote down everything, everything. I could not express too much. And how proud I was to read it. Then I no longer could. I would stare at a blank page, and that would appear far more expressive than my own emptiness.'

The man yawned again. He was not bored, however, but very happy. He, too, was rather exhausted by what had happened, but his physical exhaustion was sealing up the memory of it.

'While I am engaged on this expedition,' he said, 'I will, of course, keep a journal, that you will read afterwards, and follow me step by step.'

Even his pride had grown tired and childlike.

'The official journal of the expedition,' murmured the young woman, not ironically, to the tired child.

'Yes. The official journal,' he repeated, in grave agreement.

It was obvious that she would read it with that interest women took in the achievements of men.

Ah, I must pray for him, she said, for he will be in need of it.

He was inexplicably flattered by her no longer communicative presence in the darkness, and very contented.

Then Mrs Bonner had emerged from the square light, and was puckering up her face at darkness, and trying to read its mind.

She called:

'Laura! Laura, dear, where are you? Laur-*a*.'

So that her niece felt it her duty to approach. In leaving, she barely touched Voss upon the hand. He was not sure whether he was intended to go or stay, but followed immediately.

They came out into the light almost together. Almost as if they had been sleep-walking, Aunt Emmy feared.

'My dear child, you will be frozen,' she began to complain, and frowned.

But as if she did not see Voss.

'In this treacherous wind.'

With that wretched man.

She half-arranged an invisible shawl as a protection against her own distress in such a situation.

'Miss Hollier particularly wants to hear you play the Field nocturne, the one with the pretty tune towards the end, you know, that I so much like.'

They went into the rosy room, where Uncle had built his hands into a gable, and was explaining to Mr Palfreyman, whose eyeballs had grit behind them, the dangerous hold the sectarians, not to say Roman Catholics, already had upon the Colony. It was strange that things spiritual should make Mr Bonner's flesh swell.

Laura Trevelyan immediately sat down at the piano, and gave rather a flat rendering of the Field nocturne.

The German, who had followed the ladies into the room, stood biting his lips, unconscious of the awkward, even embarrassing attitude of his body, listening, or so it appeared, as if the music propounded some idea above the level of its agreeable mediocrity. Then he went and flung himself down, boorishly, Miss Hollier remarked afterwards to a friend, flung himself upon an upright sofa that did not respond to him. He sat or sprawled there, passing his hand intermittently over his forehead and his closed eyes, and remained more or less oblivious after Laura had left the piano.

So he spent what remained of the evening. He himself could not have told exactly of what he was thinking. He would have liked to give, what he was not sure, if he had been able, if he had not destroyed this himself with deliberate ruthlessness in the beginning. In its absence there remained, in the lit room, a shimmering of music, and of the immense distances towards which he already trudged.

5

THE morning Johann Ulrich Voss and his party were due to
sail to Newcastle on the first stage of their attempt to cross the
continent, a fair number of friends and inquisitive strangers was
converging on the Circular Wharf. It was a still, glassy morning,
from which the wind had but recently fallen after blowing
almost continuously for three whole days. It would rise again,
however, said those who knew instinctively of such things; it
would rise later that afternoon, and more than likely take the
Osprey out.

So there was a quiet conviction of preparation in the lovely
morning, although at sight of green water lolling round the sides
of ships and little blunt boats, all belief in oceans should have
been suspended. Life was grown humane. No one would be
crucified on any such amiable trees as those pressed along the
northern shore. On all sides of the landscape there was evident at
present a passionless beauty that recurred even in the works of
men. Houses were honester, more genial, it seemed, in the crude
attempt to fulfil their purpose. Then, there was the long, lean
ship, smelling of fresh tar, of hemp, of salt, and a cargo of seed
potatoes with the earth still on them. This ship that would carry
the party on the first and gentle lap of their immense journey,
and which had been evolved by some most happy conjunction
of art and science, could never have known conflict of canvas, or
so it appeared.

Most tackle had already been conveyed aboard, either the
previous evening, or early on the present day, before the drunk-
ards had begun to stir on the ruts of the streets, while cows with
full udders were still filing towards the fringes of the town. The
stars were not yet gone when Voss stuck his head into his cold
shirt. His skin was soon taut. His light-coloured eyes, which were
often surprisingly communicative to simple people, had made
Mrs Thompson cry as she stood in her nightgown at the leave-
taking, though, of course, as on all such occasions, she was
remembering the dead. Topp, in nightcap, still puffy, and also

93

moved, shook his lodger by the hand, but would come at the last, he insisted, to the ship's side. Then Voss climbed upon the cart of an Irish emancipist, and was driven to the water. The straggly grass, wherever the town had not suppressed it, was full of dew.

All that morning Voss was coming and going at the ship. Some spoke to him as he passed, asked for directions, asked to be commanded. Some did not see him, but took him for granted. He was there, the leader. He had grown thinner overnight from thinking of the future. From all angles, this was so immense, he would suddenly grow exasperated and turn his back on those of his followers who were simple enough to expect explanations. It puzzled those honest people. Others would catch sight of his head and shoulders as he disappeared below deck, and feel relieved, because they were unable to resolve their relationship with such a man, yet even these were glad of his presence, unseen and hateful though he was. Others still were racked by the spasms of a jealous love.

Harry Robarts, who had got there earliest after his leader, to be ignored, would have felt lost in that perfect but oblivious scene, if later that morning he had not caught sight of Mr Palfreyman, the ornithologist, who was attempting to bring on board a number of awkward specimen cases, that a cynical carter had dumped upon the wharf and left. This kind of situation would rouse Harry's gratitude and ardour. Only when serving was he purposeful.

So he came down, as quick as his boots would let him, his simple soul open to receive the superior will of whatever master. He touched his cap, and rather jerkily, said:

'Why, Mr Palfreyman, sir, I will lend a hand with these 'ere articles, if you is agreeable. It passes the time to be of use, when it is all strange, like.'

Some would have taken Harry Robarts for servile. He had been sworn at, in fact, by certain individuals of that town. But the only concession made to the judgement of his critics was in the mottling and deepening of his skin, now a clear bronze, that had once been innocent pink. Otherwise, the lad continued to give of himself without shame, because it was in his nature to.

'Yes, well, thank you, Harry. It is civil of you. If you please,' said the ornithologist, who was taken by surprise.

The latter was, after all, a stiff, insignificant man, it appeared. Certainly, if there were no reason why he should assert himself, he might go whole days without being noticed. During the recent interval of preparation and expectation he had withdrawn to his own thoughts, and was only now emerging, as ropes were being freed, the voices of sailors calling to one another, wagons backing, landsmen swearing, bodies sweating. His grey eyes were now looking about him, and at the boxes which the boy proposed to lift. One of the man's cheeks twitched, but once, and very shadowily.

'These are most impracticable cases for muleback, but I am taking them because, in other ways, they suit my purpose. Do you see, Harry?'

'Yes, sir,' said the boy.

He did not, but felt that he was being drawn into some confidence which was good and warm, and which promised contentment for the future.

Or was this wrong?

The boy looked over his shoulder, but did not see anyone. He had been guilty of a lapse, he suspected, in enjoying those moments of warm fellowship in the sun. Somewhere he had learnt that man's first duty is to suffer.

The gentlemen, however, appeared to be ignorant of that lesson, as he bent over his cases, opened their flaps, and explained certain advantages of their design, which was his own, he suggested, smiling.

'And these sections are for the skins which I shall prepare,' Mr Palfreyman was saying; 'and these little compartments for the specimens of eggs. Where are you from, boy?' he asked.

The lad did not answer. He could have been absorbed.

'You are not from London,' the ornithologist pondered.

Then Harry Roberts began to mumble.

'From thereabouts,' he said.

As if it mattered. Now the blue sky was hateful.

'We have that in common,' the rather grey Mr Palfreyman replied, and would have continued, as a disguise, in that vein of enthusiasm which men tap for boys.

Then both of them knew that it did not convince. That they had become equal. They were perhaps glad. They would melt together more fiercely under that blue sky. Or burn to ashes.

They realized, standing on the wharf, that the orderly, grey, past life was of no significance. They had reached that point at which they would be offered up, in varying degrees, to chaos or to heroism. So they were shaking with their discovery, beside the water, as the crude, presumptuous town stretched out behind them, was reeling on its man-made foundations in the sour earth. Nothing was tried yet, or established, only promised.

Such glimpses are, of course, a matter of seconds, and Harry Robarts had shoved back his cap of somewhat scruffy kangaroo hide, and sliced his nose with a finger, and said:

'Well, sir, this will not make us a shirt.'

He had begun to pile the cases, of fresh-smelling wood. By the strength of his body alone, he was a giant. So he was proud for a little. But the rather delicate ornithologist remained humble. While the boy's animal nature enabled him to take refuge from revelation in physical strength, the man was compelled to shoulder the invisible burden of the whole shapeless future as his soul had briefly understood it.

Soon they were stumbling about below deck, looking for a place in which to lay the cases. The boy did not ask for more than to be led; the man, more sensible of strange surroundings, was also more noticeably diffident. Interrupting a conversation with the mate and boatswain over some matter of space and stores, Voss did glance for a moment at the incongruous pair, and recalled the scene on London River, which seemed to be repeating itself. Then Palfreyman, too, is weak, he realized.

Finally, the ornithologist and the boy stowed their cases in a dark corner beside the bundles of bridles and the mounds of pack-saddles. Their relationship was cut now. Harry, who had been set working, would return for another load. But Palfreyman began to wander in free captivity, amongst the blunt-toed, hairy sailors, all of whom had the power and knowledge to control unmanageable objects. It was only really through humility that his own strength was restored to him. Some of those sailors began to recognize it, and wondered how they could repair their error after they had shoved aside his apparently frail and useless body.

One man, apparently under the impression that restitution can only be made in a state of complete nakedness, resolved to part with a secret that he had told to no one. After thinking it over a while, and observing the gentleman's face, and breathing, and spitting, he dropped the sail he was mending and took Palfreyman aside.

On that night of which he wished to speak, the sailor said, he happened to be full of the rum. It was not a habit with him, but it had occurred on some occasions, of which this was one. He had been walking on the outskirts of the town at no great distance from the house of a friend, whose wife, he suddenly noticed, was passing by. As his condition was not far enough advanced to give offence (he was never on no account so far gone as to be falling-drunk), he accompanied the wife of his friend a little of the way, making conversation that was agreeable to both parties. When, it seemed, they had lain down beneath a tree, and were taking advantage of each other's bodies.

The sailor had fallen asleep, he said, in some quandary of pleasure or guilt, and when he had woke, the woman was gone.

Now it was his worry whether he had dreamed a dream, or not, for whenever he met the wife of his friend she made no sign. What was he to believe? the sailor asked, and looked at the convenient stranger, into whose keeping he was not afraid to give himself.

'If it happened in a dream that was not distinguishable from the life, it is still a matter for your conscience,' Palfreyman replied. 'You wished to live what you dreamed.'

But the sailor was troubled.

'Then, a man is caught all ways,' he said, putting his hand in his chest, and scratching the hair of it.

'But if it happened,' he continued, and began to be consoled, 'if it happened that the woman really had a part in it, then she was as much to blame, and never making so much as a sign.'

'If the woman took part in it, in fact,' Palfreyman said, 'she is a bad woman.'

'But in a dream?' the sailor mused.

'It is you that are bad,' laughed Palfreyman.

'Still, it was a good dream,' the sailor said. 'And she would have been willing, I know, if she was that willing in any dream.'

The sailor's logic was made infallible by the dreamy accompaniment of green water soothing the wooden side of the ship.

I cannot blame the fellow, even if I condemn his morality, Palfreyman saw. The man had become more important than his ambiguous problem, which their association, elbow to elbow at the ship's bulwark, did, in fact, seem to have solved.

It happened in this position that Palfreyman was reminded of his conversation with Voss as they stood in the Botanic Gardens at the rail of the little bridge. He realized that he did not wish to recall this scene, or that until now he had chosen to take refuge, as the sailor had, in a second possibility. Voss, he began to know, is the ugly rock upon which truth must batter itself to survive. If I am to justify myself, he said, I must condemn the morality and love the man.

The sailor had begun to sense some repugnance.

'But you do not think ill of me?' he asked. 'Not altogether?'

Then Palfreyman, looking into the open pores of the man's skin, wished that all difficulties might wear the complexion of this simple sailor.

'I am glad to have heard your story,' he said, 'and hope to have learnt something from you.'

So that the sailor was puzzled, and returned to that work in which he had been engaged, of mending a sail.

Presently Palfreyman was addressed, and found that his colleague Le Mesurier had come up, somewhat dandified, considering the circumstances, in nankeen trousers, and a blue coat with aggressive buttons.

'Then we are off at last to *do*,' Le Mesurier said, though without a trace of that cynicism which he usually affected.

'Yes.'

Palfreyman smiled, but did not at once come out of himself to meet the young man.

The latter remained unperturbed. Whether it was the radiant morning, or the presence of human kindliness, Le Mesurier did feel that something might eventuate from such beginnings, and expressed his thoughts along those lines.

But the ornithologist cleared his throat.

'It is early days yet to say.'

'You are an old hand, and cautious,' Le Mesurier replied;

'whereas I am a man of beginnings. They are my delusion. Or my vice. I have never got very far beyond indulging it.'

Palfreyman, who could not easily visualize a life without dedication, asked:

'But tell me, Frank, what have you achieved? I refuse to believe there is not *something*.'

'I am always about to act positively,' Le Mesurier answered wryly. 'There is some purpose in me, if only I can hit upon it. But my whole life has been an investigation, shall we say, of ways. For that reason I will not give you my history. It is too fragmentary; you would be made dizzy. And this colony is fatal to anyone of my bent. There are such prospects. How can I make a fortune from merino sheep, when at the same time there is a dream of gold, or of some inland sea floating with tropical birds? Then, sometimes, it seems that all these faults and hesitations, all the worst evil in me is gathering itself together into a solid core, and that I shall bring forth something of great beauty. This I call my oyster delusion.'

Then he laughed.

'You will think I am drunk, Mr Palfreyman. You will not believe in my pearl.'

'I will believe in it,' said the quiet man, 'when you bring it to me in your hand, and I can see and touch it.'

Le Mesurier was not put out. The morning, shimmering and floating, was for the moment pearl enough. Listening to the humdrum grind of enterprise, of vehicles and voices in the pearly distance, he was amazed that he could have hated this genial town. But with the impact of departure it had become at last visible, as landscapes will. The past is illusion, or miasma. So the leaves of the young Moreton Bay figs were now opening their actual hand. Two aboriginal women, dressed in the poorest shifts of clothing, but the most distinguished silence, were seated on the dirt beside the wharf, broiling on a fire of coals the fish that they had caught. And a little boy, introduced especially into this regretful picture, was selling hot mutton pies that he carried in a wooden box. He was walking, and calling, and dawdling, and looking, and picking his snub nose. The little boy would not have asked to live in any other surroundings. He belonged to that place.

The nostalgia of the scene smote Frank Le Mesurier, who feared that what he was abandoning might be the actuality for which he had always craved.

Palfreyman, irritated by the young man in spite of his intention not to be (he would make amends, he promised himself, at a later date), was watching with pleasure the approach of a party on horseback, that had negotiated the streets which petered out on the eastern slope, and had begun to cross the white space that opened out before the wharf.

'I must leave you for a little, Frank,' he said, with kindness covering relief, 'and speak to some friends who are arriving.'

Le Mesurier agreed, in silence, that this should happen. His dark, surly nature had resumed possession. Palfreyman, who had friends of his own, was no longer any friend of his. Human beings, like intentions, he could never possess for long. So, surlily, darkly, he watched the other descend the gang-plank towards an encounter which made him a positive part of that place. Even Palfreyman. Le Mesurier would have condemned his former friend's neat and oblivious back, if he had not known that, for some reason, the ornithologist could not be thus wounded.

The party that was approaching, and of which the horses' flanks were shining with a splendid light, forelocks flirting with the breeze of motion, rings and links of accoutrements jingling and glancing, nostrils distended with expectation, and blowing foam, was also of some importance, it began to appear. As they came on, sailors' eyes took the opportunity to observe a gentleman and two ladies, and farther back, an officer in scarlet, managing his mount with enormous virtuosity. If his horse was strong, the officer was stronger. It was not clear what the latter's intentions were, but his performance was accomplished.

One of the ladies, young and pretty, too, in expensive habit, reined back in a glare of dust.

'Tom!' she called. 'Oh, do be careful, Tom!'

She spoke with a coaxing warmth, without a trace of annoyance, in the voice of one who was still in love.

Nor did the officer quite swear, but answered in tones of curbed exasperation, vibrating with a manly tenderness:

'This is the *hardest* mouth in *all* New South *Wales!*'

Drawing down the corners of his own, ruddy, masculine mouth, he jerked with all his strength at the snaffle.

They continued to advance.

There was the brick-coloured, elderly gentleman, swelling on his freshly soft-soaped saddle. His well-made calves controlled his solid hack. His hat was of the best beaver, and a firm fistful of reins proclaimed authority. The gentleman was looking about him from under indulgent lids, at the ship, and at those menial yet not uncongenial beings who were engaged in loading her – such was the frankly democratic *bonhomie* of the gentleman in the high hat. Years of sun had made him easier. Or was it the first suspicion that he might not be the master?

They came on.

A little to one side, and indifferent to her black mare, whose brilliant neck and head were raised at the tumbled wharfside scene, rode the second of the young ladies. She was singularly still upon her horse, as if she hoped in this way to remain un-noticed, whereas it did but attract attention.

At least, it was to this one that the eyes of the more inquisitive sailors and labourers returned from devouring the details which they understood. All the other figures were of their own flesh and thought. This one, though she did raise her face and smile guardedly at the sun, or life, acted according to some theory of bounty, or because it was time to do so. The men were frowning at her, not in anger, but in concentration, as they picked at warts on their skins, and at lice in their hair, or on other familiar parts of them. They were unsuspectingly afraid of what they could not touch. The young woman, leaping the gunnel on her black horse, could easily have surprised them, and inflicted wounds.

But at the same time, this girl – she was not above twenty, or leastways, little more – appeared to hesitate in some respects, for all the cold confidence of her rather waxy skin. She would not speak easily, as ladies were taught in all circumstances to do. The stiff panels of her black habit were boarding her up.

'It is a grand sight, Laura,' said the stout gentleman, less for his niece than for himself.

'Nobody, I think, could fail to be impressed by these ships,' replied the dutiful girl.

How insipid I am, she felt, and bit her pale lip. It was no consolation to remember that fire of almost an inspired kindling would burn in her at times; it is the moment, unfortunately, that counts. So she began secretly to torture her handful of reins, and the little crop that she held in the same hand, and which was a pretty though silly thing, with head of mother-o'-pearl, that she carried because it had been given, and she cherished the memory of the donor, an old man whom she had not seen since her childhood. But that it was a useless sort of whip, she had known for several years.

'That one is a sour-faced lass,' observed the sailor who had spoken to Palfreyman.

'I have not got your eyes, Dick. I cannot see good,' said his mate. 'She is a lady, though.'

'Sour-faced is sour-faced. There is no difference if it be a lady.'

'There is, Dick, you know. It is somethink that you cannot put yer hand on.'

'I would not have somethun that I cannot touch.'

'You would not be invited.'

'I am for the rights of the common man,' grumbled the sailor who had dreamed the dream.

'All right, Dick,' said his mate. 'I do not gainsay your rights, only there are some corners into which they will not penetrate. This lady will have some gentleman, with which she will fit together like the regular dovetails. It is the way you are made.'

'Ha-ha!' laughed the dreamer. 'It comes down to that, though.'

'It comes down?' said his mate, whom the habit of thought and a lifetime on the open sea had raised from native simplicity to a plane of simple understanding. 'You are like a big cat, Dick. And that is just what ladies do not take to, some big stray tom smoodgin' round their skirts. Ladies like to fall in love. This one, you can see, has done no different.'

'How in love, though? How do you know? When you cannot see furr, and her ridin' down on a horse, at a distance, for the first time. Eh?'

'It is in their nature, and what they do to pass the time, when they are not readin' books, and blowin' into the fingers of their

102

gloves. I have seen ladies in windows. I have watched um writin' letters, and puttin' on their extry hair. In those circumstances, Dick, you do get to know whatever it is they are up to.'

'Well,' decided Dick, 'you are a sly one, after all. And lookin' in at windows.'

The cavalcade, which had crossed the white and glaring space before the wharf, was reining in the other side of such crates and cargo stuff as had not yet been loaded, amongst the straggling groups of early spectators, men who had taken off their coats in the warm sun, and their women who were wearing everything. The riders drew to a standstill, and were exchanging politenesses with the ornithologist, who was by now arrived at their stirrup-irons.

'I can imagine your emotions, Palfreyman, on such an occasion,' said the merchant.

How people act or feel on specific occasions had been reduced for Mr Bonner to the way in which he had been told people do act and feel. Within this rather rudimentary, if rigid, structure of behaviour, he himself did also behave with jolly or grave precision, according to rule. For such souls, the history primers and the newspapers will continue to be written.

Now he was enjoying the motions suited to the occasion, and although he took it for granted that others must be similarly moved, he would not really have cared if they were not. His own feelings were so positive they did not require reinforcing.

Palfreyman, who had opened his mouth a couple of times, could not find sufficiently innocent words.

'It is too soon,' he began at last, but left off.

The merchant, however, was not waiting on answers.

'Only the wind is needed,' he said anxiously. 'There is no wind. Or not to speak of.'

While his cobby horse kept him revolving, he was able to consider all quarters of the compass.

'I am told we may expect the change at three o'clock,' Palfreyman contributed, how unnecessarily, he himself knew.

'The change? The wind,' recollected the merchant. 'Oh, yes. The brickfielder commonly gets up round three o'clock of an afternoon.'

And at once, he began to shrug his shoulders, as if his excellent coat did not fit, or else it was some other physical discomfort, of rheumatism perhaps.

'Where is Voss, though?' he asked, looking about him in hopes of not seeing.

'Mr Voss is below.' Now Palfreyman had no intention of being disloyal, but did smile. 'He is about some business of seeing that the equipment is safely stowed.'

'In a battle between German precision and German mysticism,' laughed Lieutenant Radclyffe with kindly unkindness. 'Wonder which will win.'

Battles of his own were still fresh, although he was not thinking at that moment of his conversation with Laura Trevelyan at the dinner-party. He would forget the causes of his suffering while continuing to suffer. He was like a man in his sleep, who will lunge out at an actual mosquito, but return always to his more convincing dream. Still, the mosquito continues to buzz, and if, for Tom Radclyffe, Laura was that mosquito, by some calculation of the sleeping man, Voss was the sting.

So he must take steps to protect himself.

'When Voss is concerned,' the Lieutenant laughed, 'I will put my money on the clouds of theory rather than the knife-edge of practice.'

'I have to admit there have been few signs of method,' blurted the merchant with frightful daring, though he did not look over his shoulder.

It began to seem terrible to Palfreyman that Voss should be the subject of criticism. If he himself criticized, he did so in private, and in a state of some considerable distress.

'His methods are not those of other men, perhaps,' his principles forced him to say.

How dull it is when people cease to talk about *things,* sighed Belle Bonner, whose glance had begun to stray, and did seize most sensuously on the sight of a red apple from which a little boy was tearing the flesh with noisy bite.

'No,' said Mr Bonner, realizing his slip. 'He is different from other men. How different, only time will show. I am encouraged that you are confident, Palfreyman. It justifies my own initial confidence in Mr Voss.'

Palfreyman was sorry for the merchant, who chewed beef more happily than words.

'In any case,' said the man on foot, who should have been at a disadvantage, 'Mr Voss has every confidence in himself, and that is the chief necessity.'

This more or less brought the discussion to a close, which was as well, for several spectators looked as if they might learn to interpret the moon-language that was being spoken. Mr Bonner dismounted and, after giving the reins of his horse to the subordinate Palfreyman to hold, soon restored his spirits to the full by going about and looking at actual objects. The rich man glowed to find himself once more in possession of the physical world.

Laura Trevelyan, who had listened to the conversation, was grateful that the rather inconspicuous, she had thought even characterless ornithologist, with whom she had never exchanged more than half a dozen necessarily polite words, had been the champion of the man whom, on the whole, in spite of her intentions, yes, she despised. Now she wanted desperately, she felt, to talk to the German's friend, in spite of the German himself, purely, she told herself, out of admiration for moral strength. So she waited upon an opportunity.

This came quickly, but not without humiliation. It might have been expected, she decided later, of anyone foolish enough to expose herself to a scene as humiliating as that which had taken place so recently in the garden. Now this other, certainly minor, but still distasteful incident occurred.

The elegant riding-crop that Laura Trevelyan was carrying in her hand, fell, by purest accident as it happened, though to any observer it must have appeared the most obvious design, at the feet of Mr Palfreyman, who bent down, of course, and in a rush of blood, and all politeness, returned the little whip to its owner.

'I see the handle is of some Eastern design,' Palfreyman remarked.

He made it very quickly into something of scientific interest.

'Yes. Indian, I believe. It was given to me when I was a child by a sea-captain, an acquaintance of my uncle's, whose ship would sometimes call at Sydney.'

The young woman was looking most intently at the object of

her shame, but could not concentrate enough. Hot, insufferable waves were surging in her contracted throat. Moreover, she could not remember with clearness her motives for wishing to speak, however discreetly, to this man.

'It is a pity to use such a thing, and perhaps break it,' Palfreyman said. 'Would it not be seen to greater advantage in a cabinet?'

Sensing that the young woman was emotionally upset, he treated the riding-crop with exaggerated solicitude, which made her sorrier for herself, and him to wonder what secrets she was withholding from him. There was no reason to suppose that he was of greater importance to her than he had been on the night of the party. He would not allow himself to believe that she was in any way using him. Palfreyman, who was a man of some intuition, did not understand the female sex, in spite of his respect for it.

Nothing was altogether satisfactory, Laura felt, who continued to look at her little whip. She was no longer pale, however, and her cheeks and mouth had filled out, with self-pity, it could have been.

'It is not of great use,' she said, 'and not of exceptional beauty. I no longer give it much thought, except to bring it. From habit, you know. In the beginning it pleased me because it was something unusual, and foreign. I liked to think I might visit foreign places, such as the one from which my present had come. I would dream about the Indies. Mauritius, Zanzibar. Names should be charms, Mr Palfreyman. I used to hope that, by saying some of them often enough, I might evoke reality.'

All the while her black mare was pawing up the dust, some of which, she noticed from a distance, was settling on the hem of her skirt.

'But I did not succeed. Most probably I shall never travel. Oh, I am content, of course. Our life is full of simple diversions. Only I envy the people who enjoy the freedom to make journeys.'

'Even this journey? Of dust, and flies, and dying horses?'

The young woman, whose hand appeared to be rejecting the glare, or some particles of grit that had gathered on her face, said slowly:

'Of course, I realize. I am not purely romantic.'

She laughed in rather a hard manner.

'There will be dangers, I know. Won't there?'

She began to search him, he saw, as if she suspected a knife might be hidden somewhere. A knife intended for herself.

'On any expedition of this nature, there are always dangers,' Palfreyman answered dryly.

'Yes,' she said.

Her own lips, that other emotions had been filling, were grown thin, and dry.

'Oh, I would welcome dangers,' she said. 'One must not expect to avoid suffering. And the chance is equal for everyone. Is that not so?'

'Yes,' he said, wondering.

'Then' – she laughed a hard laugh – 'if it is all equal.'

But Palfreyman was not convinced by what he heard and saw.

'Though I do not care to think about the horses,' she admitted, patting her mare's neck. 'It is different for men. Even a man of little or no religious faith. He creates his own logic.'

She spoke with such force of feeling, of contempt, or tenderness, that her hand was trembling on the horse's skin. Palfreyman observed the stitching on her glove.

'And is, therefore, less to be pitied,' she said or, rather, begged.

Remembering a contentment she had experienced in the garden either from illumination or exhaustion, after the daemon had withdrawn from her, the dry mouth of any dying man was a thing of horror.

The girl's lips, in spite of her youth, were dry and cracked, Palfreyman noticed with surprise.

Then the world of light was taking possession, the breeze becoming wind, and making the dust skip. The whole shore was splintering into grit and mica, as down from the town several equipages drove, with flashing of paint and metal, and drew near, bringing patrons or sceptics, and their wives, in clothes to proclaim their wealth and, consequently, importance.

So that Palfreyman and Miss Trevelyan were reduced to a somewhat dark eddy on the gay stream of trite encounters and light laughter that had soon enveloped them. They looked about them out of almost cavernous eyes, before Palfreyman could conform. He was the first, of course, because less involved. He suspected he would not become involved with any human being, but was reserved as a repository for confidences, until the final shattering would scatter all secrets into the dust. He looked at the hair of the young woman where it was gathered back smoothly, though not perfectly, from those tender places in front of the ears, and was saddened.

'Here are your friends,' he said, and smiled, twitching the rein of the horse he was holding. 'I must leave you to them. There are one or two things that need my attention.'

'Friends?' she repeated, and was rising out of her dark dream. 'I know nobody very well. That is, of course, we have very many acquaintances.'

She was looking about her out of her woken eyes.

Then she noticed the sad ones of the small man who was fidgeting on foot, and who had prevailed at last upon a lad to take the rein of her uncle's horse.

'I am most grateful to you,' she said, 'for our conversation. I shall remember it.'

'Has it told you anything?' he asked lightly.

It was easy now that he was going.

'Not,' she said, 'not in words.'

Now she was become too wooden to struggle any further in the effort to express herself. She seemed altogether humble and contrite, small, even hunched, she who had been proud, on her powerful horse.

'Laura,' cried Belle, from the back of her old, gentle gelding, 'the Wades are here, and the Kirbys, and Nelly and Polly McMorran. Poor Nelly has sprained her ankle, and will not come down from the carriage.'

Belle Bonner was looking and looking, drinking up the crowd with her eyes, that were always thirsty for people with whom she was slightly acquainted.

'And here is Mr Voss himself,' Lieutenant Radclyffe announced. 'He has shaken the moths out of those whiskers for the occasion.'

Laura did turn then, too suddenly, for it alarmed her horse into springing sideways. But she was moulded to it by her will, Palfreyman saw, and she possessed, besides, an excellent pair of hands.

The Lieutenant heard, but did not interpret the long, agonized hiss of breath.

'Sit her, Laura!' he laughed.

How he disliked the thin line of her lips, from which forked words would dart at him on occasion, but which were now taut.

'Laura, can you control her?' called the frightened Belle.

'Yes,' breathed Laura Trevelyan, on her calmer, but still trembling, mare.

She looked towards Palfreyman. As he withdrew through the already considerable crowd, he received the impression of a drowning that he was unable to avert, in a dream through which he was sucked inevitably back.

Ah, Laura was crying out, bending down through that same dream, extending her hand in its black glove; you are my only friend, and I cannot reach you.

As it had to be, he left her to it. And she continued to sit sculpturally upon her mastered horse, of which the complicated veins were throbbing with blood and frustration.

Voss, who was by now walking amongst the crowd, had recovered authority, presence, joviality even, and worldliness. He was looking into the eyes of his patrons and forcing their glances eventually to drop, which did please and impress them, convincing them of the safety of the money they had invested in him. As for the ladies, some shivered. His sleeve brushed them as he passed. In one instance, surprisingly, he kissed the hand of a rich tradesman's elderly wife, who withdrew her member delightedly, looked round, and giggled, showing the gaps in her side teeth.

What kind of man is he? wondered the public, who would never know. If he was already more of a statue than a man, they really did not care, for he would satisfy their longing to perch something on a column, in a square or gardens, as a memorial to their own achievement. They did, moreover, prefer to cast him in bronze than to investigate his soul, because all dark things made them uneasy, and even on a morning of historic adventure, in bright, primary colours, the shadow was sewn to the ends of his trousers, where the heels of his boots had frayed them.

Yet his face was a lesson in open hilarity.

'No, no, no, Mr Kirby,' he was saying. 'If I fail, I will write your name and that of your good wife upon a piece of paper and seal it in a bottle and bury it beside me, so that they will be perpetuated in Australian soil.'

Even death and eternity he translated into a joke at which people might laugh by sunlight.

The simplicity of it all was making him enjoy himself. The terrible simplicity of people who have not yet been hurt, and whom it is not possible to love, he thought, and explored his laughing lips with his tongue.

Some of those present were patting him on the back, just to touch him.

Oh yes, he was enjoying himself.

Only once did Voss ask: Is all this happening to me, a little boy, clinging to the *Heide* by the soles of his boots, beneath a rack of cloud and a net of twisted trees?

At the wharf the sun was shining. It was the lovely, lyrical, spring sun, that had not yet become a gong.

Mr Bonner had returned from his stroll, and was standing between the German and his own horses. His back was square, his calves imperious. Laura would have been glad to shelter behind her uncle's back, if it had not also been, on final consideration, pathetic.

'You will take every opportunity of sending back dispatches, of keeping us informed' – he was issuing orders to his servant, saying the same thing over and over again in many different ways, as was his habit, to increase his own confidence.

Voss was smiling and nodding, to humour the man who considered himself the master.

And he patted the Lieutenant on the knee, beside whose horse he was passing, and raised his hat to the young ladies, as it was expected of him. None could have found fault with him on that morning.

Only that he did not raise his eyes higher than the saddle-flaps, Laura Trevelyan observed. She did not, however, censure this behaviour; she was, in fact, bitterly glad. She was perspiring. Her face must surely be greasy, and her jaw so controlled that she would have assumed the long, stubborn look which frequently displeased her in mirrors. It was her most characteristic expression, she had begun to suspect, after long and fruitless search for a better, without realizing that beauty is something others must surprise.

As she sat upon her horse, knowledge of her superficiality and ugliness was crushing her.

Mr Bonner, who had been trying all this time to take the German aside, to talk to him intimately, to possess him in front of all the others, was growing more and more preposterous, as he frowned, and shook the jowls of his heavy face, and made little stamping movements with his heel, which caused his spurs to jingle, and emphasized his opulent calves.

Finally he did succeed.

'I want you to feel you may depend upon me,' he said, when he had hedged the German off against a crude wooden barrow on which lay some stone-coloured pumpkins, one of them split open in a blaze of orange. 'Any requests that you care to make, I shall be only too willing to consider. Your family, for instance, you have not mentioned, but they are my responsibility, you know, if, in the event of, if you will only inform me of their whereabouts, write me a letter, you could, when you reach Rhine Towers, with any personal instructions.'

It was badly expressed, if honestly intended. Mr Bonner *was* honest, but also demanded submission, which he was not always certain of getting. So he picked at the German's lapel, hoping to effect a closer relationship by touch, and it transpired that the crowd, at least, was impressed. Little ripples of admiration ran along the faces, as they appreciated the daring of this citizen whose hand was upon the foreign explorer. Mr Bonner's anxiety subsided. He did now honestly love the man, who at times had appeared hateful to him, and scraggy. The merchant's eye grew moist over a fresh relationship that he had created by magnanimity and his own hand.

Voss did not find this relationship distasteful, for he could not believe in it. It was not even ludicrous. It was simply unreal.

He fingered the seeds of the orange pumpkin, and considered what the merchant had said about his family.

'My family,' he began, arranging the pointed seeds of the pumpkin. 'It is long since I corresponded with them. Do you not think that such arrangements of birth are incidental, even if

III

in the beginning we try to persuade ourselves it is otherwise, and are grateful for the warmth, because still weak and bewildered? We have not yet learnt to admit that destiny works independently of the womb.'

Mr Bonner looked at the clear eyes, and did not understand.

'Oh, well,' he said. 'Does it, though? Does it? Who can say?'

Not Mr Bonner.

'But I will write, I expect, when it is time. My father is an old man. He is a timber merchant. He is perhaps dead. My mother is a very sentimental woman. Her own mother was Swedish, and the house is full of painted clocks. *Na, ja,*' he said, 'striking at different times.'

This lack of synchronization alone was threatening to upset him. He smelled the stovy air of old, winter houses, and flesh of human relationships, a dreadful, cloying tyranny, to which he was succumbing.

Resentment of the past forced him out of himself, and he looked up into the face of that girl whose hands had been tearing the flesh of camellias. For an instant their minds were again wrestling together, and he experienced the melancholy pleasure of rejecting her offered prayers.

Laura Trevelyan was sitting her horse with a hard pride, it seemed, rather than with that humility which she had desired to achieve.

She is a cold, hard girl, he decided, and I could almost love her.

The less discriminate sunlight did.

Then Laura Trevelyan had to turn her face away from the glare, that was making her eyes glitter, or from the form of the German, that was filling her whole field of vision. I am, after all, too weak to withstand tortures, her eyes seemed to say.

And he turned away, too, no longer interested.

Just at that point the crowd parted to admit an open landau that was arriving with every sign of official importance. The liveries would have snubbed the most intrepid radical. Some mouths frankly hung open for the gold, and for the dash of scarlet that blazed and rocked above the black lacquer.

It was the Governor himself, some maintained.

But those who knew better were contemptuous of such ignorance, as if the Governor himself would arrive upon the scene in an unescorted vehicle.

Those who knew most, who were in touch with the Household, or whose cousin, even, had dined once at the vice-regal table, said that His Excellency was confined with a severe cold, and that this was Colonel Featherstonhaugh come to deputize for him at the leave-taking.

It was, in fact, the Colonel, together with some young anonymous Lieutenant, of sterling origins and pink skin, that apologized at every pore. The Colonel, however, was a man of self-opinion, of rigidity, and least possible flesh. He waited for the German to be led up and, because it was a duty, would acquit himself, it was suggested, with all dignity. His personal feelings were controlled behind his whiskers, or perhaps not quite; it was possible to tell he was an Englishman.

His Excellency the Governor wished Mr Voss and the expedition God-speed and a safe return, the Colonel said, with the littlest assistance from his fleshless face, which was of a rich purple where the hair allowed it to appear.

And he clasped the German's hand in a gloveful of bones.

Colonel Featherstonhaugh did say many other things. Indeed, when a space had been cleared, he made a speech, about God, and soil, and flag, and Our Young, Illustrious Queen, as had been prepared for him. The numerous grave and appreciative persons who were surrounding the Colonel lent weight to his appropriate words. There were, for instance, at least three members of the Legislative Council, a Bishop, a Judge, officers in the Army, besides patrons of the expedition, and citizens whose wealth had begun to make them acceptable, in spite of their unfortunate past and persistent clumsiness with knife and fork. Important heads were bared, stiff necks were bent into attitudes that suggested humble attention. It was a brave sight, and suddenly also moving. For all those figures of cloth and linen, of worthy British flesh and blood, and the souls tied to them, temporarily, like tentative balloons, by the precious grace of life, might, of that sudden, have been cardboard or little wooden things, as their importance in the scene receded, and there predominated the great tongue of blue water, the brooding, indigenous trees, and sky clutching at all.

So that Mr Voss, the German, listening with the others to that talk of soil, flag, and Illustrious Queen, in music of speech at least, for he had taken refuge in his own foreignness as a protection from sense of words, was looking rightly sardonic. He was compelled to shift his gaze from the faces of men, and to cast it out into space. Any other attitude would have been hypocritical, but, on the other hand, no one else present was justified in aspiring to that infinite blue.

When Colonel Featherstonhaugh's speech had unwound, right down to the last inch of buckram, and the Queen had been saved, in song and with loyal hats, and the pink, young Lieutenant, whose name was Charlie Tatham, Tom Radclyffe remembered, had become entangled in an important personage with his sword, Mr Voss roused himself, and in his usual, stiff, reluctant manner, presented to His Excellency's envoy Mr Palfreyman and Frank Le Mesurier, who were at his side, Mr Bonner, and other supporters of the expedition – or rather, some of these last more or less presented themselves, as they were in the habit of dining with, and on several occasions had even got drunk with, the Colonel.

Then a horse neighed, dropped its fragrant dung, and life was resumed.

As the spectators were circulating again, making every effort to whirl the leader of the expedition out of one another's grasp, Mr Bonner realized that he had finally lost control of his plaything, and began to sulk. It seemed to him that nobody had paid sufficient tribute to his initial generosity, without which the present function would not have been taking place.

'Well, Bonner,' said the Colonel, in whose vicinity he was left standing, and who now saw fit to extend some measure of informal joviality to the Colonials amongst whom his lot was temporarily cast, 'there is little for ordinary mortals like you and me to do. It is up to the Almighty and the wind.'

'Oh, the wind,' exclaimed Mr Bonner, looking gloomily at the sky, 'the wind suits itself when it comes to filling canvas. We shall be kept here mumbling the same words till tomorrow at dark. That is the wind all over.'

The Colonel, who had no intention of remaining five minutes beyond official necessity, smiled his conception of a jolly smile.

'Then it is up to the Almighty, eh, Bonner?'

And he summoned his Lieutenant to summon their vehicle, that he might abandon the whole damn rout, and dispatch his dinner. His duty done, his long legs folded up, the door of the landau closed, the Colonel looked about him from under his eyebrows with the superiority of his class and rank. Not even the Almighty would have denied that.

Then he was driven away, and almost everybody, certainly Mr Bonner, was glad.

Feeling suddenly released from any further obligation whatsoever, the latter was determined to punish someone, and resolved to do it in this manner.

'Our presence here is superfluous,' he decided, 'now that we have paid our respects. So let us take it that we may slip away.'

'Oh, papa!' Belle cried.

'I will ride round by the store. Palethorpe is an excellent fellow, but will depend to his dying day on someone else's judgement.'

'But Papa, the ship,' pleaded Belle, who was again a little girl, 'we shall not see her sail!'

Mr Bonner did not say: Damn the ship.

'You, Mr Radclyffe, will escort the ladies home, where Mrs Bonner will have been expecting them this little while.'

The Lieutenant, who was still in a position where he must appear exemplary, answered:

'Yes, sir.'

'Then, at least,' protested Belle, 'let us shake hands with Mr Voss, who is our friend, whether we like him particularly or not. Papa, surely you agree that this would be only right? Laura?'

But Laura said:

'If Uncle will shake hands, I feel nothing further will be necessary.'

'How peculiar everybody is,' Belle remarked.

She was only just beginning to suspect rooms that she might not enter.

'I wish I was free,' she paused, and pointed, 'like that black woman. I would stay and wait for the wind. I would wait all night if need be. And watch the ship out.'

'Does it mean so much to you?' asked Tom Radclyffe, who

was bored by Belle for the first time, and realized that similar occasions would occur.

'Nothing,' she cried.

'You are exciting yourself, Belle,' said her father, who did not consider that his daughter or his niece needed to be understood.

'It is not what the ship means to me,' said Belle.

It was that she had been made drunk by life, and the mysterious wine that spilled from the souls of those she loved, but whom, perhaps, she would never know.

'I do not care for the ship,' she persisted, 'or anyone in her. Do you, Laura?'

Laura Trevelyan was looking down.

From this jagged situation the party was saved by Voss himself, who came up and said to Mr Bonner with a spontaneous thoughtfulness which was unexpected:

'I regret that my departure must be causing you so much inconvenience, but I have not learnt yet to influence the wind.'

Mr Bonner, who had begun to wonder what he could influence, and whether even his daughter was giving him the slip, laughed, and said:

'We were on the point of disappearing. You would not have noticed it in these circumstances.'

The German squeezed Mr Bonner's hand, which made the latter sorrier for his situation. The way people treated him.

'I will remember your kindness,' Voss said.

He could have become fond of this mediocre man.

I will not give him the opportunity, Mr Bonner thought, on sensing it.

'If you should find yourself in need of anything,' he hastened to say, 'you will inform us.'

His mind snatched at packing-needles.

Belle was happier now that the departure was taking a more personal shape.

'You may send me a black's spear,' she called, and laughed, 'with blood on it.'

Her lips were young and red. Her own blood raced. Her thoughts moved in pictures.

'Indeed, I shall remember this,' the important explorer called back, and laughed too.

'Good-bye, Tom,' he continued, grasping the Lieutenant, who had bent down from his horse, and offered his hand with rather aggressive manliness to preclude all possible sentiment; one never knew with foreigners.

'Good-bye, old Voss,' Tom Radclyffe said. 'We shall plan some suitable debauchery against your return. In five years' time.'

He was forced to shout the last words, because his big horse had begun to plunge and strain, as the horses of Tom Radclyffe did, whenever their master took the centre of the stage.

'In five years' time,' his strong teeth flashed.

Foam was flying.

'With a beard over my arm,' laughed Voss, matching his friend's animal spirits with a less convincing abandon of his own.

All this was spoken as he was touching other hands. The fingers of Belle Bonner slid through his. The hands of women, even of the younger ones, he took as a matter of course, but always as an afterthought.

'Tom! Do, please, take care! Belle Bonner begged. 'That horrible horse!'

One woman screamed, whose cheek was lashed by horsehair — she felt it in her mouth, a coarse, stinging dustiness. Her bonnet had become disarranged.

While everybody was apologizing, and Voss was smiling and watching, still rather pleased with that scene of horseplay in which he had acted a minor but agreeably unexpected part, he was reaching up and taking Miss Trevelyan's hand, which the glove made quite impersonal. Fascinated by the movement and colour, the turmoil and laughter, the confusion of the good woman who had bit upon the horse's nasty tail, he did contrive to shake hands, if only after a fashion.

As soon as a decent interval had elapsed, Laura withdrew her hand. If Voss did not notice, it was because he was absorbed.

There is no reason why it should be otherwise, Laura told herself. But shivered.

'Belle,' she called, in a white voice, as low as she could make it above the noise, 'let us go now. Everything has been said.'

Soon the party was riding away, and Voss looked after them,

and realized that he had not spoken to Laura Trevelyan. He watched the coil of hair in the nape of her neck, which revealed nothing, and her shoulders which suggested none of the strength she had displayed on that strange evening in the garden.

He stood there wetting his lips in the crowd, as if he were about to call some last remark; but what? And, of course, his words would not have blown so far. Still, when Frank Le Mesurier fetched him to settle some matter that had to be decided, the lines of his face did appear somewhat relaxed.

'Can you not sometimes make a decision in my absence, Frank?' he asked.

'What is this, sir?' exclaimed the amazed Le Mesurier. 'When would my decisions have been accepted?'

But Voss only laughed.

All that forenoon the crowd loitered, waiting for the wind. Some were swearing at the dust, some had got drunk, and were in danger of being taken up. One individual in particular was falling-drunk. His hat — that was gone; but on no account would he be parted from a little keg, which he carried like a baby in his arms.

He would be ashamed in the morning, one honest body remarked.

'It is me own business,' he heard enough to reply, 'and this is the last time, so let me alone.'

'It is always the last time with the likes of you,' the lady said. 'I know from experience and a husband. Who is dead of it, poor soul.'

'I will not be dead of this,' drooled the man. 'Or if I am, it is a lovely way to die.'

The lady, morbidly attached to a situation over which she had no control, was sucking such teeth as remained to her.

'It is a scandal,' she said, of that which she could not leave be.

'Why, if it is not Mr Turner,' interrupted Harry Robarts, who had come up.

'Who is that accusin' me now?' complained the man. 'Oh, it is you, boy,' he said more quietly.

'We had all forgot you, Mr Turner, an' if the wind had rose, you would have had no part in the expedition; the ship would have sailed.'

'It is not my fate,' said Turner. 'The wind is with me. Or against, is it?'

Either way, he blew out such a quantity from his own body, that the lady who had been solicitous for him, removed herself at speed.

'Come now, Mr Turner,' said the boy, 'you are not acting as you ought. Come on board quiet like, with me, an' lay down for a bit. Then you will feel better.'

'I do not feel bad,' insisted Turner.

But he came as best he could, with his little keg, and fell down a hatchway without breaking his neck, and lay there.

Once, only, as the ship began to move later that afternoon, he rose up in a dream, and cried :

'Mr Voss, you are killing us! Give me the knife, please. Ahhhhh! The butter! The butter! It is not my turn to die.'

So he was saved up out of his dreams, and preserved for the future.

*

The future? Laura Trevelyan could not bear to think of it, even though the present, through which the riding party moved, was still to some extent an unpleasant dream. They were riding home, however. Tea trees were scratching them, a stink of stale fish was rising out of Woolloomoolloo, and an Irish person, wife of the boatswain, it transpired, ran out of a humpy to ask whether they did not have news of *Osprey*. The boatswain's wife, with a baby clawing at her bodice, and several little boys at heel, had every belief in that life.

After escorting them as far as Potts Point, Mr Radclyffe left the young ladies to change their habits for loose gowns and a kind of informal, private beauty, that admirably suited the spring afternoon in which they finished a luncheon of cold meat and bread and honey. But the dream persisted disturbingly. Laura Trevelyan, drawing back her lips to bite the slice of bread and honey, saw whole rows of sailors' blackened teeth gaping from a gunnel. The knife with which she slashed the butter, had a mottled, slippery handle, and could have been made from horse's hoof.

Afterwards the two cousins went up to Laura's room.

'I am going to rest,' the latter announced.

'So will I,' said Belle. 'I will lie here with you.'

Which she had never done before.

So the two girls lay down, in some way grateful for each other, even in uneasy sleep, which was half present, half future, almost wholly apprehensive. Even Belle, touching her own hot cheek, was conscious of the future, not as the gauze that it had always been in the past, but as some inexorable marble thing. It was forming.

Tom, she was saying, men fall in love, over and over again, but it is always with themselves.

Do you really think to escape? he asked. You will not, even though I may sometimes wish it. It is Laura who will escape, by putting on canvas. She has sailed.

Belle Bonner sat up.

'She has sailed.'

But it was Rose Portion speaking.

'What?' asked Belle, whose face was in an afternoon fever.

'Oh, miss, the ship. *Osprey*,' said Rose, who had come in a hurry, with a dish of preserved cumquats in her hand.

Laura still lay in long folds of uneasy marble. Her hand was curled, and could have been carved, if it had not been for a twitching.

'Miss? Miss Laura!' called Rose. 'It is the ship. It is such a sight.'

Belle touched her cousin.

The two women who were awake realized that the event was somehow of greater concern to the third who was still asleep.

Laura Trevelyan woke then, raised herself upon straight arms, got up, and went out without word or second thought to the long balcony. Her skirt, which was of a pale colour and infinite afternoon coolness, streamed behind her.

There, indeed, was the ship.

The wind was moving *Osprey* out towards the Heads. The blue water, now ruffled up, was full of little white waves. It had become an animal of evident furriness, but still only playful, because the mood was a recent one. *Osprey* continued in her pride of superior strength. She was not yet shaken.

'Yes, they have got away,' said Laura, in a clear, glad, flat voice.

Her face also was rather flat for that moment, just as its expression of gladness, which she had flung on while rising from her sleep, was inadequate and transparent; it did not quite conceal.

'Oh, I will pray for them,' exclaimed Rose Portion, clutching the saucer with the cumquats.

'But you do not know them,' said Belle, to whom her maid's concern was consequently absurd.

'I do not need to know them.'

'They may not need praying for. It is ridiculous.'

Rose did not answer.

The three women watched the ship.

Laura Trevelyan threw back the sleeve of her creamy gown, as if it had been heavy.

'Do you think Mr Palfreyman is nice?' Belle Bonner asked.

'From what little I have seen of him, I think exceptionally nice,' her cousin replied.

'But quiet.'

'He says whatever has to be said.'

The women were watching the ship.

'He is a man of education, I expect,' said Belle. 'Not an ignorant colonial savage. Like us.'

'Oh, miss!' protested Rose.

'But he is kind,' Belle continued. 'And kind people do not mind.'

'Oh, Belle, do not chatter so!' said Laura.

'But is it not true?'

'All that you have said. Though beside the point.'

The three women watched the ship.

Presently Rose Portion, who had taken upon herself that chastening which was intended for Miss Belle, said in a whisper, holding her stomach:

'These are a few cumquats that I was bringin' to you for a taste, when I saw the ship had sailed.'

And she set the saucer, with two forks, upon a little bamboo table, and went softly away.

Neither girl thanked the woman for her trouble, except in spirit, for the words had been absorbed from them.

Wind and sea were tossing the slow ship. Gusts of that same wind, now fresh, now warm, troubled the garden, and carried the scents of pine and jasmine into the long balcony. The two young women could not have told whether they were quickened or drugged, until a kind of feverish melancholy began to take possession of them. Their bodies shivered in their thin gowns; their minds were exposed to the keenest barbs of thought; and the whole scene that their vision embraced became distinct and dancing, beautiful but sad.

Yet, it seemed to Laura Trevelyan, those moments of her life which had been of most importance were both indistinct and ugly. The incident with the German in the garden had been indescribably ugly, untidy, painful. She could not help recalling that, and in doing so, there came into her mouth a bad taste, as of blood oozing, as if she had lost a tooth. She bit her lip, but was reminded of his rather pointed teeth as he stood talking that morning at the wharf.

Then Belle, who was finally overwhelmed by the moist, wind-blown afternoon, began to be afraid.

'Laura,' she said, very quietly.

She was as determined to press against her cousin, as the latter was to hold her off.

But Belle could not bear it. She was both afraid, and filled with a desire to mingle with what she did not understand, which was the future, perhaps, hence her necessity.

'Laura,' she asked, 'what has come over us? What is happening?'

She was crying, and pressing herself against the mysterious body of her cousin.

'It is nothing. It is you who imagine,' said Laura, resisting with her voice, with all her might.

Persistent touch was terrifying to her.

But neither could resist the force of that afternoon. Seeking protection, they were swept together, in softest sympathy.

'Tell me, Laura,' cried Belle, 'what is it?'

Her hot tears shocked the other's colder skin.

'But I cannot,' Laura cried, 'when there is nothing – nothing to tell.'

As they rocked together on the balcony, in the shaggy arms of the honest trees, in the bosom of the all-possessing wind, they were soothed to some extent, and the light, touching the cumquats on the little bamboo table, turned these into precious stones, the perfection of which gave further cause for hope.

6

OSPREY anchored after what would have been an uneventful voyage, if, during it, Turner had not woken from his drunken sleep in an almost disordered state of mind, babbling of some knife that he had in his possession and must find immediately. After rummaging through his box and tumbling his things, it had come to light, of black, bone handle and rather elegant blade. It was unlucky, he insisted, and come by in strange circumstances. The man was quite frenzied, till he had run to the side and flung the knife into the waves. Then he grew calmer, and the vessel was carried on and reached Newcastle.

It was evening when the party landed. They were met, as arranged, by Mr Sanderson, and taken to an inn on the outskirts of the town, where, he suggested, they would enjoy greater peace. Nobody objected. They were at the mercy of anyone at this stage. Voss drove with Mr Sanderson. They could not yet find living words, but offered dry communications which did not really convey, and were an embarrassment to each other. By the time they entered the yard of the inn, they had chosen silence as a state preferable to conversation. However, neither man was resentful, and they were drawn closer together by having to face the anomalous life of the inn, as they got down into the yellow patches of light, the scent of urine and roasting meats, the barking of a pointer, and a tangle of woolly advice from the inevitable drunkard.

Their sojourn at the inn was of the briefest, for Mr Sanderson had provided horses, and it was his intention that they should proceed the following morning to his station at Rhine Towers, a journey of several days, while such equipment as the party had brought from Sydney would follow by bullock-wagon, at easier pace.

Voss accepted this most reasonable plan, and, on the morning after landing, joined his host in heading the cavalcade that started out from Newcastle. None was more elated than young Harry Robarts, who had never been astride a horse before, and who was soon surveying from his eminence the fat lands of the settlers, and snuffing up the aromatic scents of the mysterious, blue bush, that rose up as they approached, and enveloped, and silenced. Soon there was only the clinking of metal, the calling of birds, and the aching of Harry's thighs, that ticked regularly as a clock, in hot, monotonous, endless time.

'Oh, Gawd,' he moaned and rolled from side to side in attempts to ease himself.

But there was no relief. There were the pastures, there was the bush. There was the hot, red sun of Harry Robarts' face set in his prickly head.

The country was by no means new to Voss, who had returned by land from Moreton Bay and the North, yet, on this significant occasion, he observed all things as if for the first time. It was a gentle, healing landscape in those parts. So he was looking about him with contented eye, drinking deep draughts of a most simple medicine. Sometimes they would leave the road, from the stones of which their horses' feet had been striking little angry sparks, and take short cuts instead along the bush tracks, walking on leaves and silence. It was not the volcanic silence of solitary travel through infinity. The German had experienced this and had been exhausted by it, winding deeper into himself, into blacker thickets of thorns. Through this bushland, men had already blazed a way. Pale scars showed in the sides of the hairy trees. Voss was merely following now, and could almost have accepted this solution as the only desirable one. The world of gods was becoming a world of men. Men wound behind him, heads mostly down, in single file. He was no longer irritated by their coughing. Ahead of him sat the long, thin, civilized back of his host.

'The country round here is divided up, for the greater part, into small holdings. That is to say, until we reach the boundaries of Rhine Towers, and Dulverton, which is the property of Ralph Angus,' explained Sanderson, who would sometimes become embarrassed by silence, and feel it his duty to instruct his guests.

At places, in clearings, little, wild, rosy children would approach the track, and stand with their noses running, and lips curled in natural wonder. Their homespun frocks made them look stiffer. An aura of timelessness enveloped their rooted bodies. They would not speak, of course, to destroy any such illusion. They stood, and looked, out of their relentless blue, or hot chocolate eyes, till the rump of the last horse had all but disappeared. Then these children would run along the track in the wake of the riders, jumping the mounds of yellow dung, shouting and sniffing, as if they had known the horsemen all along, and always been brave.

Only less timid by a little were the mothers, who would run out, shaking the structure of a slab or wattle hut, dashing the suds from their arms, or returning to its brown bodice the big breast that had been giving suck. In spite of their initial enthusiasm, the mothers would stop short, and stand in the disturbed silence, after mumbling a few guilty words. It was for husbands to speak to emissaries from the world. So the squatters themselves would come up, in boots they had cobbled during winter nights. Their adam's apples moved stiffly with some intelligence of weather, flocks, or crops. As they had hewn, painfully, an existence out of the scrub and rocks, so they proceeded to hew the words out of a poor vocabulary.

Voss appeared to glow.

'These are good people. One can see,' he said. 'Have they all been free settlers?'

'Some. Some are emancipists,' Sanderson replied from over his shoulder. 'There are both kinds. And there are good and bad of each.'

Because he was a better man than Voss, he also had fewer transitory illusions. Just then, exalted by hopes of regeneration, the German was ready to believe that all men were good.

'It goes without saying there are such distinctions,' he agreed, but with the air of suffering of one who has been misunderstood by a superficial companion. 'If you will look into the skin of a beautiful young lady, you will see perhaps one or two blemishes: a patch of slight inflammation, let us say, the holes of the pores, even a pimple. But this is not to deny the essence of her beauty. Will you not concur?'

'If it is a question of essence,' Sanderson replied, with appropriate gravity.

The way he was placed, Voss could see only his host's back, which was that long, discreet, civilized one already mentioned.

Sanderson was a man of a certain culture, which his passionate search for truth had rid of intellectual ostentation. In another age the landowner might have become a monk, and from there gone on to be a hermit. In the mid nineteenth century, an English gentleman and devoted husband did not behave in such a manner, so he renounced Belgravia for New South Wales, and learned to mortify himself in other ways. Because he was rich and among the first to arrive, he had acquired a goodish slice of land. After this victory of worldly pride, almost unavoidable perhaps in anyone of his class, humility had set in. He did live most simply, together with his modest wife. They were seldom idle, unless the reading of books, after the candles were lit, be considered idleness. This was the one thing people held against the Sandersons, and it certainly did seem vain and peculiar. They had whole rows of books, bound in leather, and were for ever devouring them. They would pick out passages for each other as if they had been titbits of tender meat, and afterwards shine with almost physical pleasure. Beyond this, there was nothing to which a man might take exception. Sanderson tended his flocks and herds like any other Christian. If he was more prosperous than most, one did not notice it unduly, and both he and his wife would wash their servants' feet in many thoughtful and imperceptible ways.

'We are how many miles now from your property?' Voss would ask on and off.

And Sanderson would tell.

'I am most anxious to see it,' Voss said invariably.

Places yet unvisited can become an obsession, promising final peace, all goodness. So the fallible man in Voss was yearning after Rhine Towers, investing it with those graces which one hopes to find at the heart of every mirage, entering its mythical buildings, kindling a great fire in the expectant hearth. Its name glittered for him, as he rode repeating it to himself.

Sanderson accepted the eccentricity of his guest's inquiries, because there was much of which he had been forewarned, even though his informant's account seemed to diverge somewhat from fact. The German wore a blandness of expression, and appeared to be endowed with a simplicity of mind that was, indeed, unexpected. They rode on. In the clear, passionless afternoons of spring, the landowner wondered what evidence of passion he had anticipated. But his own mind could not conceive darkness. They forded streams in which nothing was hidden. A truth of sunlight was dappling the innocent grass. In this light, he felt, all that is secret must be exposed. But he could not accuse the German of a nature different from his own.

It was true, too, that there was no difference – at that moment, and in that place. An admirable courtliness and forbearance had possessed Voss. He would ride back along the line informing himself on the welfare of his party, point out features of interest, ask opinions, offer suggestions, and return to his position in file behind his host, there to drink fresh draughts of his new friend's benevolence, for which, it appeared, he had a perpetual thirst.

All but Sanderson were in some way conscious of this.

Harry Robarts accepted gladly that his idol should deceive their host by borrowing the latter's character. This was not theft, that Mr Voss had demonstrated to be honest. But Le Mesurier and Turner sniffed, as dogs that have been caught before by kind words, and then kicked. And Palfreyman looked and listened, in conflict between the scientific study of behaviour, and his instinctive craving to believe that man is right, even if, to establish this, he would have to prove that he himself had been wrong.

Late in the afternoon of their arrival, the party descended from the hills into a river valley, of which the brown water ran with evening murmur and brown fish snoozed upon the stones. Now the horses pricked their ears and arched their necks tirelessly. They were all nervous veins as they stepped out along the pleasant valley. They were so certain. Which did, indeed, inspire even strangers with a certain confidence and sense of homecoming.

Soon domestic cows had run to look, and horned rams, dragging their sex amongst the clover, were being brought to fold by

127

a youthful shepherd. But it was the valley itself which drew Voss. Its mineral splendours were increased in that light. As bronze retreated, veins of silver loomed in the gullies, knobs of amethyst and sapphire glowed on the hills, until the horseman rounded that bastion which fortified from sight the ultimate stronghold of beauty.

'*Achhh!*' cried Voss, upon seeing.

Sanderson laughed almost sheepishly.

'Those rocks, on that bit of a hill up there, are the "Towers" from which the place takes its name.'

'It is quite correct,' said the German. 'It is a castle.'

This was for the moment pure gold. The purple stream of evening flowing at its base almost drowned Voss. Snatches of memory racing through him made it seem the more intolerable that he might not finally sink, but would rise as from other drownings on the same calamitous raft.

Sanderson, too, was bringing him back, throwing him simple, wooden words.

'You can see the homestead. Down there in the willows. That is the shed where we shear our sheep. The store, over by the elm. And the men's cottages. We are quite a community, you see. They are even building a church.'

Skeins of mist, or smoke, had tangled with the purple shadows. Dogs dashed out on plumes of dust, to mingle with the company of riders, and bark till almost choked by their own tongues. The men were silent, however, from the magnificence through which they had passed, and at the prospect of new acquaintanceships. Some grew afraid. Young Harry Robarts began to shiver in a cold sweat, and Turner, who had now been sober several days, feared that in his nakedness he might not survive further hazards of experience. Even Palfreyman realized he had failed that day to pray to God, and must forfeit what progress he had made on the road where progress is perhaps illusory. So he was hanging back, and would not have associated with his fellows if it had been possible to avoid them.

A woman in grey dress and white apron, holding a little girl by the hand, approached, and spoke with gravity and great sweetness.

'Welcome, Mr Voss, to Rhine Towers.' To which immediately

she added, not without a smiling confusion: 'Everybody is, of course, welcome.'

Sanderson, who had jumped down, touched his wife very briefly, and this woman, of indeterminate age, was obviously strengthened. For a second, it was seen, she forgot other duties. Then her husband called, and two grooms came, parting the fronds of the willows, to take the horses.

'Come on, Voss. They will be seen to,' Sanderson announced. 'Are you so in love with the saddle? Come inside, and we shall hope to make you comfortable.'

'Yes,' said Voss.

But he continued to sit, thoughtful, with his mouth folded in.

The serpent has slid even into this paradise, Frank Le Mesurier realized, and sighed.

Everyone was expecting something.

'I did not think to impose upon you to this extent, Mr Sanderson,' the German released his lip and replied. 'It would embarrass me to think such a large party should inconvenience you by intruding under your roof-tree. I would prefer to camp down somewhere in the neighbourhood with my men, with our own blankets, beside a bivouac fire.'

Mrs Sanderson looked at her husband, who had turned rather pale.

'It would not enter my head,' said the latter.

Since it had entered the German's, his eyes shone with bitter pleasure. Now the beauty of their approach to Rhine Towers appeared to have been a tragic one, of which the last fragments were crumbling in the dusk. He had been wrong to surrender to sensuous delights, and must now suffer accordingly.

Those to whom such mortification remained a mystery, groaned and shifted in their saddles. Those who were more enlightened, composed their mouths.

'But the beds are all aired,' ventured the bewildered Mrs Sanderson.

Voss's jaws were straining under the hurt he had done to the others, and, more exquisitely, to himself.

It was doubtful whether even the admirable Sanderson could have led them out of the impasse to which they had come, when Palfreyman sighed deeply, and began to crumple forward, and to slide down, which shocked the company into doing some-thing. Everyone was taking part. Everyone breathed relief, except Palfreyman himself.

'Is he ill?' asked Mrs Sanderson. 'Poor man, it could be ex-haustion.'

As they carried the unconscious Palfreyman towards the house, Voss related how his colleague had sustained a fall from a horse a short time ago, and although pronounced fit, it was not his personal opinion that Palfreyman was sufficiently recovered to take part in the expedition. Voss kept wiping his neck with a handkerchief, but seemed to find no relief. His explanations assumed the tone of threats.

When they reached the veranda of the house, which was a low-built, slab edifice, in colour a faded yellow ochre, with whitewashed posts and window-frames, a thick-set strong-look-ing individual appeared and took the body of the unconscious man, although nobody had asked him to do so.

To Mr Sanderson, it appeared perfectly natural.

'This is Mr Palfreyman, the ornithologist. Who has fainted,' he explained for the benefit of the stranger. 'He has not long re-covered from an illness. Take him to the corner room, if you will, so that my wife and I shall be near him, and able to give attention.'

Regaining consciousness soon after in a strange room, Palfrey-man's chief concern was to find someone to whom he might apologize. At his pillow was standing rather a thick-set man, to whom he was preparing to speak, when the individual went away.

The incident of the ornithologist's collapse did at least cut the knot: in the confusion, explanations and comradeship that fol-lowed, Voss and Le Mesurier had also accepted quarters in the house, while Turner and Harry Robarts had been led off to the back by the grooms. Nobody referred to the strange objections raised by Voss. It was possible that he himself had forgotten, until such times as he would torment himself by reviving painful memories of all his past perversities.

Such night-growths withered quickly at the roots in that house, in which little children ran clattering and calling over the stone floors, maids came with loaves of yellow bread and stiffly laundered napkins, and dogs were whining and pointing at the smells of baking meats. In the big, low-ceilinged room in which the company was to eat, a fire of ironbark had been kindled. The clear, golden light flickered in patterns on the white cloth, until the advent of several mellow lamps. Finally, Mrs Sanderson herself, who had obeyed vanity to the extent of doing something different to her hair, brought her own contribution of light, and a branch of home-made candles to set upon the mantelpiece.

While they were waiting, their host had poured wine for Voss, Le Mesurier, and himself.

'From our own grapes,' he explained. 'It is one of my aims to become self-supporting.'

And he went on to draw their attention to various bowls and jugs that he had modelled himself in local clay, and on which his wife had painted designs and then fired in their own kiln. If the clear colours and honest forms of their pottery had, in the one case, run, in the other, been distorted by the intense heat in which that had been tried, its poignance had increased.

That was the quality which predominated in the dining-room, in the whole homestead at Rhine Towers, a quality of poignance, for heights scaled painfully, or almost scaled. Incidental failure did not rob the Sandersons of success. It was perhaps the source of their perfection.

'I do congratulate you for your remarkable achievement here in the wilderness,' said Voss, whose wine was hot in his mouth. 'And envy, too.'

Sanderson replied rather harshly.

'It is for anyone to achieve who wishes to.'

Voss himself knew this.

'But achievements differ in different men. It is not for me, unfortunately so, to build a solid house and live in it the kind of life that is lived in such houses. That is why' – and he began guzzling his wine – 'it is disturbing,' he said. 'Honest people can destroy most effectually such foundations as some of us have.'

He put down his glass.

'I cannot express myself in English.'

Mrs Sanderson, who had sensed more than her husband would allow himself to, looked unhappy. She held her thin, though strong, hands to the fire, so that they looked transparent, and said:

'It is time the others came.'

Le Mesurier, also seated at the hearth, and sensible of his leader's mood even as their hostess was, bent down then and picked up a little girl in his arms.

'What do you like best?' he asked, with no trace of that cynicism with which he would protect himself from the omniscience of children.

The child answered, out of what had never really been a doubt:

'Treacle tart.'

She was fingering the skin of his face, gravely, as he held her, and drowning him in her eyes. Of all the enchantments at work in that room, in which the fire was crackling and a dog hunting dream hares, this was perhaps the most powerful – until Angus broke the spell.

It was immediately apparent that this must be Angus who had burst in. He would be forgiven almost anything, even his wealth and his ignorance, by all but the most disgruntled, for handsome, clumsy, oblivious young men, together with thoroughbred horses and gun-dogs, cannot be held responsible. Because his face concealed nothing, withdrawn souls felt guilty for their secrets, and hastened to make amends by coming into the open. He was so amiable, reddish of hair, and ruddy of skin, with a smile that was particularly white.

'You are late, of course, Ralph,' Sanderson did not complain; 'but I suppose punctuality is past praying for.' For the benefit of Voss, he added: 'This is a *second* Ralph. I am the first.'

The thought of being duplicated, even in name, seemed to give great pleasure to the host.

Voss accepted the handsome young man with some caution, remembering that Angus had been promised to his expedition. He did not, however, confess to this knowledge, just as Angus thought better than to mention the agreement that had been reached. Mentally they were stalking round each other as they stood making conversation with their hosts.

'I think if we ring for Mr Judd,' Mrs Sanderson finally decided.

The bell echoed through Voss. Remembering the convict to

whom Mr Bonner had referred, the German realized it was this
that he dreaded most of all.

Presently Palfreyman appeared, walking fraily, his lips composed, but a dark yellow in colour. At his side was the thick-set
man who had taken possession of him on arrival.

'Do you think this is wise?' Sanderson asked.

'Perfectly,' smiled Palfreyman. 'It was a passing weakness.
That is all. I have rested these two hours on a good bed, and Mr
Judd has very kindly fed me with rum out of a spoon.'

So the thick-set individual was Judd.

He was there now, not far from Palfreyman's elbow. He
seemed to have appointed himself nurse, which the patient
accepted as a natural arrangement.

Judd was introduced to Voss, and the two men shook hands.

The former convict was in every way discreet, which was the
more noticeable in anyone of his bulk and strength. He was, in
fact, a union of strength and delicacy, like some gnarled trees
that have been tortured and twisted by time and weather into
exaggerated shapes, but of which the leaves still quiver at each
change, and constantly shed shy, subtle scents. He was rather
grizzled, deeply wrinkled on the back of his neck. It was difficult
to estimate his age, but he was not old. He was quietly, even well
spoken. What he knew could have been considerable, though
would not escape from him, one suspected, even if pincers were
brought to bear. Not that he mistrusted men. Rather had the
injustice and contempt that he had experienced during a certain
period sealed him up. Risen from the tomb of that dead life, he
could not yet bring himself to recognize it as a miracle, and
perhaps he would not, and perhaps it was not.

'Now that we are all here, let us sit down at once,' Mrs Sanderson suggested. 'I expect you are hungry, Mr Angus.'

'I am always hungry,' said the agreeable young man, but
somewhat tight-lipped.

For Mrs Sanderson was disposing her guests at the table.

'And you, Mr Angus there. And Mr Judd.'

Angus was all vagueness and colour as his hand touched the
back of the chair. Whereas Mr Judd seemed possessed of a sad
irony for some situation that he had experienced before.

Voss realized then that they were about to sit down with the former convict, and that the prospect occupied the young land-owner's mind to the exclusion of all other thought or feeling. The German wondered whether his own crimes, to which he would admit on days of candour, exceeded those that Judd had committed. Here he might possess, he felt, a salve for some future sore. But he quickly threw it away. His own distaste was rising. He did not object to Judd as a convict, but already sus-pected him as a man.

'Come, then,' said Mr Sanderson irritably, 'is nobody going to sit down?'

Because he was daring them not to, and because of the respect they bore him as an unquestionably superior being, everybody did sit, while saving up their grievances.

Then the girls were bringing a big soup, and thick, homely plates.

'I understand Mr Judd is a squatter in these parts' – the German did not quite accuse.

His face professed kindness, but was prepared to examine any visible wounds.

The emancipist barely turned his eyes, and opened his mouth. He expected his host to save him, which Sanderson hastened to do.

'Mr Judd has taken up a few acres on our boundary,' he explained. 'So you see, we are close neighbours. Fortunately for us, as it means we are able to take advantage of his assistance and advice.'

Judd began to eat his soup, which was of a milky, potatoey consistence, speckled with sweet herbs, and eminently soothing. The convict was taking Sanderson's defence of him for granted, or so it seemed. Some of those present adjusted their opinion of him from that instant, considering that they themselves would have spoken up. But Judd continued to eat his soup. The opinion of others did not affect him any more.

The company enjoyed their dinner. They had a big, crisp, crinkled saddle of baked mutton, and a dish of fresh, scented plums, and conversation, which by degrees, and with the warmth of wine, sounded agreeable to everyone.

The evening progressed. It would not be one in which to dis-cuss matters of importance. This was implicit in the light and temper of it. Mrs Sanderson kept her guests deliberately on the surface, and began to enjoy herself, remembering parties of her girlhood, with music and games. She became quite flushed, and looked frequently at her husband, who was preventing the collision of their friends by his own methods. He had begun to give some account of their existence at Rhine Towers, since they arrived there on bullock wagons, with all their possessions and their white skins, and were at first burnt, then blistered, finally calloused, but above all, grappled for ever to their land by the strong habits of everyday life that they formed upon it. Many simple images were conveyed most vividly to the minds of his audience, there to stay, as he told of prime beasts, a favourite gun, springs of cold water he had found in the hills, or a wild dog he had failed to tame. Once, treading through the bracken, his horse's hoof had struck against a human skull, probably that of some convict, escaped from the coastal settlements in search of the paradise those unfortunates used to believe existed in the North.

The narrator presented the skull with such detachment that Ralph Angus could almost feel the downy bracken growing through the sockets of his own eyes.

Judd, too, observed the skull, in silence. His silences, Voss could feel at times, were most formidable.

After an interval, when the company was broken into groups in the tattered firelight, or dozed singly and fitfully between the flickering of eyelids, the German approached the convict, who was seated just a little to one side, and resolved to talk to him. Leaning with his forearm against the wall, and crossing his ankles in prim support, always leaning, and yet with a kind of awkward formality, he said:

'Tell me, Mr Judd, you own this property, and yet see fit to leave it for so long a period as the expedition will require?'

For he would offer the convict a loophole.

'Yes,' answered the solid man. 'I have an able wife, and two boys who were brought up to hardship.'

No shadow of doubt was revealed in this reply.

'You must feel very strongly on the necessity for such voyages of discovery,' said Voss, always looking down at Judd.

The explorer recalled finding on his previous journey a mass of limestone, broken by nature into forms that were almost human, and filled with a similar, slow, brooding innocence.

The convict said:

'I have had some experience of the country to the north-west. As you have been told. And I consider it my duty to offer my services to the Colony on the strength of that experience.'

'In spite of certain injustices of the Crown?'

The German was honestly interested in such a conundrum of human behaviour. Although an expert in perversity, this had a strangeness that even he did not understand. So he continued to look at the emancipist, as though their positions were reversed, and Judd were the foreigner in that land.

Judd was moving his lips.

'In spite of – yes, in spite of it,' he replied, and did not look at Voss.

'I shall take pleasure in knowing you better in the course of time,' the German said.

The emancipist made a wry mouth, and sound of regret or doubt, of which Voss, preoccupied with his own deficiencies, remained unaware. Indeed, the pleasure he promised himself in learning to understand Judd did seem illusory, for rock cannot know rock, stone cannot come together with stone, except in conflict. And Voss, it would appear, was in the nature of a second monolith, of more friable stone, of nervous splinters, and dark mineral deposits, the purposes of which were not easily assessed.

Judd excused himself, saying:

'I am a simple man.'

Which can read: *most complex,* Voss suspected.

'But I am pledged to give of my best. If it is only with my hands. You see, I have received no education worth speaking of. I have not read the books. All my gifts are for practical things. Then, too, I have a "bush sense", it has been proved. So there, sir, are my qualifications in a nutshell. Oh, I forgot to mention endurance. But that goes without saying. I have survived till now.'

All these words were placed upon one another broodily, like stones.

Voss, who was looking down all the time upon the man's massive, grizzled head, could not feel superior, only uneasy at times.

It was necessary for him to enjoy complete freedom, whereas this weight had begun to threaten him. So he was chewing his moustache, nervously, his mouth quite bitter from a determination to resist, his head spinning, as he entered in advance that vast, expectant country, whether of stone deserts, veiled mountains, or voluptuous, fleshy forests. But his. His soul must experience first, as by some spiritual *droit de seigneur,* the excruciating passage into its interior. Nobody here, he suspected, looking round, had explored his own mind to the extent that would enable him to bear such experience. Except perhaps the convict, whose mind he could not read. The convict had been tempered in hell, and, as he had said, survived.

Mr Sanderson, who was very sensitive to the limits of human intercourse, now got up, kicked together the remainder of the burnt logs, startled a dog or two, and suggested that his guests should turn in, so that they might inspect his property in the morning with renewed strength. Young Angus at once jumped up, to return as he had come, on horseback, to his own station, and to avoid by an immediate start the company of Judd. For both these men had but ridden in for the evening, to make the acquaintance of the other members of the expedition, which would be camped at Rhine Towers at least a week, resting, choosing horses, and assembling the mules that would act as baggage animals on the journey.

As the hoofs of the horse ridden by Angus spattered away into the darkness, Mr Sanderson stood on the steps of the house with a lantern to guide his other departing guest to the gate. Of the rest, only Voss and Palfreyman were with him, for Le Mesurier, by some radiant discovery of vocation, was helping their hostess carry sleeping children to their beds.

Now Palfreyman, who had been silentest of all those present since his weakness wrested him from their company earlier in the evening, was looking at the stars, and said:

'I am glad that my knowledge of astronomy is very poor.'

'Why so?' asked Voss.

'To understand the stars would spoil their appearance.'

Voss snorted for the defencelessness of such a statement, which might permanently prevent him from taking Palfreyman into account.

Yet the German himself appreciated a poetry of the stars, as did each of the other men, a different one. It was the simplicity, hence the ridiculousness, of Palfreyman's words that caused Voss inwardly to rage, and those stars at which he happened to be staring, to flash with cold fire.

'There will be frost again tonight,' shivered Sanderson, and the lantern shook.

'Are you all right then, sir?' asked Judd, lowering his voice, and touching Palfreyman on the elbow.

'Why, yes, I was never better,' said Palfreyman, who had forgotten his earlier indisposition.

The two men were speaking for each other, so the tone of their voices suggested. Something, Voss realized, had been established between them.

Then he almost experienced a state of panic for his own isolation – it was never to him that people were saying good-bye – and he had come down another step in an attempt to see what was in the faces of the convict and the ornithologist.

If he had but known, Palfreyman was remembering how, earlier that evening, the convict had brought him a shallow iron basin of water, and a lump of crude, yellow soap, and although this humble man had waited on him, they had gratefully sensed they were equal in each other's eyes.

Now Voss, looking from one to the other, was trying to trap their shy secret, but could not succeed. There was a flickering of light, of willow trees.

In consequence, he said, with rather too anxious a warmth:

'Good-bye, Mr Judd. I will come in search of you one day. Before we leave. I would see your land.'

But the emancipist murmured, and got upon his horse, and went.

Why, then, have I been foolish? the German asked himself; no man is strong who depends upon others. And as he went inside, he thought of the contempt he bore Palfreyman.

He has been rubbed up again in some way, Sanderson saw, as they were saying good night.

Indeed, Voss was scarcely present at any of that ceremony, nor saw the face of his host, who went away at last to his own room.

'Do you think Mr Voss will be able to endure the sufferings of an explorer?' asked his wife, who was brushing her hair by candlelight.

'He subjects himself continually to such mental suffering, he well may,' the husband answered.

'But a great explorer is above human suffering, for his men's eyes, at least.'

'That is where he may come to grief. Not that his suffering is human. But other men will interpret it as such.'

'I fear he may be ill,' Mrs Sanderson ventured.

She came and laid her cheek against her husband's. That others did not share the perfection of their life would fill her at times with a sense of guilt, and now especially was she guilty, by such golden light.

'Have you been watching him to that extent?' laughed her husband.

'It is not necessary to watch. One can feel it. I wish it were possible to heal him.'

'Rocks will not gash him deeper, nor sun cauterize more searingly than human kindness,' said her husband with affectionate sententiousness.

Going to bed in the best room the Sandersons could offer, between exquisitely clean sheets and a lingering scent of verbena, Voss was not long with his body, and those thoughts which had been buzzing like blowflies in his head. At once the hills were enfolding him. All that he had observed, now survived by touch. So he was touching those same hills and was not surprised at their suave flesh. That which would have been reprehensible, nauseating, frightening in life, was permissible, even desirable, in sleep. And could solve, as well as dis-solve. He took the hand to read it out aloud, whatever might be printed on it. Here there were hills, too. They would not be gone around. That is the hill of love, his voice said, as if it had been most natural. That, she pointed, was burnt in the fire of the kiln as I pushed the clay in, and, insignificant though it is, will show for life. Then, roughly, he threw away the hand, which broke into pieces. Even in dreams he was deceived by the appearance of things, and had taken the wrong hand. Here it is, she said without grudge, and brought him another, which had not been baked. It was of white

139

grain. It still had, most terribly, most poignantly, its semblance of flesh. So he shut it up in his bosom. He was afraid to look at it again. Till she bent down from her horse. The woman with the thumping breasts, who had almost got trampled, and whose teeth had been currying black horsehair, began to shout: Laura, Laura. For assistance. All that happens, happens in spite of the horsehair woman, who is, in fact, stuffed. Laura is smiling. They are sharing this knowledge. Then, how are names lost, which the hands have known by touch, and faces, like laborious, raw jugs? Laura is the name. But the name, all is lost, the veil is blowing, the wind. Is it not the same stuff with which the hills are shrouded, and of which the white word is, *ach, Musselin, natürlich*, but what else?

In the grey light and first house-sounds, Voss woke and lay with his face against the pillow, whose innocent down was disputing possession of him with the day. For a while the man lay there, trying to remember what he had dreamt, but failing. Irritated at first, he then remembered that it is enough to have dreamt. So he continued to lie, and the faded dream was still part of him. It was, he sensed, responsible for the state of complete well-being which possessed him, at least for that hour.

Sanderson himself brought a jug of hot water, and stood it in the basin. It pleased him to wait upon his guests in small ways, once he had learnt that this is the true way. But he did not address the German, as it was still too early. At that hour of day words might defile the pure pleasure of living.

Voss lay and listened to the people of the house begin to go about their business. Some of the girls were exchanging the plain, country dreams they had dreamt. They were giggling, and slapping, and protesting, until their mistress hushed them, and told them to bring brooms and buckets. The man heard the scratch and slop from these utensils as industry increased. He heard the methodical skirts of the mistress ever passing in the passage.

During the days which followed, the healing air of Rhine Towers worked upon Voss almost to the extent his hosts would have wished. In company with the amiable Mr Sanderson, he rode slowly about the paddocks, inspecting horses, mules, and a few head of cattle that they would take North for their requirements. (Additional beasts, a mob of sheep, and a herd of goats were awaiting them on the Downs, at Mr Boyle's.)

While their leader was thus engaged, other members of the party were occupied in different ways: mending their clothes, writing in their journals, snoozing, casting flies for fish, chewing the long juicy grass, or yarning to the hands and Mrs Sanderson's disbelieving maids. When Voss appeared, however, they would jump to it, eager to obey what now seemed to them his perfectly reasonable commands. All responsibility was taken from them by his presence, a fact of which they were most appreciative at this stage. They did not have to think, but could screw up their eyes at the sun. He was the leader.

At times the German was quite fatherly, too. This was a part strange enough for him to fancy. Authenticity was added by the first grey hairs which were appearing in his beard; those lines round the eyes were, of course, the signs of kindliness; while the eyes themselves encouraged confidences, of a sort that most men would think twice about giving into the keeping of anyone else.

During the stay at Rhine Towers, some of them did tell the German. For instance, Harry Robarts confessed how his father had hung him by the ankles, with chains, above a fire of sea-coals, to watch the sweat run out of him. Turner was next. The sun slowed his voice dangerously the day he told of the house in Kentish Town, in which, it was suggested, he had lodged, in which some man had died, in which people were looking at himself, and looking at him, on landings and stairs, until he had run away rather than endure their eyes, and had come of his own free will to this country, where others were expiating their sins by force. After he had told, Turner looked at Voss, sideways, but the sun was too hot for him to regret possible rashness just then.

Voss received these confidences, and locked them up quickly, both because they were valuable and because it repelled him to share the sins of human vermin on their infected wall. Yet that same disgust drove him to invite further confidences.

There was one, though, who would not tell. There was Frank Le Mesurier.

The German realized he had seen little of the young man since their arrival at Rhine Towers, and on one occasion went so far as to say so.

'How you employ your time, Frank, is something of a mystery,' he said, and smiled.

The young man was embarrassed.

'What can I say?' he answered. 'Whatever I do, I have nothing to hide.'

Because, he had, of course, something.

'I was joking,' said the German, kindly. 'This is a period of rest. You do right to use it.'

But he looked at the young man, who went outside soon after.

Already the evening of his arrival, upon scenes of splendour such as he had known to exist but never met, Frank Le Mesurier had begun to change. The sun's sinking had dissolved all hardnesses. Darkness, however, had not fallen; it seemed, rather, to well forth, like the beating and throbbing of heart and pulse in the young man's body, to possess the expectant hills. Only the admirable house resisted. Later that night he had gone outside to watch the light from the lamps and candles, with which every window appeared to be filled. Isolation made that rather humble light both moving and desirable. So the days began to explain. Grasses were melting and murmuring. A child laid its cheek against him. The sun, magnificently imperious, was yet a simple circle that allowed him to enter, with the result that he was both blinded and illuminated.

Finally, on one occasion, he had run into the cool, still room that he was occupying during their visit, and rummaged inside his pack for an old journal which an insignificance of facts had caused him to abandon, and had sat there for a moment with the book held in his daring fingers. So he began.

All that this man had not lived began to be written down. His failures took shape, but in flowers, and mountains, and in words of love, which he had never before expressed, and which, for that reason, had the truth of innocence. When his poem was written, it was burning on the paper. At last, he had done this. But although he was the stronger for it, he put his poem away, afraid that someone might accuse him of a weakness. Often he took it out, and if some of it had died, for then, there opened out of it other avenues of light. It was always changing, as that world of appearances which had given him his poem. Yet, its structure was unchanged.

So, he was truly strong.

Sometimes he longed to reveal his strength to some other man, but was held back from doing so.

Frank is hiding something, Voss saw.

Two days before they were to leave for the North-west, the German was compelled to take a horse and go in the direction in which they said Judd's selection lay. For some of the distance a faint road led across bare flats. Silly sheep on wooden legs stood and stamped at the horseman from amongst the patches of rusty sorrel. A shepherd was watching from the doorway of his wattle hut. Then the grey road petered out into a bush track, which could have been a shallow watercourse carved between the boulders and the trees. On the night he had returned from Sanderson's homestead, Judd must have trusted to providence and the instincts of his horse, though the track exhilarated Voss by day. He no longer rode consciously, but was carried onward by sensation. He was touching the bark of those trees that were closest to him (they were, in fact, very close; he could see the gummy scabs on healed wounds, and ants faring through the fibre forests). He was singing, too, in his own language, some shining song, of sunlight and of waterfalls. As the words of the song were few, or those with which he was familiar, they would recur, which stressed their shape, and emphasized their mystical errand in the silence of the grey bush.

Presently the path, which had reached a razorback, bristling with burnt stumps, wound suddenly, violently, through a crop of shiny, black rocks, and plunged down. The saddle shot forward over the horse's withers. The sober gelding propped on his four legs, before himself starting down. All was, indeed, headed downward. The world was slanted that way, a herd of goats clinging to it. The hoofs of these animals clicked, their horns slashed, their pellets spattered, as they slit the scrub open, or nibbled at the blades of grey grass. Yellow eyes looked only once at the rider. Then the goats were dashing down, down, down, deeper than all else. Soon their bobbing tails were lost.

The horse had faith that paths do lead somewhere, and did follow, but the country itself was legendary. Birds plunged songless through the leaves in heavy flight. Dark birds, mostly. It was strange that such soft things could explode the silence, but they did, most vehemently, by their mere passage through it.

Voss was jubilant as brass. Cymbals clapped drunkenly. Now he had forgotten words, but sang his jubilation in a cracked bass, that would not have disgraced temples, because dedicated to God.

Yes. GOTT. He had remembered. He had sung it. It rang out, shatteringly, like a trumpet blast.

Even the depths lead upward to that throne, meandered his inspired thoughts. He straightened his shoulders, lying back along the croup of the crazily descending horse. It had become quite clear from the man's face that he accepted his own divinity. If it was less clear, he was equally convinced that all others must accept. After he had submitted himself to further trial, and, if necessary, immolation.

I shall worship you, suddenly said the voice of the cold girl.

It was she who had wrestled with him in the garden, trying to throw him by some Christian guile, or prayers offered.

I shall pray *for* you, she said then.

'*Jesus*,' murmured the man, making it sweet, soft, pitiful. Because ineffectual.

Then he laughed, and spat it out.

Almost at once, Voss realized that he was righting himself upon the saddle because it was no longer necessary to lean back. They had come to the bottom, and there was a woman looking at him.

The old gelding stood on the flat bottom of a rock enclosure, directly at the foot of the mountain. Almost wholly enfolded by rocky cliffs, this considerable pocket opened out farther on, gently, cautiously, it could be seen, into a blue and noble plain.

But, for the present, it was the foreground that prevailed. In it the woman stood watching, after the manner of animals, like the horse which had come down from the mountain, and the herd of brown goats, which was now gathering gravely on its own ground.

'I am seeking for a Mr Judd,' said Voss, to whom alone, of all those present, he himself was not strange.

'Ah,' said the woman, stirring. 'This is his place. But he is not here.'

'He will come, though.'

'Yes,' she said. 'Oh, yes.'

She was standing in front of a house, or hut, of bleached slabs, that melted into the live trunks of the surrounding trees. The interstices of the slab hut had been daubed with a yellow clay, but this, too, had weathered, and formed part of a natural disguise. Only smoke gave some sign of human occupation, drifting out of the chimney, always taking fresh shapes.

'You are his wife, perhaps?' suggested Voss.

The woman, who was bending a twig, waited for it to snap, and said :

'Yes.'

Thus she realized time was passing.

'I am in the middle of making the butter,' she said, or tossed out. 'I cannot leave it. You can hitch the horse over there.'

She walked, or stamped, round the side of the hut, a heavy woman, in whom purpose took the place of grace. Some of the goats were following her. She went inside a smaller hut, from which there soon came the sound of butter tumbling crumbly in a wooden churn, awkward, but created.

Walking on numb legs, Voss went over presently to the smaller hut. He had every intention of examining the woman as if she had been an animal. She was, though.

By this time she had lifted the butter from the churn, and was pressing and squeezing, squelching with her strong hands, not all as labour, but some for pleasure. There was a milky perspiration still upon the mound of white butter.

'He will not be long,' she said, after she had prepared her voice for the adventure. 'He is down at the lamb-marking with the two boys. They should have finished yesterday, only the dusk come while there was a few left.'

Then she paused. Her throat had contracted. All her strength was in her red hands.

'Why is the butter white?' asked Voss.

'It is the goats.' She laughed.

Some of these had come in, and were nibbling at the stranger's buttons.

'He is going on this great expedition,' continued the woman after some pause. 'You know, to find an inland sea. Or is it gold?' She laughed, because she knew better.

'Was your husband telling you that?' the stranger asked.

'I do not remember,' said the woman, rubbing at a cheek with her shoulder, at a hair, or gnat. 'I heard somewhere. People talk. They tell you things.'

'What will you do when your husband goes?'

'What I always do.'

She was washing the butter. The lapping of the water would not allow the silence to wrap her for very long. She reduced the butter, then built it up again, a solid fortress of it.

'I will be here,' she said, 'for ever now.'

'Have you no wish for further experience of life?'

She was suspicious of the words the stranger used. An educated gentleman.

'What else would I want to know?' she asked, staring at her fat butter.

'Or revisit loved places?'

'Ah,' she said, lifting her head, and the shadows hanging from it, slyly sniffing the air at some ale-house corner, but almost immediately she dropped the lids over her searing eyes. 'No,' she said, sulkily. 'I do not love any other place, anyways enough to go back. This is my place.'

When she raised her eyes again, he did believe it. Her glance would not betray the honest shape of her possessions. These were her true eyes, looking through ferns at all wonders, animal-black, not wishing to interpret.

'*He* is restless, though,' she continued, brisker, laughingly. 'He is a man. Men know more about things. And want to know more. He has got a telescope to look at the stars, and would tell you about them if you asked him; they are no concern of mine. The stars!' She laughed. 'He is a quiet one. But deep. Sits there by the coals, and feels his knuckles. I would never know all what he knows. Nor would not ask. And make things! He can put a gun together, and a clock, only the clock is broke now for good. It was no fault of his; something essential, he says, is missing. So we watch the sun now.'

She had begun to slap the butter with broad wooden pats, that left a nice grain upon it.

'Sir, there would be no man more suitable than him to lead this great expedition, not if they had thought a hundred years.'

The stranger heard the thwack.

The woman raised her head again, with that same cunning which had shown itself once before, plumb in the middle of her honesty.

'Would you, perhaps, have an interest in the expedition, that you are come to see him?'

'Yes,' said the stranger. 'Voss.'

And did click his heels together funny, the woman related ever after.

'Ah, I heard tell.'

Her voice was trailing.

'Sir,' she said, blunt, 'I am a woman that gets little practice with talkin', and that is why it has been comin' out of me by the yard. It is one of my weaknesses. In those days, they would punish me for it. I was often reported. But no one can say I do not work.'

And she hit the butter.

Voss laughed and, looking through the doorway, remarked:

'Here, I do believe, is the leader of the expedition.'

'Sir,' decided the woman, coming round the sturdy bench, 'that is something he would never claim. It was me, truly, sir. Because all men will lead, some of the time, anyways, even the meanest of 'em. It is in their nature. And some are gifted different, whether it is for shootin' the wicks off candles, or divinin' water, or catchin' rats. You will be well advised to let them have their glory, take it from me.'

Just then her lord approached, accompanied by their sons, a pair of strapping boys, each bare to the middle. All three were spotted with dry blood, and had a smell upon them, of young, waxy lambs.

When the German and the convict had come together, neither was certain how to proceed. The sons of the latter knew that this meeting was no concern of theirs, so stood stroking their bare skins, their faces grown wooden.

The mother had gone inside.

'I am ridden in this direction, because I have wished to see your place,' the German began.

'My place is of no consequence,' the other answered.

He began to bring the visitor out of earshot of his family, because he was a different person in conversation with acquaintances.

'I like to see people, how they live,' said Voss. 'They become easier to understand.'

The convict laughed, as far as his straight mouth would let him.

'I am nothing to understand.'

His expression was guilty, but he could also have been pleased.

They walked on through a grove of saplings, that stirred, and bent, and invited strolling. Beyond stood a shed where the family shore their flock in season, very plain, of the same grey slabs, with races for the sheep to enter by, the pens below, of wattle and split posts, as in the Old Country. In one corner there was something resembling a gallows, furnished with ropes and pulleys. It was one of those erections that will rise up against the sky on immense evenings, though the present occasion, with its lambs'-wool clouds and pink sun, was not of that scale.

'What is that gibbet?' asked Voss to revive the conversation.

'Gibbet?' flashed the man, very bloodshot.

Then, when he had seen, he explained with his usual decent calm.

'That is where we kill. You can string a sheep up there. Or a beast.'

They continued, as if by agreement, to stroll along the edge of the plain, but in the shadow of the sheltering mountain, until it became apparent the squatter had purposely led his guest to a cleft where a spring welled into a basin of amber water. Black, rocky masses, green, skeleton ferns, the pale features of men, all fluctuated in the mirror of water. Taking off his shirt, Judd got upon his knees, and was washing off the lambs' blood with a piece of crude soap already there on a rock ledge.

He is strong, mused Voss, considering not so much the thick body as some strength of silence of which the man was possessed.

'When we first come here,' Judd began dreamily, 'this was all we had.' He lathered himself with dreamy soap. 'I mean, we got here in a dray, along the plain that runs to the South. We had an axe, of course, and a bag of flour, and shovels and things. We had the mattresses. But nothing of importance. I never owned anything of value, except once a gold chain, that got took off me in the street. At home.'

He was lathering his neck and his armpits, which made the dream seem silky, subtler.

'Then, here was this spring. We found it.'

It was, indeed, as seductive as the lesser jewels. (Is not the poetry of topaz or moonstone more nostalgic than that of diamonds?) Looking at those wet pebbles over which the water was welling, Voss could have put one in his pocket, as if he had been still a boy.

'I soon was owner of the spring,' said Judd, mopping himself. 'I would come and sit here of an evening.'

Circles expanding on the precious water made it seem possible that this was the centre of the earth.

'Then, you wish to leave all this, all that you have found, and all that you have made, for the possibility of nothing?' Voss asked, as softly as his foot, which was probing the brown crooks of ferns.

He was very thoughtful.

Judd, who had sluiced himself quickly and brutally, once it had come to that point, had turned round, and was groping for his shirt. The man's back, the German saw, was laced with scars, of an ugly purple, and the shameful white of renewed skin.

'Yes,' said Judd.

He was looking at the water.

'It is not mine,' he said, 'any more than that gold chain, which somebody shook in the street. And when they would take the cat to me, I would know that these bones were not mine, neither. Oh, sir, I have nothing to lose, and everything to find.'

In some agitation, which was only just visible in that thick body and still mind, he began to hurry his visitor away. They walked across the rather harsh bush grass, and skirted a clearing in which, on a rock platform, on a tripod, was the telescope that the convict's wife had mentioned. It was a somewhat larger instrument than Voss had visualized.

'What is that?' he asked, in spite of knowing.

149

Judd murmured.

'That is a telescope,' he said, 'that I rigged up to look at the stars. But you would not see nothing. It is too weak.'

He hurried the visitor past. He did not wish to communicate anything further, and was, moreover, ashamed of himself for any speculation upon which he had ventured. He was noted, rather, for his practical resourcefulness and physical strength. These were the qualities which had recommended him to Mr Sanderson.

When they had reached hut and horse, Voss held out his hand, and said:

'We shall assemble at Rhine Towers the day over tomorrow.

'The day *after* tomorrow,' laughed Judd, with strong teeth.

They were liking each other now.

As the light was already bronzed, Voss did not delay in mounting his horse, and was soon climbing the sharp ridge that lay between there and Sandersons'.

That night his hosts told him something of the Judds' history, in no sustained narrative, however, for what they knew had been put together from fragments, some of which, they admitted, did not fit together. For what crime Judd had been transported, they were not certain, but, on arrival in the Colony, he had been subjected to the greatest brutality and most rigorous kinds of physical labour. He had attempted once to escape, but had been dragged back while still upon the lower slopes of the mountains, through the intervention of God, it would seem, considering the fate of those who remained at large. On another occasion, involved in a mutiny, the ringleaders of which were summarily shot, Judd had been overlooked, again, it would appear, by divine favour. As one of those unfortunate beings who took part in the premature colonization of Moreton Bay, he had met his wife, herself a convict. There were those who doubted whether their union had received the blessings of the Church. If this were true, it had not prevented the tie from enduring many years since the first touch of hands under the giant grasses and teeming moisture of Moreton Bay. The latter part of their sentences the Judds had served more happily in the employment of a Judge-Advocate at Sydney, and it was from his home and upon his recommendation that they had received their pardons.

Voss listened to this with some, though not with great, interest, because he had not discovered it for himself.

But Palfreyman was greatly moved.

'I will not easily forget,' he said, 'my first meeting with the man, and the almost Christlike humility with which he tended one responsible, in a sense, for all his sufferings.'

Voss jerked his head.

'Your sentiments, Mr Palfreyman, are sometimes stirred to sickliness. However great your sympathy for this individual, it is unreasonable to want to take upon yourself the guilt of a felon, which it must be admitted, he was, to greater or lesser degree.'

Palfreyman looked at Voss.

'I cannot overcome my convictions, for you, or for anyone, Mr Voss.'

Voss got up. His black boots were squeaking.

'I detest humility,' he said. 'Is man so ignoble that he must lie in the dust, like worms? If this is repentance, sin is less ugly.'

He appeared to be greatly agitated. His skin was a dark yellow in the candlelight. His darker lips were rather twisted.

Palfreyman did not answer. He had composed his hands into an inviolable ball.

Afterwards Voss relented, but most of all towards himself. He was looking about somewhat jerkily in that half-lit room in which his words had fallen. There was a faint tinkling of crystal drops, suspended by silver wires from the sockets of the candlesticks.

Now, in this tinkly silence, he began also to excuse himself after a fashion to Mrs Sanderson, who had averted her face halfway through the foregoing scene, which, obviously, she had found most distasteful.

Ignoring his apologies, she said, however, very kindly:

'I recommend you to drink a cup of warm milk before you retire to bed. When one is over-tired, it works wonders.'

Voss did not think he would accept her advice, but his eyes were for the moment grateful.

He is a handsome man, of a kind, she saw again, and, I do believe, asking to be saved. She wondered whether she would one day mention this to her husband.

That night Voss dreamed of the goat butter, in which the convict's wife was about to mould a face. But which face? It was imperative to know. The necessity made his skin run with sweat, long after the inconclusive dream was done, and he lay there turning and tossing in the grey impersonality of sleep.

Next day, their last at Rhine Towers, was a gentle one. On such occasions are last testaments composed. Much was forgiven. The men spent hours conversing with little children. The day had never been more beautiful in that valley, nor had withdrawn more quickly from it in long robes of gold, and blue, and purple.

Just at evening, Voss had gone down to the river of ghostly trout. He was purged since yesterday, possessed even of some of the humility which Palfreyman extolled as a virtue. Standing by the brown waters of the friendly river as it purled and swirled over the stones, and looking back to where the house was fastened, so it appeared, to the bank, with much hopefulness and trust by human hands, the man was drawn nostalgically towards that strength of innocence which normally he would have condemned as ignorance, or suspected as a cloak to cover guile.

So, watching the clumsily-conceived but eventually beautiful house, of which the material structure had begun to dissolve, windows flower with the blurry clocks of candlelight, he could remember the elbows of the young woman as she sat at the piano and played through some insignificant nocturne. Woodenly. For all her grace and superficial self-possession, her cold mouth and warm eye, her small ears, which he now recalled in extraordinary detail, down to the last transparent curve, it was in the quality of rather stubborn innocence that her greatest strength lay. She herself was probably unconscious of what he had but now discovered. So, too, in the baleful garden, when she was indeed a wooden woman, of some ugliness, but strength, her words had struck deeper for their clumsy innocence, and could have delivered, as he had feared, or desired, a *coup de grâce*.

He continued to think about the young woman, there on the banks of the river, where the points of her wooden elbows glimmered in the dusk. Then, as it was time and he was tired, he climbed the slope and returned into the house.

Later that night, Voss searched in his valise for paper and his box of pens, and, after seating himself within range of a pair of candles, at a convenient little table covered with a cloth that Mrs Sanderson herself had worked, began to write to those of his patrons who wished to be kept informed, whenever possible, of his movements: rather pompous letters, which they expected, and of which he was capable.

Then, when he had done, he took pen again, almost immediately, and was writing with what would have appeared to an observer in a public room as an intensity of purpose, combined, if it were not so contradictory, with a strange lack of personal control.

Voss wrote recklessly upon the neat sheet of paper:

Rhine Towers,
Oct., 1845

Dear Miss Trevelyan,

It will be surprising for you at this stage to receive such a letter from me, but my recollections of you, together with the peaceful beauty of this country where we have even passed several days of idyllic unemployment in the hands of the most considerate of hosts, have compelled me to put pen to paper, and unite by conscious thought and sentiment all that would appear to have been present by fragments in my mind. For, it would seem that, beneath the cares of responsible preparation for this great expedition, and the many agreeable incidents of the journey thus far, I have ever been aware of your friendliness, and sincere interest in our welfare, as well as the great value I myself place upon our connexion, however slight this may present itself at first, and subordinate in the plan of life that fate has prepared for each of us.

I would hesitate to express my feelings in such personal terms, if I were not aware already of your moral strength and discernment, and that you have happily grasped certain grounds of my character. The gifts of destiny cannot be returned. That which I am intended to fulfil must be fulfilled. Consequently, I am aware that a companion must stumble almost daily over the savage rocks of circumstance, but that a companion of strength and judgement, such as I have already perceived to exist, would be forearmed against destruction.

Materially, I have nothing to offer. I am convinced, however, that my mission will be accomplished; this I would pledge against any quantity of gold or bonds. Dear Miss Trevelyan, *do not pray for me,* but I would ask you to join me in thought, and exercise of will, daily, hourly, until I may return to you, the victor.

In the meantime, also, I would ask your allowance that I may write to your Uncle, Mr Bonner, with necessary formality, for your hand.

So, I have little more to say at this late hour, and tomorrow start by lanternlight. At Jildra, the property of Mr Boyle on the Darling Downs, I can receive your answer, if you are so agreeable. Weigh carefully every possible consideration, but do not overweigh, for Jildra is my last chance!

From Jildra also I hope to write you interesting details of flora and fauna encountered, and to include some account of our behaviour on the march. I will give this now to Mr Sanderson, whose men descend periodically by wagon to Newcastle, and hope that from there it will be dispatched with all possible speed and safety into your kind hands.

Yours most respectfully,
JOHANN ULRICH VOSS

Next morning, while the lamps of friendship hovered touchingly in the dew and darkness, and naked voices offered parting advice, the company began to move northward, with the intention of crossing New England. It was a good season, and the land continued remarkably green, or greyish-green, or blue-grey, the blue of smoke or distance. These were sparkling, jingling days, in which sleek horses, blundering cattle, even the sour-heeled mules had no immediate cause for regret. Men shouted to their mates, their voices whipping the blue air, or else were silent, smiling to themselves, dozing in their well-greased saddles under the yellow sun, as they rubbed forward in a body, over open country, or in Indian file, through the bush. At this stage they were still in love with one another. It could not have been otherwise in that radiance of light. The very stirrup-irons were singing of personal hopes.

As the party advanced, settlers came down to show it kindnesses, or to hang about, if too shy, with every sign of respectful curiosity. The especial object of all these individuals was to catch a glimpse of the foreigner, with whom, of course, even the boldest did not presume to communicate on account of the peculiarities of his speech. However careful he was to imitate their own, the settlers preferred to address a member of his party; the honour of his presence was enough. The foreigner himself remained indifferent. Seated on his horse and intent on inner matters, he would stare imperiously over the heads of men, possessing the whole country with his eyes. In those eyes the hills and valleys lay still, but expectant, or responded in ripples of leaf and grass, dutifully, to their bridegroom the sun, till all vision overflowed with the liquid gold of complete union.

The demands Voss made on his freshly-formed relationship were frequent and consuming, but, although exhausted by an excess of sensuousness, it was a period of great happiness to him and, in consequence, of unexplained happiness to everyone else.

7

THE source of irritation had been removed from Mr Bonner with departure of the expedition. Now he could enjoy its purpose, now that it was becoming history, hence impersonal. To such as Mr Bonner, the life we live is not a part of history; life is too personal, and history is not. So the merchant returned to those personal pleasures, of house and family, business and equipage, and quite considerable bank account. If customers or friends ever alluded to that other matter of exploration for which Mr Bonner had, in fact, been personally responsible, he would smile what was an ethereal smile, for one so hearty, and materialist, and self-willed, and proceed to hold forth, between the chinking of the money in his pocket, on the historical consequences of such an expedition. But thanks be, it no longer directly concerned him. The Crusades were not more remote. No doubt he would have subscribed to a Crusade, just as he would continue, if called upon, to support the expedition, but in hard cash, and not in sufferings of spirit. While approving of any attempt to save the souls of other men, he did appreciate the comfort of his own.

The comforts, both material and spiritual, so conveniently confused in comfortable minds, inspired the merchant's residence. Of solid stone, this had stood unshaken hitherto. As a house it was not so much magnificent as eminently suitable, and sometimes, by pure chance, even appeared imaginative, in spite of the plethora of formal, shiny shrubs, the laurels, for instance, and the camellias that Uncle had planted in the beginning. The science of horticulture had failed to exorcise the spirit of the place. The wands and fronds of native things intruded still, paperbarks and various gums, of mysterious hot scents, and attentive silences: shadowy trees that, paradoxically, enticed the eyes away from an excess of substance. Moreover, the accents of poetry were constantly creeping in through the throats of doves, and sometimes young ladies might be seen, sampling strawberries from the netted beds, or engaged in needlework in a little latticed summer-house, or playing croquet with the military, but later, in the afternoon, when the hoops made long shadows on the crisp grass.

The Bonners' garden was a natural setting for young ladies, observers were aware, particularly for the niece, who was of a more solitary nature, and given to dabbling in flowers – in a ladylike manner, of course – when the climate permitted. In the mornings and the evenings she would be seen to cut the spring roses, and lay them in the long, open-ended basket, which the maid would be carrying for that purpose. The maid was almost always at her heels. People said that Miss Trevelyan demanded many little, often unreasonable, services, which was only to be expected of such an imperious young person, and a snob.

She was quite unlike Miss Belle. On those suffocating days when the change would not come, and the feet crushed a scent out of the fallen camphor leaves, Miss Belle would be crying out loud, and fanning herself, and pushing back her hair to be rid of its weight, but would not escape, it was seen by people passing the other side of the wall; Miss Belle remained dripping gold. Or in the grey gales of afternoon, when at last they came, the great round gusts that smote the camphor trees, Miss Belle would catch up her skirt, and run at the wind, and drink it, and feel it inside her dress, and shout, even, until her mother or cousin would hush her. Yes, Miss Belle was the lively one.

So the life of the garden merged with the thoughts of the passers-by. The flickery muslins and the brooding leaves obsessed the more speculative. Indistinct voices would follow them to distant quarters of the town, almost always the voices of

ladies, devoted to those pursuits to which ladies do devote themselves, because they must pass the time.

'Oh dear, I would write a letter,' Belle might say, 'if I had not
written to everyone.'

She had, too, but she did receive in return many informative
letters from other girls.

'I would not know to whom I might write,' Laura replied on
such an occasion.

They were sitting in the latticed summer-house, from which
the wistaria from China hung its buzzing, drunken heads.

'But there is everyone,' Belle replied. 'There is Chattie Wilson,
and Lucy Cox, and Nelly McMorran. And everyone.'

'Or that I would find a subject of sufficient interest.'

'That is not necessary,' said Belle. 'One simply writes.'

Time was heavy, although, in the afternoon, Tom would
come.

'Papa is surprised he has had no word from the expedition,'
Belle rattled, to save herself. 'He would not expect, of course,
civility from Mr Voss, but he did fancy Mr Sanderson might
keep him informed, on that stage of the journey at least.'

'It is early yet,' suggested Laura, who was sketching the
garden from an angle that had only recently occurred to
her.

'Or Mr Palfreyman,' said Belle. 'Mr Palfreyman could, and
ought to, write.'

She did not look at her cousin.

Laura frowned at the garden.

'It is not his duty. He is not the leader of the expedition.'

'Dear Lolly,' sighed Belle, taking her cousin's hand as if it
had been a cat to cuddle.

'You are absurd, Belle,' laughed Laura, to whom perspective
was a problem.

'But you found Mr Palfreyman agreeable. You admitted it
yourself. The day the ship sailed.' For Belle Bonner, her cousin
was a fascinating mystery, whether sketching from the summer-
house or taking her leave of suspected admirers. 'Such an amiable man, Mamma considers.'

'Most amiable,' Laura agreed.

'Even Tom feels – because I have asked him – that Mr Palfreyman is so *good*. Of delicate constitution, perhaps. Still, delicacy of health can make a man considerate of others.'

Laura was entertained.

'Is that also Tom's opinion?'

'No. Mamma's.' Belle blushed.

'Then, poor Mr Palfreyman has been discussed.'

'Dear Laura, I could be so happy.' Belle caressed her cousin's hand.

It was exasperating. She would have forced those she loved to eat of sweets she had not yet tasted.

But Laura laughed. She withdrew her hand, and took the pencil to her sketch, and ploughed it with one long, dark line, almost through the paper.

'You have spoilt your sketch!' cried Belle.

'Yes,' said Laura. 'It was an insipid thing.'

She crumpled it up, and dared her dear Belle.

At that season, Laura's glistening, green laughter was threaded through the days. These were warm, though not yet oppressive, full of the clovey scent of pinks, with harsh whiffs of torn gum-leaves, dissipated by the wind, and married with perfume of roses, in passionate gusts. Heady days. Green was garlanding the windows, the posts of balconies, the knobs of gateways, in celebration.

In celebration of what, others did not know, except that there was something. They were looking at Laura for some sign, as she moved in the garden, in a crush of cool flowers, or appeared suddenly in doorways, in the sound of her skirts, or under trel-lises, trailing a dappled shadow, or at windows, that she threw open suddenly, her arms flying upward after the sash, to stay suspended there a second, the greenish flesh of those stalks glimmering against vines. All these acts were joyful, without reveal-ing. Her mouth did not so much smile, as wonder.

For Laura herself had not yet grasped the full sense of that season, only that it was fuller than ever before, and that the flesh of roses was becoming personal, as she cut the long, pointed buds, or heavy blooms that would fall by evening. She had to take all, even the big, blowing ones.

'Those will make a mess, miss,' Rose Portion did protest once. She was holding the basket.

'Yes,' said Laura. 'I am aware of that.'

'Tt-tt-tt!' sighed the brown woman. 'All over the tables and carpets. A mess of rose petals.'

But the girl was dazed by roses. She continued to cut the big heads, in which bees were rummaging. She bent to reach others, till roselight was flooding her face, and she was forced to lower the lids of her eyes against the glare of roses. Then she became caught. It was one of the older, the more involved, the staggier bushes, of sinewy black wood. She was held. Neither one way nor the other was it possible to move, however she shook the tough bush. She began to laugh, mirthlessly, out of exasperation for her powerlessness, and call:

'Help me, Rose! Where are you? Do something!'

The woman set down the basket then, and freed her mistress easily.

The girl was laughing, though blushing, because she was really rather annoyed.

'Can you see whether I am torn?' she asked.

'Not that I can notice,' Rose replied, 'but I expect.'

Controlling her wind, the woman picked up the basket. This business of flowers was not her work, but it pleased her to do it, and since she had grown heavy, the people of the house humoured her.

Although Mrs Bonner, who had just come out upon the balcony, stood frowning down. At the back of her mind, there was always Rose.

Once Mrs Bonner had gone to her niece at an awkward and unexpected moment, as the latter was practising a new piece, and sat beside her, and said, there and then:

'We must really think, Laura, what is to be done about Rose. I understand there is a Mrs Lauderdale, who has founded some institution to provide for women in that condition, during, or perhaps it is for afterwards, the unfortunate children, I do not know, but must consult Mrs Pringle, and think.'

Then Aunt Emmy looked right up into her niece's face, as if she had been a tree with something hiding in it, and not a young woman engaged upon an arpeggio.

'Yes, Aunt. Of course,' said Laura, who suffered all the difficulties of music.

Laura is selfish, Mrs Bonner sighed.

'Nobody will help me,' she murmured.

So she went away.

Now Laura could see her aunt upon the balcony, threading the ribbon through a clean cap, but looking, instead, at Rose.

Rose looked, and saw, and understood – there was very little she did not – and said:

'There is Mrs Bonner. She could be wanting something of me.'

'I do not think so,' said Laura firmly.

Laura Trevelyan had given much consideration to the question of Rose Portion, but the answer to it was withheld. She did not fret like her aunt, although it concerned her personally, she sensed, even more personally. For personal reasons, therefore, she would continue to give the matter thought, although her faith in reason was already less. She would prepare her mind, shall we say, to receive revelations. This preoccupation, which was also quasi-physical, persisted at all times, though most in the overflowing garden, of big, intemperate roses, with the pregnant woman at her side. At such times, the two shadows were joined upon the ground. Heavy with the weight of golden sun, the girl could feel the woman's pulse ticking in her own body, and was, in consequence, calmer than she had ever been, quietly joyful, and resigned. As she strolled towards the house, holding her parasol against the glare, though devoured by the tigerish sun, she trusted in their common flesh. The body, she was finally convinced, must sense the only true solution.

Mrs Bonner, on the balcony, sensing her own limitations, tweaked the ribbon through the starched cap, and went inside.

'They have not yet heard from that German,' said Rose Portion, whose habit it was to state facts, rather than commit a possible indiscretion by asking.

'Not yet,' Laura Trevelyan replied.

She had bared her teeth, it seemed, somewhat convulsively – it could have been the violent glare – and the tips of her teeth were quite transparent.

'Not yet,' she said, and mumbled: 'But perhaps we shall hear, perhaps this evening.'

Although it was spoken more slowly than she had intended, in her mind it sprang like a shiver. Her mouth was dry.

'Ah, I cannot understand that man,' said Rose.

'How?' asked Laura. 'Not understand?'

'It is his speech, I suppose. Though half the time I think he does not understand himself, even in his own language.'

Laura did not answer, but was listening to breath, footsteps, pauses, and pauses were the loudest.

'No more can I understand his eyes,' breathed Rose. 'You should understand a man by his eyes, if by no other avenue.'

Then she cleared her throat, because she had said too much.

They were entering the house by way of the conservatory, in which little ferns rang with bells of moisture, and the teeth of the palm were sawing at the spider's silk. Here the heat was so intense that the women's breath was taken from them. Their faces were barely swimming forward between the walls of watery glass. Their features clove painfully the green gloom on which hairy branches swayed.

'I can understand him,' said Laura, 'if not with my reason.' She was drugged.

'Even when I cannot agree with him, I can understand him.'

The other woman drew her breath with difficulty.

As they passed into the house, the girl put her hands to her temples in an ecstasy of coolness. When she could not understand, she would pray for him, though of recent nights happiness had made her dumb, and prayer grows, rather, out of wretchedness.

The same evening, when Mr Bonner returned early, as was his habit now, into the house of roses, it happened that his niece was first to meet him, as she passed through the hall on some errand to the pantry. After kissing her at the required moment, for in matters of affection the merchant was something of a ritualist, he did remark:

'News has come at last from the expedition, today, by the Newcastle packet. They are arrived at Sanderson's. Or were at his place. They will have left by now for the Downs.

'So that is that,' he added, disparagingly, or so it sounded.

The truth was: anything that intruded on the daily round, even events anticipated, or news long hoped for, embittered Mr Bonner.

'And all is well?' Laura asked.

'All are in good heart,' corrected her uncle. 'Though it is early days yet, to be sure. Living off the fat of the land.'

How glad he was to be in his own home, and there was no prospect of his having to suffer.

The feet of the young woman were passing on the stone floor of the hall. They made a cool, impersonal sound.

'Oh, and Laura, there is a letter that has come with mine. It is in the same hand, of Mr Voss. You had better have it.'

'A letter,' she repeated, but without surprise, and took it before going on her way.

When she had done what she had intended, Laura Trevelyan went straight up to her room, which, although open to her aunt and her cousin, already contained so much of her secret life, she was not afraid of adding to it. So, after she had sat down and broken the lumpy seal, she unfolded the paper, and began to read rapidly.

That evening, over dessert, when they were discussing the news that had been received, Mrs Bonner asked:

'Would you say, from his letter, that Mr Voss appears satisfied at last with the way his affairs are progressing?'

Mrs Bonner would almost dare a person to be dissatisfied, provided it was not herself.

'Yes,' said her husband, as though he were intending no. 'I gather he is displeased at the inclusion of Judd, more than ever now that he has met him and can find no reason for objecting.'

'What sort of a man is Judd?' asked Mrs Bonner.

'A very quiet, a very reasonable man, I gather from Sanderson. And lion-hearted. Of great courage and physical strength.'

'Then, it is the lion in him that Mr Voss is objecting to,' said Belle, who was bored at this, and would become a silly little girl for her own entertainment.

Her hands, that she held above the finger-bowl, dripped inelegantly with the juice of early peaches.

'For perhaps the lion will gobble him up,' she giggled. 'But, poor lion, I could wish him better than bones and black hair.'

'Belle!' Her mother frowned.

And a girl, almost married, who could not learn to eat a peach!

Mr Bonner moved his mouth as if he had a peachstone in it.

'That could be,' he said, approving, and would himself have spread a net to assist the lion. 'But what impression,' he continued, 'did Laura's letter give?'

'Laura's letter?' asked Mrs Bonner and Belle.

'Yes,' said the merchant. 'Mr Voss was kind enough to write to Laura by the same packet. Did you not share the news, Laura?'

The young woman moved her plate slightly, on which were the downy skins of peaches, almost bloody in that light.

'Yes, I did receive a letter,' she answered. 'It was just a short note. Written in friendship. It contains civilities rather than positive news. It did not occur to me to share anything of so little general interest.'

To Mrs Bonner it was peculiar.

To Belle it was something into which animal instinct would burrow at leisure.

But Mr Bonner thought that he detected in his niece signs of unusual dismay, and wondered whether he ought to hurt her, both for her own, and the common safety. Besides acting as a corrective, domestic cruelty could be a mild and pleasing form of sport.

Immediately after this, they pushed back their chairs and went into another room.

And the days swelled with that sensuous beauty which was already inherent in them. I did, of course, know, Laura Trevelyan decided, but remained nevertheless bewildered. By the heavy heads of roses that stunned the intruder beneath trellises. By the scent of ripe peaches, throbbing in long leaves, and falling; they were too heavy, too ripe. Feet treading through the wiry grass were trampling flesh, it seemed, but exquisitely complaisant, perfumed with peach.

Or she closed her eyes, and they rode northward together between the small hills, some green and soft, with the feathers of young corn ruffled on their sides, others hard and blue as sapphires. As the two visionaries rode, their teeth were shining and flashing, for their faces, anonymous with love, were turned, naturally, towards each other, and they did, from time to time, catch such irrelevantly personal glimpses. What they were saying had not yet been translated out of the air, the rustling of corn, and the resilient cries of birds. As they rode on, all metal was twining together, of stirrup-irons, for instance, and the bits in the mouths of their horses. Leather was not the least potent of the scents of their journey, and at evening the head would sink down into the pillow of the warm, wet saddle. The hands of the blind had polished the pommels to the silkiness of ivory.

This was a period of great happiness for Laura Trevelyan, her only known happiness, it seemed. Of course, the other side of her eyelids, there were many possibilities waiting to harm her. If she would open. But she did not.

Except to write. She realized that she had not written the letter.

She sat down one afternoon at her desk. The shutters were closed. Even here was the season's prevailing scent, of live roses, and the rustling ones, and cloves. She began to write. It was easier than she had expected, as if she had acquired virtuosity in an art. So the chips of marble mounted, as the words were carved out, deep, and final.

When she had dried the paper in its own breeze, and folded, and sealed it, she cried a little, and felt the better for it. She lay on her bed for some time, behind the shutters, in the green afternoon, until the woman came, and asked:

'Are you not coming down, miss? There are some calls. It has been the wife of Justice Smart, and now it is Mrs Pringle, with Miss Una, in a pale pink bonnet.'

Then the girl, who in the past had barely suffered her maid to touch her, on account of a physical aversion such contact invariably caused, suddenly reached out and put her arms round the waist of the swelling woman, and buried her face in the apron, in the sleeping child, to express what emotion it was difficult to tell.

'Ah, miss!' hissed Rose Portion, more in horror over the unorthodoxy of it, than for the stab she experienced in her belly.

Later they would both be glad, but now the girl, realizing she had just done something awkward and strange, jumped up from the bed and began to change into a better dress.

It was Una Pringle, who, seated in the drawing-room on a little, tight-buttoned, slippery chair, first caught sight of Laura through the doorway as she was descending the hall stairs. Down, down, down. Through that, and every subsequent afternoon, of which, it was obvious, she would be the mistress. Una Pringle stopped breathing. She had always hated Laura Trevelyan, and would now hate her more than ever.

8

By now the tall grass was almost dry, so that there issued from it a sharper sighing when the wind blew. The wind bent the grass into tawny waves, on the crests of which floated the last survivors of flowers, and shrivelled and were sucked under by the swell. All day the horses and the cattle swam through this grass sea. Their barrels rolled and gurgled. All night the beasts were glutting themselves on dew and grass, but in the dreams of men the waves of grass and the waves of sleep were soon one. Dogs curled in pockets of the grass, shivered and bristled as they floated on their own dreams.

It was the dogs that first confirmed the German's opinion that they must be in the vicinity of Jildra. On a certain evening, as the expedition continued to advance, the dogs had begun to whine, and gulp, and lift their legs repeatedly. Their muzzles had grown leaner, the eyes were bulging from their skulls, when, with very little further warning, suddenly foreign tails, then the bodies of foreign dogs were emerging from the grass. Thus having come together, the two parties of animals were stalking round and round, in stiff, shocked silence, awaiting some sign.

The members of the expedition had shaded their eyes with their hands, as an extension to the already broad brims of their hats, and eventually one of them, Mr Judd it was, remarked that he could see a man approaching on horseback above the waving grass. Other eyes were soon focused on this figure, who came on through the red light, firmly clamped by the thighs to the body of his strong, chestnut horse. As he advanced, erect, moving in the saddle just enough to emphasize the arrogance of ownership, it was disclosed that the man himself was of a reddish, chestnut colour, intensified by the evening sun.

There he was, at last, reining in. The suspicious horse snorted.

'Boyle is my name,' announced the man, on thick lips, holding out a hand that did not waver.

'Of Jildra,' added Voss.

'That is correct.'

No further civilities were expended on the meeting, but Mr Boyle turned his horse and proceeded to escort the party along the track he had made by his coming. The band of sweating horses, straight mules, lowing, heavy-headed cattle, and parched, tingling men went on towards Jildra. By the time the homestead was reached, the western sky was of a blood red. The foreground had almost foundered, through which ran the figures of a number of individuals, if they were not animated, black sticks, to receive the reins from the hands of the new arrivals. Smoke was ascending, and dust fom the broad road the animals had trampled, together with the vapours of night. All was confused, nor did the approaching unity of darkness promise great consolation.

Mr Brendan Boyle was of that order of males who will destroy any distinction with which they have been born, because it accuses them, they feel, and they cannot bear the shame of it. In consequence, the station-owner had torn the boards off Homer to chock the leg of the table, and such other books as he had inherited, or even bought in idealistic youth, now provided material for spills, or could hope at best to be ignored, except by insects, dust, and mould. In his house, or shack of undaubed slab, that admitted day- and starlight in their turn, several pieces of smooth Irish silver stood cheek by jowl with pocked iron, the former dented somewhat savagely, in reprisal it seemed, for elegance. The dirt floor was littered with crumbs and crusts of bread. Birds and mice could always be relied upon to carry off a certain amount of this rubbish, but some lay there until it became petrified by time, or was ground to dust under the hard feet of those black women who satisfied the crude requirements of Brendan Boyle.

'This is my mansion,' indicated the latter, waving a lantern so that the room rocked, and the dimples which came when he spoke flickered on either side of his mouth. 'I suggest that you,

Mr Voss, and one or two others, peg your claims here on the floor, and allow me the pleasures of conversation, while the rest of the party enjoy the luxury of their own tents. There are plenty of blacks here, bustin' themselves with meat and damper, who will lend a hand. Here, Jem, where the deuce,' he grumbled, and shouted, and went outside, causing the whole neighbourhood of grass and trees frantically to rock in that same disturbed lantern-light.

Voss and Palfreyman, who were left standing in the skeleton shack, in the smell of old, hard bread and that morning's ash, did not regret that this was the last hospitality civilization would offer them.

Later, when these two had shared with their host a lump of salt beef and some cold potatoes, which a pair of shrieking black women, naked as the night, had set on the table's edge, he proceeded to make the conversation he craved, or rather, to disgorge out of his still handsome throat chunks of words, and opinions he was not used to confess to other men in all that vastness.

'It is ten years now since I came to this something country,' said Brendan Boyle, swilling the rum, to which he seemed addicted, from an ugly, iron pannikin. 'I have done nicely,' he said, fascinated by the eddies in his pot of rum, 'as nicely as most people, and will do better; yet it is the apparent poverty of one's surroundings that proves in the end to be the attraction. This is something that many refuse to understand. Nor will they accept that, to explore the depths of one's own repulsive nature is more than irresistible – it is necessary.'

He had opened the shirt on the hair of his chest, and had sat forward, and was holding his head in his hands, and was twitching with his mouth to release the words, or some personal daemon.

'To peel down to the last layer,' he yawned. 'There is always another, and yet another, of more exquisite subtlety. Of course, every man has his own obsession. Yours would be, it seems, to overcome distance, but in much the same way, of deeper layers, of irresistible disaster. I can guarantee,' he said, stabbing the table with two taut fingers, 'that you will be given every opportunity of indulging yourself to the west of here. In stones and thorns. Why, anyone who is disposed can celebrate a high old Mass, I do promise, with the skull of a blackfeller and his own blood, in Central Australia.

'High Harry!' he laughed, more for himself, and added, in a sigh: 'Ah, dear!'

Palfreyman, who had been shifting about, thought that he would turn in, and Voss, who was growing increasingly glum, agreed that this could be a solution.

'If that is the extent of your ambition,' said Brendan Boyle, and spat upon the floor.

His two guests got between their blankets, where they were, while himself was gone out on last errands.

The anatomy of the house was such that, by night, it resembled a warped skeleton, so that, for a long time, Voss lay looking at the stars on the other side of that cage of bones.

Meanwhile, Mr Boyle had returned to the room which he was pleased to refer to as the Bedchamber, beyond the chimneypiece, and which was the only other room of the house. He was blundering about a good deal, and making animal noises, and exploring the darkness for its distinctive grain. His bed, it seemed, was full of giggles.

Palfreyman was already asleep, but Voss continued to stare at the restless stars until he was no longer able to identify himself.

Next morning, when host and guest of honour were standing together upon the veranda, it was possible to compare the two men – at least their outward appearances, since their souls were temporarily gathered in. Now Brendan Boyle was reminiscent of the big, rude, red potatoes, the shapely ones, but hard, with the fine red dust coating them, which is akin to the patina the man had encouraged to coat those persistent traces of aristocracy. Where these lingered formally, as in the head and throat, of course he could not destroy them. There they were; it was both sickening and sad for him. But his hands, as he spoke, or on any occasion, waited, were stroking the accretion of red dust on the bare skin of his forearms. It could have afforded him some pleasure, but his eyes, which were of a cold, unchanging green, would not convey his feelings by daylight.

At his host's side, on the rudimentary veranda, which was all splinters, just as it had been split, stood the German, also in disguise. Blackened and yellowed by the sun, dried in the wind, he now resembled some root, of dark and esoteric purpose. Whereas the first man was composed of sensual forms, intended to be touched, flesh to be rubbed against flesh, it would not be presumed to use the second except in a moment of absolute necessity, and then with extreme caution. He stood there moistening his lips, and would have repudiated kinship with other men if it had been offered. In the presence of almost every one of his companions, and particularly in the company of Brendan Boyle, he was drawn closer to the landscape, the seldom motionless sea of grass, the twisted trees in grey and black, the sky ever increasing in its rage of blue; and of that landscape, always, he would become the centre.

The two men were evidently expecting something or someone to appear. The host was balancing on the veranda's edge and, from annoyance at being made to wait, could very easily have toppled off. The delicate wobbling of his barely controlled body made him look ridiculous.

'I cannot recommend these blacks as infallible guides and reliable companions,' Mr Boyle was saying. 'Like all aboriginals they will blow with the wind, or turn into lizards when they are bored with their existing shapes. But these two fellers do know the tribes and the country for a considerable distance to the west. Or so they tell a man. Standards of truth, of course, vary.' Then, realizing, he added: 'But you do not know their lingo. Dugald – that is the elder feller – has a little English. But you will not be able to make much of an exchange.'

'In general,' Voss replied, 'it is necessary to communicate without knowledge of the language.'

Then the two men were looking and laughing at each other insolently, their faces screwed up, their eyes splintering. Each would consider he had gained the point.

Before they had recovered themselves, two blacks came round the corner of the house. Their bare feet made upon the earth only a slight, but very particular sound, which, to the German's ears, at once established their ownership.

'Well, now, since they have condescended,' said Mr Boyle, who was not really of bad temper; if he raised his voice to a bellow, it was only because he was addressing blacks, and it made his meaning clear. 'You, Dugald, you, Jackie,' he said, 'I tell you this Mr Voss go far places,' waving his arm towards the west, 'find new country, do good all of us, black and white feller. You stick to Mr Voss do you hear, even if you drop, you old beggar.'

Then he laughed, and spoke to the men in a few phrases of their own tongue, in a very English accent, to which they listened with that same politeness with which they received intelligence in any shape or form.

The elder native was most serious and formal. He was wearing what appeared to be a very old and floury swallowtail coat, but deficient in one tail. His black skin, which had been gathered by age into a net of finest grey wrinkles, was not tramelled further, except by a piece of bark-cloth, the colour of nature, in an appropriate place. A similar piece of cloth did cover his colleague a little; otherwise, the latter was naked, of a youthful, oily skin, and flattened features. This one, Jackie, was really quite young. He stood about with the delicacy of a young girl, looking away while absorbing all details, listening with his skin, and quivering his reactions. It was not possible to address him directly, nor would he answer, but through his mouthpiece, Dugald.

In other circumstances, Voss would have liked to talk to these creatures. Alone, he and the blacks would have communicated with one another by skin and silence, just as dust is not impenetrable and the message of sticks can be interpreted after hours of intimacy. But in the presence of Brendan Boyle, the German was the victim of his European, or even his human inheritance. So he got down from the shaky step, and advanced on the old black with his rather stiff, habitual gait and said:

'This is for Dugald.'

It was a brass button that he happened to have in his pocket, and which had come off a tunic, of military, though otherwise forgotten origin.

The old man was very still, holding the token with the tips of his fingers, as if dimly aware in himself of an answer to the white man's mysticism. He could have been a thinking stick, on which the ash had cooled after purification by fire, so wooden was his old, scarified, cauterized body, with its cap of grey, brittle ash. Inside the eyes moved some memory of myth or smoke.

The youth, on the other hand, had been brought to animal

life. Lights shone in his skin, and his throat was rippling with language. He was giggling and gulping. He could have eaten the brass button.

On an afterthought, Voss again put his hand in his pocket and offered Jackie a clasp-knife that he was carrying.

'*Na, Junge,*' he said, with a friendliness that could not avoid solemnity.

Jackie, however, would not receive, except by the hand of his mentor, and then was shivering with awful joy as he stood staring at the knife on his own palm.

Voss, too, was translated. The numerous creases in his black trousers appeared to have been sculptured for eternity.

As all of this scene was a bit unexpected, not to say peculiar, to Brendan Boyle, the latter was itching to cut it short.

He jabbed with a finger in the old man's shoulder-blade, and said :

'Plenty valuable button. You take good care.'

After which, he spat, and was easing his clothes.

Boyle then proposed to Voss that they should spend the morning inspecting the sheep and goats he had selected for use of the expedition, and which would probably be found somewhere in the vicinity of a string of waterholes a mile or two north of the homestead. Voss agreed. It soon became clear that he and his host were continually humouring each other. In this way each hoped to hide the indifference he felt towards his companion, though each remained humorously aware that the other was conscious of his attitude. The agreeable part was that neither harboured actual dislike. No one could have disliked Brendan Boyle in spite of his peculiarities, and he was quite incapable of disliking for long anyone but himself.

So they set out from the slatternly settlement of Jildra, to which Voss had grown reconciled, just as he had come to accept certain qualities of his host. The smoky setting of the early morning was not unpleasing, even touching. Columns of blue smoke were ascending, a long cloud was lying flat above them, and the wisps of smoky grass, suggested an evanescence of the solid earth, of shack and tents, iron and hessian, flesh and bone, even of the rather substantial Brendan Boyle. They rode out of the jumble of grey sheds, past several gunyas, at which black women were standing, and little, red-haired boys with toy spears. Over the skins of the natives, the smoke played, and through. A yellowish woman, of spreading breasts, sat giving suck to a puppy.

'Dirty beggars,' coughed Mr Boyle – it was the smoke, 'but a man could not do without them.'

Voss did not reply to what appeared, in his host's case, obvious.

The two men rode on, in hats and beards, which strangely enough had not been adopted as disguises. In that flat country of secret colours, their figures were small, even when viewed in the foreground. Their great horses had become as children's ponies. It was the light that prevailed, and distance, which, after all, was a massing of light, and the mobs of cockatoos, which exploded, and broke into flashes of clattering, shrieking, white and sulphur light. Trees, too, were but illusory substance, for they would quickly turn to shadow, which is another shape of the ever-protean light.

Later in the morning, when the air was beginning to solidify, the two riders were roused from themselves by sight of the promised waterholes. These might have been described more accurately as mud-pans, or lilyfields, from which several grave pelicans rose at once, and were making off on wings of creaking basket-work.

'There are the sheep now,' said the station-owner, pointing.

These dirty maggots were at first scarcely visible in the yellow grass, but did eventually move enough, and mill round, and stamp.

'They are a rough lot,' said Boyle, 'but so is your undertaking. I am glad it is you,' he had to add, sniggering, because in very many ways he was a schoolboy.

'It is almost always impossible to convince other men of one's own necessities,' Voss said. 'Do you believe you were convincing to us last night when you attempted to explain yours?'

'I? What?' exclaimed Boyle, and wondered whether his obscurer self had been caught in some indecent confession, or even act; he suspected it, but could not remember. 'What a man lets out at night, you know, is a different thing from what he would say by day.'

He was protesting, and redder, as he searched his mind.

'I cannot think what you are referring to,' he concluded.

On such a mild and bountiful morning, Voss would not reveal what it was.

All this time the sheep, in their yellow wool and wrinkles, went on milling round and round, trying to find, or to escape from one another. Two black shepherds, at a distance, gave no indication of wanting to come any closer.

'There, I think, are the goats,' indicated Voss.

'What? Oh, yes, the goats,' Boyle replied.

About a hundred of these animals had gathered on the farther bank of a second waterhole, where they were climbing and slithering on the hulks of fallen trees, stretching their necks to pull at the fronds of live leaves, scratching at remote pockets of their bodies with the tips of their horns, skull bashing, or ruminating dreamily. As the horsemen approached, the goat-mind was undecided whether to stay or run. Several did remain, and were staring up, their lips smiling, looking right into the faces of the men, even into their souls beyond, but with expressions of politeness.

'Descendants of the original goat,' Boyle commented rather crossly.

'Probably,' answered Voss, who liked them.

One aged doe had searched his mind with such thoroughness as to discover in it part of his secret, that he was, in fact, only in appearance man.

He held out his hand towards her subtle beard, but she was gone, and all of them, with hilarious noises, and a rain of black dung.

'Come on,' said Boyle.

If he could have attacked or accused his guest in some way, he would have, but the German had assumed a protective cloak of benevolence. As they rode homeward, the many questions that the latter asked, all dealing with the flora and fauna of the place, were unexceptionable, expressed with that air of simple benevolence. His face wore a flat smile, and there were little lines of kindness at the outer corners of his eyes.

Yet there was something, Boyle knew. He rode, answering the German's questions, but absently flicking at his horse's shoulder with the skein of reins.

During the remainder of their sojourn at Jildra, Boyle tried to read the faces of the German's men for some clue to their leader's nature and intentions. But they, if they knew, would not be read, or else were spell-ridden in the hot, brown landscape. As they went about the tasks that had been allotted to them, such business as arises during an interval of preparation and rest, the men appeared to have little existence of their own, unless it was a deeply buried one. There was Palfreyman, in a cabbage-tree hat that made him look smaller, with a clean, white hand-kerchief to protect his neck and throat, but which exposed, rather, his own innocence and delicacy. There he was, riding out, an old woman of a man, with the boy Robarts perhaps, and one or two natives, to secure the ornithological specimens which he would then clean and prepare by candlelight. Nothing more simplified than Palfreyman. So, too, the others were tranquilly occupied. Judd had become an immense rump as he busied him-self at shoeing horses. Others were oiling firearms, greasing leather, sharpening axes, or sewing on buttons.

Except once or twice, nothing untoward occurred. On one occasion, to give the exceptions, Boyle had gone into the men's tent, admittedly to satisfy his curiosity, and there was Frank Le Mesurier, sprawled out upon his red blanket, writing in a note-book. As Boyle was a big man, he was forced to stoop to enter the rather low-slung, oiled calico tent, then to stand hunched. He was so obvious that he made no attempt to behave casually. The blood was too thick in his fingers. Le Mesurier stopped writing, and rolled over on his book, which he could not hide effectively, because it had been seen.

'Where is Mr Voss?' asked Boyle.

Although he had not been looking for Voss, it was true the German was always somewhere in his mind.

'I do not know,' answered the young man, darkly returning the intruder's stare. 'He has gone out somewhere,' he added in a hollow voice, which suggested that the speaker had but recently woken.

Then Boyle squatted down, as an opportunity seemed to be offering itself.

'Have you known him long?' he asked.

'Yes,' Le Mesurier answered at once, and at once began to

hesitate. 'Well, no,' he corrected, prodding at a seam of the tent with his stump of lead pencil. 'Let me see now. I knew Mr Voss at Sydney.'

Then he blushed and was confused.

'It was much longer than that,' he said. 'It was on board the ship. Which does make it a very long time.'

Boyle's suspicion increased. What was this young man trying to hide? Had he, perhaps, participated, or was he still participating in the German's crime?

Le Mesurier lay there blushing dark, and resenting the intrusion more than ever. Now, as on that evening under the scrubby trees of the Domain, he felt that he did share something of his leader's nature, which he must conceal, as, in fact, he was hiding the notebook that contained the most secret part of himself.

Boyle suspected this, but could no more snatch away the book than tear out by bleeding roots those other secrets of personality.

'I was thinking of taking the gun down to the river, to look for a few duck that I saw making that way. Will you come, Frank?' he now asked.

He wanted to kill something.

The young man agreed to come, rolled over, and grabbed for his hat. In the folds of the blanket there was no sign of the notebook that both knew to be there.

So they went down to the river, which had almost dried since the last rain. A brown heat was descending like a flat lid. Jildra, with its squalid pleasures of black flesh and acres of concealed wealth, was reduced to a panful of dust and stinking mud, in which Brendan Boyle himself had chosen to stick.

Once during those days, the latter approached Voss and almost asked to take part in the expedition, as if death in unpredictable circumstances were suddenly preferable to slow rotting.

Instead, they discussed water-bags.

This man has a favour to ask, the German knew, and in consequence grew wily. All, sooner or later, sensed his divinity and became dependent upon him. There was young Ralph Angus, Sanderson's grazier-neighbour, blushing like a girl to ask an opinion. The armour of youth and his physical strength had not protected him against discovery of his own ignorance during the journey north. Turner was abject, of course, and Harry Robarts an imbecile. But Angus might prove a worthy sacrifice. The young bull of pagan rites, he would bellow and cast up his brown, stupid eyes before submitting.

Of all the company, Judd remained least changed. Voss was encouraging, but amused. The day he found the convict tarring a horse's swollen pastern, the German's upper lip was as long in amused appreciation as a hornet is in legs. He looked at the stooping man, and said :

'Is it a solution you are putting, Mr Judd?'

'It is,' replied the latter, chasing some insect away from his face with his tar-free arm.

'You have not omitted the oil?' asked Voss.

'No,' said Judd.

Voss was whistling a little tune of insect music.

'That is excellent,' he said.

He continued to whistle until, Judd could feel, he was drifting on. Then the convict's empirical nature was glad of the stench of tar, and the heat which was for ever descending and ironing the dust still flatter.

Heavy moons hung above Jildra at that season. There was a golden moon, of placid, swollen belly. There were the ugly, bronze, male moons, threateningly lopsided. One night of wind and dust, there was a pale moonstone, or, as rags of cloud polished its face, delicate glass instrument, on which the needle barely fluttered, indicating the direction that some starry destiny must take. The dreams of men were influenced by the various moons, with the result that they were burying their faces in the pregnant moon-women, or shaking their bronze fists at any threat to their virility. Their dreams eluded them, however, under the indicator of that magnetic moon. The white dust poured out from between their fingers, as they turned and turned on hairy blankets that provoked their nakedness. On the other hand, there were some who lay and listened to their own eyelids grate endlessly.

Such was the predicament of Palfreyman on one particularly white night. Unable to sleep, he had passed the time reviewing houses in which he had lived, minor indignities he had suffered, and one tremendous joy, a white eagle fluttering for a moment on the branch of a dead tree and almost blotting out the sky with the span of its wings.

The sound of the strong feathers, heard again above the squeak of mice and groans of sleep in Boyle's squalid shack, had almost freed the wakeful Palfreyman, when Voss rose. There he was, striped by moonlight and darkness, the stale air moving round him, very softly. Voss himself did not move. Rather was he moved by a dream, Palfreyman sensed. Through some trick of moonlight or uncertainty of behaviour, the head became detached for a second and appeared to have been fixed upon a beam of the wooden wall. The mouth and the eyes were visible. Palfreyman shivered. Ah, Christ is an evil dream, he feared, and all my life I have been deceived. After the bones of the naked Christ had been drawn through the fœtid room, by sheets of moonlight, and out the doorway, the fully conscious witness continued to lie on his blanket, face to face with his own short-comings and his greatest error.

But there was an end to this unhappiness, he was surprised to find. The moonlight returned Voss to the room. As he was moved back, his bones were creaking, and his skin had erupted in a greenish verdigris.

Palfreyman nearly put out his hand, to recall them both to their normal relationship, but was restrained by an access of cold.

Next morning he remarked:

'Mr Voss, do you know you were sleep-walking last night?'

The German was engaged in putting on his socks, his backbone exposed to his accuser.

'I have never been known to, before. Never,' he replied, but most irritably, as if refusing a crime with which he had been unjustly charged.

Boyle, who had just then come through the partition, scratching an armpit, felt compelled to say:

'We welcome you, Voss, through the gate of human weaknesses.'

And was glad at last. He remembered how the yellow woman had flattened her belly against him the other side of sleep.

But Voss was grumbling. He had grown livid. All that day he remained bones rather than flesh.

177

All his days were wasting away in precise acts. His feet were heavy with dust as he tramped between shed, tent, and stockyard. Now his distaste for men returned, especially for those with whom he had surrounded himself, or, to be more accurate, with whom an ignorant jackass had surrounded him against his will. Blank faces, like so many paper kites, themselves earthbound, or at most twitching in the warm shallows of atmosphere, dangling a vertebral tail, could prevent him soaring towards the apotheosis for which he was reserved. To what extent others had entangled him in the string of human limitation, he had grown desperate in wondering.

So he was chewing his pen over that journal of acts and facts, which he did keep meticulously, he was holding a narrow oblong of clean, folded paper to protect the page from other eyes and dust, at the moment when Boyle came into the room, crunching over stale bread, smelling of sweat, and said:

'Now, Voss, I do not want to meddle in anybody's affairs, but I would suggest you are missing the best of a good season by delaying.'

'Yes. Yes,' said Voss, flicking at the page with the paper shield that he held between his long, clean bones of fingers. And frowning. 'In two, three days we shall be prepared to leave. I have a report to write,' he added.

'I do not want to suggest you are in any way *de trop*,' said his host, and could have become sentimental, for anyone at all, even for this scraggy guest whom he did not understand, suspected, and at times had even disliked.

Boyle was not resentful. Of loving flesh, he could not have wished for better than a close companion on the same dungheap, to sit beside, and touch.

'Understand that, old man,' he said, patting the German on the knee.

Voss frowned at the dust which had spurted through the open doorway and dirtied his clean paper. It was about sundown, and the blaze of light was blinding him.

'I do not intend to inconvenience you above a day or two,' he repeated.

With these words, spoken thus, for a second time, he realized that he was staking all. Thus, he could blame no one else for his own human weakness. He had delivered up his throat to the long, cold, glistening braids of her hair, and was truly strangling in them.

'That is very reasonable,' commented Boyle. 'And Thorndike should be here by then. A black from Cubanong has just come in. Thorndike has arrived there. If they have sent up anything for you, as an afterthought, Thorndike will have it.'

'Who is this Thorndike?' the German asked, although he was not interested in knowing more.

'That is difficult to answer. Thorndike is just a man. Comes and goes. Does a job here and there. He is of no importance, but useful. Brings things, you know. Mail.'

The simplicity of the clay-coloured landscape was very moving to the German. For a moment everything was distinct. In the foreground some dead trees, restored to life by the absence of hate, were glowing with flesh of rosy light. All life was dependent on the thin lips of light, compressed, yet breathing at the rim of the world.

'That will be convenient then, and I shall leave at once on the arrival of Thorndike.'

Never had an issue of greater importance been decided so conclusively by an apparently insignificant event.

'Take it easy, though,' laughed Boyle, who began to suspect that other spurs had been applied to his particular friend.

'Oh, it is natural to regret the waste of time,' Voss shrugged and fenced. 'And to wish to make amends for it.'

So he explained, but did not tell, absorbed as he was in his discovery: that each visible object has been created for purposes of love, that the stones, even, are smoother for the dust.

As darkness fell upon a world emptied for its complete reception, the German began to tremble in a cold sweat, with the consequence that, when the black woman brought the inevitable leg of charred mutton, he announced to his astonished host:

'I do not think I will eat tonight. I am suffering from some derangement of the intestines.'

And avoided further explanation under cover of the difficulties of language.

For an hour or more he proceeded to pace up and down by himself, only interrupting his walk to stoop and pat the station dogs. These animals were quick to sense a desire to express tenderness, and, indeed, he was shaking with it.

To what extent would he be weakened? He could not help but wonder, fear, and finally resent.

As they waited for Thorndike, the strange moons continued to hang above Jildra, and even by day there would appear to be a closed eye, which signified the presence of a moon. Voss was for ever biting his whiskers and cracked lips. How thirsty the days were already, the ground opening in cracked mouths, in spite of that good rain, which people will always tell you has fallen. The German would go to the water-bag, and drink down pannikins full of the tepid canvassy water, which flushed his stomach. He already felt physically sick. Somewhere behind his knee-cap a time was beating, as he waited for the man Thorndike to arrive.

Early on a certain morning, the leader was suddenly moved to issue orders.

'I will have all cattle, goats, and sheep that we are taking with us, mustered and driven into the vicinity of the homestead,' he announced to Boyle. 'Dugald and Jackie must go with Turner and the boy. Ralph' – he addressed the young grazier – 'I will put in charge of these operations. Tomorrow we will make a start.'

'You are not waiting, then, for this feller Thorndike?' Boyle asked.

'Yes,' said Voss. 'It is certain. He will come before evening.'

Boyle was rather diverted by this intelligence.

'The smoke messages have got going?' he inquired lazily.

'Mr Judd,' Voss called, going out into the languid morning of young, silky air, 'I wish you to make a careful count of all fire-arms, tools, instruments, *und so weiter*, that nothing is over-looked. You, and Frank, will see that horses and mules are brought in and securely hobbled tonight.'

Soon dogs were barking, children laughing, threads of dust weaving in and out of one another as a pattern began to form upon the bare earth at Jildra. Harry Robarts was by now brave enough to jab spurs into his horse's sides, so that it would leap into action and execute proud and important figures. Harry him-self had become leaner, for the distance had thinned him out.

Yet, paradoxically, his once empty face was filled with those distances. They possessed, but they eluded him; he was still, and perhaps would remain always, lost.

Now, however, Harry and those with him were riding forth. Their purposes were set in motion.

Mr Judd went immediately, with his quartermaster stride, and began to account for such tackle as was in his charge. Frank Le Mesurier had already spotted the mules and horses, and their attachment of tails, occupied in the shade some little distance off. He would ride over later, as they moved to open pastures with the cool, and turn them with his whip, and they would drum the depths out of the earth as they raced up the flat towards the homestead, and pull up sharp at the yards, on their knees almost. The sky would be peacock coloured then.

In the heat, after the men had left to muster, Mr Judd was proceeding methodically. He had a scrap of crumpled paper, on which he would make his own signs. There was a stub of lead pencil in his mouth. One of his thumbs had been badly crushed by a sledge-hammer long ago, and had grown, in place of a nail, a hard, yellow horn. Now as he worked, he experienced a sense of true pride, out of respect for what he was handling, for those objects, in iron, wood, or glass did greatly influence the course of earthly life. He could love a good axe or knife, and would oil and sharpen it with tender care. As for the instruments of navigation, the mysticism of figures from which they were inseparable made him yet more worshipful. Pointing to somewhere always just beyond his reach, the lovely quivering of rapt needles was more delicate than that of ferns. All that was essential, most secret, was contained for Judd, like his own spring-water, in a nest of ferns.

Sometimes he would breathe upon the glass of those instruments, and rub it with the cushiony part of his hand, of which the hard whorls of skin and fate were, by comparison, indelicate.

But now he complained:

'Frank, I cannot find that big prismatic compass in the wooden frame.'

'It cannot have got far, a big thing like that,' answered Le Mesurier, who was not greatly interested.

'These blacks would thieve any mortal thing, I would not be surprised,' the convict said.

He was sweating, as big men will, in sheets, but his upper lip was marked by little stationary points of exasperation, anxiety, even cold despair.

He was looking everywhere for that compass.

'Frank,' he said, 'it has got me bested. It will not be found.'

Then he went down to the gunyas, and cursed the black gins that were squatted there, looking in one another's hair, laughing with, and tumbling the small, red-haired children. The black gins did not understand. Their breasts became sullen.

To Judd, the peculiar problem of the lost instrument was as intricate as the labyrinth of heat, through which he trudged back.

Mr Voss was furious, of course, because he had been expecting something, if not necessarily this.

Judd went away.

In the late afternoon when the other men rode in, and were watering their horses and coiling their whips, they were closely questioned, but there was not a single one could honestly feel the compass concerned him personally. At best amused, at worst they were irritated at having to turn out their packs.

Voss, who had come down to the tents, a prophetic figure in his dark clothes, said that the instrument must be found.

Boyle, too, had come across. He had questioned the blacks at the camp, and was pretty certain no native was withholding the prismatic compass.

'Then there is no explanation,' Judd cried, and flung his own saddle-bags from side to side, so that some of the onlookers were put in mind of the flapping, of a pair of great, desperate wings.

'It is as if I was dreaming,' the convict protested.

For almost all, the situation had begun to assume the terrible relevant irrelevance of some dreams. They stood rooted in the urgent need to find the compass.

Which Judd, it now appeared, was drawing out of his own saddle-bag.

'But I never put it there,' said his shocked voice. 'There was no reason.'

His strong face was weak.

'No reason,' he added, 'that I can think of.'

But he would continue to fossick in desperation through his memories of all evil dreams.

Voss had turned and walked away. The incident was closed, if not to his positive advantage, to the detriment of some human being. Yet, there were times when he did long to love that which he desired to humiliate. He recalled, for instance, the convict's wife, whose simplicity was subtle enough to survive his proving of her lie. He remembered, with some feeling, the telescope that Judd himself had rigged up, and found unequal to its purpose of exploring the stars. Associated with such thoughts, of human failure and deceit, the German's shoulders narrowed as he Humped across the dusty yard. Judd's humiliation over the discovered compass forced him up the side-tracks of pity, until, suddenly, he jibbed. Delusion beckoned. His throne glittered achingly.

Down at the tents, Judd said:

'Mr Palfreyman, I did not put that compass there.'

'I believe you,' answered Palfreyman.

'There was no reason.'

There is always a reason, Palfreyman corrected silently, and would continue to search for this one.

Their stay at Jildra had become for the ornithologist a season of sleep-walking, dominated by his dream – it could have been – of tortured moonlight and rustling shadow, that retrospect had cast in lead. This brooding statue stumped horribly for him under the glass moon, but although Palfreyman watched – in fact, he continued to do so long after they had moved on – Voss the man did not walk again.

And now, at Jildra, something else was about to happen. Blacks scented it first upon the evening air, and dogs were half inclined to snarl, half to fool with one another. Then some of the white men, who had washed their necks and faces of dust, and who were smelling of dried water and soap, and an aggressive, crude cleanliness, came up formally from the tents to announce that a team was approaching. Distantly already the barking of strange dogs was going off like pop-guns, and the dogs of Jildra had begun to whine and to bite at one another's shoulders, to express their joy and solidarity.

'It is Thorndike, then,' said Voss, running out without a hat, which left the white of his forehead exposed: he could have been emerging from a mask.

'Damn me, if you were not right,' contributed Boyle.

The latter was now permanently good-tempered, indifferent, acceptant, and, above all, amused.

In time the team was straining into Jildra, with that gallantry of animals reaching a goal. The bullocks groaned to a stop, and were turning up their eyes, dilating their nostrils, and, to the last, resisting the heavy yokes with their necks.

Thorndike, a scrawny, bloodshot individual, did not make any great show of pleasure, so insignificant and regular were his habits. Nor did he pay much attention to the German, about whom people had been talking; he merely handed over, as he had undertaken. For Thorndike brought, in addition to the expected provisions for Jildra, an axe that had been left behind at the station of a Mr McKenzie with whom the expedition had camped some miles farther back, as well as a bundle of mail, tied with a bow of string, for the German cove.

Voss took the mail, and was striking his leg with it as he asked Thorndike questions, flat ones about his journey and the weather, at which the other rasped back in some amusement. Thorndike had never seen a German, but was determined not to look at this one. So he spat, and worked his adam's apple, and went about freeing his bullocks.

Presently, Voss went inside and untied his letters.

There were instructions and digressions, naturally, by Mr Bonner. There was a friendly line from Sanderson; newspapers; and a lady had contributed a fly-veil, made by her own hands, out of knotted, green silk.

There was also the letter, it would appear, from Miss Trevelyan.

When he had read or examined all else, throwing pieces of intelligence to his host, who had by this time pushed back his plate, and was picking his teeth and mastering his wind, Voss did break the seal of Miss Trevelyan's letter, and was hunching himself, and spreading and smoothing the paper, as if it had been so crumpled, he must induce it physically to deliver up its text.

Finally he read:

Dear Mr Voss,

I must hasten to thank you for your letter, which arrived at its destination several days ago, by Newcastle packet. If the length of time needed for mine to reach you should make you suspect an utter unwillingness on my part to reply, you must take into account great and exonerating distances, as well as the fact that I have been compelled by the substance of what you have written to give it the deepest possible consideration. Even after such thought, I confess it is not clear what answer one in my position would be expected to return, and, since it is one of my most stubborn *weaknesses* to try to reach conclusions without the benefit of advice, I must, I fear, remain at least temporarily confused.

Your letter was unexpected, to say the least of it: that anybody possessed of your contempt for human frailty should make so un-equivocal a proposition to one so well endowed with that same frailty! For, on at least one memorable occasion, you did not attempt to conceal your opinion that I was a person quite pitiably weak in character. Having formed a similar estimate of myself, I could not very well reject your judgement, even though the truth one has per-ceived is, if anything, more distasteful when confirmed by the mind of another, a mind, moreover, that one has held in some esteem. That you made me suffer, I cannot deny, but the outcome or purpose of that suffering still remains to be understood. In the meantime, if nothing else, my lamentable frailty does accuse my arrogance.

Arrogance is surely the quality that caused us to recognize each other. Nobody within memory, I have realized since, dared so much as to *disturb* my pride, except in puppyish ways. Men, I am inclined to think, are frightened if their self-importance does not impress. You, at least, were not frightened, but ignored me so coldly that I was the one to become alarmed – of my insignificance and isolation.

So, Mr Voss, we have reached a stage where I am called upon to consider my destroyer as my saviour! I must take on trust those tender feelings you profess, and which I cannot trace clearly through the labyrinth of our relationship. Can you wonder that I am con-fused? All the more since I have remained almost morbidly *sensitive to the welfare* of one whose virtues do not outweigh the many *faults I have continued to despise.*

Now the question is: can two such faulty beings endure to face each other, almost as in a looking-glass? Have you foreseen the possible outcome? And have you not, perhaps, mistaken a critical monster for a compliant mouse?

I, personally, to assume a most unseemly candour, would be prepared to wrestle with our mutual hatefulness, but mutually, let it be understood. For I do respect some odd streak of humanity that *will* appear in you in spite of all your efforts (after reading poetry, for instance, or listening to music, while your eyes are still closed), just as I regret most humbly my own wretched failures to conquer my unworthiness.

Only on this level, let it be understood, that we may *pray together* for salvation, shall you ask my Uncle to accept your intentions, that is, if you still intend.

In any event, Mr Voss, I do thank you once again for your kind letter, and shall intercede as ever for your safety and your happiness.

> Your sincere,
> LAURA TREVELYAN

Then Boyle, who had been dozing in a pleasant apathy of tobacco and half-digested meat, opened his eyes, and asked:

'Nothing bad, I hope, Voss?'

'Why should it be bad? No,' said the German, who was getting up, and mislaying and dropping other papers. 'On the contrary, I have received nothing but favourable news.'

And he tied the string tightly and methodically on his papers.

'I am glad of that,' answered Boyle. 'Nothing can upset a man's digestion like doubtful news. For that reason, I am glad I no longer receive letters, except those in black and white.'

'None of my acquaintances is in the habit of corresponding with coloured inks,' said Voss. 'I think I will turn in soon, Boyle, so as to make this early start that we have anticipated.'

Now he went out into the darkness, ostensibly to issue last orders to his men, though in fact to hide himself, and failed in his real purpose, as he embraced the past tremblingly beneath a vast audience of stars.

On his return he began to notice Palfreyman, who had been there all the time, seated within the candlelight, sketching for his own pleasure a big, dreamy lily propped in a tin mug.

'What is this?' asked Voss, with unduly warm interest.

'It is a lily,' said Palfreyman, with grave concentration on his silvery sketch, 'which I found in the red soil along the second of the waterholes.'

Voss made a lazy guess at the variety.

'With these seeds?' asked Palfreyman.

Voss squinted. They were of a distinct shape, like testes, attached to the rather virginal flower.

When the German had undressed and was lying in his blanket, he and Palfreyman began to recall other botanical specimens they had found, of unorthodox seed formation. Boyle had retired by now, and it was a pleasant, drowsy conversation that drifted between the two men, containing friendship, because it made no effort to.

Perhaps it is I who am frequently to blame, Palfreyman decided, and would not move for fear of breaking the spell.

'Will you not go to bed, Palfreyman?' Voss yawned at last. 'We start tomorrow early.'

'It is the lily,' Palfreyman said, and sighed. 'We may never see it again in all its freshness.'

Voss yawned.

'It may be very common.'

'It may,' Palfreyman agreed.

Their voices were somehow complementary to each other. Like lovers.

Then Voss began to float, and those words last received. But *together*. Written words take some time to thaw, but the words of lilies were now flowing in full summer water, whether it was the water or the leaves of water, and dark hairs of roots plastered on the mouth as water blew across. Now they were swimming so close they were joined together at the waist, and were the same flesh of lilies, their mouths, together, were drowning in the same love-stream. I do not wish this yet, or *nie nie nie, niemals. Nein.* You will, she said, if you will cut and examine the word. *Together* is filled with little cells. And cuts open with a knife. It is a see seed. But I do not. All human obligations are painful, Mr Johann Ulrich, until they are learnt, variety by variety. But gold is painful, crushing, and cold on the forehead, while wholly desirable, because immaculate. Only resist the Christ-thorn. Tear out the black thing by the roots before it has taken hold. She was humbly grateful for it, however. In her kneeling position, she continued to bathe her hair in all flesh, whether of imperial lilies, or the black, putrefying, human kind.

After one of those pauses, in which the sleeper dries up, in which his tongue is a little pebble, and the blanket is grafted on his side, he said:

I do accept the terms. It was the sweat that prevented me from seeing them.

You are in no position to accept. It is the woman who unmakes men, to make saints.

Mutual. It is all mutual.

It was his tongue that would not come unstuck.

You have gained that point, the mouth was laughing.

Two *zusammen* should gain by numbers, but lose in fact. Numbers weaken.

The weaker is stronger, O Voooos.

So that the sleeper sat up, the better to look into the mouth of the lily. Instead, he found darkness and the smell of a wick, for Palfreyman was finished, and had gone to bed.

Then Voss lay down again, and pretended his sleep had not been interrupted, for he did not wish to be told that he had spoken during his dream. He was dubiously happy. He remembered whole lines of Laura Trevelyan's letter. And her voice speaking. He would have liked to be told, in that voice, what to do next, since consummation is not an end in itself.

Next morning, in a tunnel of red light and bowed grass, Voss took his leave of Boyle, who, as the cavalcade moved forward with a surge of sacrificial animals and dedicated men, stood for a long time looking sorrowfully like something that had been abandoned on the edge of life. An old boot, in fact.

With very little warning the day opened like a square-cut, blazing jewel on the expedition, holding it almost stationary in the prison of that blue brilliance. Its progress and humble dust did begin to seem rather pitiable. The goats were obviously bewildered by the extreme imprudence of man. The sheep, on the other hand, could have possessed some understanding of foolishness, as they pushed on scraggily, staggily, through the tussocks, leaving bits of wool on the bushes, their pulsating throats already resigned. Round and about moved the magnificent men, correcting any blunders on the part of the cattle, in whose horns the long whips were frequently entwined. The men were impressing themselves, although towards noon their sense of purpose was less definite, and what had been a compact mob of moiling beasts had worn into a thin trickle.

So that after the midday halt, which was spent in the shade of some brigalow scrub, Voss called his men and divided his strength into several parts, of sheep together with goats, of cattle, and of pack animals. Thenceforth they followed at their several speeds the river-bed which Boyle had identified for Voss as the C—. Voss himself rode forward with the two blacks, Dugald and Jackie, and in that way was freed momentarily from further responsibility, and strengthened by his vision of uninterrupted space.

He was happiest with his loyal subjects.

'You were foolish to bring along that fine coat,' he said to the old native. 'Now, if you lose your life, you will lose your coat too.'

Then he laughed.

The old native followed suit, bouncing lightly on his grey horse. No one had ever spoken to him like this. There was a certain absence of the expected in the white man's words which made him shy, however.

The white man was singing:

> *'Eine blosse Seele ritt hinaus*
> *Dem Blau' ent-ge-gen. . . .'*

He would pause, and think, and continue to sing.

> *'Sein Rock flog frei.*
> *Sein Schimmel mit den Wol-ken*
> *Um die Ehre rrrann. . . .'*

He was very pleased with his song. He was singing it at the sky.

> *'Nur der edle Rock zu Schaden kam,*
> *Die Fetzen fie-len,*
> *Den Hi-im-mel ent-lang.'*

All the time the young native was keeping up a chatter to his mentor, Dugald, who was lost between several worlds.

The white man was laughing.

'Ach, Dugald, Wörter haben keine Bedeutung. Sinnlos!

'Nonsense,' he added, and asked: 'Do you understand *nonsense?*'

Dugald smiled. He was shy. But they were happy together.

By now the light had softened and was beginning to reveal more. Voss thought how he would talk eventually with Laura Trevelyan, how they had never spoken together using the truly humble words that convey the innermost reality: bread, for instance, or water. Obsessed by the struggle between their two souls, they had threatened each other with the flashing weapons of abstract reasoning, while overlooking the common need for sustenance. But now we shall understand each other, he said, glancing about. At that hour fulfilment did appear to prevail, in the dry river, with its recurring pot-holes of greenish-brown water, in the drifts of white flood grass tinkling on bushes, in the ugly, thumping lizards and modest birds. Through the marriage of light and shadow, in the infinite distances of that dun country of which he was taking possession, all, finally, would be resolved.

His almost voluptuously hopeful vision was broken by the younger native, who had slithered from his horse into a saucer of bare earth, and was there belabouring something with a stick. The lights in his skin were flickering frenziedly.

'Jackie kill lizard,' Dugald explained.

It was, in fact, one of the short, knobbly-tailed lizards. Surrendering up its life quickly and decently to the grinning Jackie, it lay with its paler belly exposed. A very little of its dark blood had trickled out of the battered mouth.

The three men rode on. The two blacks were chattering to each other. The naked Jackie dangled the stiff lizard by its tail.

'What will he do with the lizard?' Voss asked of Dugald.

The old man popped a bony finger into his mouth. All his grey stubble laughed.

'It is really good to eat?' asked the German.

Dugald restricted that possibility by waving the same, long, black stick of a finger.

'Blackfeller.' He laughed.

And Jackie joined in.

The two blacks jogged along, a little to one side of Voss, as if the subjects of his new kingdom preferred to keep their distance. They could even have been rejecting him. Their voices were for each other, and twining with the dust.

Other figures were beginning to appear, their shadows first, followed by a suggestion of skin wedded to the trunk of a tree. Then, at a bend in the river's bed, the dusty bodies of men undoubtedly emerged. Dugald and Jackie averted their faces. Their cheeks were sulking as they rode. Once the old man did exchange words with some of those who had come, but tentative language, of a great formality and coldness. The strange natives looked at the white man, through the flies, and the whisks of grey leaves, with which they brushed them away. The explorer would have liked to talk to these individuals, to have shown them suitable kindness, and to have received their homage. But they disappeared. Once or twice he called to his escorts, who had decided, apparently, not to hear. They were riding faster now. The increased pace robbed the white man's voice of its roundness: it flickered flimsily with the motion of his horse. If he turned in the saddle, and attempted to communicate directly with the strange blacks, he found himself beckoning to those same shadows which had accompanied their approach.

This was, of course, a temporary state of affairs. New hope convinced him that he would interpret the needs of all men, the souls of rocks, even. In that more tender light the bare flesh of rocks was promisingly gentle.

As evening was approaching, he resolved to camp there in the elbow of the river, and sent the natives back to convey his intention to the other members of the party. In consequence the leader was left alone for some little time, and then the immensity of his presumption did accuse him. The dome of silence was devoid of all furniture, even of a throne. So he began pulling logs together, smashing sticks, crumbling scrub, and was building their first fire. Sympathy, brilliance, warmth did not, however, immediately leap forth, only a rather disappointing flame. It was a very human fire. Walking up and down, its maker was overcome by the distance between aspiration and human nature. The latter, it appeared, was almost inescapable, like those men whose dust he could already see. Fidgeting in a similar dust, his spurs accused him of his own failures.

Of which we must make the most, Laura Trevelyan implied.

From where he was standing, he could watch the secret place at the nape of her neck, of infinite creaminess, and the swathe of greeny-white veil round the hard, dark crown of her hat. He had never yet dared to touch, except through those formal gestures society expects, or else, the formless, self-explanatory liberties of sleep. Human relationships are vast as deserts: they demand all daring, she seemed to suggest. And here was the little fire that he had made. How it flickered on the smile of this girl, or woman, as she was becoming. Her throat and shoulders were both convincing and convinced. He could not see the eyes, however. Because, she said, you cannot remember. It was true. He remembered her chiefly by the words and ideas they had offered each other, and by a certain poignance of her Italian hand. So that her form remained indistinct. While suggestive of hopefulness. As she turned her rather pointed face with the unremembered eyes. He did not encourage her to approach, for he was afraid that he might receive the impression of ungainliness, dressed as she was in her thick, travel-stained habit.

Then the cries of men and animals began to break in.

Ralph Angus had cantered up, and was at once correctly informative.

'Mr Voss, sir,' he said, and his brick-coloured skin was very respectful, 'the sheep are quite done up. They are a mile back, still.'

'Good, Ralph,' replied the German. 'You will take Dugald or Jackie and camp near them tonight. It is late now. We shall see in the morning.'

Judd the convict was more reproachful, who came up then behind the spent cattle.

'We did ought to camp earlier, sir,' said Judd, but still respectful.

'Yes, yes,' Voss agreed. 'We have come far. It is a mistake not to camp earlier. You are correct, Judd. If you are offering me advice I shall take it for the next occasion.'

Judd had not expected to be thus mollified by reasonableness and smiles.

With the exception of Turner, who was grumbling because his thighs were chafed, everybody was contented at the sight of fire. Cattle lumbered to a standstill, holding their masks close to the ground. Horses rubbed their faces on their wet legs. A mule dragged at the branches of a tree. And the men, though white about the mouth from thirst, jumped down, and at once assumed ownership of that corner of the dusk.

After Mr Judd had mixed flour and water, and hidden it in the ashes, and taken from that unpromising bed a huge, rude loaf, and they had cut themselves chunks of salt beef, an offering from Boyle of Jildra, and were burning their mouths on the red tea, there was little else to be desired.

'Except that tea without milk,' Turner grumbled, 'is not much above medicine.'

'If you will walk back a mile in the dark,' suggested Voss, 'to where the goats are camped with Mr Angus, you may have your milk, Turner, if you care to pull it.'

Some people considered this a joke of the leader's, and laughed accordingly, but Turner spat out the bitter tea-leaves, which tasted of metal, besides.

'Poor old Turner,' laughed Harry Robarts. 'You are out of luck. Better turn in.'

The boy could not stop, but continued to laugh beneath the stars. The apparent simplicity of space had deceived his rather simple mind. He was free, of past, and future. His hilarious body had forgotten its constricting clothes.

'Turn in, Turner! Eh?'

He was so pleased, this large boy, of laughing throat.

But Turner had turned sour. He was harbouring a grievance, against no one in particular.

'I will turn in, all right,' he answered. 'What else would I do?'

For a long time that night Harry Robarts continued to enjoy the joke that he had heard and the joke that he had made. Lying with his head in the crook of his arm, he discovered, moreover, that he could draw a line through certain stars, and create figures of constellations. He was dazzled in the end, if not delirious with stars. Their official names, which Mr Voss had taught him on board, he had long since chosen to forget, for the stars themselves are more personal than their names. Then he who had been dazzled became puzzled. It seemed that he had not spoken with Mr Voss for several days. So that someone else fell asleep with a grievance, and in his sleep licked the hand, licked with the tongue of a dog, down to the last grain of consoling salt, but was fretful rather than comforted.

The country round them reduced most personal hopes and fears until these were of little account. An eternity of days was opening for the men, who would wake, and scramble up with a kind of sheepish respect for their surroundings. Dew was clogging the landscape. Spiders had sewn the bushes together. And then there were those last, intolerably melancholy stars, that cling to a white sky, and will not be put out except by force.

After breakfast, which was similar to other meals, of salt meat, or of meat lately killed, with the tea they made from scum of waterholes, or from the same stuff brought on in canvas, Voss, attended by Judd, would take readings from their instruments, and attempt to assess their current position. Judd would bring out from their cloths those trembling devices in glass and steel and quicksilver. Judd was the keeper of instruments, Voss indulging his subordinate's passion with the kindness of a superior being. He himself would sit with the large notebook upon his knees, recording in exquisite characters and figures, in black ink, the legend. Sometimes similarly black, similarly exquisite spiders replete from their dew-feast, would trample in his hair, and have to be brushed off. These small insects could affront him most severely. By this time the air was no longer smelling of dew; it had begun again to smell of dust. Men were buckling girths, and swearing oaths through thinner lips. As the sun mounted, the skin was tightening on their skulls. Some of them winced, and averted their eyes from those flashing instruments with which Voss and Judd professed to be plotting, in opposition to Providence. The sceptics would ride on, however, because they were committed to it, and because by now their minds and limbs had accepted a certain ritual of inspired motion.

So they advanced into that country which now possessed them, looking back in amazement at their actual lives, in which they had got drunk, lain with women under placid trees, thought to offer their souls to God, or driven the knife into His image, some other man.

194

Then, suddenly, Voss looked in his journal and saw that the following day would be Christmas. By some instinct for self-preservation, he would not have spoken of it, and most of his men, dependent on him for every judgement or calculation, would have ridden quietly by.

Palfreyman realized, but as he was not a man to act, an observer, rather, or sufferer of life, he was waiting to see.

If, in the case of Voss, it was the instinct for self-preservation that warned him to avoid Christmas, in Judd's case it was the instinct for self-assertion that caused him to remember. Since his death by whips and iron, he had aspired longingly at times to be reborn, and when more hopefully than at that season, at which, he sensed now, they had arrived. If he had not succeeded all those years, in the loving bosom of his family, it was perhaps because he was shy of eyes that had witnessed something of his sufferings. But to these mates, and even to the knowing German, he was a stone man. Then it would be easier, given the opportunity, to crack open and disclose all manner of unexpected ores, even a whole human being.

So the emancipist was expectant. He was always urging his horse forward, and hesitating, and reining it back. He must only choose the moment, but would speak soon, he knew. His shirt was shining and transparent with sweat, over the old wounds, and clumsy labouring of great ribs, as he tidied the edges of his mob of cattle, and watched the point at which the German was riding with Mr Palfreyman. The backs of the two gentlemen ahead remained quite flat and unconscious, while the figure of Judd, labouring always with his cattle and his thoughts, loomed like sculpture.

They had entered, as it happened, a valley sculptured in red rock and quartz, in which a river ran, rather shallow and emotional, but a river of live water such as they could remember, through the valley of wet grass. Heat appeared to intensify the green of a variety of splendid trees, some sprouting with hair or swords, others slowly succumbing to a fleshy jasmine, of which the arms were wound round and round their limbs. These deadly garlands were quite festive in immediate effect, as they glimmered against the bodies of their hosts. The breath of jasmine cajoled the air. Platters of leaves presented gifts of moisture. And there were the birds. Their revels were filling the air with cries and feathers, rackety screams of utter abandon, flashes of saffron, bursts of crimson, although there were also other more sombre birds that would fly silently into the thoughts of men like dreadful arrows.

When it was almost noon, and the valley had narrowed to a neck, the convict left his cattle, which were tired and unwilling, and rode forward.

He said:

'Mr Voss, I reckon it is near Christmas. If it is not tomorrow, it is soon after.'

Then they listened to the silence.

If he had been given to irony, Palfreyman would have indulged in it at this point, but as he was not, he looked at the grass, and waited.

'Yes, you are correct, Judd,' said Voss.

The birds were screaming and ascending in red riot.

'It is tomorrow,' said the German precisely.

All round this group hung the heat in sheets of damp silence.

'It did not occur to me to mention it,' said Voss. 'You know, in such circumstances.'

He let his hand fall limply, as if his own body were as much to blame.

'But if this festival will mean anything to you, Judd, personally, or to any of the other men, then certainly must we celebrate it.'

'I would like to celebrate Christmas, sir,' said Judd.

Once he would have looked to Palfreyman, even last week he might have, but did not now. This rather massive man, sitting astride his caked horse, was not in need of support for the present.

Instead, it was Palfreyman who felt the need to follow. He hastened to add:

'I, too, would like to celebrate Christmas.'

It was perfectly natural that any Christian should wish to join the emancipated convict at this season of complete emancipation, yet Voss, who feared union, most of all one in which he himself might become involved, suspected snares.

'Good,' he said, wetting his lips, and smiling painfully. 'Then, what would you suggest, Judd?'

He waited to hear something he would hate.

'I would suggest, sir, that we call a halt just where we are. It is a pleasant spot,' the convict said, and indeed, it was reflected in his face, a place of large leaves and consoling water. 'If you agree, I will kill a sheep, that we will eat tomorrow. I will make a pudding or two, not the real thing, like, but to deceive ourselves. I am not going to suggest, sir, how we should spend Christmas Day. Every man will have his own ideas.'

'We could read the service,' he did add, as a careful after-thought.

'Let us, at least, call the halt,' said Voss, and, riding into the shadow of a tree, flung his hat down, then himself.

Judd took command. His face was glad, Palfreyman saw. Calling to his mates as they approached, throwing out his thick, hairy arm, signalling to them to dispose of beasts and baggage in a final halt, the convict had become a man of stature. Little signs of hopefulness were playing round his mouth amongst the lively points of perspiration. The strength of innocence can but increase, Palfreyman realized, and was himself glad.

Then, as he was exhausted by the luxuriance of unwonted green, by the habitual heat, as well as by the challenge of souls that he had just witnessed, the ornithologist went and joined the German in the shadow of his tree.

'It is not splendid?' asked Voss, admiring the prospect of sculptural red rocks and tapestries of musical green which the valley contained.

Palfreyman agreed.

'Ennobling and eternal,' persisted the German. 'This I can apprehend.'

Because it is mine, by illusion, it was implied, and so the ornithologist sensed. By now, moreover, the latter had learnt to read the eyes.

'Yet, to drag in the miserable fetish that this man has insisted on! Of Jesus Christ!'

The vision that rose before the German's eyes was, indeed, most horrible. The racked flesh had begun to suppurate, the soul had emerged, and gone flapping down the ages with slow, suffocating beat of wings.

As the great hawk flew down the valley, Turner did take a shot at it, but missed. It was the glare he blamed.

During the afternoon Voss continued in his journal the copious and satisfying record of their journey through his country, and succeeded in bringing the narrative up to date. As he sat writing upon his knees, the scrub was smouldering with his shirt of crimson flannel, the parting present of his friend and patron, Edmund Bonner. If there were times when the German's eyes suggested that their fire might eventually break out and consume his wiry frame, as true fire will lick up a patch of tortured scrub, in a puff of smoke and a pistol shot, on this occasion he was ever looking up and out, with, on the whole, an expression of benevolent amusement for that scene in which his men were preparing a feast.

'Do you appreciate with me the spectacle of such pagan survivals?' he called once to Palfreyman, and laughed.

For Judd had seized the lamb, or stained wether, and plunged the knife into its throat, and the blood had spurted out. Several of his laughing audience were splashed.

Judd himself was painted liberally with the blood of the kicking sheep. Afterwards he hung its still carcass on a tree, and fetched its innards out, while the others lay in the grass, and felt the sweat stiffen on them, and talked together peacefully, or thought, or chewed the stems of the fat grass. Although they appeared to ignore the butcher, they were implicitly but the circumference of that grassy circle. Judd was the centre, as he plunged his arms into the blue cavern of the sheep.

Watching from his distance, Voss remembered the picnic by the sea, at which he had spoken with Laura Trevelyan, and they had made a circle of their own. As he saw it now, perfection is always circular, enclosed. So that Judd's circle was enviable. Too late, Laura said, or it was the shiny, indigenous leaves in which a little breeze had started up. All the immediate world was soon swimming in the same liquid green. She was clothed in it. Green shadows almost disguised her face, where she walked amongst the men, to whom, it appeared, she was known, as others were always known to one another, from childhood, or by instinct.

Only he was the passing acquaintance, at whom she did glance once, since it was unavoidable. Then he noticed how her greenish flesh was spotted with blood from that same sheep, and that she would laugh at, and understand the jokes shared with others, while he continued to express himself in foreign words, in whichever language he used, his own included.

Laura Trevelyan understood perfectly all the preliminaries of Judd's feast. It would be quite simple, humble, as she saw it; they would eat the meat with their hands, all of them, together, and in that way, it would become an act of praise.

As the day grew to an end, and preparations for the feast were completed, Voss grew angry and depressed.

The same night, after the fires had been lit, and the carcass of the sheep that would be eaten for Christmas was a sliver of white on the dark tree, Judd took fat, and tossed the liver in a pan, and when it was done, brought it to his leader.

'Here is a fine piece of liver, sir, done as nice as you would see it.'

But Voss said:

'Thank you, Judd. I cannot. It is the heat. I will not eat tonight.'

He could not. The liver stank.

When Judd went away, which he did as respectfully as ever, he had a glittery look in his eye, and pitched the liver to the dogs.

Left alone, Voss groaned. He would not, could not learn, nor accept humility, even though this was amongst the conditions she had made in the letter that was now living in him. For some time, he sat with his head in his hands. He did truly suffer.

Except for the dogs scratching and sighing, the night had grown silent, the fires had fallen into embers, when grass began to rustle, feet approached the leader, and there was Turner's face upon the darkness.

Why did I bring the man? Voss wondered.

'Look at this, sir,' Turner invited.

'What is it?' asked Voss.

Then he saw it was the handle of the frying-pan.

'Well?' he asked. 'How does this concern me? Is it of any interest?'

'It was him,' laughed Turner.

'Who?'

'The cook, or Jack-of-all-trades. Lord God Almighty!'

'I am not interested. You are foolish, Turner. Go to bed.'

'I am not all that foolish.' Turner laughed in going.

He should have been drunk, but his stomach would sometimes turn sour without all that assistance.

As he prepared for sleep, Voss continued to feel incensed against the miserable fellow. Though it was Judd who had roused his anger. It is Turner, he said, but he knew that it was Judd.

And Turner knew, in the tent that was shared by several.

Some were already snoring as Judd lay fidgeting against the pillow of his saddle.

'Listen, Albert,' Turner said. 'You are awake, I can hear that.'

He rolled over, so that his long thin body was close against the thicker one. His long face was very close.

'Remember that there compass, that was lost at Jildra, or not lost, it was in your bag?'

Judd did not have to remember, for he had not forgotten.

'It was put there, see, on a moonlight night, by a certain Prussian gentleman, who was innocent on account of he was *sleep*-walkin'.'

'I do not believe it,' Judd said.

'No more do I,' Turner continued. 'He was as naked as moonlight, and bony as the Lord. But his eyes did not convince this one.'

'You did not tell,' said Judd. 'Not till now.'

'I have been caught before,' Turner replied. 'And this was valuable.'

'I do not believe it,' said Judd. 'Go to sleep.'

Turner laughed, and rolled over.

Judd lay in that position until his bones had set, but did also sleep at last.

Then everyone was sleeping, or waking, to remember that it would soon be Christmas, and fall into a deeper sleep.

About midnight, however, wild dogs had begun to howl, which woke the dogs of the expedition, and these were soon moaning back in answer. The night was grown rather black, but with a flickering of yellow from a distant storm. A thin wind ran along the crest of things, together with the high yelping of the increasingly uneasy camp dogs.

Himself disturbed, Voss got up at last, and stumbled in search of their two native guides, tracing them by the embers of their fire, against which they were rolled like animals. Their eyes were open, he could see, upon some great activity of their minds. If only he could have penetrated to that distance, he would have felt more satisfied.

Dugald, the old man, immediately turned away his face, and said, before other words could be spoken:

'I sick, sick.'

And was rubbing his belly under the remnants of his ridiculous swallowtail coat.

'Have you heard something, Dugald, perhaps? Could it be wild dogs?'

'No dogs,' said Dugald.

These sounds were made, he explained, by blackfellows who intended mischief.

Just then there fell a few big drops of flat rain, and there was a sudden thumping of the earth, and protesting of grass.

'That is cattle,' said Voss.

It could have been the sound of cattle in motion, of frightened cattle, a little farther up the valley where the herd had been left to graze.

'Blackfeller no good this place,' Dugald moaned.

Voss now returned to his tent, and fetched a gun. He called to the two natives.

'You come, Dugald, Jackie. We go look cattle.'

But the two men were fascinated by the fire. They turned their faces from the darkness, and stared closer into the coals, rubbing their cheeks against the dust. Darkness is a place of evil, so, wisely, they avoided it.

Voss continued up the valley for what seemed like some considerable distance, encountering only a vast, dark humidity. Once a cow and calf propped, and snorted at him, and lumbered away. There was no further sign of cattle.

'*Nutzlos*,' he said, coldly furious, and discharged his weapon once or twice in the direction the herd must have taken.

When he returned, Le Mesurier and Palfreyman had come out, awakened by the shots and a hysteria of dogs.

'It is probable that blacks have driven off the cattle,' Voss announced. 'There is nothing we can do for the present.'

Beside their fire Dugald and Jackie were listening to these words. The voice of the white man could have been issuing from the earth.

So Christmas began.

In the morning, it was learnt that more than half the cattle had been driven off. Dugald, who had resumed possession of his ancient grace and a kind of sad resourcefulness, said that Jackie would take his horse and search – Jackie had eyes for stolen cattle – and Voss accepted this suggestion as a temporary measure, if not a way out of their dilemma.

The others were secretly glad that, for the moment at least, they need not exert themselves on such a radiant, pigeon-coloured morning. After breakfast – a subdued, though contenting meal – Harry Robarts fetched out a flag they had brought with them, and fastened it to a sapling-staff, from which it hung rather dank. At once somebody began to mumble, then almost all joined in, and they were singing '*God Save the Queen*'.

The German in his crimson shirt observed them with amusement, but quite kindly, holding himself erect by instinct, if not from approval.

Afterwards, Mr Palfreyman produced his prayer-book, and declared his intention of reading the Church of England service.

Then Voss said :

'It may not be the wish of everyone, Palfreyman, to be forced to worship in this way. It is preferable if each man does his own part, and reads in his own book. There,' he concluded, looking at them.

It was not altogether unreasonable, and Palfreyman made himself condemn certain of his own thoughts.

Soon, one or two who possessed prayer-books had taken them out, and were attempting to follow the words, in that place where the wild jasmine was sweetly stifling a sense of duty, and the most dogged devotions were shot through with a glint of parrots. Turner, frankly, whittled wood, and recalled how the rum was far more efficacious than prayer as a means of refreshment. Judd went away.

'The old beggar,' Turner was quick to call. 'What will yer ma say? Church is not out.'

'I have things to do,' Judd mumbled. 'There is the mutton.'

'Then, I will come and lend a hand,' Turner proposed.

But he was not encouraged by the convict, who went from there, shambling and mumbling.

'There is no need,' he said, surlily. 'I have my own methods, and will be ready by noon.'

So that Ralph Angus looked up from his dry book, and his mouth was full and moist in anticipation.

Judd was soon hidden by the blessed scrub. He who could squeeze the meaning out of a line by pressing on it with his finger-nail, always hastened to remove himself from the presence of true initiates when they were at their books. All the scraps of knowledge with which he was filled, all those raw hunks of life that, for choice, or by force, he had swallowed down, were reduced by the great mystery of words to the most shameful matter. Words were not the servants of life, but life, rather, was the slave of words. So the black print of other people's books became a swarm of victorious ants that carried off a man's self-respect. So he wandered through the bush on that morning, and was only soothed at last by leaves and silence.

Then he was glad again. He would have expressed that gladness, but could not, except by letting the smooth leaves lie upon his stubbly face, except by being of the stillness. In this way he offered his praise. For a short space the soul returned to his body, from which it had been driven out by whips, and he stood there looking through inspired eyes into the undergrowth.

When Harry Roberts discovered Judd, the latter was already at work upon the sheep's carcass. He was cursing the flies.

'Urchhh!' cried the disgusted boy.

'Why, Harry,' said Judd, 'those are only maggots.'

'And what about our dinner?'

'Why, it will be on your plates, as promised.'

'Maggots and all?'

'Maggots knock off very easy,' Judd replied.

He was, even now, engaged in knocking them off.

'Filthy stuff!' cried the boy.

Certainly the meat was already of rather a green appearance as the result of such a damp heat.

'You wait and see,' coaxed the convict. 'You will be surprised. If you do not eat your mutton, then I will eat my hat.'

But the boy was not consoled.

'My stomach is turned up,' he complained.

'Not everyone is queasy by nature,' answered Judd. 'Still, Harry, I will ask you not to mention this to anyone else.'

Other incidents prevented the boy from breaking his promise.

During the morning a party of blacks appeared, first as shreds of shy bark glimpsed between the trunks of the trees, but always drifting, until, finally, they halted in human form upon the outskirts of the camp.

'Did you ever see such a filthy race?' asked Ralph Angus, whose strength and looks prevented him from recognizing anything except in his own admirable image.

'We do not understand them yet,' said Le Mesurier.

The latter's doubts and discoveries could have been leading him towards the age of wisdom.

'You are morbid, I believe, Frank,' Angus said, and laughed.

He was all for driving out the wretched mob of cattle thieves.

The blacks were watching. Some of the men even grew noble in the stillness of their concentration and posture of their attenuated limbs. Their faces betrayed a kind of longing. Others, though, and particularly the old, could have been wallowing beforehand in the dust; they had the dusty, grey-black skins of lizards. Several of the women present had had the hair burnt from their heads. The women were altogether hairless, for those other parts which should have been covered, had been exposed by plucking. By some perversity of innocence, however, it did seem to emphasize the modesty of those who had been plucked. They had nothing left to hide.

Turner, naturally, was provoked to immoderate laughter, and was shouting:

'What will you bid for the molls, Mr Le Mesurier?'

And when Le Mesurier was silent:

'Or are they not to your taste?'

Finally, he took the handle of the iron frying-pan, which he still had about him from the previous night, and presented it to one of the more impressive blacks.

'You sell wife,' he demanded. 'I buy. But the pretty one. The one that has not been singed right off.'

Everyone was by this time repelled by Turner, and by the blacks that had so inspired him.

The blacks themselves were disgusted by those of his gestures which conveyed a meaning. Several of the males made hissing noises, and the pan-handle was flung down.

Hearing the scuffling and flumping that followed, and curses from Turner, and gibberish of natives, the German had come out of his tent, and entered into the situation.

'Turner,' he said, 'your behaviour will always live down to what I would expect. You will please me by not molesting these people who are my guests.'

Someone who had begun to snigger did not continue. It was often thus in the presence of Voss. His laborious attitudes would fill the foreground and become the right ones.

Now he approached the black whose instincts had rejected Turner's offer, and, holding out his hand, said stiffly:

'Here is my hand in friendship.'

At first the blackfellow was reluctant, but then took the hand as if it had been some inanimate object of barter, and was turning it over, examining its grain, the pattern of veins, and, on its palm, the lines of fate. It was obvious he could not estimate its value.

Each of the white men was transfixed by the strangeness of this ceremony. It would seem that all human relationships hung in the balance, subject to fresh evaluation by Voss and the black.

Then the native dropped the hand. There was too much here for him to accept. Although something of this nature had been expected by his companions, Voss appeared somewhat saddened by the reception his gesture had received.

'They are at that stage when they can only appreciate material things,' he said in some surprise.

It was he who was in the wrong, to expect of his people – for as such he persisted in considering them – more than they were capable of giving, and, acknowledging his mistake, he promptly instructed the boy to fetch a bag of flour.

'At least, sir,' said Ralph Angus, 'let us question them on the subject of the stolen cattle.'

Dugald did exchange with the natives a few, unhappy, private words. Then all was mystery, in a concert of black silence.

'No know,' said Dugald, in that sick voice he would adopt for any of his failures.

By this time the boy had lugged the flour into their presence, and Dugald was ordered to explain its virtues. This he did briefly, as people will confess unwillingly to the lunacy of some relative.

The blacks were chattering, and plunging their hands into the flour, and giving floury smiles. Then they swooped upon the bag, and departed through the valley, laughing. While yet in sight, some altercation of a semi-humorous nature arose, and many hands were tugging at the bag. One old woman was seizing handfuls of the flour and pouring it upon her head. She stood there, for a moment, in veils of flour, an ancient bride, and screamed because it tickled. They were all laughing then, and running through a rain of flour, after which they trailed the empty bag, until it was dropped, finally, in ignoble rags.

Such an abuse could have been felt most keenly by Voss, the benefactor, if at that moment the smells of roasting mutton had not arisen.

'It is the dinner,' cried Harry Robarts, quite forgetting the earlier stages of its preparation.

Judd had fixed the carcass above the coals of a fire, in a kind of shallow trench, and now the golden sheep was rustling with juices and spitting fat. Slabs of hot meat were presently hacked off for the whole company, who for once omitted to gnaw the bones before throwing them to the dogs. All were soon bursting, but still contrived to stuff down some of the hard puddings that Judd had improvised out of flour and currants, and boiled in water; even these were good on that day. Afterwards the men lay in the grass, and embroidered on their past lives, stories such as nobody believed, but to which they listened contentedly.

Even Voss descended from his eminence, and was reviewing the past through benevolent gauze.

'I can remember in the house of my parents a green stove. It was composed of green tiles, you understand, of which the decoration was rampant lions, though they more resembled thin cats, it occurred to me as a boy.'

Everybody listened to the German. Exhausted by food, mellow with Christmas, they no longer demanded narrative, but preferred the lantern slides of recollection. Into these still, detached pictures entered the simplest members of the party as into their own states of mind.

'Round that green stove we would sit on Christmas Evening: the relatives, some acquaintances, old women living off friendship, one or two boys apprenticed by my father. We would sing the Christmas songs. There was always a tree, a *Tannenbaum*, smelling as such trees will when they bleed from fresh wounds. Between all this festivity, and sweet things that were passing round, and the hot wine, I would hear the streets. It was the snow, filling and filling the empty streets, until we were lost, it seemed, in Christmas.'

The German paused.

'So,' he said. 'It was not altogether different. Except for the snow, *selbstverständlich*. There was the snow.'

'And except that we are not lost,' Judd felt compelled to add.

Some of them laughed, and said they were not so sure. At that moment they would not have cared.

'What did you use to eat, sir?' asked Harry Robarts.

'At Christmas, a goose. But on the Christmas Evening, always a fine carp.'

'What is a carp, sir?'

But how could the German answer, who was so far distant?

In the cool of the evening, when those who had been feasting rose from their stupor of meat and dreams, Voss asked Judd to come with him, and they took horses, and rode out in the direction in which Jackie had gone to look for the lost cattle. It was not long before they had left behind all trace of that pleasant valley where they were camped, entering a dead country, in which the horses were continually stumbling, for they would plunge their feet into burrows or hidden pot-holes, and sink up to the pasterns in the crumbly earth.

Once in the course of this hard going, the horse which Voss was riding shied at a snake. The fact that it was a live one was surprising, for all else in the landscape appeared to be dead. The horse was immediately protesting, with his breath and his fore-lock, and the whites of his eyes. In that sudden leap, the German's left temple and part of his forehead were scored by the branch of a dead tree, nothing serious, indeed, he would not have thought anything more of the matter, if the blood had not begun to trickle down into his eyes.

'You should attend to it, sir,' said Judd, on noticing that his leader was brushing away the blood.

'It is nothing,' Voss replied.

And frowned. With the result that the blood was again gushing, and tumbling down into his eyes.

'Wait,' said Judd.

Astonishingly, Voss did. They were both reining in. They were jumping down upon the ground. The convict took a handkerchief that he had but lately washed in the river at the place where they were encamped, and with which he was now preparing to bind the German's head.

Should I let him? wondered the latter.

But he was already submitting. He was bowing his head. He could smell the smell of the crumpled, but spotless handkerchief, which had been dried on spikes of grass, at leisure, in the sun. He could hear the convict's breathing, very close.

'Is that too tight, sir?' Judd was asking.

Although expert in being of service to others, frequently on such occasions he would experience a weakness so delicious that his skilful hands would bungle.

'That is right. As it is,' said Voss.

To surrender itself into other hands is one of the temptations of mortal flesh, the German knew, and shivered for an instant.

'Do you say that somebody is passing over your grave?' he laughed.

'There is some such saying,' replied the convict, whose eyes were examining his work with a detached affection.

When they had remounted and were riding on, Voss wondered how much of himself he had given into her hands. For he had become aware that the mouth of the young woman was smiling. It was unusually full and compassionate. Approbation must have gone to his head, for he continued unashamedly to contemplate her pleasure, and to extract from it pleasure of his own. They were basking in the same radiance, which had begun to emanate from the hitherto lustreless earth.

'We will find it pretty rough going from now on, I expect, sir,' interrupted Judd, who was ploughing forward somewhat in advance.

'I have every confidence in our company,' said the German.

They rode on, and it could have been the gentle silence of evening that made them both grateful.

Not long after this, on the banks of a dry creek, they came upon Jackie with seven head of cattle, or what remained of the lost herd.

'You look all over?' exploded the infuriated Voss.

'All over,' said Jackie, reasoning that this was what the white man wished to hear.

'We could fan out in the morning, the whole lot of us,' suggested Judd, 'and perhaps snap up a few more.'

As it was growing late, nothing else could be done for the present, but fall in behind the exasperating rumps of the recovered few, and return to camp.

In the morning the convict's plan was adopted by all but Palfreyman, who was occupied with the ornithological specimens he had taken while in the valley. He sat at work beneath a tree, brushing the flies off his neatly folded birds with a switch of leaves. So that the German was irritated to see him.

'Perhaps it is as well you should remain, Palfreyman,' he did say, contemplatively, 'to guard against possible marauders.'

But he continued to be furious with all, especially with Gyp, the big, half-Newfoundland bitch, that got beneath his horse's feet, and then shrieked.

Except that they discovered the hacked carcasses of two steers, the search for the missing cattle proved fruitless, and after several days it was decided to strike camp and push on without them. Only Palfreyman, it now appeared, had profited by their stay in that pleasant place, for the interlude of Christmas had faded, Turner was suffering from a fever, and two of the others from insect bites. Palfreyman had to try hard to conceal his personal contentment, but did not succeed in hiding it from Voss.

'What shall we do,' grumbled the latter, 'when the back of the last mule is broken under the corpses of birds?'

Palfreyman accepted this as a joke.

And they pushed on.

They were riding eternally over the humped and hateful earth, which the sun had seared until the spent and crumbly stuff was become highly treacherous. It was, indeed, the bare crust of the earth. Several of the sheep determined to lie down upon it and die. Their carcasses did not have much to offer, though the blacks would frizzle the innards and skin, and stuff these delicacies down their throats. The white men, whose appetites were deadened by dust, would swallow a few leathery strips of leg, or gnaw from habit at the wizened chops. Their own stomachs were shrivelling up. In the white light of dawn, horses and cattle would be nosing the ground for any suggestion of leaf, any blade of grass, or little pocket of rock from which to suck the dew. The ghosts of things haunted here, and in that early light the men and animals which had arrived were but adding to the ghost-life of the place.

But it is what we expected, the German assured himself.

His features had grown thinner, his eyes, of that pale, pure blue, were the clearer for this confirmation of vision by fact.

Once they came across a party of blacks, trooping gaily over the grey earth. The blacks approached, laughing, and showing their white teeth. Unlike their fellows farther back, they proceeded to hail Dugald and Jackie. An exchange of cheerful civilities was taking place; then the thin line straggled on into the vastness. The women were carrying nets and children, but the men were free.

It was afterwards learnt from Dugald that the party was on its way to eat the fruit of the bunya bunya.

'Where?' asked Le Mesurier, to whom those dark trees promised paradise.

'Very far. Blackfeller walk,' answered Dugald, growing sad. 'Many sleeps,' he added.

So the white men continued westward through what could have been their own perpetual sleep, and the fruit of the mystic bunya bunya contracted in their mouths.

Several days from there they came to a ridge, of hills even, at which a brigalow scrub whipped their flesh back to waking. Mules began to buck. The udders of those goats which had kidded were slashed and torn by twigs, and the glassy eyes of the most rational of all animals were seeing far too clearly as they advanced into chaos. On the farther side of the ridge, however, there was the suggestion of a creek, that is to say, a string of pools, filled with brown water or scum, for which the expedition made with all the speed it could muster, and but for curses, and skill in horsemanship, would have been trapped in it.

As it was, two of the more obstinate mules succeeded in becoming bogged, and were only dragged out by concerted strength at the end of their leading ropes, and blows on the rump from the torn-off branch of a tree.

One of these animals, it was seen, had staked itself. Dark blood was mingling on its fetlock with the slime of mud. It limped ostentatiously.

Voss approached the animal with that directness which comes from controlled distaste, a thin figure possessed by will, and was immediately lying on his back, his face even thinner.

Most of his party appeared as if drugged by circumstance, but Palfreyman was quick to dismount and run to their leader.

'What is it, Mr Voss?'

'It has got me in the stomach. The devil of a thing!' the German did manage to convey, as he lay twisting his lips.

At this point Judd arrived at his side, and the tortured man was carried back up the slope, and laid in the shade of some scrub, over which the convict rigged a sheet of canvas as additional shelter.

As the German continued to bite his lips, and seemed incapable of uttering any but his own language, Judd took it upon himself to call a halt, and they camped there several days, treating the sick, for the fever-ridden Turner had contracted the diarrhoea, from the milk of a goat, he insisted, and there was, besides, the staked mule.

Judd had soon organized the camp. He sent the supple Jackie out along a log to scoop the scum-water with a pannikin. Dugald unearthed the roots of trees, from which he shook a quantity of crystal water. Soon all were meagrely refreshed. Only the beasts were dissatisfied with their portion of scum; they would stand and murmur, with their heads held low, nosing for celestial dew.

One evening when the pain had begun to leave him, and the skin of his face was less yellow, Voss sent for Judd and thanked him formally.

'For your personal attention, Mr Judd, and kindness,' said the stiff German, who was still stretched upon the ground like a breathing corpse, looking from beneath his eyelids.

'A man does what he can,' said Judd, and would have accepted the cat rather than the scourge of recognition.

'But with no water,' he blurted.

A most shameful tenderness was taking the shape out of his mouth.

He had, indeed, been forced to boil in a pot of scum the rags he had used to foment the German's belly. Tinged by the mule's hoof with saffron and purple, this part of his anatomy must originally have been ivory in colour, very thin, moreover, and private, so that, as he worked, the convict had been forced continually to turn his head, and turn his head, to look out into the haze, and thus avoid violating further the privacy, that almost sacrosanctity of which he was aware.

Voss, who had felt more exposed on some less physical occasions, despised all sickness; he despised physical strength; he despised, though secretly, even the compassion he had sensed in the ministrations of Judd. His own strength, he felt, could not decrease with physical debility. But, was Judd's power increased by compassion?

He was continually observing the convict as the latter applied the miserable hot rags, and now, from beneath his eyelids, as he thanked the man for his services.

'And particularly for seeing fit to assume command.'

Judd stood there.

'I did not take command, not intentional like.'

'But it is for this that I commend you,' answered Voss, looking ever deeper into Judd.

'I did round up a few mules,' the convict confessed. 'And tell the men to see as the canvas was pegged down. And kill a beast. And send the blacks to look for water. Because I am a practical man.'

'And mules must be rounded up. And men, men must be driven, although they blind themselves to the truth.'

Then the convict protested with great vehemence:

'Not men. It is not so with men.'

This man was shaking, as if the wounds were opening in him.

'Good, Judd,' laughed Voss. 'I will exonerate you from any such designs.'

But when the fellow had gone away, he continued to suspect him of exercising great power, though within human limits. For compassion, a feminine virtue, or even grace, of some sensual origin, was undoubtedly human, and did limit will.

So the German was despising what he most desired: to peel the whale-bone off the lily stem and bruise the mouth of flesh.

Ah, he cried, rubbing his face against the leather of the saddle-bag.

Then he lay more tranquilly upon the barren hillside. He thought about the woman whose consent was making her his wife. All twisted lusts had gone out of his body and the stunted trees. The sky was flowering at that hour, and the distant fields of vision. He lay breathing gently in this union of earth with light. He lay thinking of the wife from whose hands he would accept salvation, if he were intended to renounce the crown of fire for the ring of gentle gold. That was the perpetual question which grappled him as coldly as iron.

In a few days Voss was up. His will walked erect, if not yet his emaciated body. As the others were cured of their ills, Turner of all but the grumbles, and the offending mule of its lameness, the German called Judd and Palfreyman and informed them of his decision to make a start on the following morning.

It was a relief to put an end to inactivity on that scrubby slope. Life starts afresh with each fresh journey, even into the dust. So the forenoon and evening were filled with lively preparation.

Only Dugald was squatting inactive on the ashy fringe of a small fire. The old native was more than ever a man of ash and charred wood; his brittle hams might have crumbled at a touch.

'What is it, Dugald?' asked the German. 'Are you not pleased?'

'Blackfeller old,' said the old man, in a voice that was his oldest. 'This feller too old.'

How the notes of lamentation twangled on his bone harp.

'This feller sick. Sick old. Wanta go back Jildra. This no place old feller die.'

'I will not let you die, Dugald,' Voss consoled lightly.

'You let Mr Voss die. You no stop Dugald,' answered the old black, looking gravely at the white man.

'How *let myself die?*'

'Not now. No ready. You no stop when ready.'

This melancholy conversation that was taking place at the fire's edge had its gaiety for Voss.

'You old devil,' he laughed, 'you will see us all put in the ground.'

Then the old man himself began to laugh.

'No here,' he laughed ashily. 'Jildra. Jildra good place. Please,' he said, quickly, quietly. 'I go away Jildra.'

But the German dismissed that possibility with his hand, and walked on.

The old man continued to nurse what was, indeed, a sickness of foreboding and fear. He was holding his old ashen head as he squatted by the fire. The hostile spirits of unfamiliar places were tormenting him.

Later, in the camp which had begun already to dissolve in anticipation of the morning's move, Voss caught something of the old native's melancholy, and began to look about at their blackened pots, at the leather tackle which sweat had hardened, and those presumptuous notebooks in which he was scribbling the factual details of their journey. Then the palms of his hands knew a great helplessness. The white sky, for it was again evening, was filled with empty cocoons of cloud, fragile and ephemeral to all appearance, but into which he would have climbed, if he had been able. As he could not, he continued to walk about the camp, and his men looked up from whatever work they were engaged upon, searching his face with the eyes of children who have not yet learnt to reject appearances.

So Voss, who was exhausted, besides, by the illness from which he had not fully recovered, went and sat by his own fire.

'Dugald!' he called, when he had decided, and taken paper.

The breeze was lifting the stiff paper, and rattling it slightly against his knee, as if it had been bark or twig, but, without his protection, would have scrabbled and tormented it, for such white constancy is anathema to the mouths of dust.

The old native came.

'Dugald,' said Voss, who was by this time somewhat feverish, or irritated, '*hör' wohl zu*. Tomorrow morning you will leave for Jildra. *Verstanden?* You will take the horse from Mr Turner. He old, poor horse, better to stay Jildra.'

'Yes,' laughed Dugald. 'Old man same belong Jildra.'

'That is exact,' the German said. '*Warte nur*. Give Dugald's horse to Mr Turner.'

'Yes,' murmured the old black, who was now preparing to suffer all else with patience.

'I write paper, give Dugald letter,' Voss explained.

How the unborn letter rattled against his knees.

'Dugald take same letter Mr Boyle.'

His words were lead bullets.

'Now do you understand?'

'Yes,' said the old man.

Darkness sighed.

When he was alone again, the German spread the sheet of paper, on which the whole darkness converged, spread it on the boards of a notebook, and was prepared to write. His knees were trembling, but, of course, he had been ill. And firelight flickers. Dugald had been gone a long time, but Voss still hovered over the heading of his letter. Had he been in fullest possession of himself, he would have consulted his neat journal and copied down their latest estimated position. He was not, however, at that moment, self-possessed. He was sitting in the middle of nowhere. Which, naturally, was of too fantastical a nature, too expressive of his nothingness. Yet, out of nothing, he did finally begin, smiling painfully at the prospect of certain words, of which the sentiments remained unfamiliar.

Voss wrote:

My dear Laura, . . .

Addressing her thus intimately, as if he knew her, again the man hesitated. He knew that part of himself, the weakest, of which was born the necessity for this woman. With the latter he was acquainted from several cold conversations and one heated argument. They had met, besides, by flashes of intuition and in dreams. Whether or not such knowledge, haunting and personal though it was from some aspects, sufficiently justified his attitude, he touched the L gently with his pen, and so continued:

... *Your letter* has brought me great happiness. I will not say my only happiness, since I am underway to accomplish my also great, and long-conceived ambition. All these prizes falling to me at last make me at times confused, so that you will see you have inspired some degree of that humility which you so admire and in me have wished for! If I cannot admire this quality in other men, or consider it except as weakness in myself, I am yet accepting it for your sake.

There are many points of criticism in your letter that I could answer, but do not here in the circumstances in which I am placed, for those arguments appear to me rather as subjects for the tea-table, and here I have no such furniture from behind which I might make a stand. Indeed, we are reduced almost to infinity. In consequence, I will pass instead to those of your sentiments which, you profess, underlie your arguments, and which have been the cause of so much cordial happiness, while accompanying me these many weeks. That we should love each other, LAURA, does at last appear inevitable and fitting, as I sit here alone in this immense country. No ordinary *House* could have contained my feelings, but this great one in which greater longings are ever free to grow.

Do I take too much for granted, my dearest wife? I have forgotten, perhaps, some of the pretences, living and dreaming as I do, but life and dreams of such far-reaching splendour you will surely share them, even in your quiet room. So we are riding together across the plains, we sit together in this black night, I reach over and touch your cheek (not for the first time). You see that separation has brought us far, far closer. Could we perhaps converse with each other at last, expressing inexpressible ideas with simple words?

I will send this shameful letter tomorrow by an old native, to Jildra, to Mr Boyle, together with all necessary information on the progress of the expedition for your Uncle, and the formal request of his niece's hand. I would postpone this, Laura, to enjoy our privacy a little longer. Such a precious secret will be stolen only too soon. Am I mad? It is the gold that I have found in these rocks, in these desert places. Or I am delirious still, having been kicked in the stomach by a mule before several days, and suffered considerable pain.

You need not fear that I have not received every attention in my sickness, my chief Angel (a rather hairy one) being Mr Judd, an emancipist convict and neighbour of Mr Sanderson's, of whom I recollect it was also spoken at your Uncle's. Judd is what people call a *good man*. He is not a professional saint, as is Mr Palfreyman. He is a tentative one, ever trying his dubious strength, if not in one way, then, in another. It is tempting to love such a man, but I cannot kill myself quite off, even though you would wish it, my dearest Laura. I am reserved for further struggles, to wrestle with rocks, to bleed if necessary, to ascend. Yes, I do not intend to stop short of the Throne for the pleasure of grovelling on lacerated knees in company with Judd and Palfreyman. As for yourself, take care! At the risk of incurring your serious disapproval, I will raise you up to the far more rational position at my side.

So, we have our visions. Frank Le Mesurier has experienced something of importance that he is keeping hidden from me. On the other hand, Harry Roberts must tell all, while growing simpler, I sometimes feel, with distance. His simplicity is such, he could well arrive at that plane where great mysteries are revealed. Or else become an imbecile.

If I have not described every tree, every bird, every native encountered, it is because all these details are in writing for those who will not see beyond the facts. For you, our other journey, that you are now condemned to share, to its most glorious, or bitterest end.

I send you my wishes, and venture by now also to include my love, since distance has united us thus closely. This is the true marriage, I know. We have wrestled with the gristle and the bones before daring to assume the flesh.

Your
JOHANN ULRICH VOSS

In the morning, when the now shrunken cavalcade pushed westward, Dugald took the old horse which had been assigned to him, and which was gone in the feet, with girth galls, and saddle sores besides. The native was still standing at the stirrup looking shy when the last of the surviving sheep and a heavy, palpitating cow had shambled past. The men had finished calling, some correctly, others affectionately, one obscenely, to the old black. Now, all were gone, except the dust, and Voss.

'Good-bye, Dugald,' said the German from his horse, bending down, and offering a hand.

Then the old man, who was unskilled in similar gestures, took the hand with both his, but dropped it, overwhelmed by the difference in skin, while laughing for happiness. His face was filled with little moons of greyish wrinkles.

'You will go direct to Jildra,' said the German, but making it a generous command.

'Orright, Jildra,' laughed the old man.

'You will not loiter, and waste time.'

But the old man could only laugh, because time did not exist. The arches of the German's feet were exasperated in the stirrup-irons.

'You will give those letters to Mr Boyle. You understand?'

'Orright,' Dugald laughed.

'Letters safe?' asked the man in bursting veins.

'Safe. Safe,' echoed the scarecrow.

He put them in a pocket of his swallowtail coat. They were looking very white there.

'Well,' cried the writer of them, *'was stehst du noch da? Los!'*

The black mounted. Kicking his bare heels into the sides of the skinny horse, he persuaded it to stumble away.

Then Voss turned and rode in the direction of the others. Always at that hour he was a thin man juggling impotently with hopes. Those great, empty mornings were terrible until the ball of the sun was tossed skyward.

*

Dugald continued to ride. Several days he spent jogging on the back of the old horse, which sighed frequently, and no longer swished its tail at flies.

The old man, who was contented at last, sang to himself as he rode along:

> 'Water is good,
> Water is good. . . .'

The truth of this filtered fitfully through the blazing land.

Sometimes the old man would jump down at the butt of certain trees, and dig until he reached the roots, and break them open, and suck out the water. Sometimes he would cut sections of these precious pipes, and shake the moisture into the cup of his hand, for the old horse to sup. The hairs of the drawn muzzle tickled his withered skin most agreeably.

The old man killed and ate goannas. He ate a small, dun-coloured rat. As he had reached an age when it was permissible for him to eat almost all foods, it was a pity so little offered itself.

He experienced great longings, and often trembled at night, and thrust his skin against the protecting fire.

When the horse lay down and died, one afternoon in the bed of a dry creek, the black was not unduly concerned. If anything, his responsibilities were less. Before abandoning the dead horse, he cut out the tongue and ate it. Then he tore a stirrup-leather off the saddle, and went forward swinging it, so that the iron at the end described great, lovely arcs against the sky.

The veins of the old, rusty man were gradually filling with marvellous life, as his numbness of recent weeks relented; and in time he arrived at good country of grass and water. He came to a lake in which black women were diving for lily roots. In the dreamlike state he had entered, it seemed natural that these women should be members of his own tribe, and that they should be laughing and chattering with him as he squatted by the water's edge, watching their hair tangle with the stalks of lilies, and black breasts jostle the white cups. Nor was it unnatural that the strong young huntsmen of the tribe, when they burst through the wiry trees, clattering with spears and nullas, should show contempt, until they realized this was a man full of the wisdom and dignity that is derived from long and important journeys. Then they listened to him.

Only his swallowtail coat, by now a thing of several strips, was no longer dignified enough, with the result that the tallest huntsman solemnly tore off one of the strips, followed by a pocket.

Remembering the white man's letters, Dugald retrieved the pocket, and took them out. The shreds of his coat fell, and he was standing in his wrinkles and his bark-cloth. If the coat was no longer essential, then how much less was the conscience he had worn in the days of the whites? One young woman, of flashing teeth, had come very close, and was tasting a fragment of sealing-wax. She shrieked, and spat it out.

With great dignity and some sadness, Dugald broke the remaining seals, and shook out the papers until the black writing was exposed. There were some who were disappointed to see but the pictures of fern roots. A warrior hit the paper with his spear.

People were growing impatient and annoyed, as they waited for the old man to tell.

These papers contained the thoughts of which the whites wished to be rid, explained the traveller, by inspiration: the sad thoughts, the bad, the thoughts that were too heavy, or in any way hurtful. These came out through the white man's writing-stick, down upon paper, and were sent away.

Away, away, the crowd began to menace and call.

The old man folded the papers. With the solemnity of one who has interpreted a mystery, he tore them into little pieces.

How they fluttered.

The women were screaming, and escaping from the white man's bad thoughts.

Some of the men were laughing.

Only Dugald was sad and still, as the pieces of paper fluttered round him and settled on the grass, like a mob of cockatoos.

Then the men took their weapons, and the women their nets, and their dillybags, and children, and they all trooped away to the north, where at that season of the year there was much wild life and a plentiful supply of yams. The old man went with them, of course, because they were his people, and they were going in that direction. They went walking through the good grass, and the present absorbed them utterly.

9

MRS BONNER had come out in a rash, due to the particularly humid summer, or to the shortage of green vegetables at Sydney (neither would she be robbed), or sometimes she would attribute her physical distress – privately, in case any of her family should laugh – attribute it to the impossible situation in which she had been placed by the pregnancy of her servant, Rose Portion. For Rose was still with them, very heavy, very shameful. Mrs Bonner would refer to her maid's condition as *Rose's illness*. It was intolerable, as was her own helplessness.

'I understood,' said Mrs Bonner to her friend, Mrs Pringle,

'that there was this institution of Mrs Lauderdale's for fallen women, but I find, on making inquiries, it is not for those who exhibit, shall we say, material proof of having fallen.'

Mrs Bonner dabbed her lip.

'I really do not know what to suggest,' sighed Mrs Pringle, who was herself legitimately pregnant, and who could take no serious interest in a convict woman's fall.

'In a normal family,' complained Mrs Bonner, 'responsibility for such matters would not be left entirely on one's hands.'

'Oh, but Mrs Bonner, no family is *normal*,' Mrs Pringle cried. 'Is it not?'

This did not comfort as it should have.

'Children are little animals that begin to think by thinking of themselves. A spaniel is more satisfactory.'

Mrs Bonner looked shocked.

'I will not deny that children are dear little things,' conceded Mrs Pringle, who had a lot of them.

'Nobody would expect a tender child to offer mature advice,' Mrs Bonner pursued, 'but a husband should and does think.'

'A husband does think,' Mrs Pringle agreed, 'but that, again, is a different kind of thinking. I believe, between ourselves, Mrs Bonner, that these machines of which all the talk is at Home would never have been invented, if men were not *in sympathy*, so to speak, to a *great extent*. I believe that many men, even respectable ones, are *themselves machines*.'

'Really, Mrs Pringle?' Mrs Bonner exclaimed. 'I would not suspect Mr Bonner of this, though he does not think my way; nor will he offer suggestions.'

Mrs Bonner was again unhappy.

'It is I who must bear the burden of Rose.'

Ah, Rose, Rose, always Rose, sighed Mrs Pringle. Mrs Bonner had become quite tedious.

'We must think of something for the wretched soul,' said the kind friend, and hoped with that to close the subject.

Mrs Bonner, who was a tidy woman, would have turned her maid into the street and learnt to think no more about it, if her family might not have reminded her. In the circumstances, she did not dare, and the question of Rose's future continued nagging at her martyred mind.

One afternoon of deepest summer, when a brickfielder was blowing, and the hideous native trees were fiendish, and the air had turned brown, Mrs Bonner developed a migraine, and became positively hysterical. She flung herself too hard upon that upright sofa in the drawing-room, on which it was her habit to arrange people to listen to music, and was sobbing between gusts of eau de Cologne.

'But what is it, Aunt Emmy?' asked her niece, who had swirled in.

They were alone on that afternoon, except for the heavy Rose, since Belle had been driven to the Lending Library, and Mr Bonner was not yet returned from the establishment in George Street, and Cassie and Edith had started, unwisely, on a picnic with acquaintances while the gale was still threatening.

'What is it?' Laura asked, and was smacking the backs of her aunt's hands.

'I do not know,' Mrs Bonner replied.

For, it was everything.

'It is nothing,' she choked. 'It is the dust. It is those dreadful trees, which I can only wish all cut down.'

Waves of resentment surged through Mrs Bonner.

'It is that Rose,' she cried, as wind struck its greatest blow hitherto, and sashes rattled. 'For whom we must all suffer. And cannot receive, in our own home, except our most intimate acquaintance. Because of Rose. And Belle, I am ashamed, must see this everlasting Rose. To say nothing of the young girl in the kitchen, to whom it is an example that could well influence her whole life.'

'There, Aunt,' said Laura Trevelyan, and produced her own green smelling-bottle.

'Then it *is* Rose,' she added.

'I will not deny I am distracted,' Mrs Bonner sobbed, but drier.

The younger woman had sat down, and, after she had reconciled her watered silk to the rather awkward little chair, announced with a composure that might have been rehearsed.

'I think, Aunt, that I have a plan.'

Mrs Bonner sniffed so sharp that her nostrils were cut by hartshorn.

'Ah, dear Laura,' she gasped. 'I knew you would.' And

coughed. 'I believe you have had one all the time, and for some reason that I do not understand, chose to be naughty.'

The young woman was very grave, yet calm, on her wave of grey silk that she was smoothing and coaxing.

I do not understand Laura, Mrs Bonner remembered, not without apprehension.

'What is your plan?' she asked.

The young woman was taking her time. She was quite pregnant with some idea waiting to be born. She would not be hurt by any precipitate behaviour of others. She was shielding herself.

And so, she lowered the lids of her mild, yet watchful eyes. At the same time, her engrossed expression did allow her to smile, a smile of great sweetness. Aunt Emmy had to admit: Laura's face has melted.

Laura said:

'It is a plan, and it is not a plan. At least, it is the beginning of one, which will grow if circumstances permit.'

'Oh,' said Mrs Bonner, who had hoped for a strong box in which to lock her annoyances. 'It is not a *secret* plan, I hope?'

'It is so simple that I am afraid you may not call it a plan at all.'

'Tell me,' Mrs Bonner begged.

'I cannot tell you, except the beginning of it, because the end has still to come. But, for a start, I have brought Rose down from the attic into the spare room.'

'Into the best room!' Mrs Bonner hissed.

'She will stay there quietly. I will take her all her meals on a tray. It will be a matter of a few days, by Rose's calculations. I have engaged a midwife, of good reputation, from inquiries I have made, who lives in a cottage in Woolloomooloo, and whose name, you must appreciate it, is Mrs Child.'

'In the best room!' Mrs Bonner cried.

'What is all this?' asked the merchant, who had come in.

'That dreadful woman,' cried his wife, 'is to have her . . . Rose Portion in the best room! Laura has done it, and behind my back.'

For Mr Bonner, who hated disturbance, awful prospects were opening in his own house. He listened to the sound of dresses. Complexions were accusing him. He was surrounded by women.

'Laura,' he began, seizing any weapon, however blunted, 'I cannot believe that you have been so thoughtless.'

Like most people, Mr Bonner cherished the opinion that he alone considered others.

'On the contrary, I have given the matter considerable thought,' replied the wretched Laura, 'and am haunted by a similar situation in which I am having my baby in an attic, or worse, in the street.'

'Your *baby*?' asked her uncle, in a white voice.

'Laura is suffering from an unhealthy imagination. That is all, Mr Bonner,' explained the aunt. 'Oh, dear, oh, dear.'

The young woman had grown very hard inside her murmurous silk of dove grey.

'Lord, give me patience,' she said. 'If truth is not acceptable, it becomes the *imagination* of others.'

'From one who has been treated as a daughter!' cried Aunt Emmy.

'It is obvious that she prefers to forget,' added the uncle, who was not as impressive as he should have been; frequently he would find himself bringing up the rear.

'When one is unhappy, one does forget,' Laura admitted. 'Threats and injustices overshadow all the comfortable advantages.'

Beyond the window-pane, trees were fluctuating, the brown world was heaving. Even in the nice room, despite the protest of horsehair and pampas grass, the dust was settling on reflections and in the grain of taffeta, or ran with the perspiration, or the tears, on ladies' faces.

For, it had grown stuffy, and Aunt Emmy was crying again.

'I do not understand,' she protested, 'the necessity to be miserable when one need not be.'

'But we need not, Aunt Emmy,' cried Laura.

At times she was very quick, glancing, her eyes glittering.

'Do you not understand the importance of this life which we are going to bring into our house? Regardless of its origin. It is a life. It is my life, your life, anybody's life. It is life. I am so happy for it. And frightened. That something may destroy this *proof* of life. Some thoughtlessness. Poor Rose, she does not care a bit about her baby, yet. She will, of course. In the meantime, I must protect it from everyone. Until it can speak for itself. Aunt, dear, if you will only wait to hear.'

Mrs Bonner sighed.

'I cannot let myself be won over against my reason, Laura. Babies are, of course, very pretty. *But.*'

Mrs Bonner had, as yet, refused to visualize this baby, and smell the smell of warm flannel.

'Then I appeal to you, Uncle,' said Laura, cruelly.

In argument her hand had become an ivory fist, but she herself was again softening. She had a certain waxiness, observed her uncle, who would walk in his garden in the evening amongst those camellia bushes he had planted as a young man.

'To you, Uncle,' Laura was saying.

'I?' exclaimed Mr Bonner, exposed. 'I, of course, agree with your aunt. Though there is something to be said, one must confess, for your argument, Laura, at least, shall we say, in its general principle. One must applaud the humanity of your viewpoint. It is the allegory that I do not go much on. You know I am a plain man.'

'Then, for goodness' sake, let us prune my argument of allegory,' Laura hastened to reply. 'Let it be quite naked. Let us receive this poor child into the world with love. That is argument enough. Or I will love it, if necessary. As if it had been mine. Let me. Let me.'

'You are overwrought, Laura,' said Mr Bonner.

His wife smiled bitterly.

'I am excited,' Laura agreed, 'by my great hopes.'

'I do not see,' began Mr Bonner, who would tire of things temporarily, and was now, in fact, thinking of his glass of rum and water, 'I do not see how we can help but allow this misguided wretch to give birth to her child under our roof, unless we break the precepts that our religious faith teaches us. As it is too late to effect an arrangement combining the practical with the humane, let us hope that in time the Supreme Being will lead us out of our predicament. I do not doubt we shall find some honest woman who will see the advantage of accepting the child, especially if accompanied by a small consideration. The unhappy mother will be more difficult to dispose of, although, in this also, I am confident we shall be guided to act in a right way.'

Laura Trevelyan lowered her eyes.

'I do not know what to say,' admitted Mrs Bonner, uncertain whether to feel offended at her own husband's defection, or chastened by his magnanimity.

The poor woman was racked by hartshorn and dampened by emotion. Those little curls, which she still affected from a former fashion, and which rain or sea air always compelled her to revive, had by now lost their necessary frizz, and were hanging upon her forehead like the tails of dead mice.

'I am at a loss,' she said.

'Dear Aunt Emmy,' the younger woman consoled, 'you will recover. And discover.'

As her collapsed aunt continued to sit with the smelling-bottle in her lap, the niece added:

'I must ask you to replace the stopper in the little bottle, otherwise its virtue will be exhausted.'

So Laura Trevelyan left the presence of these relations, who were again her good parents. She did truly love them.

In her condition, she could have loved all men, as, indeed, she would love the baby. She walked through the house protecting her achievement, in her sensuous, full dress of grey watered silk. Of singing silk. Her heart was full. Sitting in the same room with her dull and heavy maid, the mistress did not lose her buoyancy. She was cutting out flannel, making garments for the baby they would have. Her steely scissors flew, and she would gather up snippets of ribbon and braid, and fasten together little, bright bundles of trivial conversation. The maid would listen, but dully. The latter became leaden as her time approached, and she would perhaps have sunk, if it had not been for the trust she put in her mistress.

'Now that the wind has died, let us take our walk in the garden, Rose,' decided the mistress.

And the maid followed, trustingly.

They would walk in the garden, in the dusk, by mysterious, involved paths that the mistress chose. In the wilder, scrubbier parts of the garden, the skirts of the two women would catch upon the fallen bark and twigs. Sometimes Laura Trevelyan would tear the bark in scrolls from the native trees, and attempt to unroll them before they broke, or she would tear the leaves, and crush them, and smell them, in her hands smelling of ants.

Then, in the mysterious garden, obsessed by its harsh scents, she would be closest to the unborn child, and to the love of her husband. Darkness and leaves screened the most intimate forms, the most secret thoughts. Soon he will write, she told herself. As if words were necessary. Long before pen had been put to paper, and paper settled on the grass in its final metamorphosis, she had entered the state of implicit trust. In the evening garden, their trusting bodies glimmered together, always altering their shape, as the light inspired, then devoured. Or they would sit, and again it could have been the forms of two women, looking at each other, as the one tried to remember the eyes of her husband. If she could have looked deeper, deeper, deep enough.

Once she had felt the child kick inside her, and she bit her lip for the certainty, the shape her love had taken.

'Oh, it is cold,' Rose Portion was moaning. 'It is cold.'

Fear compelled her to drag her mistress back.

'On the contrary,' murmured Laura, 'it is warm tonight. Far too warm, in fact.'

But she was returned to her actual body.

Then the young woman took the stiff, cold hand of her maid, and led her indoors.

One evening, as Rose Portion was seated by the lamp, picking over some work that she had taken into her lap to pacify her mistress, she looked up quite suddenly. A savage hand had carved the lines deeper in her grey face, which, under light, was more than ever that of a dumb animal.

'Oh, miss, I cannot bear it,' breathed Rose.

'You shall,' said Laura, getting up.

The woman clenched her teeth, until the grey sweat ran in the channels of her face. It was as if the breath were being torn out of her.

'It is time,' said Laura.

'I do not know,' Rose replied. 'At least, it is the pains. I would die if I could.'

Then Laura sent Jim Prentice with the brougham to fetch

the midwife, who arrived shortly, with an infallible knowledge of the world and a leather bag.

Mrs Child was a small woman with eyes so sharp and black they could have strayed down from amongst the other jet ornaments accumulated on her bonnet. For reasons of policy, she began by ignoring the patient, while enumerating to Miss Trevelyan those articles she would need in the course of operations. And all the time, the midwife was glancing here and there, as if she had been in the furniture trade, instead of belonging to her own particular branch of the conjuring profession. For Mrs Child knew: however discreet the eyes, and modest the behaviour, solid mahogany and figured brocade must be taken into account. So she reckoned up, accordingly.

Now, when she had removed her bonnet and disposed of her pelisse, the midwife deigned to notice the patient. She ran at Rose, with all her curls a-jingle, and gave her what could have been a pinch.

'You, Mrs Portion,' shouted this jolly soul, 'your trouble is a little one, that you will be calling a blessing by tomorrow night.'

The pregnant woman, who was holding her arms rigid across her belly, gave a long, terrible moan.

So that Mrs Bonner shuddered, in the little, far parlour, which they seldom used, and where she had hoped not to hear.

The midwife sucked her teeth.

'There, dear. You must not fight against receiving such a wonderful gift. Woman truly vindicated, as a reverend gentleman once put it. But I do not reckon your time is come, unless I do not know my business, and nobody can accuse me of that. I would say, at a guess, in another two, or three, even, or it could be four hours. Now, miss, would it be possible for me to take some light refreshment? I always dine early, to be ready to give service, seeing as the night air seems to work upon the poor things.'

While Mrs Child was demolishing a nice mutton chop, together with a liberal portion of baked custard, and describing for the benefit of Cassie the details of the more spectacular cases to which she had been called, Laura Trevelyan made the necessary preparations. She was exalted now.

'On the good carpet!' wailed Mrs Bonner in her distant parlour.

'I have put newspaper,' replied her niece. 'At least four layers of the *Herald*.'

But the aunt was not consoled. In her isolation, for her husband had remembered a message he had failed to deliver to a friend, and kind Mrs Pringle had carried off their daughter Belle for as long as circumstances required, Mrs Bonner had been reading a sermon, and just now was offering a prayer, for the poor sufferer, which signified: herself. So she passed the evening, in the green-backed mirror, in her stuffy room.

Then a great cry was shattering all the glass in the house. The walls were falling. Flesh subsided only gradually upon the ridge of the spine, to be shocked further at sound of the midwife bouncing up the stairs like an indiarubber ball. She was a very tough small woman, it seemed, who proceeded to wrestle with life itself for the remainder of the night.

In the spare room the kindly lamplight had grown inordinately hard. Nothing was any longer hid, nor would the Brussels carpet muffle. The midwife had the woman sitting on an upright chair, from which her solid gown hung in long, petrified folds. Now that the agony had begun, the girl who had willed it was herself stunned into stone. The knot of her hands was carved upon her waist, as she stood in her corner and listened to doom writing upon a slate.

Only the midwife continued to move, round and about, with the resilience of rubber.

'Hands on the arms of the chair, dear,' she advised. 'You would bless me for it, if you only knew.'

But the woman in labour shrieked.

A flow of endless time began to fill the room. Laura Trevelyan would have prayed, but found that her mind was stuck to the roof of her mouth.

Even the lowing beast was, in the end, stilled.

'It is the head that is giving the trouble,' Mrs Child remarked, as, her face averted in considerable delicacy of curls, she fumbled and bungled under Rose Portion's gown. 'If you are not an obstropulous little wretch!'

The mother was beyond caring as she drowned in that sea.

In spite of her stone limbs, Laura Trevelyan could have screamed with pain. Her throat was bursting with it. They would all be strangled by the darkness, she suspected, when a curious transformation of their faces began at last to take place. Their livid, living stone was turning, by divine mercy, into flesh. The shutters were slashed with grey. Its thin stuff lay upon the newspapers with which the carpet was spread.

It is moving, we are moving, we are saved, Laura Trevelyan would have cried, if all sound had not continued frozen inside her throat. The supreme agony of joy was twisted, twisting, twisting.

Then the dawn was shrieking with jubilation. For it had begun to live. The cocks were shrilling. Doves began to soothe. Sleepers wrapped their dreams closer about them, and participated in great events. The red light was flowing out along the veins of the morning.

Laura Trevelyan bit the inside of her cheek, as the child came away from her body.

'There,' said the midwife. 'Safe and sound.'

'A little girl,' she added with a yawn, as if the sex of the children she created was immaterial.

The actual mother fell back with little blubbering noises for her own poor flesh. She had just drunk the dregs of pain, and her mouth was still too full to answer the cries of her new-born child.

But Laura Trevelyan came forward, and took the red baby, and when she had immersed it in her waiting love, and cleaned it, and swaddled it in fresh flannel, the midwife had to laugh, and comment:

'Well, you are that drawn, dear, about the face, anyone would think it was you had just been delivered of the bonny thing.'

Laura did not hear. All superficial sounds were swallowed up in her own songs.

Later, she carried the baby through the drowsy morning to that remote room in which her aunt had chosen to do penance. But Mrs Bonner's cap had slipped. Day had caught her dozing in a chair. She woke up. She said:

'I knew I would not be able to sleep for the terrible noise. So I sat in the chair, and waited.'

'And here is the baby,' said Laura, stooping.

'Oh, dear,' said Aunt Emmy. 'What is it?'

'It is a girl.'

'Another girl!'

Mrs Bonner lamented the boys she did not have, and whom, she liked to think, she would have managed and understood.

'We must do the best by her, then,' she sighed. 'Until her future has been settled.'

As for the baby, she had but exchanged one room for another, or so it seemed. She was still curled, with her instincts, in the transparent, pink cocoon of protective love, upon which a vague future could have no possible effect.

Mrs Bonner searched greedily for some evidence of discomfort or sickliness in the sleeping child, of ugly dangers threatening it, but found no more than a bruise or two. Nature had favoured the baby that lay so unperturbed in Laura's arms. Then Mrs Bonner looked in the latter's face and was a bit afraid, as if she had been present at a miracle. She did not know what to make of it.

Nor did Laura attempt to explain her own state, even to herself. Those ensuing days she was exhausted, but content. They were the baby's days. There was a golden fuzz of morning in the garden. She could not bring herself to tread upon the tender flesh of rose petals that were showered at her feet. To avoid this, she would walk round by another way, though it meant running the gauntlet of the sun. Then her duty was most delicious. She was the living shield, that rejoiced to deflect the most savage blows. Other pains, of desert suns, of letters unwritten, of the touch of his man's hands, with their queer pronounced finger-joints, would fluctuate, as she carried her baby along the golden tunnels of light.

There was no doubt that the child was hers; nor did the blood mother protest, lying on her hot pillows in the shuttered, best room. Rose Portion took all for granted. She would receive the child and feed it at her breast whenever she was told. She would look from her distance at its crinkled face. It was obvious that she had paid the penalty for some monstrous sin, but not the most seductive religion, not even her own baby, could have convinced her the sinner is pardoned. So the flies stood transfixed on wiry legs in the corners of the baby's eyes. So the wool lace on the backs of the chairs stared back with a Gothic splendour. All was marvellous, but sculpture, to the frozen woman. Her stiff mouth would not move. Her hands had reached the position of infinite acceptance.

Then the mistress would begin to frown for the maid's omissions.

'Look, Rose, at the flies on Baby's face. Disgusting things! They could do her some harm,' she would scold in true concern. 'We must ask Mr Bonner to bring us a gossamer from town.'

She herself would take up the baby in its parcel of expensive clothes, and rock it in her arms, or hold it to her shoulder, to listen to its bubbles. The mistress was very soon appeased. She forgot her irritating maid on recovering her child. The young woman would glow and throb with the warmth of the baby, whereas the maid, on surrendering her share in its transparent life, was content to relapse into her own opaque flesh, in its dull shroud of days, into which she had been sewn by circumstance.

'What will you call the baby?' Belle Bonner asked her cousin.

'I do not know,' said Laura Trevelyan. 'We must ask Rose.'

'Poor Rose!' said Belle.

'Why *poor*?' asked Laura, quickly.

Belle laughed. She could not say.

Since her return from the Pringles', the tawny Belle was also changed. She was a lioness prowling in the passages. Laura had escaped, she felt, leaving her alone in the empty cage.

Laura, however, would often remember, and look back affectionately at Belle.

'Let us go together,' she tried now to make amends, and touched, 'let us go and ask Rose.'

Belle smiled sadly, but did consent to come, at a distance.

'Rose,' began Laura, very kindly, 'what would you like to call your baby?'

Rose, who had risen from her bed, but continued to sit in the cool room, waiting to recover her strength, did not hesitate.

'Mercy,' she said.

Belle laughed, and Laura blushed.

'That is a modest name,' replied Belle.

'Mercy, and nothing more?' asked Laura.

'Nothing,' said Rose.

She cleared her throat. She looked down. She would have been better left alone.

'I can see Mercy all in grey,' Belle sang dreamily.

For the future was a dream.

'You take Mercy, Rose, for a little,' suggested Laura, offering the parcel of her child.

'She is as well with you, miss,' said the woman, quite unmoved and positive.

'You are suited to each other,' she added.

It did, indeed, seem as though this grey-skinned woman were made of a different stuff.

So that Laura felt wrung.

'But if people should laugh at "Mercy",' she had to protest, 'could we not give her a second name? Mary, for instance?'

'Ah, people!' Rose replied.

Then Laura knew that she herself must suffer any derision or opprobrium.

During this intercourse Belle was to some extent mollified by discovering Mercy to be the most amusing creature.

'A whole chain of dreadful bubbles! Give her to me, Lolly,' she insisted.

'Then if Mercy it must be, I will speak to my uncle, and ask him to arrange with Mr Plumpton,' Laura said. 'There is no reason why the christening should not take place at once.'

'Thank you, miss,' said Rose.

So it was arranged.

But the morning that Mercy was dressed for the font, they began to suspect that her mother had overslept, and on going at last to rouse her maid, Laura Trevelyan discovered that she was gone.

Rose Portion had turned aside her face. The watery blood had stained the pillow, her leather tongue was already stiff, in fact, this poor animal had suffered her last indignity, with the result that the girl who had arrived breathless, blooming with expectation and the roses she had pinned at her throat, was herself turned yellow by the hot wind of death. She was chafing her arms for some time beside the bed. She was gulping uglily, and touching the poor, living hair of the dead woman, her friend and servant.

The christening of Mercy was, very properly, postponed. Instead, her mother was buried at the Sand Hills after a day or two had elapsed, and to that burying-ground the Bonners drove, in the family carriage and a hired fly, for there was the grateful Mr Plumpton to be considered, and Cassie, who was remembering Ireland, and Edith, the young girl, her red knuckles stuffed for the occasion into a first pair of gloves. The mourners smelled of fresh crêpe, supplied by the George Street store, and of the refreshment with which some of the weaker had fortified themselves. These sad smells were soon straying amongst those of baked ivy and thirsty privet at the cemetery gates, where there was an urn, besides, in which someone had left half a dozen apples to rot. The poor, sandy soil soon provided most difficult going, especially for the women, whose heels sank, and whose skirts dragged dreadfully. There were times when it seemed to the ordinarily unimpeded Belle that they were making hardly any progress; nor could the merchant help but suspect, while holding up his distressed wife, that the sun was burning a hole in his back. As for Mrs Bonner, she did suffer a good deal, less in sorrow for her dead servant, than from the presence, the very weight of Death, for while she had been struggling up the crumbly slope, recalling the different illnesses that had carried off her relatives and friends, He had mounted pick-a-back, and there He rode, regardless of a lady's feelings.

Rather an isolated part of the cemetery had been chosen for the grave of Rose Portion, the emancipist servant, but, of course, as the conciliatory Mr Plumpton pointed out, the whole ground would in time be opened up. So they straggled on towards the mound, and a tree from which wind or insects had torn the foliage, leaving its essential form, or bones.

Now, when the party stood before the grave, and sun and wind were fighting for possession of the black clothes, it was Laura Trevelyan who saw clearest. The bright new box tossed and bumped as they lowered it. Then there was a thump and a spurt of sand, to reply to such human life as persisted in its arrogance. The girl who was watching flung aside the bitter hair that was blowing across her mouth. The terrible body of the dead woman, with its steady nostrils and its carved hands, was altogether resigned, she saw again, through the intervening lid. But what of her own expectant soul, or tender roseflesh of the child? Each grain of merciless sand suggested to the girl that her days of joy had been, in a sense, illusory.

While the thin young clergyman was strewing words, great clouds the colour of bruises were being rolled across the sky from the direction of the ocean. There was such a swirling and whirling that the earth itself pulled loose, all was moving, and the mourners lowered their heads, and braced their feeble legs to prevent themselves from being sent spinning.

Only Laura Trevelyan appeared to stand motionless upon a little hummock.

Laura is so cold, Aunt Emmy lamented. She shivered inside her hot dress, and tried desperately to cling to some comfort of the parson's words.

But Laura was calm rather than cold, as, all around her, the mourners surrendered up their faces to the fear of anonymity, and above, the clouds were loading lead to aim at men. After the first shock of discovery, it had been exhilarating to know that terrestrial safety is not assured, and that solid earth does eventually swirl beneath the feet. Then, when the wind had cut the last shred of flesh from the girl's bones, and was whistling in the little cage that remained, she began even to experience a shrill happiness, to sing the wounds her flesh would never suffer. Yet, such was their weakness, her bones continued to crave earthly love, to hold his skull against the hollow where her heart had been. It appeared that pure happiness must await the final crumbling, when love would enter into love, becoming an endlessness, blowing at last, indivisible, indistinguishable, over the brown earth.

'We can do no more for Rose,' Mr Bonner was saying; otherwise everyone might have continued to stand.

When she had resumed her body, and noticed the little mound that they had made for her friend, the clods of earth accused Laura's exaltation, and she went away quickly after the others, holding her clumsy skirt.

As soon as they reached the vehicles, the ladies and the servants climbed inside. They were congratulating one another with elaborate relief that the threatening storm had not burst. But they looked nowhere in particular, certainly not at one another, for the skin of their cheeks had dried, and was feeling too tight. As Jim Prentice and the man from the livery stable were gathering up the reins, Mr Bonner led the parson behind the carriage to pay his fee. Hungry Mr Plumpton, whose name did not fit his form, had been standing there for some other purpose, he would have liked it to appear, but did also have to eat. Mr Bonner rewarded him substantially, for he was only too relieved to escape. And the young parson became gay. The shadow of death was lifted, and all were smelling the sea breeze and the good chaff which the horses had beslavered in their nosebags.

Life resumes possession thus simply. Mr Bonner was again stalking in the midst of his smoothly ordered women, in his impregnable stone house. Laura Trevelyan's baby grew. She washed it, and powdered it, and wrapped it up tight, but with that humility which lately she had learnt, or rediscovered, for humility is short-lived, and must be born again in anguish.

Similar phases mark the cycle of love. Could I forget my own husband? Laura asked, as she nursed the baby that was playing with her chin. Yet, she did forget, frequently for whole days, and then was conscience-stricken. As one takes one's own face for granted, so it was, at least she hoped, staring at her reflection in the glass. He is never farther removed, she said, looking at her own, woman's face. Moreover, there was the baby, that visible token of the love with which she was filled. So a mother will persuade herself.

One evening after she had put her baby in its cot, and deceived it into sleeping, she had gone down and found her uncle talking to a stranger in the hall.

Mr Bonner was saying:

'Then, if you call on Thursday, I will have the letter written.'

Noticing his niece, he mentioned:

'This is Mr Bagot, Laura. He leaves on Friday for Moreton Bay, and will find a means of sending a letter through to Jildra. I shall, of course, take this opportunity of communicating with the expedition. One never knows but that Voss may see his way to get in touch with Mr Boyle.'

Soon afterwards, the otherwise unimportant stranger left the house.

'It would only be civil,' Laura ventured, 'if I, too, were to send a line.'

'Nothing is lost by civility,' her uncle agreed, absently. 'But is it necessary in this case?'

'My dear Uncle, a great deal that is unnecessary is also nice. You are not nourished by your glass of rum and water, but I am glad to think you can enjoy it.'

'Eh?' said Mr Bonner. 'That is beside the point. But write, Laura, by all means, if it will give you pleasure.'

He was preoccupied.

'Thank you, Uncle dear,' Laura laughed, and kissed him. 'To give pleasure to Mr Voss was my intention.'

She went away then, refreshed by her inspired deception.

In the few days that remained till Thursday, Laura Trevelyan composed several tender, humorous, clever, even perfect letters, as she went about, or sat and watched the hem of her skirt. Soon, she said, I shall write it down, and then the last evening was upon her, and all the clumsiness of words.

She sat at her little desk, which had, in fact, been built for a child, in bird's-eye maple, an uncle's present for a fifteenth birthday. She took her pen from out of the conglomeration of writing tools, most of which she never used. She dropped the ink eraser. Seated before her exercise, she was both stiff and childish, sullen almost. She felt that she would bungle this, but did begin in that Italian hand, which was, mercifully, her automatic writing:

> Potts Point,
> – March, 1846

Dear Johann Ulrich Voss,

      If I address you by so many names, it is because I do not dare confess to my favourite, for my choice might indicate some weakness that you have not already suspected. You will find, I fear, that I am all *weaknesses,* when I would like you to admire me for my *strength! . . .*

Now her blood began to flow. Her shoulders were the wings of birds. Her mind was a bower-bird, greedy for the shells and coloured glass that would transform the drab and ordinary.

How I wish my sentiments were worthy of communication, and, not content with *one* gift, I would ask for the *genius* to express them. Then I would dazzle you with the glitter of diamonds, although I am inclined to believe I would adopt something less precious, but more mysterious; moonstone, I think, would be my stone. . . .

Was she being affected? She thought perhaps she was, but enjoyed the opportunity. She loved the shape of words, and taste, even of the acid drops.

I imagine how you must frown at the frivolousness of this letter, but now that I have begun, I cannot deny myself the luxury of writing as it comes, almost with recklessness, to one who knows me scarcely at all, yet (and this is what is awful) who has complete possession of the most secret part of me. You have taken the important, essential core of the apple, including (one must not forget) the nasty pips, and *scales* (I do not know what you call those little things) which must be spat out.

There it is! I hope you will continue to think kindly of me, dearest Ulrich (I have now confessed that, too!), and cherish the blemishes on my character.

I will tell you more truths. I have thought about you, and thought about you, until recently I found, to my honest disgust, that you were no longer uppermost in my mind. This disconcerting discovery was turned to advantage, however, on my realizing that you had become a necessary part of me. I do truthfully believe that you are always lurking somewhere on the fringes of my dreams, though I seldom see your face, and cannot even distinguish your form. I only know it is you, *I know,* just as I have sat beside you beneath certain trees, although I could not describe their shape, nor recite their Latin names. I have touched their bark, however.

Oh dear, if I could but describe in simple words the immensity of simple knowledge.

We are close to each other, my dearest, and shall strengthen each other. Better than that I cannot do.

I must tell you of something pathetic that occurred lately, and which has affected us all. You may remember a woman called Rose Portion, an emancipist servant, employed here in my uncle's house. Rose recently had a child, by whom, I cannot bring myself to say, but a pretty little girl called Mercy. On Rose's dying a few weeks after giving birth to her baby, never having recovered, we are now positive, from the ministrations of an ignorant and rapacious midwife, I took this child, and am caring for her as if she were my own. Together with yourself, she is my greatest joy. Can you understand, dear Ulrich? She is my consolation, my token of love.

If I continue to dwell unduly upon the death of Rose, it is because of the great impression it left upon me, the morning I found her lying in her bed, and again, at the funeral. We buried her at the Sand Hills on an indescribable day, of heat, and cloud, and wind. As I stood there (I hesitate to write you all this, except that it is the truth), as I stood, the material part of myself became quite superfluous, while my understanding seemed to enter into wind, earth, the ocean beyond, even the soul of our poor, dead maid. I was nowhere and everywhere at once. I was destroyed, yet living more intensely than actual sunlight, so that I no longer feared the face of Death as I had found it on the pillow. If I suffered, it was to understand the devotion and suffering of Rose, to love whom had always been an effort!

Finally, I believe I have begun to understand this great country, which we have been presumptuous enough to call *ours,* and with which I shall be content to grow since the day we buried Rose. For part of me has now gone into it. Do you know that a country does not develop through the prosperity of a few landowners and merchants, but out of the suffering of the humble? I could now lay my head on the ugliest rock in the land and feel at rest.

My dear Ulrich, I am not really so proud as to claim to be humble, although I do attempt, continually, to humble myself. Do you also? I understand you are entitled, as a man, to a greater share of pride, but would like to see you humbled. Otherwise, I am afraid for you. *Two cannot share one throne.* Even I would not wash your feet if I might wash His. Of that I am now certain, however great my need of you may be. Let us understand this, and serve *together.*

How many people pass over that word, I wonder, and take it for granted. I will tell you something. In my foolishness I had made up my mind to work it in wool, for what purpose I had not decided, but to embroider it in some way for my own pleasure. First, I sketched the design on paper, and had actually begun in a variety of coloured wools: blue for distance, brown for the earth, crimson, why, I cannot say, except that I am obsessed by that colour. However, as I worked, the letters were soon blazing at me with such intensity that the most witless person alive must have understood their significance. So I put the work away, and now it is smouldering in the darkness of a cupboard.

My dearest, at this distance, what can I do to soften your sufferings, but love you truly. Now that you have left behind the rich and hospitable country you have described, probably for some heartless desert, I pray that you are not filled with doubts. The moments of severest trial are surely the obscure details of a design that will be made clear at last – if we can endure till then, and for that purpose are we given to one another.

Although my own happiness is *incomplete,* we continue here in a state of undisturbed small pleasures: picnics; morning calls (which you so despise, I seem to remember); a Mr McWhirter gave a lecture on the *Wonders of India* at the School of Arts at which my Aunt E. slept and toppled over. My Cousin Belle Bonner will dance her feet right off before she marries Lieut. Radclyffe. That event, for which we are already busily preparing, should take place in the early spring. There is every indication that Belle will reap all the rewards for her sweetness and beauty. I do hope so, for I love her dearly. Mr Radclyffe is resigning his commission, and they plan to settle on some land he has taken up in the Hunter Valley, at no great distance, I understand, from your friends the Sandersons.

Now, dear, I can only pray that this will reach you, which I must finish without further ado, as my Uncle is calling from below and Mr Bagot (our messenger to Moreton Bay) is impatient to leave.

I thank you for your kindness, and your thoughts, and await most anxiously the letter I know you will hasten to send me at the first opportunity for doing so.

Ever your sincere
LAURA TREVELYAN

'Laura!' they were calling. 'Laura! Mr Bagot cannot wait.'

'I am coming,' cried Laura's dry voice, which rattled the window-panes, 'in one minute.'

But she had to read first.

Then she was appalled.

'Oh,' she protested, 'I am not as bad as all this.'

As she blistered her fingers on the sealing-wax.

Immediately, her childishness, prolixity, immodesty, blasphemy, and affectations were intensified. They were opened up like wounds at which she would be for ever probing.

'Laura!'

Yet, at the time, I was sincere, she persisted, from the depths of her disillusion.

Her own opinion did not console, however, and she went from her room, carrying in her hands extinguished fire.

10

SEVERAL of the mules had disappeared. Unlike such major disasters as the theft of the cattle on Christmas Eve, and the quiet death of the first sheep, with its neck outstretched along the ground, the latest incident was passed over lightly by the members of the expedition. Riding on towards the west, they were, naturally, the lighter for each loss, and so, must gain more easily on that future which remained a dusty golden to each pair of eyes.

They rode, and they came eventually to a ridge of abrupt hills, dappled and dancing with quartz, at the foot of which some black women were digging with their sticks for yams. Such meetings had come to be accepted by all. The blacks squatted on their haunches, and stared up at the men that were passing, of whom they had heard, or whom they had even seen before. Once, the women would have run screaming. Now they scratched their long breasts, and squinted from under their bat's-skin hands. Unafraid of bark or mud, they examined these caked and matted men, whose smell issued less from their glands than from the dust they were wearing, and whose eyes were dried pools. As for the men, obsessed by their dream of distance and the future, they glanced at the women as they would into crevices in hot, black rock, and rode on.

By some process of chemical choice, the cavalcade had resolved itself into immutable component parts. No one denied that Mr Voss was the first, the burning element, that consumed obstacles, as well as indifference in others. All round the leader ranged the native boy, like quicksilver, if he had not been bronze. Jackie was always killing things, or scenting a water-hole, or seeing smoke in the distance, or just shambling off on his horse and standing on the fringes of liberty.

Some way behind the advance party would come the spare horses and the pack-mules driven by Le Mesurier and Palfreyman. These two exchanged all manner of kindnesses and sympathy, but not their thoughts. Palfreyman was not sure which god Le Mesurier worshipped. Le Mesurier would address Palfreyman very distinctly, and smile encouragingly out of his dark lips, as if the ornithologist had been a foreigner. Well, he was, too, in that he was another man. Grown paler beneath the scales of salt, Palfreyman was sad, who would have melted with other men in love. Whenever he failed, he would blame himself, for he was by now persuaded of his inability to communicate, a shortcoming that made him more miserable, in that the salvation of others could have depended on him.

Sometimes Palfreyman would leave Le Mesurier to bring on their mob of mules and horses, and ride ahead with the apparent intention of joining Voss. Then, keeping a discreet distance, he would wait for his leader to call him forward. But the German would not. He despised the ornithologist, for obvious reasons, which Palfreyman himself knew. Of rather delicate constitution, failures of this nature, together with the pains of prolonged travel, would often cause the latter to suffer tortures. So he would force upon himself all kinds of menial tasks, as penance for his disgraceful weakness. He would scour the fat from their cooking utensils with handfuls of the dry, powdery earth; he would strain the scum from any water they found; he even treated Turner, who had broken out in boils, presenting an appearance of the most abject human misery.

All this the ornithologist taught himself to endure, and the voice of Voss saying:

'Mr Palfreyman, in his capacity of Jesus Christ, lances the boils.'

Mercifully, such incidents could occur only at their resting-places, dubious oases in the shimmering plain of motion. For the most part, personal feelings were numbed by the action of the animals that carried the party on.

Behind the spare horses and the pack-mules would stumble the few skeletons of cattle, with Judd in attendance, and Harry Robarts. The convict could coax a flagging beast most marvellously. These shocking steers and one or two udderless cows would have laid down long ago, if little reflections of the man's will had not continued to flicker in their fixed eyes. As from his cattle, the beef had dwindled from the man, but he was still large, because big-boned. Heavy, too, he would change horse frequently, to rest the back of the one he had been riding. If his frame appeared to have suffered less than that of any other human member of the expedition, undoubtedly this was because his earlier life had tempered it. His mind, moreover, had returned to his good body, and was now in firm possession, devoted to all those objects on which the party was dependent, as well as to the animals in his charge.

Judd remained, besides, intensely interested in natural forms. For instance, he would pick at the black fruit of trees to release the seed; with the rough skin of his hand, he would rub a hot, white bone, whether of man or animal, as if to re-create its flesh; he would trace with the toe of his boot a footprint in the dust to learn its shape and mission. Afterwards, he would climb back upon his horse, and sit there looking indestructible. Seldom did the action of the sun reduce him to dreams of the future. Judd, it would sometimes appear, was himself an element.

Once Voss and Jackie had discovered in some trees a platform of leafy saplings fastened together with strips of bark. They were still examining it when Judd and Harry caught them up.

'These dead men,' the native boy explained, and it was gathered that his people laid their dead upon such platforms, and would leave them there for the spirits to depart.

'All go,' said the blackfellow. 'All.'

As he placed his hands together, in the shape of a pointed seed, against his own breast, and opened them skyward with a great whooshing of explanation, so that the silky, white soul did actually escape, and lose itself in the whirling circles of the blue sky, his smile was radiant.

Those who had heard and witnessed were thoughtful as they rode on. It was easy in that landscape to encourage thoughts of death.

But the thick Judd, whose own soul had achieved fulfilment not by escaping from his body, but by returning to it, preferred to interpret the aboriginal illusion in terms of life. He who was wedded to earthly things would often invoke them as he rode along, and so, on the day they began to climb those quartz hills, he was thinking of his wife, who smelled of bread and soap, and who had the mole beside her nose, with the three little hairs sprouting from it. This he now saw with wonder, and much more from the years they had lived together, before he woke. Yet, he had got life in his sleep. His sons were evidence enough of that. Golden-skinned, they galloped the horses bareback down to water, and folded sheep at smoky dusk, and cut the lambs' tails in season, with the blood spurting in little fountains into their laughing mouths. Suddenly his ribs were aching, and the welts of old punishment. The cat of love smote him in the hands of his great sons.

In his craving for earthly love, Judd struck the stirrup-iron of Harry Robarts rather roughly with his own, and bruised Harry's knee with his, for they were riding side by side.

'Move over, son,' the man complained. 'You are riding that close we will be joined for ever at the stirrup-irons.'

The boy lowered his eyes, and removed himself.

'It was not a-purpose,' he sulked.

'Whichever way, it is not safe,' said Judd.

He had developed an affection for the sawney boy. It was out of pity, so he explained it, and in camp would cut for him choicer bits of starved mutton, or dried beef, and put them on the lad's plate, and go away. Formed by circumstances, their relationship remained upon the whole respectful, although the boy was inclined to accept it for want of a better, and the man, often impatient, was sometimes even contemptuous of his mate.

Now, as they rode together, it appeared that the boy was still thinking of the tree-platform recently discovered, and of the migration of aboriginal souls, for he murmured tentatively, dreamily:

'Did you notice it go, Mr Judd, when Jackie opened his hands?'

'Notice what?' asked the man.

'It was a white bird, like, very quick.'

'Now, you have been seeing things,' said the man.

The boy sniggered, and slapped at his horse's withers with the bundle of reins.

'Did you not see?' he persisted.

'*Naó!*' said the man.

Then a steer stumbled, and fell, and they pushed and kicked

it to its feet again. When it was walking, Judd resumed their conversation.

'You had better tell Mr Voss of this here experience of yours, Harry, with birds. It would interest him.'

For, if wax has to be wax, then it is difficult to resist a squeeze, and Judd was only human.

'Not Mr Voss,' said Harry. 'Not on your life.'

'Mr Voss would understand such things,' smiled Judd.

'That is why I would not tell him.'

'Or he would take it out on yer for ever.'

'Yes,' Harry replied.

It was obvious that all possibilities were contained for him in the single form of Voss.

Judd had become as silent as a piece of leather. He would have liked to give the boy a present, and remembered a magnifying-glass with ebony handle that he had kept for years, in a shammy leather bag, in a box.

They were riding and drowsing in perpetual dust, and stumbling on the rocky sides of the hills they were ascending, when Judd reached over and grabbed something from the trunk of a tree.

'There you are, Harry,' he said, and offered his closed, hairy hand. 'There is a present for yer.'

In the absence of ebony he was forced to such measures.

'What is it?' asked the boy, advancing his own hand, but cautiously.

'No,' laughed Judd, blushing under dirt. 'Open your mouth, shut your eyes.'

Then, when his suggestion had been followed, he popped a little lump of gum into the lad's open mouth.

'Aoh!' cried Harry, wrinkling up.

'No,' insisted Judd. 'Go on.'

He was putting into his own mouth a similar knot of gum, to demonstrate his faith in the token, or else they would both die of it.

So they rode, and sucked the gum, which was almost quite insipid in flavour, if slightly bitter. Yet, they were both to some extent soothed and united by its substance and their act, and were prodding the rumps of the broken cattle gently with their toes, as they rode back and forth in their oblique ascent of the glaring hill, until the boy glanced up, and there was Voss, looking not at him, but forward into the distance from a crag.

As the lad stared at his leader, the sun's rays striking the surrounding rocks gave the impression that the German was at the point of splintering into light. There he sat, errant, immaculate, but ephemeral, if he had not been supernal.

'We will never get that far,' muttered the gloomy Harry Robarts.

'He would not want you to,' said Judd.

But the boy would have jumped from his horse, and torn his knees open on the rock. As it was, aware of some disloyalty to his leader, he spat out the remains of the bitter, and now offensive gum.

'I will stick closer than anyone, in the end,' said Harry. 'I will sit under the platform. I will learn languages.'

'That is mad talk,' protested Judd.

Both were uneasy over what had been said, because either it could have been the truth, or only half of it, and which was worse it was difficult to tell.

'Mad,' repeated Judd, hitting his horse with the hard, dirty flat of his hand. 'First birds, and now languages. What languages will you learn, Harry? German?' He had to laugh.

'It does not matter; German or any other. I will learn to speak what Mr Voss will understand, and tell what I have inside of me.'

'What purpose will it serve?' asked Judd, looking at the closed rock.

He had grown gloomy.

'Some people can write it down,' continued the boy. 'But I cannot write no more than speak. Not like Mr Le Mesurier. He has written it. I seen the book.'

'Oh?' said Judd. 'What has he written?'

'How do I know?' cried the exasperated Harry. 'If I cannot read but big print.'

So that man and boy were plunging heavily on identical horses amongst the rocks.

'He is keeping a journal,' the man decided, finally. 'Like Mr Voss.'

'It is not that,' said the boy. 'He has a different look. I have watched him writing it.'

'Then we will see, I expect, some day,' sighed the man.

'Not us,' sneered the boy. 'These here deserts will see it, the pages blowing about, till the sun has burnt 'em. We will not be here.'

'I will not die. Though I may not know enough to read,' said the man through his blunt teeth.

'We will all die.'

'You are mad, Harry!' cried Judd.

'I know as I am somewhat simple,' confessed the boy, 'and cannot put things good.'

He had even forgotten Voss, who, when he looked again, was gone over the other side, and in his place were the swords of the sun, slashing at the quartz, and with less spectacular effect at a long, soft cloud of celestial wool, such as the men would not have imagined after looking so long at the dirty stuff on their own sheeps' wretched backs. However, the cloud itself grew dirtier with the afternoon, and was increasing, and changing uglily.

Towards evening, men, horses, mules, and cattle had crossed the ridge, and were gathered at a point where a gully, descending upon a plain, joined the dry bed of a river.

'Sure enough it will rain,' said the men, whose eyes were already shining with moisture, and lips filling, while horses whinnied painfully, and blunt noses of cattle were snuffing.

In hopes that the river would be restored, it was thought to camp there where they were, and to beat a retreat if necessary to higher ground.

'There are still the sheep, though,' remembered Palfreyman.

Then, with his arm, Voss flung away the sheep.

'We must abandon these,' he frowned. 'They do not keep up. They are costly in time.'

Because rain must fall at the expense of time, he frowned even at the clouds which would soon revive his own skin.

'Given feed and water, the sheep will travel faster,' Judd submitted.

'No,' said Voss. 'No. There are too few. It is not worth it.'

A flash of green lightning cut the brown air.

'All sheep must be sacrificed,' shouted the German against the thunder, and inhaled until it began to appear he might burst. Then he added, more practically: 'There is nothing to prevent Ralph and Turner from killing a couple for our own use. We will dry the mutton and carry it on.'

The hills were jumbling and rocking.

'Somebody must inform Ralph,' the German continued to shout, of necessity, at those others who were unbuckling girths, unknotting knots, hobbling horses, or stretching pathetic squares of canvas, to cover their unwillingness to return across the ridge.

'Let me see,' reflected the Voss who was as exultant as the storm.

He was never so hateful as when identifying weakness, and now, in this brown storm, almost anybody could have been accused.

Then, strangely, he altered his approach.

'You, Frank, will better go,' he ordered Le Mesurier, but making it a conspiracy between themselves.

For he had already sensed, early in their association, that the young man was possessed of a gristly will, or daemon, not unlike his own. Now, smiling his approval, the German's lips were tinged with the green of lightning.

Le Mesurier, however, did not return the smile, but got upon his horse, which had remained saddled, in readiness, it seemed, and went.

From the beginning, the rider had to urge his horse. As the almost dislocated withers in front of him proceeded to toil back up the ridge, the mare's ears remained sad, her body had become a slab, or muleflesh, for horses do associate themselves with the more rational behaviour of men, mules with none. Through the irrational, brown dusk, premature by two hours, man and horse were moving. Clouds were now so close their weave was visible, bundles of ever dirtier stuff, that were swirling and fraying, even tearing in places on the rock summit. Rocks of thunder were rolling together, so that at times the man did duck his head to avoid collision with the approaching storm, and in doing so, the brim of his hat became more ridiculously ineffectual, beating on his eyelids, and causing him pain.

Then he dragged the hat off, and stuffed it into his saddle-bag. At once his matted hair began to stream out, and as the wind

248

encircled the pale, upper half of his forehead, he seemed to be relieved of some of the responsibility of human personality. The wind was filling his mouth and running down through the acceptant funnel of his throat, till he was completely possessed by it; his heart was thunder, and the jagged nerves of lightning were radiating from his own body.

But it was not until the farther side of the ridge, going down, and he was singing the storm up out of him, that the rain came, first with a few whips, then with the release of cold, grey light and solid water, and he was immersed in the mystery of it, he was dissolved, he was running into crannies, and sucked into the mouths of the earth, and disputed, and distributed, but again and again, for some purpose, was made one by the strength of a will not his own.

Angus and Turner, who had crawled under a rock ledge, which provided almost a small, uncomfortable cave at the foot of the hills, looked out as darkness fell, and saw Frank Le Mesurier descending the slope. They called, and he headed towards them, the mare carefully picking her way.

The faces of the troglodytes were shiny like their own rock, as their skins had become soaked before reaching shelter. To the messenger who had just descended through the cloud, they also looked repulsively human. Sheep were huddling in the deluge, in which some of them had lain down with the obvious intention never to rise. Against rocks and scrub, lean goats were flattening their sides. The goats were most shocked by the uncompromising rain.

Le Mesurier delivered his message without dismounting.

'Well, you had better hobble your nag, Frank, and come inside. It is good in here, and you will be one more to carry a supply of mutton in the morning.'

Thanks to their rock roof, and a handful of comparatively dry sticks, the drovers had even succeeded in starting a modest fire, and had begun to put away some stale damper and shreds of fibrous meat to the accompaniment of its sputtering. They were happy, their eyes suggested, but within human limits, so that Le Mesurier, who had been admitted to infinity at times, did not wish to enter their circle.

'No,' he said. 'I shall go straight back.'

'You are mad,' shouted Angus, who had learnt to cherish his own limitations as a sure proof of sanity.

'You will break your bally neck in the dark,' shrieked Turner, hoping to encourage that possibility by his warning.

Then the lightning leapt again. For a moment the green horseman looked down at the faces of the two human animals in their kennel of rocks. However, as wind and rain were stopping mouths, he did not open his, but turned his spindly horse. Nor did he know how to address those individuals into whose souls he saw most clearly; he was too startled by them.

The mare was whinging but hopeful as she started back through the teeth of rocks. The rider gave her her head, and trusted to her instinct. By this time he was rather sunken, as if he had been so firmly contained by his envelope, that he had failed to burst out and rise to the heights of the storm. And now Voss began to go with him, never far distant, taunting him for his failures, for his inability to split open rock, and discover the final secret. Frank, I will tell you, said his mentor, you are filled with the hallucinations of intellectual power : I could assist you perhaps, who enjoy the knowledge that comes with sovereignty over every province of illusion, that is to say, spiritual power; indeed, as you may have suspected, I am I am I am. . . .

But the young man had been submitted to such a tumult of the elements, and now, of his own emotions, he failed to catch the divine Word, only the roll of thunder departing upon the drums of wax. So he shook his numbed head, until his ears rattled.

Voss was grinning. The rider could see the mouth, for the rain had been folded away into the outer darkness. All around there was a sighing of wind, and a moon, the loveliest of all hallucinations, had slid into being. Its disc spun, and was buried, and recovered, cutting the mad, white hair of the clouds.

On the edge of the ridge, the mare paused for a while, and was swaying, and raising her head. Then she plunged down towards what, she knew, was certainty. But in that interval of rest upon the summit, Voss and the rider had touched hands, the same glint of decomposition and moonlight started from the sockets of their eyes and from their teeth, and their two souls were united in the face of inferior realities.

So like clings to like, and will be saved, or is damned.

Riding down the other side, the young man conceived a poem, in which the silky seed that fell in milky rain from the Moon was raised up by the Sun's laying his hands upon it. His flat hands, with their conspicuously swollen knuckles, were creative, it was proved, if one dared accept their blessing. One did dare, and at once it was seen that the world of fire and the world of ice were the same world of light; whereupon, for the first time in history, the third, and dark planet was illuminated.

As he let himself be carried down the shining hillside, that was shown to be strewn with snares of jet now that the moon was fully risen, Le Mesurier was shivering. He who had carried the sun for a moment in his breast was frozen in his own moonlight. His teeth were tumbling like lumps of sugar. Any hope of salvation was, ironically, an earthly one, a little smudge of light from a candle-end, from behind a skin of canvas, at the foot of the hill.

More ironically still, the light came from the tent of Voss, who was writing in his journal, like a methodical man. The others, on that night of rain and discomfort, had made an effort to overcome the darkness, but had fallen at once into a steamy sleep; they had not bothered even to sort out the bodies, and were bundled all hugger-mugger in the second tent.

'Is that you, Frank?' called Voss.

'Yes,' said Le Mesurier, addressing the luminous canvas.

'Did you give this message?' the German asked.

'Yes.'

'In what way will the sheep behave, when they are finally abandoned?' the light asked. 'Do you suppose they will be in any way aware, as they stand amongst those bushes? The silence, for one thing, will sound more intense as it penetrates the wool. Still, there will be water, and grass, and they will drink and graze before they lie down and die. It is, in any case, perfectly normal for sheep to die.'

'Yes.'

'And we shall enjoy the advantage of the mutton from those that Ralph and Turner kill. We shall dry the meat in the sun. If there is a sun. Do you suppose, Frank, that the weather will permit of drying the meat?'

But Le Mesurier had gone.

And Voss, the man who was left alone, continued after a while to write in his journal.

After hobbling his tired mare, Le Mesurier, the still-possessed, bundled into the second tent, in which the others were sleeping, their white bellies afloat upon the darkness, together with their dreams and snores. The young man, after dropping his wet and wrinkled rags, wrapped himself in a blanket, but continued to shiver. He was tortuously stooped in the low tent, as in a womb. When he had rummaged in his pack, and found a little candle-end – very precious – and the rather dented tinder-box, and the flame was at last trembling on the wick, he lay down, but still shivering and gritting his teeth, struggling in the grip of a fever, it would appear.

Watching through his eyelashes, Harry Robarts saw Mr Le Mesurier take out that book in which he wrote so frequently. As he tossed and shivered, he was at great pains to form the words, Harry observed. Or the man's dry mouth would suck at the air for some renewed sweetness of suffering. Until the boy, who shared the same transparent womb, longed to burst out into a life he did not know, but sensed. He was throbbing with excitement, while also afraid, as the teeth of the moon sawed away at the sodden canvas, as the slippery earth continued to heave, and the man to write in painful forms. At last Le Mesurier fell back with his head upon the saddle, and Harry Robarts watched the transparent fingers pinch the flame off the stinking wick.

Soon there was not a man awake on either side of those sharp hills, for Angus and Turner had quickly fallen into a stupor against their bit of a hissing fire.

Recently these two had become inseparable, if only through appreciation of each other's mediocrity. In consequence, neither could apprehend the nature of their relationship, and each was flattered by it. The seedy Turner, who could not see straight except by squinting, and then was crooked in his final vision, who was spewed up out of what stew nobody had ever heard, and who had begun lately to suffer from the suppurating boils, this Turner was in love with the rich young landowner, and could not let him go from his side without he felt the draught. Ralph Angus, who had been so glossy, whose whiskers in normal circumstances wore a gallant, reddish curl – he was, in fact, the colour of a chestnut horse — would have been amused at Turner's friendship if he had not become grateful for it. They could speak together, he had discovered, of little things. They would talk about the weather and the state of their stomachs, and end up feeling quite elevated by conversation. They would sigh like dogs, and enjoy the silences. If each had something to conceal, for Turner was possessed of cunning, and had been a pickpocket at times, and perhaps had even killed a man, while Angus had known the Palladian splendours — his godmother was the daughter of an earl, his nose had been wiped for him, and his father had grabbed several thousand colonial acres, by honest means — these running sores in their past lives had been mercifully healed by that nothingness to which their long journey had reduced the two friends.

On the night of rain when they had made themselves at home beneath the rock ledge, they were noticeably united, the splendid, glossy gentleman, who had by now acquired the colour and texture of a coconut, and the yellow reprobate, whose body was crying out through the mouths of his boils. After they had lit their little fire, of which the spitting alone was a comfort, they began to say kind things to each other.

'Here is a pinch of tea,' Turner said. 'You take your quart, Ralph, and brew for yerself. I have not got the stomach for even a hot cup of tea.'

'But you are eating,' Angus pointed out.

'By George, so I am. It is from habit, I assure you,' said Turner, crooking his finger a bit from proximity to the gentleman.

'Then you will drink from habit, too, idiot,' said Angus. 'Or I will pour it into the ground.'

'If you please, then,' said Turner, with genteel resignation.

The quart pot was soon sighing on the damp sticks. As the scum rose from the water, the men would knock it off. Each was seated tailorwise, sticking the fragments of food into his mouth, and staring far too intently at the pot, the alternative of which would have been his mate's face.

It was at this point and from this position that they had looked out and seen the horseman descending the hill.

What they had always suspected, the lightning at once made evident: that the rider was not of their own kind. Even before he was gone, each of the cave-dwellers was raging, and longing to communicate his rage. They were brought together closer than before. Each wondered what the other had seen, although neither would have dared to speculate on the nature of his vision. Thought is very disturbing when it lights up the mind by green flashes.

Some time after Le Mesurier had left, while Turner was still picking his teeth and digesting what he had eaten, he did remark:

'That is one I cannot cotton to, Ralph.'

The young landowner winced, and was loth to criticize a man who might possibly be considered a member of his own class.

'He is an odd sort of cove. He is different,' finally he replied.

'Not so different from some,' Turner said.

'What do you imply by that?' asked Angus, who did not care to become involved in any unpleasantness.

He was what you would call a pleasant fellow, no one had anything against him, and now he did a little repent of his rash friendship.

'Eh?' mumbled Turner, resentfully.

'What do you mean, then?'

'Voss is what I mean. And Le Mesurier.'

Angus tingled.

'In this expedition, which is what it is called,' Turner said, or whispered, rather, from habit, 'we are made up of oil and water, you might say, and will not run together, ever.'

The whites of the young grazier's eyes had remained very clear.

'I have every intention,' he said, 'of running together with Mr Voss, who is the leader of the expedition.'

'Oil and water,' Turner chanted.

The fire hissed.

'We understand each other, Ralph, you and me.'

The rich young landowner did sincerely yearn for understanding with his friend.

'As that is a quart pot, there is no mistake about it,' Turner assured him, and the black pot did look most convincing. 'But that there Le Mesurier' – how the speaker hated the name, and would roll it between his tongue and his palate, more often than not, as if to gather up a bad taste, and spit it out — 'that Le Me-*sur*-ier would keep a cove guessing for years. Then you would wake up one fine day, and find as the pot was not at all what you and me thought it to be.'

The grazier was fascinated by the pot.

'How so?'

He smiled to hide his intense interest.

'People of that kind will destroy what you and I know. It is a form of madness with them.'

The young landowner clucked with his tongue against his teeth. He was unhappy once more. A runnel of rainwater, besides, was trickling down his neck. He was for ever shifting.

'I know,' pursued Turner, 'because I have looked in the book.'

'What book?'

'Why, the book that Frank is always writing in.'

Angus was not aware that such a book existed, but pretended that he was. Thus he would conceal his ignorance of most things.

'If it is his private property,' he mumbled.

'Naow, naow, Ralph,' said Turner. 'What is that?'

The hair stood up on the back of the young man's neck. He avoided an answer.

'What was in this book?' he asked, unhappily.

'Mad things,' Turner replied, 'to blow the world up; anyhow, the world that you and me knows. Poems and things.'

'Poetry can be very enjoyable,' said Angus, who had memories of young ladies seated after dinner beside lamps.

'I do not deny that,' Turner hastened to agree; 'I am partial to a good read of it meself. But this was like, you might say, Ralph, like certain bits of the Bible. They are cut up, like, but to make trouble, not to make sense.'

As trouble was Turner's own particular province, his mouth was now watering, and his eyes shone.

'We have no right to make such comparisons, you know,' insisted Angus, whose doubts of his friend had grown great.

'Go on, Ralph,' said the latter. 'If a man don't assume his rights, nobody is going to give 'em to him.'

The young grazier looked out into the night, on which a moon had risen. Black wings were continually sweeping the surface of the silver plain. It was the wind hustling the clouds, of course.

But on several occasions during the journey, his own thoughts had developed a span that had carried them almost out of his control.

'This is what I think, Ralph,' Turner was saying, 'mind you, in confidence, seeing as how we are mates. I think that Le Mesurier will in the end turn out to be in league with Voss. It is the oil, see? And that barmy boy, why, Harry would not harm a fly, but oil, oil, see, he must go over, too.'

Ralph Angus tossed what had been his handsome head. So horses will discourage the March fly.

'I will not discuss Mr Voss,' he said. 'Besides, there is no question of *going over* to him. We are all *with* him.'

'Discuss Mr Voss?' spat Turner. 'You cannot discuss what is not. . . .'

His spittle appeared white-hot, as it curled and twisted on the embers of the lost fire.

'Do you believe in God, Ralph?' asked Turner.

'I should think there are very few individuals so miserable as not to,' answered the upright young man.

Turner might have been rehearsing such a situation all his life.

'I do not believe in God,' he said.

A water was dripping in the silver silence.

'Not in nothing that I cannot touch.'

He gave the quart an angry poke.

'Do you think as Voss was reading my thoughts when he set hisself up? But I was not deceived.'

'Are you not most unhappy?' asked Angus, whom the disclosure had shocked considerably.

'Oh, there is plenty of other things to believe in,' Turner cried, looking in anguish at his friend's face, which, however, avoided him.

'Without dependin' on God, who is the Devil, I would say, to have got us into a mess like this. There!' cried the angry man. 'That is what I think of Mr Bloomin' Voss!'

Young Ralph Angus was so shaken he felt he could no longer call upon his own considerable virility for support.

'Mr Palfreyman has faith,' he remembered, with the relief of a pious girl.

'Oh,' shrugged Turner, 'Mr Palfreyman is a good man.'

Consequently, he cancelled out.

The rocks in the moonlight were on the verge of bursting open, but failed.

'There is still Albert Judd,' murmured Turner, becoming dreamy. 'He is ours, Ralph. He will lead us out. He is a man.'

'I have every confidence in Judd,' Angus agreed, but shifted his position.

'Of course you have,' cried Turner. 'You only have to look at his hands.'

The young man, inside himself, in the most secret part of him, was disgusted. He could not have given himself into the hands of the convict. Something almost immodest was required of him.

Finally, he laughed it off, showing his immaculate, man's teeth.

'How we are talking through our hats!' he protested. 'I expect we are all become a bit mad by this.'

But Turner, whose mouth was stuck open, would have had to contradict his dreams. What remained of life was upon the lips, the slight, white rime of salt, which will also embitter dreams. He was snoring brokenly.

Then the young man realized the distance he had come from the Palladian façade and emerald turf into that desert country, and how he had sunk himself almost gratefully to the level of his sleeping companion. If he even sensed the existence of levels higher than that to which he had been born, he was left to wrinkle his forehead at them. So he drowsed, and wondered. And looked quickly at the sleeping Turner. He would have condemned his friend for his own thoughts. For just then Ralph Angus had been seated, rather, at the convict's side, and together they were mending hobble-chains. The jingly chains were delightful as a childhood game. The convict could do many simple, but fascinating things: he knew tricks, and rhymes, and could take a wart off by magic. Then the young man, who had by this time crossed right over, from the outside, into the circle of sleep, watched the hands take the rope, and lasso the chestnut horse. He had learnt it at Moreton Bay, Judd explained; while the horse fought back with all his strength, the vein bursting from his glossy neck.

*

The morning that followed the storm was set in a splendour of enamels. The two stiff men were practically strutting as they performed their early ritual. Afterwards they killed two of the more respectable sheep, or rather, Angus did, while Turner offered advice in such a way that it did seem as if he were taking part in the operation. This accomplishment he had acquired while employed as a labourer at Sydney.

Once the sheep had been dressed and cut up into convenient quarters, they loaded their horses as best they could, and prepared to carry the meat across the hills, to be dried at the main camp.

The weather and the prospect of comparative comfort had rendered Turner quite merry. As he rounded up the already skipping goats, which, it was presumed, would continue to accompany the expedition, as they had received no order to abandon them, he was belabouring his horse's rump with his hand, and singing:

> 'A-jew, a-jew kind sheep,
> The fatal hour has come. . . .'

'Poor beggars,' he added, 'how glad I am to see the last of 'em.'
And settled himself in the saddle for the ascent.

As they slowly climbed, driving their small herd of goats, Ralph Angus looked back at the brown sheep standing in the plain, but turned at once, for he did not care to show any concern over what must be considered a commodity rather than an animal. Although this young fellow was possessed of great decency, naturally there were limits to what he was permitted to reveal.

Nothing untoward occurred during the short journey, except that the two horsemen were soon caught in a black net of flies that had fallen upon the meat dangling from their saddles. This caused Turner to curse and kick, and his nag in consequence to sidle and pigroot. Each provoked the other to worse.

'By cripes,' the man screamed at the horse, 'one or other of us will break his neck, and both of us is fly-blown; I can feel the maggots strolling on me skin. Ralph, can you not feel 'em?'

Ralph made a face. As steam had begun to rise from the sodden earth, and the mind was already languishing, he decided it was unnecessary to reply to his friend. Besides, one of the advantages of such a friendship lay in the freedom to choose silence. Animals do not discuss. So the two men toiled on, each accepting the other's shortcomings in gratitude for the continued enjoyment of his own. Small figures on the same mountain, they were more alike than not.

When finally the party descended into the camp, it was found that Voss, Palfreyman, and the native boy were absent on some mission of a scientific nature, it was not specified what, and that Judd was unofficially in charge. The convict decided at once to cut the mutton into strips, and to light a fire, both to hasten the curing of their meat with smoke and to keep the flies away in the process. All of this he accomplished himself, for the others were not interested. Or else they had put themselves in his hands.

There was an air of peace at that camp, since rain had drowned many doubts. Thick, turbulent, yellow water was now flowing in the river bed. Green, too, was growing in intensity, as the spears of grass massed distinctly in the foreground, and a great, indeterminate green mist rolled up out of the distance. Added to the gurgle of water were the thousand pricking sounds of moist earth, the sound of cud in swollen cheeks of cattle, and sighs of ravaged horseflesh that looked at last fed and knowing. There was the good scent of rich, recent, greenish dung. Over all this scene, which was more a shimmer than the architecture of landscape, palpitated extraordinary butterflies. Nothing had been seen yet to compare with their colours, opening and closing, opening and closing. Indeed, by the addition of this pair of hinges, the world of semblance communicated with the world of dream.

However, the moment Judd pronounced the mutton sufficiently preserved by the combined action of smoke and sun, Voss decided they must strike camp the following morning, although there was not a man amongst them who would not have preferred to lie longer on his back and contemplate the scene. As for the German himself, he had been rejuvenated by the rain, and was making little jokes of a laborious nature. During the days of gathering green and kinder light, Laura had prevailed upon him to the extent that he had taken human form, at least temporarily.

Like the now satisfied earth, he was at last enjoying the rewards of wedlock. His face was even fat.

It happened on the eve of their departure from the camp beside the river that Voss and Palfreyman were seated in the brigalow shade much occupied with specimens they had taken. Palfreyman with the skins of a collection of birds, Voss with some of those butterflies which would shatter the monochrome by opening in it. Even dead, the butterflies were joyful.

'Tell me, Mr Palfreyman,' Voss asked, 'tell me, as a Christian, was your faith sufficient to survive until paradise was reached?'

'I am a poor sort of Christian,' replied Palfreyman, who was handling a small bird of a restrained colour. 'Besides,' he added, 'paradise may well prove to be mirage.'

'Admittedly,' laughed Voss, because it was a gay day. 'I myself am *skeptisch*,' he said, waving his hand to embrace both the present landscape and his mosaic of dead butterflies, 'although I confess to be fascinated by delusions, and by those who allow themselves to be convinced. But you, it appears, are not convinced.'

He said this quite kindly.

'I am convinced,' Palfreyman replied at last. 'I believe, although there is a great deal I take on trust, until it is proved at the end. That it will be proved, I know.'

'That is indeed faith,' said Voss, again not unkindly, because the green plain had laid its mantle on him.

'So my wife speaks,' he added, from a distance.

'Then you have a wife?' asked Palfreyman, looking up.

'No, no!' protested Voss, with apparent amusement. 'If she would exist!' He laughed. 'Such are the pitfalls of grammar. I acquire a wife by simple misuse of a tense.'

Palfreyman suspected this simplicity, while knowing grammatical error to be a source of great amusement to the German.

The latter now asked:

'And you, Palfreyman, have no wife?'

'No,' the ornithologist confessed.

'Not even a grammatical one,' his companion murmured.

This was a statement rather than a question. His mirth had obviously subsided, that laughter rickety in structure which belied the well-founded voice. People would remember the German's voice, whereas they were briefly, nervously haunted by his laughter.

Palfreyman also had exhausted a mood, it appeared, and was putting his work away, packing specimens and implements into the battered wooden cases. His celibacy was suddenly a miserable affair, that once had seemed dedicated.

'No wives,' he said, fastening a case firmly with a sharp, brass hook. 'When I am at home, I live usually with my uncle, a Hampshire clergyman, for whom my sister keeps house.'

Here Palfreyman paused in telling, and Voss, in spite of his natural inquisitiveness, hesitated to encourage more. Each man realized how little he knew of the other, for each had respected his companion's privacy out of jealousy for his own. Besides, the country had absorbed them to a great extent, and now, in the deepening shade of evening, on the edge of the brigalow scrub, they were diffident of confessing to their own lives.

Palfreyman, however, since he had dared a little, was being sucked back by the dreadful undercurrent of the past. As he could no longer hope for rescue, he continued.

'My uncle's vicarage would astonish any stranger expecting to find a house given up to normal human needs. Nor does this vicarage truly suggest the home of an inadequately rewarded, but devoted servant of God. Certainly it is noticeable for the advanced dilapidation of its grey stone, that the vines are open- ing up, or holding together, it is difficult to say which, but there are signs that the decay is not so much unavoidable as unheeded. If the roof should fall, as it well might, the neighbourhood would be roused by the most terrible shattering of glass, for the rooms are filled with glass objects, in a variety of colours, very fine and musical, or chunks with bubbles in them, and bells con- taining shells or wax flowers, to say nothing of the cases of humming birds. You see, my uncle, although a clergyman by name and intention, inherited a small fortune from a distant cousin. Some say that it was his downfall, because he could afford to be forgetful, but my sister, who is poor and dependent, suffers from the same disease – as well as from her infirmity, of which I will tell you.'

The narrator's life, it seemed, was so cluttered up, he could not easily make his way between the objects of threatened glass.

'My sister spends little enough time in the house, and probably could not remember in any detail the contents of its rooms. Dust would head her attempted list, I expect. I do not doubt her acquaintances are surprised that anyone so neat and clean, of dress and person, should be able to endure the ubiquitous dust. Moreover, thanks to my uncle's comfortable means, she enjoys the services of two maids. What her critics fail to remember is that she constantly omits to give orders to her easy-going maids, in her great hurry to rush outside, into the garden, or the woods. My sister is particularly fond of woodland and hedgerow flowers: violets, primroses, anemones, and such-like. She will venture out in the roughest weather, in an old grey cloak, to see her flowers, and will often return with an armful of the common cow-parsley that she has been unable to resist, or a string of scarlet bryony to wear round her neck.

'As my uncle's tastes are similar – he is always bringing in mosses to dry, and plants to press – the parish suffers the most shocking neglect. But the sheep remain fond of their shepherds, and will go to great lengths to protect them. I have noticed that if a man is afflicted with what one might call an honest weakness, people do tolerate that fault, and will love its victim, not in spite of, but because of it. Then, there is my sister's infirmity.'

This sat upon the brother also, the German saw.

'My sister is several years older than I. She is become rather frail, although she continues to drive herself with her astonishing will. She is a very passionate woman. She will smash things deliberately, and cry over them afterwards, and try to fit the pieces together. Some of those glass ornaments of which I spoke. Once, when I was a boy, she flew into a rage, and threw me out of an upper window. It happened like this. On hearing a suspicious silence, I had crept into the room, and found my sister at her looking-glass. She had outlined her lips completely in red ink, giving them the arch of a perfect, but horrifying mouth. I was very frightened, which impressed itself upon her the moment she noticed me, and she immediately rushed, in her passion, and pushed me through the open window. Then, when I lay upon the ground below, calling breathlessly that I had broken my back, she raced down, screaming that she had killed me, or else I would recover, and for the rest of our lives I would be her image. It was her shoulders, she meant,' Palfreyman explained. 'My sister is deformed.'

Miss Palfreyman stood over the two men. She was twisting a bunch of small flowers, violets they could have been, which were her offering, but from which the flesh was coming away in terrible jerks. Of all the blots and distortions of evening, the shadow of her hump upon the ground was the most awful.

'She was kissing me, and crying, and blaming herself, and hoping,' Palfreyman said, 'until I became more terrified of her love than of my own condition. Especially when the pain subsided, and I got up. For the fall had only knocked the wind out of me. Then my sister was ashamed. We both were. Only, she was resentful too. On thinking it over since, I am convinced that she would have liked to keep me *in her own image*, as she expressed it, so that I should be completely hers. The most I can do for her is pray constantly that I may take some of her suffering upon myself, and that I may learn to return her love in the measure that she needs. But so far, I have failed. I know when I watch her stooping on the borders of the garden, to look at flowers, or to pull a piece of southernwood or rosemary, and smell it, and throw it away, useless, and glance over her shoulder, and walk on. Or she will fly at the duties she has been neglecting: the work of the parish; and the parishioners, like uneducated people who have inherited a book they cannot read, but which flatters their pride, will be quite pleased to have her amongst them, in spite of her strangeness. None of this, unfortunately, alleviates the pain of my sister's situation. She feels that she is doomed to remain unique. I forgot to say she has had all the mirrors removed from the house, for her reflection is a double that she has grown to hate. Of course, there are all those other objects in glass, which I have mentioned, but they, she says, distort in any case.'

'And your uncle,' the German asked, 'has he not taken note of the disappearance of the looking-glasses?'

'My uncle has been engaged for many years on a key to the *Revelation of St John the Divine*. I doubt he would notice the disappearance of my sister, let alone a mirror.'

The evening in which the two men were sitting had dissolved into a vast oblivion. The grey had consumed the green mist by natural process. The men themselves were cornered by it at the roots of the tree, from where the face of each appeared to the other as desirable as rafts to shipwrecked sailors.

'Where I have failed most wretchedly,' Palfreyman continued, 'is in my inability to rescue my sister from her hallucinations. She cannot believe in the possibility of redemption for herself, because she does not feel she is acceptable to God. She is too plainly marked with the sign of His disapproval. Recently, she attempted to take her own life by opening her veins.'

'And was trailing through the rooms that are filled with the jewels of glass,' dreamed the German. 'Her hump is less notice-able in the warm, grey cloak. By the time you reached her, she was already rather weak but glittering with blood, as she spat-tered the humming birds and other musical instruments.'

'Yes.'

'And you rescued, or condemned, your sister,' Voss accused, 'by denying her the Gothic splendours of death. Her intention was glorious, but you rushed and tied a tourniquet, when all you had to offer was your own delusion.'

'You cannot destroy me, Mr Voss!' Palfreyman insisted.

'Then,' continued Voss, 'not very long after, you left for the Antipodes, and retreated farther and farther from your failures, until we are sitting beneath this tree, surrounded by hazards, certainly, but of a most impersonal kind.'

'Yes,' said Palfreyman. 'Yes.'

He broke a stick.

'I think I have realized all this,' he said. 'And that I did not have the strength to endure it. And must make amends.'

Then Voss, who had been watching his companion's blurry face, knew that Palfreyman could never rescue him, as he had almost hoped during the story of the hunchback sister. Although the brother would be saved, by the strength of his delusion, the hunchback sister, together with himself, were reserved, the German suspected, for the Gothic splendours. So the moon rose in the thicket of the brigalow, and was glittering in the eyes of the condemned.

Next morning the expedition rose, and proceeded along the southerly bank of the rejuvenated river, that wound in general direction westward. Green disguised the treacherous nature of the

264

ground, and in places, where heavier rain had fallen, there was the constant danger of pack animals becoming bogged, which did occur at intervals. Then the German's hatred of mules became ungovernable. He would ride a hundred yards off his course in order to arm himself with a branch from a tree. At such times, the animals would smell danger from a distance, and would be sweating and trembling against his return; there were even some mules that would snatch at him with their long teeth as he passed, and jangle their bits, and roll their china eyes.

Of dogs, however, Voss showed every sign of approbation, and would suffer for them, when their pads split, when their sides were torn open in battle with kangaroos, or when, in the course of the journey, they simply died off. He would watch most jealously the attempts of other men to win the affection of his dogs. Until he could bear it no longer. Then he would walk away, and had been known to throw stones at a faithless animal. In general, however, the dogs ignored the advances of anyone else. They were devoted to this one man. They could have eaten him up. So it was very satisfactory. Voss was morbidly grateful for the attentions of their hot tongues, although he would not have allowed himself to be caught returning their affection.

By this stage of the journey the number of dogs had been reduced to two, a kind of rough terrier, and Gyp, the big mongrel-Newfoundland that had given good service as a sheep-dog in the days of sheep.

'Gyp is in fine condition, sir,' Judd remarked to Voss one day as they rode along.

He knew the leader's fondness for the dog, and thought secretly to humour him in this way.

The black bitch had, indeed, flourished since the sheep had been abandoned and the ground had softened. She led a life of pleasure, and would trot back and forth on spongy feet, her long tongue lolling in pink health, her coat flashing with points of jet.

'She has never looked better,' Judd ventured to add.

'Certainly,' Voss replied.

He had ridden back for company, and now sensed that he had done wrong; he must suffer for it.

'Yes,' he said, raising his voice. 'She is eating her head off, and I have been considering for several days what must be done for the common good.'

Both men were silent for a little, watching with cold fascination the activities of the fussy dog, who was passing and re-passing, and once laughed up at them.

'I have thought to destroy her,' said the fascinated Voss, 'since we have no longer sheep, hence, no longer any earthly use for Gyp.'

Judd did not answer; but Harry Robarts, who was riding close by, at the heels of the cattle, looked up, and did protest:

'Ah, no, sir! Kill Gyp?'

He was already dry of throat and hot of eye.

Others were similarly affected when they heard of the decision. Even Turner suggested:

'We will all share a bit of grub with Gyp whenever she don't catch. She will be fed out of our ration, sir, so there will be no drain on the provisions.'

Voss was grinning painfully.

'I would like very much to be in a position to enjoy the luxury of sentiment,' he said.

Accordingly, when they made the midday halt, the German called to his dog, and she followed him a short way. When he had spoken a few words to her, and was looking into the eyes of love, he pulled the trigger. He was cold with sweat. He could have shot off his own jaw. Yet, he had done right, he convinced himself through his pain, and would do better to subject himself to further drastic discipline.

Then the man scraped a hole in which to bury his dog. As the grave was rather shallow, he placed a few stones on top, and some branches from a ragged she-oak, which he found growing there beside the river.

From a distance the members of his party could have been watching him.

'What does it matter?' said Turner at last, who had been amongst the most vociferous in Gyp's defence. 'It is only a dog, is it not? And might have become a nuisance. It could be that he has done right to kill it. Only, in these here circumstances, we are all, every one of us, dogs.'

After going about for several days like one dead, Voss was

266

virtually consoled. Burying other motives with the dogs, he decided that his act could but have been for the common good. If he had mystified his men, mystery was his personal prerogative. If Laura did not accept, it was because Laura herself was dog-eyed love.

As they rode along he explained to that loving companion who lived and breathed inside him: he had only to hold the muzzle to his own head, to win a victory over her. At night, though, his body was sick with the spasms of the dying dog. Until the continuous lovers felt for each other's hand, to hear the rings chatter together. Truly, they were married. But I cannot, he said, stirring in his sleep, both kill and have. He was tormented by the soft coat of love. So he at once left it, and walked away. He was his former skeleton, wiry and obsessed.

At night now it would rain like bullets into the embers of the fires, and the sleeping men would stir at the report on canvas, as if they had been hit. The rain fell for the most part at night, but on one occasion men and beasts were humped against it for a whole day. Their misery continued into the night, until, suddenly, the blackness opened for the cold stars.

Then it began to rain again, and did not hold up. Nobody could conceive of eternity except as rain.

Men and beasts were grown very thin as they butted with their heads against the solid rain. Some of the men were hating one another worse than ever. Animals hate less, of course, because they have never expected more. But men grow green with hatred. Green slime was slapped upon the ground across which they were floundering. On that side of the river there were trees of shiny green with long, dark lances for leaves, which threatened the eyes and eardrums. Yet, in the condition to which they had come, the men's souls were more woundable than flesh. One or two most dispirited individuals confessed to themselves that their greatest pleasure would have been to die.

For, by this season the land was cooling off; cold days would alternate with others of a fitful steaminess, while nights were unequivocally cold, in which flapped the wet rags of canvas and miserable flesh. Chills and fevers had broken out, besides. There was scarce one man who was not chafing the shreds of his shivering, frayed flesh, that had first been desiccated to the substance of salt cod. Greenish-yellow teeth were rattling in the skulls, from which men looked out, luminous, but deceived.

Frank Le Mesurier was the worst, who had begun the soonest, in fact the night of his ride across the mountains to deliver the leader's message to the shepherds. He was soon mumbling of dried peas that he could not spit out of his mouth – they were fixed there in his aching jaws – and of some treasure, great chunks of smouldering ore, that would tear his hands as he tried to fetch it out of his chest, and which he must not lose at any cost.

He had grown very frail and thin, yellow, and transparent; he had the appearance of a yellow lily, but hairy, and stinking. Noticing one day how he was swaying in his saddle, Voss ordered the young man to camp inside his own tent at the next resting-place, and himself dosed him with quinine, and wrapped him in his own blankets. He was all tenderness for the patient, as if he must show the extent of his capabilites. To dispense love, he remembered suddenly. If nobody was impressed, it was not that they suspected hypocrisy, but because they could expect anything of Voss. Or of God, for that matter. In their confused state it was difficult to distinguish act from act, motive from motive, or to question why the supreme power should be divided in two. To kiss and to kill are similar words to eyes that focus with diffi-culty. So the others watched gravely as the German tended the sick man. His back turned to them, the physician himself was trembling, from the pains with which he was racked as the result of repeated wettings, but more especially for fear that his stock of love might be exhausted, or the bungling of divinity recognized.

When evening at last came, for they had camped early on account of the indisposition of most of the company, he ordered Jackie to come with him and lasso several of the goats which had recently kidded. While the blackfellow wrestled with the caught goats, Voss milked them – it would have been ludicrously angular on a less heroic scale – and hurried back to his patient with the rain battering the foaming pot. As night fell Le Mesurier was persuaded to swallow a few mouthfuls of the warm, hairy milk, laced with rum from a little store the prudent German had been hoarding against sickness.

As the sick man tried the milk on his tongue, Voss watched

longingly, upon his hands and knees, on the tamped mud floor of the straining tent.

'Tell me, Frank,' he asked, 'do you feel any easier?'

'No,' replied the yellow face, from which a string of milk hung. 'It is very distressing. Everything fluctuates, and my mind and body will not coincide.'

As it continued to rain, the German retired early. Then their common fever filled the tent. But Voss was in some measure eased by the love he had dispensed; it had done more good to him than to the patient. So, with its white salve, he continued to anoint. She was dressed on this occasion in a hooded robe, of full, warm, grey rain, that clothed her completely, except for the face. He was able to diagnose from experience that her illness was that of ciliate paralysis. Her stone form did not protest, however. Or expect. But awaited her implicit physician. At this stage of the sickness, he said, I will administer this small white pill, which will grow inside you to gigantic proportions. Please note : the act of giving is less humiliating than that of receiving. Can you bear to receive what will entail great suffering? He saw the smile crack open in honey-coloured stone. If I have suffered the Father, she smiled, then I can suffer the Son. Immediately he sensed the matter had attained flesh-proportions, he was nauseated. He was no Moslem. His trousers were not designed for parturition. I am One, he protested, forming the big O with his convinced mouth. And threw the pill upon the ground. But she continued to smile her inexorable smile, which signified they had been married an eternity, and that stone statues will survive the years of the Turk.

Upon waking, the German saw that they were still at sea in the night of rain, bobbing and straining, with groaning of ropes and shivering of canvas, but that there was a tallow candle, one of those he had been keeping for an emergency, set in the middle of the darkness. Le Mesurier evidently had lit the candle, and was now hoping to resist chaos. The cone of yellow light was the one reality.

'Oh, I am sick, sir,' he complained, when he realized he was being observed.

'There is no need for you to tell me that, Frank,' said Voss.

'I do not know how to attend to myself. I have not the strength of a fly.'

In fact, he fell back then, to lie in his own misery.

Very soon Voss understood from the terrible stench that his companion had lost control of his bowels, and that, in the circumstances, he must turn to and clean the man. So he set about it, woodenly. Prospective saints, he decided, would have fought over such an opportunity, for green and brown, of mud, and slime, and uncontrolled faeces, and the bottomless stomach of nausea, are the true colours of hell.

When he was finished, and had set down the iron dish, he said:

'But I am no saint, Frank, and am doing this for reasons of necessity and hygiene.'

Le Mesurier was shielding his eyes.

'How you are in my debt! Do you hear?' laughed the German.

The sick man, perceiving the vestige of a joke, did glimmer and murmur. He was grateful, too.

After Voss had thrown out the contents of the dish, he administered a little rhubarb and laudanum, with the result that the patient began to doze, but every now and then his mind would come forward out of the distance.

Once he sat up, and said:

'I will repay you, I promise. I will not cheat you.'

And once:

'I will let you count it over one day, perhaps, in advance, when we are together in the cave. Shall we boil the quart, Mr Voss?'

'Not in this downpour,' answered the German. 'We would never succeed to coax the fire.'

'But in this cave,' persisted the sick man, who appeared incandescent, and added: 'You must give it to me, though. I will put it under the blanket for safety's sake.'

'Give what?' asked Voss, who was by this time drowsing again.

'The book,' said Le Mesurier. 'It is in my saddle-bag. Give it to me, Mr Voss. It is the book with marbled edges.'

Like camellias, Voss remembered.

'May I look in it?' he asked, cautiously.

To read the past? Or was it the future?

'No,' Le Mesurier said. 'It is too soon.'

Rummaging in the saddle-bag, amongst the dry crumbs of bread and splinters of petrified meat, Voss did find the book.

How powerful he was, he realized, as he knelt there holding it. Never before had he held a man's soul in his hand.

'Will you repay me with this, Frank?' he asked.

'I am not yet ready,' Le Mesurier said. 'Do you remember the other evening, under the trees in the Domain? I can only give you what you have given me. Eventually. But you do not know how it must be dragged up out of me, or you would not ask for it. Can you not see that it is bleeding at the roots?'

'Go to sleep now,' Voss advised. 'We shall speak about it another time.'

'Yes,' agreed Le Mesurier, and did seem disposed to sleep, the notebook bundled for safety under the blanket.

But he sat up again, almost at once, and began to speak with comparative lucidity, wetting his feverish lips at first, for fear they might obstruct the words:

'In the beginning I used to imagine that if I were to succeed in describing with any accuracy some thing, this little cone of light with the blurry edges, for instance, or this common panni-kin, then I would be expressing all truth. But I could not. My whole life had been a failure, lived at a most humiliating level, always purposeless, frequently degrading. Until I became aware of my power. The mystery of life is not solved by success, which is an end in itself, but in failure, in perpetual struggle, in becoming.'

Voss did not care to be told the secrets of others. He preferred to arrive at them by his own intuition, then to pounce. Now he did not have the advantage.

So he said:

'You have developed a slight fever, you know. It is better that you should try to rest.'

Also he was trembling for those secrets of his own, of which it now seemed the young man might be possessed.

'Rest!' laughed Le Mesurier. 'I must remind you again of the evening we spent together in the Domain, when we did more or less admit to our common daemon.'

The German was unable, then and there, to think of a means to stop the conflagration.

The sick man was burning on.

'Of course, we are both failures,' he said, and it could have been a confession of love.

They lay and listened to the long, slow rain, which did not quench.

'If you were not sick, Frank,' said Voss at last, 'you would not believe your own ears.'

But now the young man's eyes obviously saw.

'It is the effect of the drug,' explained Voss, who was himself fast succumbing.

'You will not remember anything of what you have said. For that reason,' he added, quite dryly, and wriggling his scraggy neck, 'I will agree that it could be true.'

So that these two were united at last.

Le Mesurier, whose mission it was, he was convinced, to extract the last drop of blood out of their relationship, leaned forward, and asked:

'Since I am invited to be present at the damnation of man, and to express faithfully all that I experience in my own mind, you will act out your part to the end?'

'There is no alternative,' Voss replied, addressing the grey-green body of his sleeping companion.

Not long afterwards the German, who had intended to examine the notebook, but refrained out of dislike, almost fear of reading his own thoughts, fell asleep, too, in the pewter-coloured light.

That morning the leader of the expedition resolved to take only the aboriginal boy and push on in search of a more suitable place in which to fortify themselves against the wet, and treat the sick. After only a couple of miles' travel they were rewarded by sight of what appeared to be the entrance to some caves on the opposite bank of the river.

'You go, Jackie,' said Voss, 'make sure this place good dry.'

But the black boy, whose naked body was shivering and chafing in a shroud of hard, wet canvas, immediately replied:

'Too black. This feller lost inside.'

'Dugald would not be frightened,' said Voss.

'Dugald no here,' answered Jackie truthfully.

Voss cursed all black swine, but at once persuaded himself it was the rain that had made him lose his temper, for he clung to a belief that these subjects of his kingdom would continue to share his sufferings long after the white men had fallen away.

As there was no avoiding it, he spurred his unhappy horse down the yellow bank of the river, and into the flood, of which the breathtaking cold swallowed every thought and emotion. Otherwise, they were drifting deliciously. No dream could have been smoother, silenter, more inevitable. But the wretched horse, it appeared, was trampling the water, or swimming, for eventually he did scratch a foothold, heave himself up, and scramble out upon the opposite bank, there to shake his sides, until his bones and those of his rider were rattling together terribly. Jackie, who had followed, holding the tail of his brown gelding, soon stood there too, smiling and chattering with cold, his nakedness running with light and water, for he had lost his canvas cloak. Of bronze rather than the iron of most other blacks, fear and cold had refined him further into an imperial gold, so that Voss was reconciled to his slave, especially since the river had been negotiated by his own courage.

'Now,' he announced, 'we will inspect the caves.'

The black boy did not refuse, but would not have gone ahead of that exorcizing magic the white man possessed. Night was terrifying, and was never quite emptied out of pockets such as these caves. He would not willingly have gone through darkness without carrying fire. Even moonlight was suspect, full of the blandishment of malicious fur, and treacherous teeth that snapped at black skin.

'Blackfeller belong by these caves,' said Jackie, beginning to scent something.

'How?' asked Voss.

The black boy could not explain his instincts, so he smiled, and swayed his head, and avoided the expectant eyes of his superior.

'We shall soon see,' said the German, stooping.

Immediately he entered, there was a flitting of bats. The bats flew out, screamed at the rain, circled, and for want of an inviting alternative, returned to their disturbed darkness. Alone in the landscape, the black boy began to feel it was probably preferable to follow the bats, and rejoin his master. How fortunate he was to have one. The rain was sighing with him.

It transpired that the caves were neither very deep nor very dark, for in addition to their general shallowness, a shaft descended through the cliffside into the most important chamber, and down this sleeve a dusty light poured. The floor was deep in dust, which deadened footfall, and made for reverence. There was a smell of dust and age, also possibly of human bodies, but ancient ones, and passionless at last.

Under the influence of the reverent light, the black boy was murmuring, but in his own tongue, because he was moved. Now the cave began to smell also of his live, youthful body. It appeared from his unguarded face and dreaming muscles that the place was full of a good magic.

Then Voss caught sight of the drawings.

'What do these signify, Jackie?' he asked.

The boy was explaining, in his own language, assisted by a forefinger.

'*Verfluchte Sprachen!*' cried the German.

For he was doubly locked in language.

As the boy continued unperturbed, the man had to recover from his lapse. He was looking.

'Snake,' Jackie explained. 'Father my father, all blackfeller.'

'*Gut,*' added the boy, for the especial benefit of the German, and the word lit the whole place.

The man was yielding himself up to the simplicity of the drawings. Henceforth all words must be deceitful, except those sanctioned by necessity, the handrail of language.

'Kangaroo,' said the boy. 'Old man,' he smiled, touching certain parts.

These were very prominent, and befitting.

Although initiated by sympathy into the mystery of the drawings, of which the details fulfilled needs most beautifully, the German did retreat from the kangaroo.

He now said, rather primly:

'*Ja. Natürlich.* But I like these better. What are they?'

These appeared to be an assembly of tortuous skeletons, or bundles of bones and blowing feathers. Voss remembered how, as a boy, he had flown kites with messages attached to their tails. Sometimes the string would break, and the released kite, if it did not disintegrate in the air, must have carried its message into far places; but, whatever the destination, he had never received a reply.

Now, however, looking at the kite-figures, his heart was hopeful.

'Men gone away all dead,' the boy explained. 'All over,' he waved his arm. 'By rock. By tree. No more men,' he said, beginning to comb the light with his dark fingers, as if it had been hair. 'No more nothink. Like this. See?' He laid his cheek upon his hands, seed-shaped, and his eyelashes were playing together. 'Wind blow big, night him white, this time these feller dead men. They come out. Usfeller no see. They everywhere.'

So that the walls of the cave were twanging with the whispers of the tangled kites. The souls of men were only waiting to come out.

'Now I understand,' said Voss gravely.

He did. To his fingertips. He felt immensely happy.

Why can it not remain like this, he wondered to the woman who was locked inside him permanently, and who would answer him through the ends of her long, dreaming hair. She suggested: the souls of those we know are perhaps no more communicative than their words, if you wind in the strings to which they are attached, and that is why it is arranged for those to break, and for the liberated souls to carry messages of hope into Bohemia, Moravia, and Saxony, if rain has not erased; in that event, the finders must content themselves with guesses.

The man in the cave should have felt wet, and aching, and cold, but the woman's smooth, instinctive soul caressed his stubborn, struggling spirit. Secretly he would have liked – or why secretly, for the boy would not have understood – he would have liked to contribute to the rock drawings, in warm ochre, the L of happiness.

But time was passing, bats were stirring, the boy had tired of the drawings, and was standing at the mouth of the cave, remembering that substantial kangaroo, of which he had stuffed into his belly the last singed squares of hide ten days previously. He was hungry now.

'*Nun wir müssen zurück*,' said the man, emerging from his thoughts.

Language did not bother the black: that is to say, generally he would not listen. Now he waited for the man to act. Then he followed.

During the afternoon the main party was conveyed as far as the providential caves, Le Mesurier still very weak, swaying on his horse, with Turner, Angus, and Harry Robarts by now also debilitated, though to a lesser degree. Arrived at the point where Voss and the native had swum the river, it was decided to build a raft on which to ferry to the opposite bank any stores that could suffer from a wetting. Accordingly, Judd began to fell some saplings, of which there were few enough in the neighbourhood, and those none too straight. However, he was able to hew down a bare necessity of timber. Rain could not quench him. Water had become his element, as his shining axehead swam through the wood. The saplings were soon bound together, and upon floats of hollow logs, by means of thongs cut from a cowhide that Judd had saved against the day when such a situation should arise.

In the meantime, the men had begun to curse and bludgeon cattle, mules, and spare horses into swimming the river. The animals were begging for mercy in piteous strains, but did finally hump themselves, and plunge. Goats were next shooed into the water after a preliminary scampering. This operation was nearer murder, for the rational creatures were crying as though the knife was in their throats; indeed, some of the murderers promptly felt the blade in their own. But the goats were bobbing and swimming. Their horns were ripping up the air in vain. Then it was seen that at least five of the animals would not scramble out. As they were carried past and away, one old horny doe was beseeching Voss, who began calling out:

'Mr Judd, have you not yet prepared the raft? We shall not be across and dried before darkness overtakes us.'

Because nothing could be done for the goats.

'Mr Judd,' he called, 'are you aware that flour will turn to paste in water? Put it on the raft, man!'

To such an extent was the German distressed by the fate of the goats, he was determined to make every member of his party hate him, as he pretended not to watch those decent animals descending into hell.

Presently it was the turn of the raft. This was launched with difficulty owing to the steepness of the bank and weight of the green wood, Turner complaining that his guts were busted open, but eventually the craft was bumping on the water, and its cargo loaded, for the most part flour, ammunition, Mr Palfreyman's ornithological specimens, and plants and insects which were the property of Voss himself. While several pairs of hands steadied the tossing timbers, Judd and Jackie swam their horses across the river, bearing ropes previously secured to the dubious craft.

At this point Voss did foresee the catastrophe that would overtake them, and did almost lift up his voice, but it was too heavy. Fascinated by the doomed raft, he continued to stare. That which he apprehended almost in physical detail had to happen, so he watched, with his chin sunk upon an old woollen comforter that the sharp change in the weather had persuaded him to wind round his neck.

Judd and the blackfellow had moored the raft to a tree on the opposite bank. The plan was that the remainder of the party should swim their horses across, and join in hauling in the ropes. But this was not to be. The current took the raft, once released by hands, and as it bobbed top-heavily at the end of the ropes, solemnly tipped it up. The scene was almost exactly as Voss, in that flash, had visualized, and by this time every member of the party, watching the ridiculous object of the raft, was convinced by his own helplessness that it had to happen thus.

'Crikey,' Turner cried at last, 'there goes our flour, that we could at least have used to paper the walls of the bally caves, for what looks like being a lengthy visit.'

Voss, who had ordered the loading of the flour, did not say anything. Nor did Judd.

Some of the party appeared not to care, but were spurring their horses recklessly down the bank, for, in any event, this most personal river still had to be crossed.

'Do you think you can manage it, Frank?' asked Palfreyman, who had already forced himself to accept the loss of his specimens as some form of retribution.

Le Mesurier, who had dismounted during the foregoing operations, was seated on a rock, holding his head. He looked very ill.

'I cannot sit any longer on a horse,' he said.

'You will have to. At least a few more hundred yards,' Palfreyman replied.

'He will hold to his horse's tail, and be drawn across,' Voss decreed, and continued to explain, and to organize.

Turner, Angus, and Harry Robarts, who were clearing the water from their dazed eyes, had formed a little group with Judd. They were sheltering against one another's bodies, and watching from the other side.

'If you are to die, Frank,' said Voss, 'it will be more comfortable to do so in the cave.'

'I do not care if I lie down here and die,' Le Mesurier answered.

But they got him to his feet.

Then the last of the party was streaming silently, slowly, across the flood. Somewhere on either flank floated Voss and Palfreyman, each holding to his horse's tail. But it was the central figure, or head, rather, that cut the breath, that played upon the imaginations of those who watched. Le Mesurier was pale as water. Some of the spectators wondered whether they had ever known him. He had plaited the yellow fingers of his left hand into the sharp, blue-black horsehair, but with his right he held above his head a notebook wrapped in a piece of waterproof sheeting. More than anything, he suggested a man engaged in celebrating the most solemn ritual.

Such an emotional intensity underlay this mystic crossing, that the intrusion of solid ground beneath his feet was a violent shock to the invalid. As the horse lunged free, the man was wrested out of his entranced state, and would have fallen into the mud but for the hands that were receiving him.

Seeing everyone delivered safe, Palfreyman would have liked to offer up a prayer, only this, he realized, would not have been politic, and moreover, since his immersion in the water, he doubted whether he could have found the words, so cold was his body, and unresponsive his faculties. In his numb confusion, his mind began to grope after some substitute for prayer with which to express his thankfulness, when he happened to catch sight of a battered quart pot, and cracked and swollen saddle-bag. These objects, of simple form and humble purpose, that exposure to the elements had emphasized, strengthened his sense of gratitude and trust to the extent that he resolved to proffer their images to God, and was at once consoled to know that his intention was acceptable.

Meanwhile, all those who could, had begun to haul on the moorings of the capsized raft, and after considerable struggle, succeeded in bringing it to shore. Any cargo that rope had re-strained while it was upside down in the water was in such a sorry condition, it was doubtful whether it could be of further use. What remained of the flour had become a bluish paste.

Then Judd approached the leader, and with unexceptionable modesty, said:

'Mr Voss, I must tell you I took the liberty to divide the flour into equal quantities. The second half has crossed the river on muleback. What condition it is in remains to be seen, but some of it may serve to fill a corner of our bellies, sir, when they are crying out for it.'

To which Voss made the formal reply:

'You did right, Judd, to have the foresight.'

But he preferred to leave it at that.

Every man of them was by now the worse for the privations he had endured, and as soon as mules and horses had been un-loaded and unsaddled, then hobbled, and turned free, the whole human company was glad to huddle in the shelter of the caves. It was only later that evening, after they had dried themselves at the fires that had been lit, and eaten a little of a skillaglee of flour which Judd had been able to prepare, that any real atten-tion was given to the rock drawings. These appeared immense as the reddish light shifted over the surface of the walls. The simplicity and truthfulness of the symbols was at times terribly apparent, to the extent that each man interpreted them accord-ing to his own needs and level.

So there was ribaldry rising out of Turner, who spat, and said:

'There is no mistaking the old man kangaroo. They have seen to that.'

He spat again, this time at the drawing itself, but the stone and ochre quickly drank his spittle down, and nobody was long humiliated.

'Women too, eh? Or is it cricket bats?'

So he was brooding in the firelight, and wondering how he might cheat his celibacy.

Ralph Angus, who was seated beside his bawdy friend, had glanced at the drawings, and almost at once looked away. The young landowner would have been afraid of what he had seen, if he had not quickly convinced himself that he was superior to it.

On the other hand, Harry Robarts understood immediately what the drawings were intended to convey. Privation, which had reduced the strength of his body, had increased his vision and simplicity of mind, so that he was treading through the withered grass with the horde of ochrous hunters. Morning stole amongst the trees, all sound wrapped in pearly fog, the kind that lies close to the earth. The pale soles of his feet were cold with dew.

Or he stood in front of another drawing, which he proceeded to interpret:

'See, this man is going to die. They have planted a spear in his heart. It has gone in at the back through the shoulder-blades.'

In fact, the little fishbone in faded red ochre had entered the wizened pear, that would soon be rattling in its cage of bones. The boy poked his finger between the bars, in order to touch the leathery thing.

'Are you sure it is through the back, Harry, that the spear entered?' the German asked, ironically.

'Oh, yes,' said Harry Robarts. 'That way you do not know it is about to happen. The others prepared a plan behind his back.'

'Other feller no like this feller. Draw picture. This feller die,' said Jackie, who was squatting with his knees under his chin.

'Convenience! You have only to draw the picture of your enemy, Turner, and he will die. It is simple as that,' Voss said, and laughed.

Although addressing Turner, he was sharing his joke with Judd and Angus, who were seated at the same fire.

But there were occasions when some people refused to share the jokes of Voss.

So the latter called to the blackfellow, and went in the rain and the dusk in search of the surviving goats, and when they had caught a couple, and drawn off the little milk they had made, busied himself for the rest of the evening with his patient, who had grown delirious since the afternoon.

Le Mesurier was moving great weights. He was groaning, and pushing the sweat off his face. He was running through forests of hair. Trees let down their tails, but, repenting of their generosity, cut through his hands as far as the last shred of weary skin. Which protested and shrieked repeatedly.

'I cannot lie and listen to this,' cried Harry Robarts, and went and hid himself in a far corner that bats had dunged, but which was preferable, in that the silence held.

Others, too, were grumbling, though decently.

Towards morning, Le Mesurier was wrestling with the great snake, his King, the divine powers of which were not disguised by the earth-colours of its scales. Friction of days had worn its fangs to a yellow-grey, but it could arch itself like a rainbow out of the mud of tribulation. At one point during his struggles, the sick man, or visionary, kissed the slime of the beast's mouth, and at once spat out a shower of diamonds.

'No one will rob me,' he shouted, and was gathering the dust with his yellow fingers, as far as the fire.

He was collecting embers, even, until Voss rose and restrained him, administering a more concentrated dose from the laudanum that remained.

In that tormented cave the German was a scraggy figure, of bare legs with random hairs upon them, but his shadow did dominate the wall.

The sleepers were ranged round two separate fires, with the exception of Palfreyman, who had spread his blanket somewhat apart, at equal distance from the two. For a long time he could not drop off, or did, but woke, and tossed, and drowsed. He would most willingly have maintained a balance; indeed, it was his one thought and desire, who was a small, weak, ineffectual man that his sister had flung upon a bed of violets. There, upon those suffocating small flowers, he had failed her kisses, but would offer himself, as another sacrifice, to other spears. The close cave intensified his personal longing. One side of him Voss, the other his lady sister, in her cloak that was the colour of ashes. Towards morning her hand, with its unnaturally pronounced finger-joints, took his hand, and they walked into the distant embers, which hurt horribly, but which he must continue to endure, as he was unfitted for anything else.

About the same hour, Voss went to the mouth of the cave. If he was shivering, in spite of the grey blanket in which he had prudently wrapped himself, it was not through diffidence, but because each morning is, like the creative act, the first. So he cracked his finger-joints, and waited. The rain was withdrawn temporarily into the great shapelessness, but a tingling of moisture suggested the presence of an earth that might absorb further punishment. First, an animal somewhere in the darkness was forced to part with its life. Then the grey was let loose to creep on subtle pads, from branch to branch, over rocks, slithering in native coils upon the surface of the waters. A protoplast of mist was slowly born, and moored unwillingly by invisible wires. There it was, gently tugging. The creator sighed, and there arose a contented little breeze, even from the mouth of the cave. Now, liquid light was allowed to pour from great receptacles. The infinitely pure, white light might have remained the masterpiece of creation, if fire had not suddenly broken out. For the sun was rising, in spite of immersion. It was challenging water, and the light of dawn, which is water of another kind. In the struggle that followed the hissing and dowsing, the sun was spinning, swimming, sinking, drowned, its livid face, a globe of water, for the rain had been brought down again, and there was, it appeared, but a single element.

The natural sequence of events soothed the superior being in his cave, to the extent that he might have fallen asleep if the gelatinous, half-created world had not loomed too close, reminding him of disagreeable things. He had to recall the soup the convict had prepared the night before from flour hidden on the backs of mules. The gelatinous mess was even less palatable in retrospect, the cook more hateful than his soup. So that the erstwhile creator was fiddling with his blanket-sleeves. Moreover, he began to have an inkling of a confession he had made, in a tent, at night, under the influence of laudanum, and in human terms.

So the divine spirit fled out, into the swirl of blown rain. The man that remained continued to watch the shiny grey soup of the prevailing flood, and for want of a better occupation, crushed an earthworm that had crawled for protection as far as the rocky platform on which he sat.

In the circumstances, it was not altogether surprising that a human figure should appear, and that this figure should develop into Judd, his head down to the new-blown rain, as he carried a quart pot.

'I could not sleep, and as it was not raining at the time,' the convict explained when he had approached, 'I decided to find the goats, and have brought back a drop of milk for Mr Le Mesurier.'

Voss was furious.

'Maybe such quantities of milk are not correct treatment for a man whose bowels are in a delicate condition.'

Judd did not answer at once. When he did, he said:

'At all events, there is the milk.'

And he set the pot upon the floor of the cave.

During the morning, Voss administered another dose from the much reduced supply of laudanum and rhubarb. Then, after debating whether to throw out the contents of Judd's quart, he decided on an opposite course. Seeing the convict seat himself in their vicinity, with the object of mending a broken bridle, the German persuaded the unwilling Le Mesurier to sip at the controversial milk, and was rewarded later by the patient's suffering an access of diarrhoea.

'Only as reason led me to expect,' commented the physician, in pouring the milk away, again under the convict's nose.

Judd, who had in his life experienced the cat, did not open his mouth.

'Or else,' said Voss, who could not let the matter drop, 'one of the goats is sick.'

Then he began to clean up the invalid's mess with equanimity, even love. Noble gestures of doubtful origin did stimulate him most of all. If they left him haggard, as from suffering – for he was aware of his human nature also – it was good that he should suffer, along with men.

So he looked deliberately at Judd. But the latter plied his saddler's needle.

If it had not been for the journals that some of them kept, it would have been difficult for the members of the expedition to sense the passage of time. The days were possessed of a similarity, of sickness, and rain, and foraging for firewood, as they dripped slowly, or blew in gusts of passionate vengeance, or stood quite still for intervals of several hours, in which the only sound was that of passive moisture. Yet, a variety of incidents did also occur, or were created out of the void of inactivity, mostly quite trivial events, but which uneasy minds invested with a light of feverish significance.

There was the morning, for instance, when their cattle disappeared, such cattle as these had become, skeletons rather, from which the hair had not yet rotted. Then each of the shaggy men who had been abandoned began to wander about distraught, with his thumbs hung from the slits of his trouser pockets, looking for tracks, for dung, for some sign. If they did not communicate their distress to one another, it was because it was too great to convey, but a stranger would have read it in any of those faces, which were by now interchangeable, as the dumb creatures shambled up and down, snuffling after the rest of the herd.

A whole two days, Voss, Judd, Angus, and the blackfellow searched the country pretty thoroughly. Of all the expedition these men were the fittest, although in the case of Voss he would not have allowed himself to appear less. An effort on his part, it was an effort also on the part of Judd to continue to admire his leader, but as the convict was a fair man, he did make that effort. So they continued to roam the water looking for the lost cattle, and from a distance their employment appeared effortless.

Then they lost Jackie.

Ralph Angus cursed.

'These blacks are all alike,' he complained, and punished his horse's mouth as the blackfellow did not offer himself. 'In no circumstances are they to be relied upon.'

'Some whites would pack their swags,' said Judd, 'if the road led anywhere.'

'I have great confidence in this boy,' Voss announced, and would continue to hope until the end, because it was most necessary for him to respect some human being.

The white men rode home, which was what the cave had become. Paths now wound from its mouth. Harry Robarts had washed his shirt, and was drying it on a string beside the fire.

The German was filled with terrible longing at this scene of homecoming. He was, after all, a man of great frailty, both physical and moral, and so, immediately upon entering the cave, he returned outside, preferring to keep company with the gusts of rain than to expose his weakness to human eyes, except possibly those of his wife.

She, however, was quite strong and admirable in her thick, man's boots beneath the muddied habit. Her hands were taking his weakness from him, into her own, supple, extraordinarily muscular ones. Yet, her face had retained the expression he remembered it to have worn when she accepted him in spite of his composite nature, and was unmistakably the face of a woman.

Ah Laura, my dear Laura, the man was begging, or protesting.

As he stood in the entrance to the cave, he was resting his forehead against a boss of cold rock.

Thus he was seen by Frank Le Mesurier, who had recovered a little of his strength, and was moving on his bed, looking for some person with whom to feel in sympathy. Now he observed their leader. The young man was glad that Voss remained unnoticed by the others, since only those who have known the lowest depths are unashamed. For some reason obscure to himself, he began also to recall, as he did frequently in those desert places, the extraordinary young woman that had ridden down to the wharfside. He remembered her swollen lips, and what had appeared at that distance to be the dark shadows under her eyes, how she had been enclosed strictly in her iron habit, and how, while inclining her head to talk with evident sincerity to Mr Palfreyman, she had remained innerly aloof.

For some reason, obscurer still, the visionary felt carried closer to his leader, as the woman rode back into his life. He lay amongst his blankets, and let the moon trample him, and was filled with love and poetry, as is only right, between the spasms of suffering.

That night, when the rather tender, netted moon rose between layers of cloud, Jackie returned, herding the lost cattle. Moonlight was glinting on the pointed horns, that at intervals could have contained the disc itself. The skin of the boy, who sat thin and terrified on his sombre horse, was inlaid with shining mother o' pearl.

They looked out and saw him.

'Here is Jackie come back,' some of them said.

At once Voss was stumbling over bodies, to reach the mouth of the cave, to corroborate.

How glad he was, then.

'One cattle no find,' said the boy, and was beginning to sulk at the darkness which had but lately frightened him.

His nakedness chafed the horse as he slithered silkily down.

'Even so, you have done well,' said the German, relieved on a scale the others did not suspect, out of all proportion to the incident.

He could not talk in front of other people, but brought a lump of damper, which was left over from their evening meal.

'There,' he said to the hollow boy, and, almost angrily: 'You will have to make do with that, because there is nothing more.'

Then the German returned abruptly to his bed, and of all those present, only the aboriginal, who was well practised in listening to silence, did not interpret their leader's behaviour as contemptuous.

Nothing was added to the incident. Voss recorded it without comment in his journal:

May 28th. Jackie returned at night with cattle, one head short. Before retiring, rewarded the boy with a ration of damper. He was quite pleased.

About this time there occurred also the incident of the mustard and cress.

Turner had been expressing himself in something like the following strain:

'What would I not give for a nice dish of greens, cabbage, or spinach, or even turnip-tops at a pinch, with the water pressed out, and a lump of fresh butter slapped on like, or marrer from a good bone. But as long as there was greens.'

Greens they had had in small quantity, a kind of fat-hen that they would boil down occasionally, but in spite of this addition to their diet, Turner had become a scurvy mess, loathsome to see, and to smell, too.

Mr Palfreyman, who had overheard the fellow's remark, remembered amongst his belongings some seeds of mustard and cress, which drought at first had prevented him from sowing, and which he had forgotten long before the weather broke.

Now, Turner was most repulsive to the rather fastidious Palfreyman, who, in normal circumstances, would have attended carefully to his hands, and changed his linen every day. In this he had been encouraged by his sister, whose clear, old-woman's skin smelled habitually of lavender water or an essence of roses that she distilled herself, and whose tables were conspicuous for their little bowls of potpourri, and presses filled with the dry sheaves of lavender or yellow, crackling verbena leaves. It was, however, this same sister from whom he had run, at least, from her passionate, consuming nature, with the result that he was never finished wondering how he might atone for his degrading attitude, the constant fear of becoming dirtied, whether morally or physically, by some human being. Until the atrocious Turner, with greenish scabs at the roots of his patchy beard, and vague record of vice, seemed to offer him a means of expiation.

Once, in the cave that smelled of ashes and sickness, the ornithologist had suggested to the man that he should shave him.

'To clean up your face and give it an opportunity of healing.'

Turner laughed.

'I can see you shaving *me*, Mr Palfreyman, in the days before we lost our way.'

'Do you not think we have found it?' Palfreyman asked.

Turner made a noise, but submitted to being shaved.

It was a terrible operation.

When it was over, Palfreyman was sweating.

'Seeing as it is Saturday night,' Turner threatened, 'I must make haste to find some moll, to lay with me on the wet grass and catch the rheumatics.'

Palfreyman flung the muck of soap and hair into the fire, where it proceeded to sizzle. His sister's virgin soul winced; or was it his own?

Then, on this later occasion, Turner had confessed to his craving for greens. Miss Palfreyman, who preferred mignonette, was also in the habit of nursing up pots of mustard and cress, her brother remembered, and that he had those seeds in his pack, in an old japanned spectacle-case. At once he conceived the idea of sowing a bed for Turner and Le Mesurier, and went out on the very same day, into the rain, to look for a suitable site, and found one in a bed of silt, in a pocket of rock, some hundred yards from the eternal cave.

Here Palfreyman sowed, and the miraculous seeds germinated, standing up on pale threads, then unfolding. It was very simple and very quick. Several times on the crucial day, the man emerged from the cave to assist at the act, the importance of which was enormous.

So that, when he found that something had cut almost half his precious seedlings, Palfreyman's eardrums were thundering. He began to watch for birds, or animals, and would hang about in the grey rain. His feet made sucking sounds as they changed position in the mud, while those seedlings which had not been cut continued to thrive in spite of the abominable conditions, and were growing even coarse.

But the ornithologist could not bring himself to cut. Curiosity and rancour prevented him. Until one day, as he watched from close by, Voss approached the vegetable bed, took a knife from his pocket, bent down, and cut a liberal tuft against the ball of his thumb. There he stood, stuffing the greenstuff into his mouth, like an animal.

Palfreyman was stunned.

'Mr Voss,' he said at last, coming forward.

'*Ach!* Mr Palfreyman!' said Voss, or mumbled greenly.

So a sleepwalker is caught, but will not understand.

'Do you not realize how this greenstuff comes to be growing here?' Palfreyman began.

'It is good,' said the German, stooping and reaping again, 'but in such small quantities, it cannot give the greatest pleasure.'

Palfreyman was on the point of asking whether the leader knew that the seed had been sown by hand of man, but desisted. He felt that he did not wish to hear his suspicions confirmed.

When Voss was finished, he cleaned the knife of any traces of green by drawing the blade between his forefinger and thumb. Then he closed it, and put it away.

'Tell me, Palfreyman,' he asked, 'are you very distressed at the loss of the specimens in the river?'

'They were immaterial,' shrugged the ornithologist.

'They were the object of your joining the expedition,' corrected Voss.

'I am inclined to think there were other reasons,' Palfreyman replied. 'And we have not yet reached the most important.'

He was sorely tried, but would not yield to the impulse to believe that his leader's behaviour or the loss of his specimens could be the ultimate in tests.

Voss was watching him.

'Shall we walk back to the cave?' Palfreyman asked.

He was determined to like this man.

Voss agreed that they could not benefit by continuing to stand about in the rain.

As they were nearing the cave he turned to Palfreyman and said:

'I want you to be candid with me. Are you of Judd's party?'

'Of Judd's *party*?'

'Yes. Judd is forming a party, which will split off from me sooner or later.'

'I will not split off,' said Palfreyman, sadly. 'I am not of any party.'

'*Ach,* you cannot afford to stand aloof.'

'Perhaps I expressed myself badly. Shall we say: I am of all parties?'

'That is worse,' cried Voss. 'You will be torn in pieces.'

'If it is necessary,' Palfreyman replied.

Voss, Palfreyman, and Laura continued to walk towards the cave. The selflessness of the other two was a terrible temptation to the German. At times he could have touched their gentle

289

devotion, which had the soft, glossy coat of a dog. At other moments, they were folded inside him, wing to wing, waiting for him to soar with them. But he would not be tempted.

'I will not consider the personal appeals of love,' he said, 'or deviate in any way from my intention to cross this country.'

Then Voss entered the cave, and Palfreyman followed, looking distressed.

As the rain continued, the prisoners were submitted to further trials, but it was still only trial by minutiae.

Whenever they remained long in any one camp, Judd invariably came into his own. He immediately found – or invented, his leader would have said – many important jobs that needed doing. He became the master of objects. So that, after they had settled into their quarters in the cave, it was not long before he decided to inspect all the leather equipment they possessed; saddles, bridles, saddle-bags, and so forth. He could be seen stitching and patching beside the slow fire, upon which a dusty yellow light descended through the shaft that served them as chimney; or else he would be mending a shirt; or he was making a series of small bags in oiled cloth for the safekeeping of their reduced stock of medicines during the interminable wet.

The flotsam Turner was fascinated by the idea of friendship with this man. Turner had lived in the streets, and made acquaintances, but the solider stuff of friendship, or the subtle colours of permanence, he had neither known nor coveted. In fact, anything that restricted sudden change had always been undesirable.

Yet, here he was, now grown wistful for the rock.

'When we return from this here expedition,' he said, stretching out and crossing his legs, for Turner was never occupied, 'and have received our bounties and applause, I will get myself rigged out in something real gentlemanly, and come on a pleasure visit, Albert, to this property you was telling us of.'

'If it is pleasure you are looking for, then you will be coming to the wrong place,' Judd replied, with evident affection for his property as it stood.

And he held up a needle and squinted to thread it.

'Oh, it is not feather beds, nor nothink of that description you need worry about,' Turner hastened to correct. 'I can doss down as good as any on the floor, in that shed, for instance, where your old woman makes the butter.'

For, through conversation, the place did exist, solidly, naggingly, in Turner's mind.

These fanciful, though humble plans tended to make Ralph Angus irritable and rather bored, for his own estate was considerable.

'You would be a square peg, if ever there was,' said the landowner, who had condescended to wax some thread for the use of Judd.

'I would not,' protested Turner. 'I would learn things.'

In a return to childhood, if necessary. Because dependent, it even seemed the only state desirable. He was carving his name upon the trunks of those dusty she oaks that grew in a ragged fringe round the shack. Although alone, he was not lonely, for he had remained, as always, within call of his friend.

'Tell us some more, Albert,' he said, as they sat in actual person in the cave. 'Tell us about the time the fire would not be held back, and burned the wool shed.'

'The wool shed?' laughed Angus.

'Yes,' said Judd, 'the shed, that is, where I and my boys shear our sheep.'

'Oh,' said the rich young man, and showed mercy.

'Tell us about the fox you brought home, and had on a chain, to tame,' Turner pursued.

'That is all,' said Judd, out of a mouthful of thread. 'I had it on a chain. I never did tame it.'

'What did you do, then?' asked Turner.

'I shot it.'

'Go on,' whispered Turner, and saw the whole incident.

'It was a sick, mangy thing,' said Angus, 'if it was the one I saw at Judd's.'

Yet, the young landowner had grown to like the lag turned squatter, and sensing this himself, Judd was made melancholy for his captive fox, which had flamed on occasions, he had seen it with his own eyes, at dusk, picketed on the edge of the scrub.

One day, not long after the lamentable incident of the mustard and cress, Voss approached the three men, who were seated together as usual at the fire. Turner and Angus, who were idle, at once began to look intently at the burning sticks, while Judd continued to patch the belly of a canvas water-bag.

'Mr Judd,' began Voss, 'I have intended now for some time that we should take steps to preserve our navigation instruments from the wet.'

He waited.

Then Judd replied, forcing the needle through the canvas:

'Nothing will preserve our instruments from the wet that they are getting.'

'How so?' asked Voss, although it was possible that he knew.

One of his knees was bent forward. It quivered very slightly.

'They were lost aboard the raft,' said Judd.

It did hurt him. He could have pricked himself to distract his mind.

'It is unfortunate,' said Voss, 'that you did not employ your instinct on the instruments, instead of upon the flour.'

'Ah, that flour!' cried Judd, suffering, as, indeed, was intended. 'Can you not leave it alone?'

This massive man was trembling.

'You are very touchy, I fear,' sighed Voss.

It was not known for certain whether he had achieved his whole purpose.

'It is a sore point with me, sir,' said Judd, 'the instruments.'

There was a hissing of water upon the fire, from one single drop, that fell with the greatest regularity through the rock sleeve, or chimney.

'There is one compass, sir,' admitted the man who was again a convict, 'that I was carrying in my own saddle-bag.'

'One compass?' said Voss. 'That will be an embarrassment if, for any reason, we are compelled to form ourselves into two parties.'

Because the implications were so insidious, nothing more was said, and he returned to that side of the cave, almost a little alcove, which he shared with Le Mesurier.

In Ralph Angus, compassion for the convict began to struggle with the conventions he had been taught to respect. Always conspicuous for his manliness, he did, however, bring himself to say:

'I must apologize to you, Judd. I mean, for the behaviour of others.'

Guilt experienced for past behaviour of his own stiffened his already wooden words.

'Huh,' spat Turner. 'To form ourselves into two parties. If there is any question of that, we are with you, Albert. With or without compass. Ain't we, Ralph?'

Angus did not answer. He did not yet know how far he was prepared to go, and was unhappy about it, although from that moment he was drawn closer to Turner and Judd.

The incident did not develop further, or so it seemed. There were other problems, of which Le Mesurier's illness was not the least. The sick man was recovering slowly, while remaining weak. He had reached the stage where he could sit up again in clothes that appeared too large, the bones of his hands locked together. He had grown very yellow, and the eyes in his hairy, melted face were become quite visionary, as he stared out from the mouth of the cave upon the world of grey water and the sticks of trees.

Now, from time to time, the rain would lift, literally, he felt, of something so permanent and solid. Then, in the stillness, the grey would blur with green. In the middle of the day the body of the drowned earth would appear to float to the surface; islands were breeding; and a black dust of birds, blowing across the sky, seemed to promise salvation.

Voss, for ever observing his patient, was encouraged one day on seeing the latter attempt to hobble.

'That is right, Frank,' he said. 'It is good that you should make efforts, so that you will be fit to push on with me when the wet season is past.

'You will?' he added.

As it had never occurred to Le Mesurier that there might be an alternative, he did not ask for explanations, but answered with a flatness that matched the blue-grey water with which the afternoon was filled.

'Of course.'

He did not look at Voss, however.

There were occasions, this fever-gutted man suspected, when his leader was not sensible of their common doom, and so, he must see for him, he must feel for him. By now he was able to read the faintest tremor of blood or earth, the recording of which was perhaps his sole surviving reason for existence.

*

Exhausted by the first few steps he had taken, he was quick to drop off that night, and Voss, after he had listened long enough to his companion's breathing, and watched the other shapes of sleep slowly form around him in the cave, decided at last to examine the notebook. This was done quite simply once the conscience had been overcome, for the book was protruding from a saddle-bag, within easy reach, and unprotected by its sleeping owner. Le Mesurier was lying in a state of fretful innocence, in the congested light from a fire as dull and still as dusty garnets.

Voss took the book. Then, he hesitated, as if about to look in a mirror and discover the deformities he most feared.

Never one to be advised by prudence except spasmodically, he did look, of course, and was at once standing in the terrible arena of childhood, deafened by the clapper of his own heart. These are the poems of a maniac, he protested rather primly, to protect himself. If the book had not been nailed to his hands, he might even have subjected the poet to some act of brutality. Instead, he had to read, one poem in particular which Le Mesurier had, in fact, called *Childhood*. Under the word was drawn a line so deep it defended like a moat.

Voss read:

When they had opened us with knives, they took out our hearts. Some wore them in their hats, some pressed them to keep for ever, some were eating them as if they had been roses, all with joy, until it was realized the flesh had begun to putrefy. Then they were afraid. They hung their flowers upon a dark tree, quickly, quickly.

As for the children, they break off their tears and put them in the parents' hands. How the tears of parents flow, their innocence returned. The dead, red flowers go gaily on the water. Beside the river, a white tablecloth is spread to celebrate the feast of children. Everyone is chattering. Bees are bumbling down the golden tunnels. Sweets of honey bribe the children to forget. Sticky mouths no longer care. Children soon forget from whom they have learnt to use the knife.

There is another side of the house on which the pine-trees stand. Contradictory messages arise, some in songs of long, low voices, some in harsh bark. We carve our intentions, but lose the key. So the trees are full of secrets and moss.

It is not known that we shall rise above the trees any afternoon we choose. We are only waiting to pin the calico wings on our backs. Parents and governesses assemble to watch, and some old people, who do perhaps see. We run, and flap, and crow, and rise — one foot? Everyone applauds, and pretends, and disperses, unaware that we have flown above the pointed trees. We enjoy the immense freedom of dreams, in which nobody believes, except as a joke, to share on coming down to breakfast.

The house of nettles is sadder. It is choked with nettles. They are growing high beneath the windows. The plaster is falling from the cornices. In the summer afternoons it rains

Men and women exchange ideas, and grow exasperated; they cannot lean farther forward, or they would. They accept that bread-and-butter knives do not cut, and have come provided with others, which are waiting in the bedrooms. Have you noticed the veins on the thick, thinking necks?

Children are not expected to think, but are allowed to suffer, and rehearse the future, even to practise kisses on the cotton counterpanes. In at the windows floats the scent of hot, wet nettles and the long summer. The yellow dressing-table drawers are smelling of emptiness. We have not aranged our things, who will not be staying long in this house.

O childhood of moonlight and monkey-puzzles, and the solid statues! How solid, I broke off an arm to prove, and the smell of the wound was the smell of gunpowder and frost. Often the footsteps were not mine that fell along the gravel paths, but yew and laurel intervened; other voices would carry my song out of my control; the faces were not the faces I knew. All were turning gravely in the dance, only I was the prisoner of stone.

When I no longer expected, then I was rewarded by knowing: so it is. We do not meet but in distances, and dreams are the distance brought close. The glossy mornings are trampling horses. The rescue-rope turns to hair. Prayer is, indeed, stronger, but what is strong?

O childhood, O illusions, time does not break your chain of coloured handkerchiefs, nor fail to produce the ruffled dove. . . .

During the reading of the poem, Voss hated and resented it. As mad people will turn in the street, and stare, and enter into a second mind, and mingle with the most personal thoughts, and understand, so this poem turned upon the reader, and he was biting his nails to find himself accused.

If he continued to glance through the notebook, and peer at the slabs of dark scribble, on the smudged pages, with the fluffy edges, he no longer did so with enthusiasm. To be perfectly honest, he did not wish to see, but must. The slow firelight was inexorable.

So his breath pursued him in his search through the blurred book. At that hour of night, sound was thin and terrible. Even the sleepers, who would stir, normally, and call to one another, were turned to rock, a dust of pale sleep lying on their rigid forms, of pale brown.

Then Voss found the poem, and was tearing the book apart, the better to see it. This poem had been headed by the poet *Conclusion,* in the same rather diffident hand, with a deep, defensive line scored underneath. He had written:

I

Man is King. They hung a robe upon him, of blue sky. His crown was molten. He rode across his kingdom of dust, which paid homage to him for a season, with jasmine, and lilies, and visions of water. They had painted his mysteries upon the rock, but, afraid of his presence, they had run away. So he accepted it. He continued to eat distance, and to raise up the sun in the morning, and the moon was his slave by night. Fevers turned him from Man into God.

II

I am looking at the map of my hand, on which the rivers rise to the North-east. I am looking at my heart, which is the centre. My blood will water the earth and make it green. Winds will carry legends of smoke; birds that have picked the eyes for visions will drop their secrets in the crevices of rock; and trees will spring up, to celebrate the godhead with their blue leaves.

III

Humility is my brigalow, that must I remember: here I shall find a thin shade in which to sit. As I grow weaker, so I shall become strong. As I shrivel, I shall recall with amazement the visions of love, of trampling horses, of drowning candles, of hungry emeralds. Only goodness is fed.

Until the sun delivered me from my body, the wind fretted my wretched ribs, my skull was split open by the green lightning.

Now that I am nothing, I am, and love is the simplest of all tongues.

IV

Then I am not God, but Man. I am God with a spear in his side.

So they take me, when the fires are lit, and the smell of smoke and ash rises above the smell of dust. The spears of failure are eating my liver, as the ant-men wait to perform their little rites.

O God, my God, if suffering is measured on the soul, then I am damned for ever.

Towards evening they tear off a leg, my sweet, disgusting flesh of marzipan. They knead my heart with skinny hands.

O God, my God, let them make from it a vessel that endures.

Flesh is for hacking, after it has stood the test of time. The poor, frayed flesh. They chase this kangaroo, and when they have cut off his pride, and gnawed his charred bones, they honour him in ochre on a wall. Where is his spirit? They say: It has gone out, it has gone away, it is everywhere.

O God, my God, I pray that you will take my spirit out of this my body's remains, and after you have scattered it, grant that it shall be everywhere, and in the rocks, and in the empty waterholes, and in true love of all men, and in you, O God, at last.

When Voss had finished this poem, he clapped the book together.

'*Irrsinn!*' said his mouth.

He was protesting very gutturally, from the back of his throat, from the deepest part of him, from the beginning of his life.

If a sick man likes to occupy himself in this fashion, he decided.

But the sane man could not assert himself enough in the close cave.

He lay down again on his blanket, and was trembling. His mouth and throat were a funnel of dry leather.

I am exhausted, he explained, physically exhausted. That is all.

There remained his will, and that was a royal instrument.

Once during the night she came to him, and held his head in her hands, but he would not look at her, although he was calling: Laura, Laura.

So a mother holds against her breast the head of a child that has been dreaming, but fails to take the dream to herself; this must remain with the child, and will recur for ever.

So Laura remained powerless in the man's dream.

11

THAT winter two ships of Her Majesty's Navy, cruising in Southern waters, put in at Sydney for the purpose of refitting, and at once it seemed to the inhabitants that, for a very long time, their lives had been wanting in some important element. Whether commerce or romance, depended upon sex and temper, but many a citizen, walking at the water's edge, in good nankeen or new merino, did entertain secret hopes, as the vessels rode woodenly upon the accommodating little waves. If one or two professional sceptics, possibly of Irish descent, remarked that *Nautilus* and *Samphire* were insignificant and very shabby, nobody listened who did not wish to; moreover, everybody knew that a coat of paint will work wonders, and that the gallant ships were already possessed of *those noble proportions and inspiring lines, which confirm one's faith in human courage and endeavour*, as one young lady recorded in her diary.

It was not long before genteel society was on terms of intimate friendship with the officers from these vessels, assuaging its own boredom and nostalgia for Home, by discovering in the strangers the finest qualities of English manhood. Pregnant though she was, Mrs Pringle, for one, could have eaten the commanding officer of *Nautilus*, with whom the official bond was Hampshire.

'I find it difficult to speak too highly of him,' she confided in Mrs Bonner. 'Such true tact and admirable firmness are seldom found united in one and the same man. Mr Pringle,' she hastened to add, 'has quite taken to him.'

'I am happy to think you have been so fortunate in your acquaintance,' murmured Mrs Bonner, who had not yet succeeded in meeting any of the visiting officers.

'Have you received them in your own house?' she inquired somewhat languidly of Mrs Pringle.

'On Friday evening, several of them,' the latter replied. 'All jolly, yet respectful young men. We prepared a punch cup, and several cold dishes. It was all so quickly arranged, my dear, there was little opportunity to send over for your girls.'

'On Friday evening,' said Mrs Bonner, 'our girls were otherwise engaged. They had been promised a fortnight to the Ebsworths, although, at the last moment, Laura refused to go.'

Then it was Mrs Pringle's turn to murmur.

'And how is the baby?'

Mrs Bonner no longer cared for Mrs Pringle, but had decided it would be politic to keep her as a friend.

'Oh yes, thank you, the baby is well,' she answered, high and bright, descending with some skill to a darker key: 'I wish I could say the same of Laura, who devotes herself to the child so unselfishly, her own health must suffer in the end.'

Mrs Pringle tilted her head in a certain polite way. Although Dear Laura's Baby had become an institution in their own immediate circle, she was aware that in other quarters unwholesome references frequently were made to Miss Trevelyan's Child.

So that it was pure magnanimity on the part of Mrs Pringle, when, at a later date, she dispatched Una with Miss Abbey to the Bonners, to suggest a picnic party.

'At short notice,' Una had composed, 'but Mamma did think you might possibly be free.'

They were all seated in the drawing-room – that is to say: Mrs Bonner, determined to disguise her gratitude; Belle, who had barely had time to put up her hair after washing it; Una Pringle, in new gloves; Miss Abbey, a governess in her late thirties; Dr Badgery, surgeon of *Nautilus*; and a midshipman so shy that nobody had caught his name. Arriving at the Pringles' on shore leave, the two latter, although not unwilling, had at once been conscripted to escort the ladies on their morning call.

'On Thursday afternoon, at Waverley,' Una Pringle continued, to fulfil her duty.

'Now, you are sure it was Thursday, dear? I cannot remember precisely what Mamma said. I have an idea it could have been

Wednesday,' interrupted Miss Abbey, who would catch thus at a conversation, as it flowed by, and hope to be carried along.

Una Pringle ignored the governess of her younger sisters.

'Mamma suggests we all gather at our house; then we shall give one another protection on the way.'

'Oh dear, do you think we shall need it?' laughed Miss Abbey, and looked at the gentlemen.

She would have liked to make a clever remark, but could not think of one.

'I mean,' she said, 'one no longer meets the ruffians one is promised.'

It was very still in the drawing-room.

Then Mrs Bonner frowned, and sighed, and let it be understood she was engaged in a kind of higher mathematics:

'Let me see. Thursday?'

She had grown contemplative of the whole of time.

'Now, had it been Wednesday, that is always inconvenient. And Friday, that would be out of the question. Miss Lassiter is to fit Belle for her dress. The wedding-dress. My daughter, Mr Badgery, is to be married, you may not have heard. To Lieutenant Radclyffe.'

'Ha!' exclaimed the surgeon of *Nautilus*, and was horrified to hear himself smack his lips.

This unexpected noise was distinguished quite clearly by all the ladies present, the kinder of whom hastened in their minds to blame the madeira, of which Mrs Bonner had offered a glass, but lately imported, too. It could have been the madeira, or the biscuit; a dry biscuit does encumber the tongue. Mrs Bonner herself examined the surgeon afresh, and saw a somewhat thick-set individual, of healthy complexion, and crisp hair. If not quite a gentleman, at least his eye was honest.

'Lieutenant Radclyffe,' the tactful hostess continued to explain, 'who will resign his commission shortly before the ceremony. The young couple propose to take up residence in the Hunter Valley.'

'Oh, Mamma, you are becoming tedious!'

Belle blushed, and did look very pretty.

'The Hunter Valley?' said the surgeon. 'I must confess to ignorance of almost everything concerning New South Wales, but hope to remedy that, with time and study. The sea-shells, I have noticed, appear to be particularly fine.'

It is a dismal fact that, to know one is not as dull as one can sound, does not help in the least.

'Dr Badgery reads books,' Una Pringle contributed.

'Ah,' Mrs Bonner accepted, 'my niece, Laura, who will be down presently, is the one for reading books. She is quite highly educated, Mr Badgery, although I do say it myself. Most men, of course, are prejudiced against education in a woman; to some it even appears unseemly, but then, on the whole, men are timid things. Please do not misunderstand me, Mr Badgery. Naturally, there are exceptions. Although, in my opinion, timidity in certain avenues does enhance manliness. Just as intellect in a woman can opiee her charm and sweetness. As in our Laura.'

Oh, Mamma, Belle barely breathed, who had not suspected her mother of such enlightenment.

'Laura is so sweet,' said Una Pringle, as she had been taught, and examined her new kid glove, which had rather a distinctive smell. 'How is the baby? Laura has a baby,' she explained kindly, for the sake of Dr Badgery.

'A baby?'

The surgeon suspected that his surprise sounded less polite than indelicate and, for the second time, was made most unhappy.

It was fortunate that the midshipman had broken his biscuit. As he gathered up the fragments from the carpet, everybody was able to stare at his big, cold-looking, boy's hands.

'Yes,' said Mrs Bonner, who was most fascinated by the midshipman's god-sent crumbs. 'A baby. It is a touching story. Laura herself will tell you.'

Thus inspired, she dared that Una Pringle to say another word, and Una did not.

It was then that Dr Badgery noticed the dark young woman entering the room, and realized that all else, though elegant in its way, had been the preliminary roll of kettle drums. All were soon looking at her, because by now she had closed the door, and was forced to face them. Equally, the strangers were forced to face Miss Trevelyan, so that the walls contained a certain feeling of suppressed thunder.

'Please sit down,' Laura did not quite command, but addressed them as a woman who had attained to a position of authority.

She had also distributed kind smiles, but as there was no further debt owing to Dr Badgery, she proceeded to talk in a low, agreeable voice to Una Pringle about the latter's brothers and sisters.

'And Grace?' Laura asked.

'Grace has had the croup. We were terrified,' Una said.

'But is better?'

'But is better.'

Dr Badgery watched Miss Trevelyan's hand, which was most pleasing, as it hung from the arm of the chair. Or withdrew itself to her lap. Or rested upon the line of her jaw. On one finger she was wearing a little agate ring, that she would twist suddenly. Her hands were never still for long, yet preserved their air of authority and grace, if not of actual beauty, for they appeared to have become reddened by some labour.

'We are forgetting,' said Laura, with an effort, 'that Dr Badgery is not entertained. He will go away with the poorest opinion of the ladies at Sydney.'

This was an affectation, of course, and in which he refused to believe.

Immediately on closing her dark lips, she saw that the stranger might have read her, so she put her handkerchief to her mouth, but without being able to hide more than the lower part of her face.

Dr Badgery was, in fact, a man of some native sensibility. He would have liked to convey his appreciation of what he had observed, but had been rendered temporarily wooden by conventions and too many ladies.

At this point the aunt, beaming for her niece's self-possession and looks, could not resist announcing:

'Mr Badgery is anxious to study the geography of New South Wales, Laura. He, too, is of an intellectual turn of mind.'

Such compliments are apt to become accusations.

'I do not make claims on the strength of one or two hobbies.' The surgeon began to bristle.

Then he gave up. It would have been exhilarating if the young woman had united with him in their common defence, but he realized that for some reason she did not wish him to continue. In fact, she was beseeching him not to involve her in any way.

His immediate respect for her wishes should have increased that understanding which obviously did exist between them, but in the case of Laura, she was embarrassed. She found herself staring at his rather coarse, though kind hand spread upon his thick, uneasy thigh. As for the surgeon, he would remember certain of her attitudes, to his own torment.

'We have forgotten the picnic, Mrs Bonner.' Una Pringle returned in disgust to the prime reason for their visit.

This man would be good enough for Laura, she decided with the brutality of which refinement is capable.

'Ah, the picnic,' said Mrs Bonner. 'Why, Una, you may tell your mother it will be delightful. For all of us.'

It did seem as though she had reserved her decision, in order to enjoy the subtle pleasure of making it at last.

Laura did not comment, although everybody expected it.

There was little more to discuss, beyond the final arrangements for meeting. Then, as silences were growing, Una Pringle rose, with the two men, to whose respectability her company was tribute. However, she ignored them thoroughly, on principle, and because her thoughts were more profitably engaged.

'Till Thursday, then.'

To this extent Laura expressed her approval of what had been arranged.

'Till Thursday,' repeated Una, laying her cheek against that of her friend.

Miss Abbey had to admire Laura's dress. She had to touch it.

'What a sweet dress,' she had to say. 'And the dearest little sprigs. Could they be heliotrope?'

The other women bore with the governess. Poor thing, she was the fourth daughter of a Bristol clergyman.

Laura made some excuse not to accompany their guests to the steps, leaving them to Belle, whose amiability seldom failed her, and to Aunt Emmy, who would have loved to receive the whole world.

Everyone seemed gratified by the general situation, although the midshipman was, in addition, relieved.

Arrived outside, this relief escaped from him in his funny,

303

clumsy, recently acquired man's voice, in remarks addressed exclusively to his shipmate. There was also the voice of the surgeon as he followed at the heels of the two ladies, along the wing, and round the corner of the house. Laura listened to them all talking. But it was the men, it was Dr Badgery who predominated. His rather rough, burry voice seemed unable to tear itself out of the thorny arms of the rosebushes which lined the path.

So that Laura Trevelyan was persuaded, guiltily, to lay aside her belt of nails, and to recline upon the most comfortable upholstery the room had to offer.

In passing to the front gate, the surgeon touched the creamy, if not the creamiest rose. The heat of the sun had saturated his thick clothes, and he was wondering a good deal.

'Did you care for that Mr Badgery?' Aunt Emmy asked at a later occasion – it was, in fact, the Wednesday, the Pringles' picnic almost upon them.

'One could not dis-like him,' Laura replied.

'By some standards, not quite a gentleman.' Aunt Emmy sighed. Then, seeming to remember, she added: 'We must not decide too hastily, however, that those standards are desirable. Men, you will learn, I think, because you are a practical girl, Laura dear, men are what women make them.'

Mrs Bonner, who was at that moment counting the silver, was very pleased with her estimation.

'Then, are we to assume that poor Dr Badgery's wife did not quite finish him off?' Laura asked, who loved to tease her aunt at moments when she most loved her.

'Such an assumption would be most foolish,' Aunt Emmy returned.

She was very angry with the forks.

'A young girl, provided she is a lady, may safely assume that a gentleman is a bachelor, until such times as those who are in a position to discover the truth inform her to the contrary.'

Then Mrs Bonner, who had made it quite clear, was again pleased.

But, on the Thursday, she was dashed.

For Belle had come downstairs alone, in a bonnet that made her dreamier.

'Where is Laura?' asked the aunt and mother, kissing from habit, but distractedly.

'I do not know,' answered Belle.

She would not tell. She was drifting upon her own cloud. She was separate now.

'Laura!' Mrs Bonner called. 'How provoking! Laura, wecannotexpectthehorsestostandindefinitelyyouknowwhatitleadsto!'

'Has Tom come?' inquired Belle, who was fitting the old gloves she wore for picnics. Her cheeks were lovely.

'As if she has not experienced the incivility of servants who are kept waiting! It is the worst of all risks. Laura!' persisted Mrs Bonner.

'Yes, Aunt,' said the niece, appearing with miraculous meekness. 'I shall not keep anyone waiting a second longer.'

'But you are not ready.'

'Because I am not going.'

'You will deprive us of such pleasure?' asked Tom Radclyffe, who had just arrived, and who was looking not at this thorny cousin, but at his own precious property.

'When we are all expected!' protested Mrs Bonner.

The latter would have gone with her leg sawn off rather than diverge by one inch from the intended course.

'My baby is suffering from the wind, and I must stay with her for the very good reason that she needs me,' Laura answered gravely.

'Have you really also learnt to deflate babies?' Tom Radclyffe asked.

But Mrs Bonner's mind had conceived a tragedy grander than the detail of the baby's wind at first suggested.

'Your baby,' she gulped. 'Give me your arm, Tom, please. I will need it.'

Then she burst into tears, and they led her to the carriage.

Laura was now free. She wiped upon her apron those hands which the observant Dr Badgery had seen to be too red, and with which she had just been washing various small articles of the baby's clothing, for she had decided in the beginning that this was a duty she must take upon herself. Now she returned upstairs.

The healthy baby had been no more than passingly fretful that afternoon. The young woman stood looking at her. No longer could anybody have doubted their relationship. They were looking at each other in the depths of their collusion, fingering each other's skin and face. They were covered with the faintest silvery webs of smiles, when the blood began to beat, the shadow swept across the mother's face, and suddenly she took up her child, and was walking up and down.

The young woman was going up and down, but, in the familiar room, amongst the stolid furniture, the two beings had been overtaken by a storm of far darker colours than human passions. As they were rocked together, tossed, and buffeted, helplessness and desperation turned the woman's skin an ugly brown. What could she do? The baby, on beginning to sense that she had been sucked into some whirlpool of supernatural dangers, could at least let out a howl for her mother to save her, and was probably convinced she would be saved. The mother, however, was unable to enjoy the comfort of any such belief and, for the moment, must be presumed lost.

'My darling, my darling,' Laura Trevelyan whispered, kissing. 'I am so afraid.'

Kisses did drug the child with an illusion of safety, and she calmed down, and eventually slept. The mother saw this mercy descend as she watched. Then it seemed to the young woman that she might pray to God for love and protection of greater adequacy, but she hesitated on realizing her own incapacity to save her trusting child. Only later in the afternoon did she become aware of the extent of her blasphemy, and was made quite hollow by it.

When finally she could bring herself to pray, she did not kneel, but crouched diffidently upon the edge of an upright chair. She formed the words very slowly and distinctly, hoping that, thus, they would transcend her mind. If she dared hope. But she did pray. Not for herself, she had abandoned herself, nor for her baby, who must, surely, be exempt at the last reckoning. She prayed for that being for whom the ark of her love was built. She prayed over and over, for JOHANN ULRICH VOSS, until, through the ordinary bread of words, she did receive divine sustenance.

That evening Laura Trevelyan sat beneath smooth hair and

listened to her aunt recount to her uncle details of the Pringles'
picnic, although none was deceived as to the true direction of
the narrative.

'The air was most bracing,' Mrs Bonner declared, still snuffing
it recklessly. 'Everyone was agreeable, and some even well-
informed, for a much-travelled man cannot fail to acquire instructive scraps of information. Did I perhaps forget to mention
that several of the officers from *Nautilus* and *Samphire* were
present? It is not surprising if I did. I am scattered from here to
Waverley. Such a jolting, and worst of all down a fiendish lane
where we were driven at last to the home of Judge de Courcy
– whose wife is a lady of the very best connexions, it appears, in
Leicestershire – and were shown their glasshouses and gardens.
In the course of this little excursion, I received a most interesting
lecture on topiary from Mr Badgery – you will have heard tell,
Mr Bonner, the surgeon of *Nautilus*, who accompanied Una
Pringle on the occasion of her last visit.'

Mr Bonner could sit whole evenings without answering his
wife, but they understood each other.

'Now, it appears, Mr Badgery is known to Mrs de Courcy,
and that he is quite well connected, through his mother, with
whom he lives when at home, for in spite of his many excellent
qualities, he has remained a bachelor.'

Laura, too, in spite of her resolutions, could have strolled
along the paths between the solid, masculine, clipped hedges,
and touched them with her hand. All that is solid is at times
nostalgic and desirable.

Mrs Bonner had paused, and was knotting a thread that her
work demanded.

'I am sorry, Laura, that I have not inquired after Mercy,' she
said. 'Earlier in the afternoon, I myself was so very much
upset.'

'I am sorry, Aunt, if we have caused you unhappiness of any
kind,' Laura replied. 'As it happened, it was only a slight indisposition. But I cannot run the risk of neglecting what I have
sworn to do.'

Mrs Bonner could not answer. At this point, however, her
husband was beginning to stir. A stranger might have failed to
perceive the subtle sympathy that did exist between the couple,

for coupled they were, even in irritation, by many tough, tangled, indestructible, instinctive links.

So, when the tea was brought in, Mr Bonner began. He stood upon the hearth, which was the centre of their house, and where a small fire of logs had been lit, because the nights remained chilly. He said:

'Now, Laura, you are a reasonable girl, and we must come to a decision about this child.'

Laura did not answer. She was cold, and had twisted her fingers together as she watched the flames writhing in the oblivious grate.

'You must realize that your own position is intolerable, however laudable your intentions, in keeping someone else's child.'

'It is unnatural that you should become so stubbornly attached. A young girl.' Mrs Bonner sighed.

'If I were a married woman,' Laura Trevelyan answered, 'I do not think it would be so very different.'

The pitiful fire was leaping out in sharp, thin, desperate tongues.

Mrs Bonner clucked.

'But a baby without a name,' she said. 'I am surprised, to say the least, that you should not find us worthy of consideration.'

'I am aware of my debt, and shall attempt to repay you,' Laura replied, 'but please, please, in any other way. As Mercy is guilty of being without a name, and this offends you, the least I can do is give her my own. I should have thought of that. Of course.'

'But consider the future, how such a step would damage your prospects,' said the uncle.

'My prospects,' cried the niece, 'are in the hands of God.'

She was holding her head. The wood-smoke was unbearable, with its poignance of distances.

Then she dragged herself forward a little in her chair, and said:

'I will suffer anything you care to inflict on me, of course. I, too, can endure.'

Mrs Bonner was looking round, in little, darting glances, at her normal room.

'Oh, she is hysterical,' she said, tugging at the innocent thread that joined her needle to the linen. And then: 'We only wish to help you, Laura dear. We love you.'

They did. Indeed, it was that which made it most terrible.

Fortunately, just then, Belle ran across the terrace and into the room. She had accompanied the Pringles home for supper, and had returned in the brougham of the two Miss Unwins who also lived at Potts Point.

'Am I interrupting an important conference?' Belle inquired, rather casually.

Mr Bonner frowned.

'Young ladies about to be married walk into a room,' said her mother. 'They do not run.'

But she added, from force of habit, and because she did always hope to be informed of something dreadful:

'What is the news?'

'The news,' said Belle, 'is that Una has decided at last to take Woburn McAllister.'

'To *take*,' protested the disgusted father, who maintained a high standard of ethics in the bosom of his family.

'Money to money. Well, that is the way,' said Mrs Bonner. 'But poor man, he is certainly in the pastoral business. To add such a silly, frizzy sheep to all those he already has.'

Her husband pointed out that Una Pringle was their friend.

'She is our friend,' said Mrs Bonner, biting her thread. 'I will not deny that. And it is by being our friend that I have got to know her.'

'I think I shall go to bed,' Belle announced, nibbling without appetite at a little biscuit that she had picked up from the silver tray. 'I am so tired.'

Her eyelids were heavy. She was a golden animal that would fall asleep immediately on curling up.

After that, everybody went. So the victim was saved up for the future.

During the weeks that followed nothing more was said, and Laura could have been happy if she had not suspected silence. She also dreamed dreams, which she would try to remember, but could not, only that she had been engaged in some activity of frenzied importance far outside her reason and her cold limbs.

If the nights were formidable, the days were bland, in which everyone was occupied with the preparations for Belle's wedding.

'I shall be married in white,' Belle had said. 'But I insist on muslin. Who ever heard of a satin bride go trapesing into the bush.'

'Muslin is practical, of course,' said Mrs Bonner, who, secretly, would have liked to shine.

And the father was disappointed, who could have afforded satin for his daughter.

This was the most important event in the merchant's house since the departure of the expedition. Miss Lassiter came. There were yards of everything, and bridesmaids who giggled a good deal, and Chattie Wilson was pricked by a pin. All these women, whether the rusty, humble ones who knelt amongst the snippets, or the dedicated virgins who stood about in absorbed, gauzy groups, all were helping to create the bride, to breathe the myth of Belle Bonner, so that few people who saw her would fail to bore posterity. As the women worked, the origins of ritual were forgotten. As they built the tiers of sacred white, they debated and perspired. They unwound cards of lace, as if it had been string. They heaped the precious on the precious, until Belle, who laughed, and submitted, and did not tire – she was such a healthy girl – became a pure, white, heavenly symbol, trembling to discover its own significance.

So the spirit of the explorer, the scarecrow that had dominated the house beyond all measure with his presence, and even haunted it after he had gone, was ruthlessly exorcized by the glistening bride. Who would think of him now, except perhaps Rose Portion, out of her simplicity, if she had been alive, the merchant, by resentful spasms, since his money was undoubtedly lost, and Laura Trevelyan. The bride had certainly forgotten that knotty man, but loved her cousin, and was wrung accordingly, as she looked down out of the mists of lace and constellations of little pearls that were gathering round her hair.

The throats of the two girls were contracting. Two cats rolled together in one ball in the sun could not have led a more intimate life, yet there was very little they had shared, with the consequence that Belle, now that they were being drawn apart, began to ransack her mind for some little favour, preferably of a secret cast, to offer her cousin as evidence of her true affection.

'Lolly,' she said, at last, 'we have not thought what I shall carry on the day. Everything will be in flower, yet nothing seems suitable. To me. You are the one who must decide.'

Laura did not hesitate.

'I would choose pear blossom.'

'But the sticks!' protested the bride. 'They will only be unmanageable, and look ugly.'

It was like Laura, herself at times stiff and awkward, to suggest anything so grotesque.

'You are not in earnest?' Belle asked.

'Yes,' said Laura.

And she looked at her cousin, who was the more poignant in that her pure poetry could transcend her rather dull doubts. The blossom was already breaking from her fingertips, and from the branches of her arms.

Then Belle knew that she must do as Laura saw it.

'Perhaps,' she said, murmuringly. 'If the wind will not dry it up before the day.'

All this, trivial in itself, was spoken over the busy heads of the women who were clustered round the bride. The two girls alone read the significance of what their hearts received, and locked it up, immediately.

At this period Mrs Bonner had every reason to feel satisfied, but her nature demanded that her whole house be in order. She must make her last attempt. With this end in view, she approached her niece one day as the latter was standing with the child in her arms, and said:

'You must come in, my dear, and meet the Asbolds.'

'The Asbolds? Who are the Asbolds?'

'They are good people who have a little property at Penrith,' Aunt Emmy replied.

But Laura began protecting herself with her own shoulders.

'I am not decent,' she complained. 'And I do not want to inflict Mercy on the kitchen.'

'Then, indecent as you are,' laughed the aunt, who was in a good humour. 'You may bring Mercy, too. They are quite simple people.'

'These Asbolds,' asked the niece, as she was swept through the house, 'are they acquaintances of long standing?'

'Not exactly,' said Mrs Bonner, 'although I have known them, well, some little while.'

Which was true. All this time Laura's wise child was looking at the older woman.

Then they went into the little, rarely used parlour, where the visitors were waiting, as befitted quite simple people from Penrith.

Mrs Asbold, who had risen and made some deferential gesture, was a large, comfortable body, with pink cheeks that the sun had as yet failed to spoil. On the other hand, her husband, who had led a life of exposure to all weathers in both countries, was already well cured; he was of seasoned red leather, and beginning to shrivel up. So clearly was honesty writ upon their faces, one felt it would have been dishonest to submit the couple to proof by questioning.

However, when everyone was seated, and shyness dissolved, a pleasant talk was begun, in the course of which Mrs Asbold had to exclaim:

'And this is the little girl. How lovely and sturdy she is.'

The baby, who had but lately gone into frocks, was indeed a model child, both in her rosy flesh, and, it appeared, in her unflinching nature.

'Would you come to me, dear?' asked Mrs Asbold, her grey-gloved hands hesitating upon her comfortable knees.

Mercy did not seem averse, and was soon planted in the visitor's lap.

'Are you as Christian as your name, eh?' asked the husband, feeling the substance of the child's cheek with his honest fingers, and grinning amiably, up to the gaps in his back teeth. 'We could do with such a little girl. Eh?'

'Oh, yes,' said the woman, as if she had been hungry all these years.

Like Mr Asbold, Laura was also smiling, but stupidly. She felt ill.

'She would be killed with kindness, I feel sure,' said Mrs Bonner, fidgeting with the ribbons of her cap.

The aunt remembered a play she had once seen in which all the actors were arranged in a semicircle, in anticipation of a scene the dramatist had most cunningly prepared, and just as he had controlled his situation, Mrs Bonner now hoped to manage hers, forgetting that she was not a dramatist, but herself an actor in the great play.

'The Asbolds,' said Aunt Emmy, looking at Laura, but lowering her eyelids and fluttering them as if there had been a glare, 'the Asbolds,' she repeated, 'have the finest herd of dairy cows at Penrith. And the prettiest house. Such pigs, too. But it is the house that would take your eye, Laura, so I am led to understand, and in the spring, with the fruit blossom. Is not the fruit blossom, Mr Asbold, looking very fine?'

'They are nice trees,' the man said.

'In such healthy, loving surroundings, a little girl could not help but grow up happy,' suggested Mrs Bonner.

Mrs Asbold wetted her lips.

'You have no children of your own?' asked Laura, whose limbs had turned against her.

'Oh, no,' said the woman, shortly.

She was looking down. She was busy with the child's short skirt, touching, and arranging, but guiltily.

'It must be a great sadness for you,' said Laura Trevelyan.

Her compassion reached the barren woman, who now looked up, and returned it.

Mrs Bonner had the impression that something was happening which she did not understand. So she said, almost archly:

'Would you not be prepared to give Mercy to Mrs Asbold, Laura?' Then, with the sobriety that the situation demanded: 'I am sure the poor child's unfortunate mother would be only too grateful to see her little one so splendidly placed.'

Laura could not answer. This is the point, she felt, at which it will be decided, one way or the other, but by some superior power. Her own mind was not equal to it.

'Will you take it, Liz?' Mr Asbold asked, doubtfully.

His wife, who was ruffling up the child's hair as she pondered, seemed to be preparing herself to commit an act of extreme brutality.

The child did not flinch.

'Yes,' said the woman, peering into the stolid eyes. 'She knows I would not hurt her. I would not hurt anyone.'

'But will you take her?' asked the man, who was anxious to be gone to things he knew.

'No,' said the woman. 'She would not be ours.'

Her mouth, in her amiable, country face, had become unexpectedly ugly, for she had committed the brutal act, only it was against herself.

'Oh, no, no,' she said. 'I will not take her.'

Getting up, she put the child quickly but considerately in the young lady's lap.

'She would have too many mothers.'

Everybody had forgotten Mrs Bonner, who was no longer of importance in that scene, except to show the Asbolds out. This she did, and immediately went upstairs.

Because she, too, was powerless, Laura Trevelyan continued to sit where left, and at first scarcely noticed the persistent Mercy. Important though it was that the child should remain, her considerable victory was by no means final. No victory is final, the unhappy Laura saw, and in her vision of further deserts was touching his face with a renewed tenderness, where the skin ended and the rather coarse beard began, until the little girl became frightened, first of her mother's eyes, then of her devouring passion, and begged to be released.

Because of her own duplicity, Mrs Bonner also was a little frightened of her niece, although they addressed each other in pleasant voices, when they were not actually avoiding, and it was easy to avoid during the days that preceded the wedding, there was such a pressure of events.

Two days before the ceremony, the Pringles gave a ball in honour of Belle Bonner, whom everybody liked. It had been decided to take the ballroom at Mr Bright's Dancing Academy in Elizabeth Street, on account of its greater convenience for those among the guests who would have to be brought by boat from the North Shore. From the hiring of such an elegant establishment, and references to other details let slip by the organizers, it became obvious that the Pringles were preparing to spend a considerable sum of money, with the result that their ball was soon all the talk, both amongst those who were invited, and even more amongst those who were not. Of the latter, some voiced the opinion that it was indelicate on the part of the hostess to show herself in her condition, until those who took her part pointed out that, in obedience to such a principle, the unfortunate lady must remain almost permanently hidden.

On the morning of the event, Mrs Pringle, by now a martyr to her heaviness, proceeded none the less to the hall, accompanied by her daughters Una and Florence, where they arranged quantities of cinerarias, or saw to it, rather, that the pots were massed artistically by two strong gardeners, while they themselves held their heads to one side, the better to judge of effects, or came forward and poked asparagus fern into every visible gap. Mr Bright, the dancing instructor, who was experienced in conducting Assemblies and such like, offered many practical suggestions, and was invaluable in ordering their execution. It was he, for instance, who engaged the orchestra, in consultation with Mr Topp. It was he who was acquainted with a lady who would save Mrs Pringle the tiresomeness of providing a supper for so many guests, although how intimately Mr Bright was connected with the catering lady, and how well he did by the arrangement, never became known. For Mrs Pringle he remained *quite omniscient* and a *tower of strength,* while his two young nephews showed commendable energy in polishing the floor, running at the shavings of candle-fat until the boards were burning under their boots, and the younger boy sustained a nasty fall.

As evening approached, the gas was lit, and activity flared up in the retiring- and refreshment-rooms, where respectable women in black were setting out such emergency aids to the comfort of ladies as eau de Cologne, lozenges, safety pins, and needles and thread, and for the entertainment of both sexes every variety of meat that the Colony could provide, in profusion without vulgarity, as well as vegetables cut into cunning shapes, and trifles and jellies shuddering under their drifts of cream.

Only the room of rooms, the ballroom, remained empty, in a state of mystical entrancement, under the blue, hissing gas, as the invisible consort in the gallery began to pick over the first, fragile notes of music. Such was the strain of stillness and expectation, it would not have been surprising if the walls had flown apart from the pressure, shattering the magic mirrors, of golden mists and blue, gaseous depths, and scattering the distinct jewels from the leaves of the cinerarias.

The Pringles' guests, however, did begin to trickle in, then to flow, and finally to pour. Everyone was there who should, as well as some who, frankly, should not have been. Several drunken individuals, for instance, got in out of the street. Their pale, tuberous faces lolled for an instant upon the banks of purple flowers, terrifying in some cases, infuriating in others, those who had succeeded in thrusting ugliness out of their own lives. Then, order was restored. Attendants put an end to the disgraceful episode by running the intruders into the night from which they had come, and they were soon forgot in the surge of military, the gallant demeanour of ships' officers, the haze of young girls that drifted along the edges of the hall or collected in cool pockets at the corners.

The music played. The company wove the first, deliberate figures of the dance.

Mrs Pringle, who had been receiving her guests in a disguise of greenery, came forward especially far to embrace her dearest friends, the Bonners. There was a clash of onyx and cornelian.

'My dear,' said Mrs Bonner, when she had extricated herself sufficiently from the toils of jewellery, 'I must congratulate you on what appears to be a triumph of taste and festivity.'

For once the scale of her enterprise prevented Mrs Pringle from drawing attention to her friend's unpunctuality.

'I must remember on some more appropriate occasion to tell you what has detained us,' Mrs Bonner whispered, and hinted, and smiled. Then, raising her voice to a rather jolly pitch: 'But delay will not detract from our enjoyment; first glances assure me of that.'

No one had ever thought to remind her at a later date of her offer to explain, so perhaps ladies do respect one another's stratagems. For Mrs Bonner, in the belief that fresh flowers will catch the eye when others are beginning to wilt, always arrived late at a ball.

'Belle is radiant,' said Mrs Pringle, accepting the part she was to play.

'Belle is looking well,' said her mother, as if she had but noticed.

'Will you not agree that she is the loveliest girl in Sydney?' asked Mrs Pringle, who could be generous.

'Poor Sydney!' protested Belle.

At times she would grimace like some ugly boy, and even this was acceptable. But, on the present occasion, she returned very quickly to her high, white cloud.

'And Laura,' added Mrs Pringle, kindly.

For Laura Trevelyan was also there.

Belle Bonner at once sailed out with Mr Pringle, an ugly man, who smelled of tobacco, but respected for his influence and money. Belle was wearing satin for tonight, smoother than the music, whiter than the silences, for most men, and even conspicuously pretty girls stopped talking as she floated near. In their absorption, those who knew her intimately would not have obtruded the reality of their relationship. They only thought to support themselves on their own, prosaic legs, and watch Belle as she danced past.

There was also Laura Trevelyan.

Laura was wearing a dress that nobody could remember when asked to do so afterwards. Only after much consideration, and with a feeling that what they were saying had been dragged up from their depths and did not properly fit their mouths, some of them replied that the dress was probably the colour of ashes, or the bark of some native tree. Of course, the dress did not match either of these descriptions. It was only that its wearer, by the gravity of her face and set of her rather proud head, did make a sombre impression. Although she replied with agreeable directness and simplicity to all those who dared address her, few did, on account of some indefinite obscurity that they sensed, but could not penetrate, or worse still, because they began to suspect the presence of darkness in their own souls. So they were for ever smoothing their skins, and ruffling up their pink or blue gauze in mirrors, before allowing themselves to be thrown together again by that mad wind of concealed music. They, the larkspurs of life, were only appreciable in masses.

At one point Laura was approached by Chattie Wilson, a plump, and rather officious girl, who was always giving good advice, who knew everything, who went everywhere, always the bridesmaid, but who had been overlooked, it seemed, because she was so obviously there.

Now Chattie asked:

'Are you not enjoying yourself, Laura?'

'Not particularly,' answered Laura. 'To be perfectly candid.'

Chattie giggled. To confess to the sin of not enjoying was something she would never have dared, so she pretended that she did not believe.

'Are you not well, perhaps? There is quite a respectable sofa in the retiring-room. Quite *clean*. You could put your feet up for a little. I will come and sit with you, if you like.'

Chattie was most anxious to be of service to her friend, for, in spite of her relentless pursuit of enjoyment, at times she did suspect that enjoyment refused as relentlessly to be pursued.

Then Laura replied:

'Are you really able to lie down on the sofa and be cured? Ah, Chattie, how I do envy you!'

This was the sort of thing that people did not like in Laura, and Chattie giggled, and dabbed with her handkerchief at the perspiration on her upper lip.

'Oh, well,' she said, and giggled again to stop the gap.

But Laura was grateful to her rather suety friend.

'Come,' she said, touching Chattie, because it cost her an effort. 'Let us stand over there and watch, near that column, where we shall not be seen.'

'Oh, dear, no,' said Chattie, for whom it was a first duty to be noticed, and was propelling her friend up a short flight of steps leading to a little dais, from which prizes were distributed after the term's dancing classes, and on which chairs had been arranged in a bower of flowers. 'One does not accept to go to a ball simply to hide behind a column.'

'Will it do us any good to sit exposed in the open, like a target?' Laura asked.

Chattie knew that targets were designed for arrows, but contained her thoughts.

'If we do not actually benefit by it, we can come to no positive harm,' she was careful to observe.

So they seated themselves.

It was Belle's night. Belle was everywhere, in her white dress, almost always and inevitably in the arms of Tom Radclyffe. Other dancers made way, encouraging her presence in their midst, as if she had been a talisman of some kind, and they would have touched her magic dress. As she danced, sometimes she would close her eyes against the music, although more often she would hold them open, expressing her love in such lucid glances that some mothers considered it immodest, and Laura, intercepting the touching honesty of that almost infinite blue, was afraid for her cousin's safety, and wanted to protect her.

Or herself. She shuddered to realize that love might not remain hidden, and was nervously turning her head this way and that. She was most alarmingly, chokingly exposed. Her neck had mottled.

When the man approached so quietly, and bowed so civilly, she could have cried out, to ward off that being who, from his very modesty and reasonableness, might possibly have understood.

'It is very kind,' she said, in a loud, ugly voice. 'Thank you. But I am not dancing.'

'I do not blame you,' he replied. 'I am never surprised at any person not wishing to dance. It is not sociable, for one thing. It is not possible to jig up and down and express one's thoughts clearly at the same time.'

'Oh,' said Laura, 'I had always been led to understand that the expression of thought was the height of unsociability.'

Chattie Wilson laughed rather bitterly. She was hating everything.

Then Laura Trevelyan introduced Dr Badgery, surgeon of *Nautilus*, to Miss Chattie Wilson, and felt that she herself was absolved from further duty.

But his expression would not leave her in peace. Although his voice would be engaged with Chattie Wilson, it was not Chattie whom he was questioning.

'Tell me, Miss Wilson,' he said, 'are you well acquainted with the country?'

'Oh, dear, no. I have been very seldom into the bush. It is

different, of course, if one marries; then it may become a matter of necessity.'

Miss Wilson did not intend to waste much time on Dr Badgery, who was neither young, nor handsome, of moderate means, she suspected, and not quite a gentleman. If she did not also recognize sympathy, it was because she was not yet desperate enough.

'I would give anything to satisfy my curiosity,' he said.

'You should join some expedition,' advised Chattie, and tried anxiously to be recognized by someone nice.

'Such as left last year,' she added, for she had been well trained, 'under the leadership of that German, Mr Voss.'

No expedition, it appeared, would be led to the rescue of Chattie Wilson.

'Ah,' said Dr Badgery. 'So I have heard. Tell me about him.'

He was looking most intently at Chattie, but would be turned at any moment, Laura knew, to intercept her distress.

'I did not make his acquaintance,' Chattie replied, but remembered at once. 'Laura did, though.'

Then Dr Badgery turned, straining a little, as well-fleshed men of forty will, and was looking at Laura with the highest hopes. He would have been singularly unsurprised at anything of an oracular nature that might have issued from the mouth of that dark young woman.

Laura, who had looked away, remained conscious of his rather heavy eyebrows.

'Did you?' he asked.

And waited.

'Yes,' she replied. 'That is to say, my uncle was one of those who subscribed to Mr Voss's expedition.'

'And what manner of man is this German?'

'I do not know,' said Laura. 'I cannot judge a person on superficial evidence. Sometimes,' she added, for she had by now lived long enough, 'it will even appear that all evidence is superficial.'

'I have heard the most extraordinary things,' said the surgeon, 'of Mr Voss.'

'Then, no doubt,' said the young woman, 'you are better informed than I.'

It was at this point that Dr Badgery realized he should ask Miss Wilson to dance, and she, for want of better opportunities, accepted graciously enough. They went down. Now the surgeon, that ordinarily jolly man, who wrote affectionate letters to young girls long after their mothers had given him up, was engulfed in the tragic hilarity of the polka, as if rivers of suffering had gushed to the surface from depths where they had remained hitherto unsuspected, or he, perhaps he alone had not tapped them.

This was before his sense of duty returned.

'Do you know Waverley?' asked the jigging surgeon.

'Oh, dear, yes. *Waverley*,' sighed, and jigged Miss Chattie Wilson. 'I know everywhere round here. Although, of course, there are some places where one cannot go.'

'I was at Waverley recently, in the garden of a Judge de Courcy. Do you know him?' asked the surgeon, who had heard it done this way.

'His wife is my aunt's second cousin.'

'Is everybody related?'

'Almost everybody.' Chattie sighed. 'Of course, there are some people who cannot be.'

'I was at Waverley with the Pringles. Miss Bonner and her mother happened to be of the party.'

'Belle,' said Chattie, 'is the sweetest thing. And so lovely. She deserves every bit of her good fortune. Nobody could envy Belle.'

'And Miss Trevelyan,' the surgeon suggested.

'Laura is sweet, too,' Chattie sighed. 'But peculiar. Laura is clever.'

They continued to dance.

Or the surgeon was again threading the dark maze of clipped hedges at Waverley. He knew that, already the first day, he was dedicated to Laura Trevelyan, whatever the nature of her subterranean sorrows. So they sailed against the dark waters, trailing hands, she holding her face away, or they walked in the labyrinth of hedges, in which, he knew from experience, they did not meet.

From where she had continued to sit, Laura Trevelyan watched the antics of the fat surgeon, an unlikely person, whom she would have learnt to love, if seas of experience and music had not flowed between them.

Then the dancers stopped, and everybody was applauding the capital music with their hot gloves.

Laura was for the moment quite separate in the roomful of human beings, but as she had outlived the age of social panic, she did not try to burrow in, and presently she saw Willie Pringle, on whom the hair had begun to sprout in unsatisfactory patches.

Willie wandered through his own party, and finally arrived at Laura.

'I do not care for a ball, Laura, do you?' the young man asked, with his silly, loose mouth.

'You are my host,' Laura answered, kindly.

'Good Lord, I do not feel like one. Not a bit. I do not know what I feel like.'

Without realizing that this is frequently the case before the yeast begins to work, his mother was in the habit of blaming his ineffectuality on the fact that he had outgrown his strength.

'Perhaps you will discover in time, and do something extraordinary,' Laura suggested.

'In a solicitor's office?'

That he would find out and do something extraordinary was an eventuality of which Willie was afraid. But, in the meantime, he enjoyed the company of older girls. Not so much to talk to, as to watch. He sensed that mysticism which their presence bred, by secrets and silences, and music of dresses. Intent upon their own iridescent lives in the corners of a ballroom, or seated in a landscape, under trees, their purely formal beauty obsessed him. Often he would turn his back upon the mirrors that could not perpetuate their images.

'Not in a solicitor's office,' he did hear Laura agree. 'If we were bounded by walls, that would be terrible.'

She seemed to emphasize the *we,* which made Willie happy, although he wrinkled his forehead prodigiously to celebrate his happiness.

'Should we dance, Laura?' he asked, in some doubt.

This was a wholly and unexpectedly delightful prospect to Laura Trevelyan.

'Do let us, Willie,' she said, laughing for the approach of tenuous pleasure. 'It will be fun.'

With Willie whom she had known since childhood. It was so blameless.

So they held hands. To move along the sunny avenues of rather pretty music, produced in the young woman such a sense of innocent happiness she did for a moment feel the pricking of tears. She glanced in a glass and saw that her eyelids had reddened in her pale face, and her nose was swollen. She was ugly tonight, but gently happy.

So the two peculiar people danced gently together. Nobody noticed them at first, except the surgeon, who had been reduced to the company of his own nagging thoughts.

Then Belle saw, and called, across several waves of other dancers, that were separating the two cousins, as at all balls.

'Laura!' Belle cried. 'I am determined to reach you.'

She swam, laughing, through the sea of tulle, and was rising from the foam in her white, shining dress. Belle's skin was permitted to be golden, while others went protecting their pink and white. At close quarters, changed back from goddess into animal, there were little, fine, golden hairs on what some people dared to refer to as *Belle Bonner's brown complexion*. Indeed, there were mothers who predicted that Belle would develop a *coarse look* later on. But she smelled still of youth and flint, sunlight could have been snoozing upon her cheeks, and, amiably, she would let herself be stroked with the clumsiest of compliments. In which she did not believe, however. She laughed them off.

Now the cousins were reunited in midstream. Tugged at and buffeted, they swayed together, they clung together, they looked in through each other's eyes, and rested there. All they saw most concerned themselves.

Until Belle had to bubble.

'Remind me to tell you,' she said, too loud, 'about Mrs de Courcy's hair. You are not moping?'

'Why should I mope?' asked Laura, whose sombre breast had begun to rustle with those peacock colours which were hers normally.

Then Belle was whisked away to dance gravely with the judge.

As Willie had wandered off, as he did on practically all occasions, particularly at balls, Laura was left with her own music, of which she dared to hum a few little, feverish phrases. The fringe of metal beads, that hung from the corsage of what had been her dull dress, glittered and chattered threateningly, and swords struck from her seemingly cavernous eyes, from beneath guarded lids.

In consequence, Tom Radclyffe was of two minds when approaching his cousin-to-be.

'I presume you are not dancing,' he began.

'If you would prefer it that way,' Laura smiled, 'I am willing to set your feelings at rest.'

She knew that Belle, who was kind by instinct, had come to some arrangement with Tom.

'You know it is not a question of that,' he blurted. 'I thought you would prefer to talk.'

'That would be worse! Would it not?' Laura laughed.

He might have ignored her more completely if he had not permitted himself to frown.

'In that case,' he said, and blushed, 'let us, rather, dance.'

Were it not for his physical strength, one might have suspected Tom Radclyffe of being a somewhat frightened man. As it was, and taking into account his military career, such a suspicion could only have been absurd.

Laura said, as she touched his sleeve:

'I cannot grow accustomed to this new disguise.'

'I cannot grow accustomed to myself,' he answered rather gloomily.

For Tom had resigned his commission, and was now plain man. That, perhaps, was most of his predicament. He was not yet reconciled to nakedness.

As they danced together, the man and woman could have been two swords holding each other.

'Will you be kind to Belle?' Laura asked. 'I could never forgive you if you were not.'

Observed in a certain light, all the dancers wore bitter smiles. The heavy fringe of beads ornamenting her relentless dress was coldly metallic under his hand.

'But Belle and I love each other.'

And men become as little children.

'He who was not in love was never hurt,' Laura said.

'Let us be reasonable,' he ordered, reasserting his masculinity. 'Because you have been hurt, it does not follow that other people must suffer the same experience. Even though you may wish it.'

'You misunderstand me,' she said.

As she was looking over his shoulder it sounded humble, and her opponent, who had but recently lost his balance, was quick to take advantage.

'You know I am an ordinary sort of fellow,' he said; he could make cunning use of his simplicity. 'My intelligence is of the practical kind. As for imagination, you will say that mine is not developed to the degree that you admire.' Such was his haste, he scarcely paused for his due reward. 'Or that I am even lacking in it. For which I am deuced glad. You see, it is a great temptation to *live off* one's imagination, as some people do.'

His voice had risen too high and left him breathless, but he no longer paused; he rushed on, in fact, right over the precipice:

'What do you expect of Voss?'

His stiff lips were grinning at his own audacity.

It was the first time that Laura Trevelyan had been faced with this phantom, and now that it had happened, the situation was made more terrible by the quarter from which it had come. The silly, invisible music was suddenly augmented by her own heartbeat. Great horns were fluctuating through the wood-and-plaster room.

'Voss?' she clattered discordantly.

Now the metal beads were molten under his fingers.

'Expect?' she responded. 'I do not expect anything of anyone, but am grateful for the crumbs.'

Tom Radclyffe did not absorb this, but was still grinning stiffly.

The two people were dancing and dancing.

Now that he was master of all, the man offered:

'If I could help you in any way, Laura, for Belle's sake.'

'You cannot help me,' Laura replied, 'for Belle's, or anybody else's sake. You could not even help me by your own inclination, of your own will, for Mr Voss, Tom, is lost.'

Tom Radclyffe was quite shocked by the ugly music, and by

the lurching movements of his partner. The truth that he had let loose made him protest and bluster.

'If it is second sight that keeps you so well informed, then we are all threatened.'

Whether from emotion, or exertion, he emphasized every other word. But Laura did not defend herself. Almost at once, she left her partner, and went straight to the retiring-room. Chattie Wilson, noticing, wondered whether she should accompany her friend, whose face was shrunk to the extent that it resembled a yellow skull.

In the resilient hall the music continued to ache until it was time for supper.

Mrs Pringle's triumph was complete when the doors were flung open and her guests burst into the supper-room. If *burst* is not a refined, it is yet an unavoidable word. For those well-conducted, but prudent people who had quietly stationed themselves in readiness, were propelled from behind by the feckless rout, which had continued to dance, and chatter, and fall in love. Suddenly the two parties were united in one thought, only differently expressed, and although the prudent were protesting, and even leaning back to restrain the flushed, impulsive horde of feckless that continued pushing from behind, their common thought did prevail, in final eruption, which brought them in a rush of churned bodies right to the edge of the long tables, threatening the rosy hams and great unctuous sirloins of bloody beef.

'It is disgraceful,' laughed Mrs Bonner, 'that a gathering of individuals from genteel homes should behave like cattle.'

However, she did really rather approve of all signs of animal health, and might have been alarmed had the company behaved like human beings.

Her friend and hostess, Mrs Pringle, who had been frightened at first, for her condition, and who had sought protection behind a most convulsive palm, now emerged, and was walking amongst her guests, with advice such as:

'Do let me press you to a little of this fish in aspic,'
or:

'I can recommend the Salad à la Roosse, Miss Hetherington.'

By her very hospitality, Mrs Pringle, who had wounded many

326

a friend in the name of friendship, was laying herself open to the most savage forms of counter-attack. Now, some of those friends might never have seen her before, while the expression of others suggested they had, indeed, recognized what they must force themselves to endure. As the resigned Mrs Pringle humbly went about her duties, always the servant of their pleasure, the guests were frowning at her from above their whiskers of crimped lettuce and lips of mayonnaise.

Of all those friends perhaps only Mrs Bonner was truly grateful, and she had grown obsequious.

'Allow me to fetch you a jelly, my dear,' she begged. 'Even if, as you say, you have no appetite, a little wine jelly, in your condition, can only fortify.'

For Mrs Bonner, with her head for figures, and her honest beginnings – it was, in fact, not generally known that she had helped her husband with the books – made a habit of reckoning up the cost, and was always flattered by magnificence.

With everyone so busily employed, it was easy for Laura to return unnoticed and take her place amongst the company. Superficially restored, her composure might have seen the evening out if, in the arrangement of things, she had not found herself standing beside Dr Badgery. The surgeon would not, however, suffer her to bite him twice, nor his attention to stray from a helping of beef, and there he might have continued to stand, ignoring the true object of his concern, if their hands had not plunged at the same unhappy moment into a basket of bread.

'Then, you enjoy yourself at dancing, Miss Trevelyan?' the surgeon asked finally, while suggesting that her answer did not signify.

'No,' she said. 'No, no, no.'

And he recognized the cries of men when their wounds are opened.

'Why must you return to that?'

Dr Badgery ate his beef, realizing he had begun to feel too deeply to trust himself upon stilts of words. On the other hand, a curious cracking sound, that his jaws always made while chewing, was now turning silence into something painfully grotesque.

'I did accept the invitations of two partners,' Laura admitted, 'one because we had been happy together, as children, the other because, for the present at least, our relationship is inescapable.'

'That is all very well,' said the surgeon, 'and sentimental, and stoical. The past is desirable, more often than not, because it can make no demands, and it is in the nature of the present to appear rough and uncharitable. But when it comes to the future, do you not feel that chances are equal?'

He had rather blunt, white teeth, set in a trap, in his crisp beard.

'I feel,' she said slowly, and was already frightened at what she was about to admit, 'that the life I am to live is already utterly beyond my control.'

Even the dependable Dr Badgery could not have rescued her from that sea, however much she might have wished it. That she did wish, must be recorded, out of respect for her rational judgement and his worthiness. But man is a rational judge only fleetingly, and worthiness is too little, or too much.

So the surgeon returned presently to his ship, and had soon restored the shape to his orderly life, except that on occasions the dark waters would seep between the timbers. Then he would welcome them, he would be drowning with her, their transparent fears would be flickering in and out of their skulls, trailing long fins of mutual colours.

Long after Dr Badgery had fallen asleep in his brassbound cabin, on the night of his last meeting in the flesh with Laura Trevelyan, the ball at Bright's Dancing Academy, Elizabeth Street, the much discussed, and finally legendary ball that the Pringles gave for Belle, continued to surge and sound. O the seas of music, the long blue dreamy rollers, and the little, rosy, frivolous waves. All was swept, all was carried up and down. To swim was the only natural act, although the eyes were smarting, as the fiddles continued to flick the golden spray, although, in the swell of dawn, question and answer floated out of reach.

'It is really too much to expect of you, dear Mrs Pringle,' said Mrs Bonner. 'Let me order the horses. Could you not simply slip away? Or, supposing I were to go amongst the dancers, and hint to one or two of the more responsible girls, that it is almost morning? I am sure they would listen to reason.'

O reason, O Mrs Bonner, speak to the roses and the mignonette. They will be trampled, rather, or float up and down in the silver seas of morning, together with the programmes and the used napkins.

'Oh, Mrs Pringle, it has been the most lovely, lovely ball,' said Belle Bonner, as she woke from her dream of dancing.

Her cheek was still hot.

'Thank you, Mrs Pringle,' smiled Laura Trevelyan, who offered a frank hand, like a man. And added: 'I have enjoyed myself so much.'

Because she was a woman, she was also dishonest whenever it was really necessary.

Then all the dancers were going. Some of the girls, although well acquainted with the Bonners, carefully guided their skirts past Laura Trevelyan, who had observed them all that night as from a promontory, her eyes outlined in black.

When the Bonners returned that morning, and had kissed, and sighed, and gone to their rooms, Laura sat down at her writing-desk, as if she had been waiting to satisfy a desire, and scrabbled in her trayful of pens, and immediately began to write:

My dear Johann Ulrich,

We have this moment come in from a ball, at which I have been so miserable for you, I must write, not knowing by what means in the world it will be possible to send the letter. Except by miracle, it will not be sent, and so, I fear, it is the height of foolishness.

But write I must. If you, my dear, cannot hope to benefit, it is most necessary for me. I suppose if I were to examine my thoughts honestly, I should find that self-pity is my greatest sin, of which I do not remember being guilty in the past. How strong one was, how weak one always is! Was the firm, upright, reliable character one seemed to have been, a myth? . . .

The reddish light of morning had begun to flow into the rooms of the sleeping house. The tender rooms were like transparent eggs, from which the protective shell had been removed.

The young woman, whose eyelids were turned to buckram, was writing in her red room. She wrote:

. . . It would seem that the human virtues, except in isolated, absolved, absurd, or oblivious individuals *are* mythical. Are you too, my dearest, a myth, as it has been suggested? . . .

The young woman, whose stiff eyelids had been made red and transparent by the unbearably lucid light of morning, began to score the paper, with quick slashes, of her stricken, scratching pen.

Ah, God, she said, I do have faith, if it is not all the time.

Odd lumps of prayer were swelling in her mouth. Her movements were crippled as she stumbled about her orderly room that the red light made dreadful. She was tearing the tough writing-paper, or attempting to, for it was of an excellent quality; her uncle saw to it that she used no other. So that, in the end, the paper remained twisted up. Her breath was rasping, or retching out of her throat.

Mercifully, she fell upon her bed soon after, recovering in sleep that beauty which was hers in private, and which, consequently, many people had never seen.

*

After a very short interval, it seemed, Belle Bonner was married to Tom Radclyffe, at St James's, on a windy day. If Mrs Bonner had swelled with the material importance of a wedding, the disbelieving father appeared much shrunken as he supported his daughter up the aisle. How Belle felt, almost nobody paused to consider, for was not the bride the symbol of all their desires? Indeed, it could have been that Belle herself did not feel, so much as vibrate, inside the shuddering white cocoon from which she would emerge a woman. A remote, a passive rapture veiled her normally human face. To Laura Trevelyan, a bridesmaid who did not match the others, there was no longer any means of communicating with her cousin. She would have resented it more, and dreaded the possibility that their intimacy might never be restored, if she, too, was not become temporarily a torpid insect along with everyone else.

So satin sighed, lozenges were discreetly sucked, and the scented organ meandered through the melodious groves of flowers.

Then, suddenly, the bells were beginning to tumble.

Everyone agreed that the Bonner wedding was the loveliest and most tasteful the Colony had witnessed. Afterwards, upon the steps, emotion and colour certainly flared high, as the wind took veil, hair, and shawl, rice stung, carriages were locked together in the crush, and the over-stuffed and excited horses relieved themselves copiously in the middle of the street. There was also an episode with a disgraceful pink satin shoe, which a high-spirited young subaltern, a second cousin of Chattie Wilson, had carried off, it was whispered, from the dressing-room of an Italian singer. Many of the women blushed for what they knew, others were crying, as if for some tragedy at which they had but lately assisted in a theatre, and a few criticized the bride for carrying a sheaf of pear-blossom, which was original, to say the least.

Standing upon the steps of the church, in the high wind, Laura Trevelyan watched her cousin, in whose oblivious arms lay the sheaf of black sticks, of which the flowerets threatened to blow away, bearing with them tenderly, whitely, imperceptibly, the myth of all happiness.

12

ALTHOUGH the past winter had proved unusually wet in almost every district, it was naturally wettest in that country in which the expedition of Johann Ulrich Voss was forcibly encamped, for men are convinced early in their lives that the excesses of nature are incited for their personal discomfiture. Some who survive the trial persuade themselves they had been aware all along, either through their instinct, or their reason, of the existence of the great design, yet it is probable that only the wisest, and most innocent, were not deceived at first.

Now, as winter became spring, the members of the expedition were beginning to crawl out of their cave and watch drowsily the grey water dwindle into yellow slime. They no longer blamed their sins for their predicament. Although physically weak, and disgusting to smell, their importance was returning by human leaps and bounds. Their weak eyes were contending with the stronger sun. Already the higher ground showed green promise of a good season. So the men were stretching their muscles, and flattering themselves, on the strength of their survival, that all the goodness which emanated from the earth was for their especial benefit, that it was even the fruit of their suffering, when one day a small, grey bird, whacking his beak against the bough of a tree which hung beside the entrance to the cave, seemed to cast some doubt upon their recovered confidence.

It was obvious that the fearless bird could not conceive that respect was due to men, not even as Turner shot him dead.

When Palfreyman remonstrated with the successful sportsman, the latter cheerfully replied:

'What's the odds! If I had not of knocked 'im off, something else would of got 'im.'

The sun was blaring with golden trumpets. Tinged with gold after weeks in the musty cave, the fellow forgot the grey louse he had always been.

So he cleared his throat and added:

'And you scientific gentlemen should know that a bird is only a bird.'

His almost foetal eyes were twinkling. Never before had he felt himself the equal of all men.

Palfreyman was distressed.

'Poor thing,' he said, touching the dead bird with the tip of his toe.

'Do not tell me you never killed a bird!' cried Turner.

Compassion in the other had caused him to scent a weakness. Now he was perhaps even a gentleman's superior.

'I have killed many, to my knowledge,' Palfreyman replied, 'and could be responsible for much that I do not realize.'

As he spoke, it seemed that he was resigning his part in the expedition.

Turner was angry. He kicked the dead bird, so that it went shooting away across the mud and water. He himself slithered off, over rocks, in search of something else to kill, but constrained still by the great expanse of wet.

Palfreyman wished that he could have employed himself in some such easy, physical way and, in so doing, have re-discovered a purpose. There comes a moment when an individual who is too honest to take refuge in the old illusion of self-importance is suspended agonizingly between the flat sky and the flat earth, and prayer is no more than a slight gumminess on the roof of the mouth.

At this period, between flood and dry, owing to some illusion of sky and water, the earth appeared very flat indeed, particularly at early morning, when the leader of the expedition, Mr Voss, would walk out to test the ground. His trousers rolled to the middle of his calves, and wearing a stout reefer jacket, for the cold was still considerable in the early hours, he would proceed awkwardly across the mud, but soon become bogged. Then he would throw his feet to the winds, to rid them of that tragic sock. In different circumstances, he could have appeared a ridiculous figure to those watching from the shingly platform in front of the cave. Now they would not have dared laugh, for fear of the sounds that might have issued out of their mouths. Nor did they speak as much as formerly. Words that did not belong to them – illuminating, true, naked words – had a habit of coming out.

When he had gone a certain distance, the leader would perceive the folly of continuing, and stand a while, motionless upon his stilts of legs, reflected in the muddy water or watery mud. Then, I must return to those men, he would realize, and the thought of it was terrible. Nothing could have been more awful than the fact that they were men.

But a crust did form at last upon the slimy surface of the earth, and the party was able finally to ride forward.

Moreover, the land was celebrating their important presence with green grass that stroked the horses' bellies, or lay down beneath them in green swathes. The horses snatched at the grass, until they were satisfied, or bloated, and the green scours had begun to run. Similarly, the eyes of the men became sated with the green of those parklands, although they continued to sing, like lovers or children, as they rode. They sang songs about animals that they remembered from childhood, or the vibrant songs they had hummed against their teeth as youths, waiting in the dusk against a stile. These latter songs were the more difficult to remember, in that they had never been sung for their words. The songs had poured forth in the beginning as the spasms and vibrations of the singers' bodies.

So love and anticipation inspired the cavalcade as it passed

333

through the green country, still practically a swamp. The passionate cries of birds exploded wonderfully overhead. The muscular forms of cool, smooth, flesh-coloured trees rose up before the advancing horsemen. Yet the men themselves, for all their freedom and their joyful songs, only remotely suggested flesh. By this time, it is true, their stock of provisions was inadequate, but an abundant supply of game had arrived to celebrate the good season. The men did take advantage of this, to catch and eat, only never more than was necessary to prolong life, for deprivation and distance had lessened their desire for food. It was foreign to their wizened stomachs. They preferred to eat dreams, but did not grow fat on these, quite the reverse.

Into this season of grass, game, and songs burst other signs of victorious life. In a patch of scrub stood a native, singing, stamping, and gesticulating with a spear, of which the barbed head suggested the snout of a crocodile. Three or four companions were grouped about the singer in the bower of scrub, but the others were more diffident, or else they lacked the gift to express their joy.

'He is doubtless a poet,' said Voss, who had grown quite excited. 'What is the subject of his song, Jackie?'

But Jackie could not, or would not say. He averted his face, beneath which his throat was swelling, either with embarrassment or longing.

The enthusiasm of their leader had made several of the white men sullen.

'There is no reason why the boy should understand their dialect,' said Ralph Angus, and was surprised that he had thought it out for himself.

Voss, however, remained smiling and childlike.

'Naturally,' he replied, bearing no grudge against the individual who had censured him. 'But I will ride over and speak with this poet.'

The stone figures of his men submitted.

Voss rode across, sustained by a belief that he must communicate intuitively with these black subjects, and finally rule them with a sympathy that was above words. In his limpid state of mind, he had no doubt that the meaning of the song would be revealed, and provide the key to all further negotiations.

But the blacks ran away, leaving the smell of their rancid bodies in the patch of scrub.

When the rejected sovereign returned, still smiling generously, and said : 'It is curious that primitive man cannot sense the sympathy emanating from relaxed muscles and a loving heart,' his followers did not laugh.

But their silence was worse. Each hair was distinct in their cavernous nostrils.

During the days that followed, mobs of blacks appeared to accompany the expedition. Although the natives never showed themselves in strength, several dark skins at a time would flicker through pale grass, or come to life amongst dead trees. At night there was frequent laughter, a breaking of sticks, more singing, and a thumping of the common earth.

Voss continued to question Jackie.

'Is there no indication of their intentions?' he asked, in some helplessness. 'Blackfeller no tell why he come, why he sing?'

They were glad, said the boy.

It seemed obvious in the sunsets of plenty. At evening the German watched a hand daub flat masses of red and orange ochre above the already yellowing grass. Each evening was a celebration of the divine munificence. Accepting this homage, the divine presence himself was flaming, if also smiling rather thinly.

Although less appreciative of cosmic effects than was his master, the black boy would have prolonged the sunset. He kept close to the German at the best of times, but now, when the night fell, he had taken to huddling outside the fly of the small tent, where the terrier had been in the habit of lying.

This dog – in appearance terrier, in fact a stout-hearted mongrel – presented to Voss in the early stages by a New England settler, had disappeared, it was suddenly noticed.

'She could have staked herself, or been ripped open by a kangaroo,' said Voss.

He wandered off, calling the lost Tinker, but soon abandoned his efforts to find her. A matter of such insignificance could not occupy his mind for long.

'Of course you know what has happened to the poor tyke,' Turner whispered to Judd.

Deliberately he chose Judd, in whom he was always confiding. Judd, however, on this occasion, did not listen to Turner's conclusions. He was enclosed in his own thoughts.

Very soon after this, the fat country through which they were passing began to thin out, first into stretches of yellow tussock, then into plains of grey saltbush, which, it was apparent, the rains had not touched. Even the occasional outcrops of quartz failed as jewellery upon the sombre bosom of that earth.

One morning Turner began to cry:

'I cannot! I cannot!'

The cores of his extinct boils were protesting at the prospect of re-entering the desert. His gums were bleeding under the pressure of emotion.

If the others barely listened, or were only mildly disgusted by his outburst, it was because each man was obsessed by the same prospect. Without an audience, Turner quietened down, and was jolted on.

'At least we shall throw off our friends the blackfellows, if they are at all rational,' observed Ralph Angus. 'No one in his senses would leave abundance to enter this desert.'

'That you would not understand, Ralph,' grinned Voss, implying that he did.

'I am entitled to my own opinions,' muttered the young man. 'But I will keep them to myself in future.'

Voss continued to grin. His flesh had been reduced to such an extent, he could no longer smile.

So the party entered the approaches to hell, with no sound but that of horses passing through a desert, and saltbush grating in a wind.

This devilish country, flat at first, soon broke up into winding gullies, not particularly deep, but steep enough to wrench the backs of the animals that had to cross them, and to wear the bodies and nerves of the men by the frantic motion that it involved. There was no avoiding chaos by detour. The gullies had to be crossed, and on the far side there was always another tortuous gully. It was as if the whole landscape had been thrown up into great earthworks defending the distance.

In the course of the assault, the faces of all those concerned began to wear an expression of abstraction. In the lyrical grasslands through which they had lately ridden, they had sung away what was left of their youth. Now, in their silence, they had even left off counting their sores. They had almost renounced their old, wicker bodies. They were very tired at sunset. Only the spirit was flickering in the skull. Whether it would leap up in a blaze of revelation, remained to be seen.

Then, one evening as they scrambled up towards a red ridge, one of the horses, or skeleton of a gelding, of which the eyes had gone milky with blight, and the crimson sores were the only signs of life, stumbled, and fell back with a thin scream into the gully, where he lay, and lunged, and continued to scream.

At once every man, with the exception of the leader, raised his voice, in curses, commands, or words of advice. All together. What they intended to achieve by their outcry, the men themselves could not have explained, except that they had been compelled to join with the horse in expression of their common agony.

Then Voss said:

'I suggest that you shoot the beast, Mr Judd.'

Judd dismounted, and, when he had unslung his gun and descended the slope, quickly dispatched the poor horse. This humane act was the only one that reason could have suggested, yet, when the convict had stripped the pack-saddle from the carcass, pulling at the leather with such force as he could still summon, almost falling back under the surviving weight of his once powerful frame, he took stones, and began to pelt the dead horse. He pelted slowly and viciously, his broad back turned to the group of his companions, and the stones made a slow, dead noise on the horse's hide.

Until Voss insisted:

'Come up, Mr Judd. It is foolish to expend your energy in this way.'

It did seem foolish. Or terrifying. Harry Robarts, who had respected, and even fallen in love with his mate, was terrified. But he, poor boy, was simple.

As soon as Judd had recovered his customary balance, and his legs had returned him to the horse he had been riding, the party struggled a little farther, climbing out upon what appeared to be a considerable plateau, arid certainly, but blessedly flat.

337

'Here I think we will camp,' decided Voss, when they had come to a few twisted trees.

He did not say more. There were occasions when, out of almost voluptuous perversity, he did respect the feelings of others.

All sat in the dusk, nursing in their mouths a little tepid water, that tasted of canvas, or a sad, departed civilization.

But Harry Robarts went wandering across the desert of the moon, stumbling quite drunkenly, and when the actual moon had risen, the tears were icy in the ravines of the boy's agèd face. Rambling and snivelling, he fell to counting such mercies as he had received, and in so doing, recalled the many acts of kindness of his mate the convict. These appeared more poignant, perhaps, since all human ties must be cut.

When, suddenly, in the mingling of dusk and moonlight, the boy realized that he was looking into animals' eyes. In the interval before fear, the situation remained objective for all concerned. Then it became better understood. The boy saw that the eyes were those of a blackfellow, squatting in a hollow beside two women, his equals in nakedness and surprise, who were engaged in coaxing a firestick into marriage with a handful of dry twigs. The attitudes of all were too innocent to be maintained. The boy stumbled back upon his heels, mumbling the curses he had learnt, the black man leaped, faster than light, blacker than darkness, into the nearest gully, followed by his two women and their almost independent breasts.

The boy was still cursing the shock he had received, and the absence of that courage which he always hoped would come to match his strength, when he heard a wailing from the natives, and from the distance, a blurred burst of answering cries. Upon telling his story afterwards, he remembered also to have caught sight of a second, more distant fire the moment before it was extinguished.

'So we did not throw off the damn blacks,' panted Harry Robarts in his own camp circle.

Voss, alone of all his party, remained persistently cheerful.

'There is no reason to believe that these natives are not of our present locality,' he said, 'and it could suggest that we have come to better country.'

Such logic persuaded those who wished to be persuaded.

'It is unreasonable,' laughed Voss, 'when we have practically ignored the presence of the natives in the past, to behave of a sudden like a number of nervous women.'

'We were strong then,' said Judd, passionately. 'And had hopes.'

'You, surely, of all men, have known before the unwisdom of abandoning hope,' the leader replied.

Seeking to comfort him with human precepts, in what was possibly an unearthly situation, the comforter alone was strengthened.

When Voss had lifted the flap of his tent and got inside, Judd the convict muttered to his own teeth :

'In those days, I knew how much and how little I was capable of. I knew where *I* was headed. Now I do not know about *us*.'

After that, everybody went to bed, with firearms ready to hand, but slept deeply, as they were exhausted.

In the morning there was a bright, cold dew upon the world, and even the travellers, as they looked out across the austere plateau, were sensible of some refreshment, if only from sleep.

Voss himself was up earliest, and was going about gathering the dew with a sponge and squeezing it into a quart pot to make use of all possible moisture for his own consumption. Palfreyman soon joined him at his work.

'It could be idyllic,' the ornithologist remarked, 'if we were to keep our heads lowered, and concentrate our whole attention on these jewels.'

'This is the way, I understand, in which some people acquire religious faith,' the German replied.

Palfreyman, whose own faith had suffered considerably, was prepared to accept the remark as punishment of a sort.

'Some people,' he agreed.

'Ah, Palfreyman,' said Voss, 'you are humble. And humility is humiliating in men. I am humiliated for you.'

As Palfreyman did not answer, he added, though more for himself :

'I suspect we shall soon learn which of us is right.'

He could have continued to humiliate his unresisting friend and to exalt himself in that metallic light, for the mornings were still relentlessly cold and conducive to sharp detachment, if an uproar of voices had not at that moment arisen from the camp nearby. On going and inquiring into it, he and Palfreyman were informed by their companions that an axe, a bridle, and the surviving compass had disappeared, indeed from under canvas, in the course of the night.

'It is these blacks, sir,' Judd protested. 'With your permission, I will go in search of them.'

'We cannot accuse the natives on no evidence,' Voss replied.

'I will soon find evidence,' said Judd.

'If they did not help themselves to our property,' Turner spluttered biliously, 'and they could have without much effort, simply by lifting the canvas, who else would have taken the things?'

Both Turner and Judd, remembering Jildra, were trembling to say more, but were held back by some lack of daring. Or was it by Voss? His strength had been increased by sight of the great, trembling Judd.

'At least, here are the natives themselves,' Palfreyman broke the awkwardness.

Everybody looked, and saw a group of several blackfellows assembled in the middle distance. The light and a feather of low-lying mist made them appear to be standing in a cloud. Thus elevated, their spare, elongated bodies, of burnt colours, gave to the scene a primitve purity that silenced most of the whites, and appealed particularly to Voss.

'Good,' he cried. 'Here is an excellent opportunity to satisfy Judd's eternal craving for material evidence.'

'I do not understand,' shouted the exasperated Judd. 'I will give as well as find evidence. I will fire a few shots right into the middle of 'em.'

'Wait, Albert. I will come with you. Dirty blacks,' contributed Turner, the spotless. 'But I must find my gun first.'

'Neither of you will do anything so foolish,' Voss said sharply. 'I will go, and you will wait here. *Na, mach,* Jackie!' he called to the native boy.

'A lot will come of your hob-nobbin' with the blacks. As always,' Judd panted. 'I cannot dream dreams no longer. Do you not see our deluded skeletons, Mr Voss?'

'If you are suffering from delusions, it is the result of our unavoidable physical condition,' said the German, rather primly.

'Arrrr,' groaned Judd.

But everyone fell silent, even Judd himself, while the aboriginals, of superior, almost godlike mien, waited upon their cloud, to pass judgement, as it were.

'As our friend Judd is jealous of my attempts to establish understanding and sympathy between the native mind and ourselves,' Voss observed finally, 'I will ask Mr Palfreyman to go amongst them, and investigate this matter of our stolen property. He, at least, is unprejudiced, and will act politic.'

Somebody sighed. It could have been Palfreyman, who was startled by this sudden exposure of himself. His skin had turned yellow.

'I am certainly unbiased,' he said, and smiled thinly. 'I shall go,' he agreed. 'I only hope that I may acquit myself truly,' he added.

There he halted. Everyone was aware that he, an educated gentleman, no longer had control over the words he was using.

'Excellent,' applauded Voss.

The circumstances to which they were reduced prevented him from wetting his lips. He was confident, however, that by a brilliant accident he had hit upon a means of revealing the true condition of a soul.

'Here,' said Judd, offering Palfreyman his own weapon.

'Will you go armed?' asked Voss, lowering his eyelids.

'No,' said Palfreyman. 'Of course not. Not armed.'

'Will you, at least, take the native?'

'I doubt whether they would understand him.'

'Scarcely,' said Voss. 'But his presence.'

'No. I will go. I will trust to my faith.'

It sounded terribly weak. Voss heard with joy, and looked secretly at the faces of the other men. These, however, were too thin to express anything positive.

Palfreyman, who was certainly very small, in what had once been his cabbage-tree hat, had begun to walk towards the cloudful of blacks, but slowly, but deliberately, with rather large strides, as if he had been confirming the length of an important plot of land. As he went forward he became perfectly detached from his surroundings, and was thinking of many disconnected incidents, of a joyful as well as an unhappy nature, of the love that he had denied his sister, of the bland morning in which he had stood holding the horse's bridle and talking to Miss Trevelyan, even of the satisfaction that he and Turner had seemed to share as he shaved the latter's suppurating face. Since it had become obvious that he was dedicated to a given end, his own celibacy could only appear natural. Over the dry earth he went, with his springy, exaggerated strides, and in this strange progress was at peace and in love with his fellows. Both sides were watching him. The aboriginals could have been trees, but the members of the expedition were so contorted by apprehension, longing, love or disgust, they had become human again. All remembered the face of Christ that they had seen at some point in their lives, either in churches or visions, before retreating from what they had not understood, the paradox of man in Christ, and Christ in man. All were obsessed by what could be the last scene for some of them. They could not advance farther.

Voss was scourging his leg with a black stick.

Palfreyman walked on.

Harry Robarts would have called out, if his voice had not been frozen.

Then, we are truly damned, Frank Le Mesurier knew, his dreams taking actual shape.

Palfreyman continued to advance.

If his faith had been strong enough, he would have known what to do, but as he was frightened, and now could think of nothing, except, he could honestly say, that he did love all men, he showed the natives the palms of his hands. These, of course, would have been quite empty, but for the fate that was written on them.

The black men looked, fascinated, at the white palms, at the curiously lidded eyes of the intruder. All, including the stranger himself, were gathered together at the core of a mystery. The blacks would soon begin to see inside the white man's skin, that was transfigured by the morning; it was growing transparent, like clear water.

Then one black man warded off the white mysteries with terrible dignity. He flung his spear. It stuck in the white man's side, and hung down, quivering. All movements now became awkward. The awkward white man stood with his toes turned in. A second black, of rather prominent muscles, and emotional behaviour, rushed forward with a short spear, or knife, it could have been, and thrust it between the white man's ribs. It was accomplished so easily.

'Ahhhhh,' Palfreyman was laughing, because still he did not know what to do.

With his toes turned in.

But clutching the pieces of his life.

The circles were whirling already, the white circles in the blue, quicker and quicker.

'Ah, Lord,' he said, upon his knees, 'if I had been stronger.'

But his voice was bubbling. His blood was aching through a hole which the flies had scented already.

Ah, Lord, Lord, his mind repeated, before tremendous pressure from above compelled him to lay down the last of his weakness. He had failed evidently.

Then Harry Robarts did scream.

Then Judd had discharged his gun, with none too accurate aim, but the muscular black was fumbling with his guts, tumbling.

Voss was shouting in a high voice.

'I forbid any man to fire, to make matters worse by shooting at this people.'

For they were his.

All the blacks had streaked from the scene, however, except the second murderer, who had stumbled, straddled a rock, toppled, before the violence of uncontrol flung him away, somewhere, into a gully.

Mr Palfreyman was already dead when the members of the expedition arrived at his side and took him up. Nor was there a single survivor who did not feel that part of him had died.

In the course of the morning a grave was dug in the excessively hard ground, by which time the eyelids of the dead man had thickened, and the black blood was clotting in his wounds. Death had turned him into wax.

Pious peasants wore their knees out worshipping similar effigies, Voss remembered with disgust. The face of Laura

343

Trevelyan, herself waxen amongst the candles, did reproach him for a moment during the orgy of mortality at which they were assisting, but he drove her off, together with the flies, and spoke very irritably, for flesh, like candles, is designed to melt.

'The sooner he is below ground, the better,' he said, 'in such heat.'

'We must read the burial service,' mumbled Judd.

'*I* prefer not to,' Voss replied.

'*I* cannot,' said Judd.

Frank Le Mesurier, whose wasted face was running with yellow sweat, declined.

'I cannot,' Judd kept repeating, as he knelt upon the stones, beside the trench in which it was intended to put the dead man, 'but would if I had the education.'

It was terrible for him to have to admit.

Finally, Ralph Angus read the service, correcting himself time and again, for the meaning of the words was too great for him to grasp; he had been brought up a gentleman.

In the case of Harry Robarts, however, truth descended upon ignorance in a blinding light. He saw into the meaning of words, and watched the white bird depart out of the hole in Mr Palfreyman's side as they lowered the body into the ground.

As for Judd, he cried for the sufferings of man, in which he had participated to some extent, if not yet in their entirety.

During the afternoon the leader went in search of the body of the black, which he said they should bury too, but members of the tribe appeared already to have crept up and removed it. So Voss returned, furious with the flies, and the devotion of Laura Trevelyan, which did not allow her to leave him unattended. She was dragging after him, across the stones. And the Christ-picture. He could have shouted.

But on coming to within a hundred yards or so of the camp, his attention was attracted by the glitter of some substance, that proved to be glass, and in it the needle of the stolen compass.

'Mr Judd!' he called in triumph.

When Judd had come, the German pointed to the patch.

'This will obviate the necessity of deciding who will take the one compass.'

He laughed, but Judd, who had already been tried too sorely,

344

stood silent, looking at the little arrow that was pointing and pointing on the bare earth.

Since the day was already far advanced, and every man, as the result of the recent disaster, aching as if he had ridden miles over the very roughest country, it was decided not to push on until the following morning. In the course of the afternoon, Judd followed the tracks of the stock, that had wandered in a direction roughly to the south of the encampment, and there found them congregated along the banks of a river, of which the course was in general dry, though there remained a few passable water-holes to which the animals had been attracted. Thin horses stood, easing a tired pastern, humbly twitching a grateful lower lip. One or two surviving goats looked at the newcomer without moving, admitting him temporarily to the fellowship of beasts.

The man-animal joined them and sat for a while upon the scorching bank. It was possibly this communion with the beasts that did finally rouse his bemused human intellect, for in their company he sensed the threat of the knife, never far distant from the animal throat.

'I will not! I will not!' he cried at last, shaking his emaciated body.

Since his own fat paddocks, not the deserts of mysticism, nor the transfiguration of Christ, are the fate of common man, he was yearning for the big breasts of his wife, that would smell of fresh-baked bread even after she had taken off her shift.

That evening, after the canvas water-bags had been filled against an early start, and the men were picking half-heartedly at a bit of damper and dried meat, Judd approached their leader, and said:

'Mr Voss, sir, I do not feel we are intended to go any farther. I have thought it over, and am turning back.'

Some of them caught their breath to hear their own thoughts expressed. They were sitting forward.

'Do you not realize you are under my leadership?' Voss asked, although quite calmly, now that it had happened.

'Not any more I am not,' Judd replied.

'You are suffering from fatigue,' pronounced the leader.

The corroboration of his worst fears was making him firm, bright, almost joyful.

'Go to bed now,' he said. 'I cannot allow myself to suspect a brave man of cowardice.'

'It is not cowardice, if there is hell before and hell behind, and nothing to choose between them,' Judd protested. 'I will go home. Even if I come to grief on the way, I am going home.'

'I do not expect more of you, then,' said Voss. 'Small minds quail before great enterprises. It is to be hoped that a small mind will stand the strain of such a return journey, and unaccompanied.'

'I am a plain man,' said Judd. 'I do not understand much beyond that plainness, but can trust my own self.'

Voss laughed. He sat culling stones out of a little pile.

'So I am going back,' Judd ended. 'And I will lead anybody that is of like mind.'

This was to be the test, then. Voss threw a hateful stone into the darkness.

At once Turner jumped up, and was straining his throat to utter the words. He was like a gristly fowl escaping from the block.

'You can count on me,' he cried too quickly, 'and Ralph will come.'

'Speak for yourself,' snapped Angus, ashamed at being stripped naked by such trash, who was, moreover, his friend.

'No doubt others will have made up their minds by morning,' Voss said. 'Gentlemen, I will wish you good night. You have several hours. The nights are still cold, and will favour thought.'

Then he crawled into his tent, and was not altogether ungainly in doing so, it was realized.

The situation did crystallize, if painfully, under the stars, and by morning each knew what he must confess. In some cases, the decision was too obvious to require putting into words. There would have been no hope for Frank Le Mesurier, for instance, on any course other than his leader's, and Voss, who had read what was written, would not have dreamt of asking for proof of loyalty. Frank was busy strapping and buckling. Somewhere he had stowed his book, that he valued still, but in which he no longer wrote, as if all were said.

Turner was gabbling. The prospect of a return to sanity had brought out the streak of madness that is hidden in all men.

'I will not eat, Albert,' he was saying craftily, 'and the load will be so much lighter for the provisions we do not have to carry. It is surprising how little a man need eat. I will be the headpiece, you will see. Food, they say, only numbs the brain.'

Just then, the German came across, and insisted upon a fair division of stores. He and Judd arranged these matters quite naturally and amicably, in the pale morning. Although they were shivering, and their teeth chattering, it was from the cold.

'And the compass!' laughed Voss, who had become a thin, distinguished, reasonable being.

'There is no need for any compass,' laughed the big, jolly Judd.

As Ralph Angus approached them, he was terribly uncertain in his certainty, and in need of that macassar, which provided half the assurance of young, personable gentlemen.

'I have decided,' he said, who had been deciding all night.

'Yes?' asked Voss, who knew, and who would have let him off.

'I have decided to throw in my lot,' said Angus, sweating in the cold, 'to go with Judd. It seems to me questionable to continue any farther into this wilderness. I have enough land,' he finished rather abruptly, and did not mention the acreage, for this would have been in bad taste.

'You are rich, then,' remarked Voss, with elaborate seriousness.

'I mean,' stuttered the unhappy young man, 'there is land enough along the coast for anyone to stake a reasonable claim.'

At that moment, his leader, as Judd the convict had become, put his strong hand on the landowner's arm and asked him to do something.

'All right,' said Ralph Angus, surlily, but with every intention of obeying.

He went to do it, and at the same moment gave his life into the keeping of Judd. As the latter's hands were capable ones, it could have been a wise move, although the young man himself felt he was betraying his class, both then, and for ever.

All was got ready in quickest time. Nobody could have criticized the almost unbroken smoothness and amiability with which their departure was prepared. When the moment came, however, movements grew abrupt and unnatural. As the two parties were separating, each man remembered how the others knew him far too intimately, with the consequence that nobody experienced any real desire to look back.

Only Harry Robarts called to his mate:

'Good-bye then, Mr Judd.'

They had forgotten about Harry, who was, of course, a lad, and a simpleton. Even Judd had forgotten, who had sensed the boy's affection, while always knowing that he must lose him.

'Ah, good-bye, Harry,' the convict replied, now that he had been accused.

When he had cleared a passage in his throat, he added rather furrily:

'You are leaving me. And I would not have expected it.'

Although it was not true.

'I would come with you,' the boy began, and hesitated.

Then why would not Harry come? There was no reason, except that it was not intended.

'I would come if I wanted to,' he shouted into his friend's face.

And began to dig his heels into the sides of his horse.

'But I do not,' he cried. 'Get on, then! Arr, get on! Or I will bust your ribs open!'

The two parties now rode in opposite directions. With the exception of Harry Robarts, whose fate was tormenting him, the spirits of all were considerably revived. The blackfellow Jackie, who rode still at the German's right hand, was grinning as he bounced upon his horse's shambly skeleton. There was a great deal the young native found incomprehensible but, at least, he was not dead. So the invisible rope that joined the cavalcade was slowly broken, and then, in the immediate landscape, nothing remained of the expedition except a small cairn of stones that marked the grave of Mr Palfreyman.

13

ALTHOUGH the money he had made was enough to have bought him absolution of his origins, Mr Bonner had never thought to aspire to gentle birth. That was a luxury he left to his wife, who did enjoy immensely both the triumphs and the punishments involved. The merchant enjoyed the money, having experienced the condition of errand lad, of blameworthy assistant, and of confidential clerk to several hard men. Ah, he did love the fortune that rendered him safe, so he considered, from attack by life, for, in the course of living, Mr Bonner had forgotten that the shell-less oyster is not more vulnerable than man. Safe in life, safe in death, the merchant liked to feel. In consequence, he had often tried to calculate, for how much, and from whom, salvation might be bought and, to ensure that his last entrance would be made through the right cedar door, had begun in secret to subscribe liberal sums to all denominations, including those of which he approved.

Intellectual, to say nothing of spiritual inquiry, was not, however, a serious occupation for a man. He was content to leave it to the women, or to some slightly comical specialist. If he had experienced yearnings of the spirit, he had come closest, though still not very close, to satisfying them by going out and thinning the buds from his camellia bushes, those fine, shiny, compact, inpenetrable shrubs that he had planted himself, and which had increased with his own magnificence. Although their flowers suffered in the end from perfection, and their reliable evergreen charms became a bore as the season progressed, that was really what he liked: the unchanging answer to his expectations. Take his God, for instance. If his God had not been a bore, Mr Bonner might have suspected Him. Instead, his respect for the Divine Will had approximated very closely to the respect in which he held his own. Associated for many years in what he had supposed an approved commerce, it had begun only now to dawn upon the draper that some cruel surprise was being prepared.

It was his niece, Laura Trevelyan, who had caused Mr Bonner's world of substance to quake.

'We hope to persuade Miss Trevelyan to try the sea-water bathing.'

On this occasion he had come round the glass partition, and waited for Palethorpe, his right hand, to close the ledger the latter had been fingering.

'What is your opinion of sea-water bathing, Palethorpe?' Mr Bonner asked, which was humble, indeed, for him.

Palethorpe, who had decided early in life that opinions were dangerous, replied rather carefully:

'It depends, sir, altogether, I should say, upon the constitution of the person concerned.'

'That could well be,' agreed his disappointed employer.

'Without studying the constitution, it would not be possible to express any opinion at all.'

Palethorpe hoped that he was saved.

But Mr Bonner churned the cash in his trouser pocket, his good money, out of which Palethorpe was paid, by all standards liberally. The merchant was generous enough, for he hated dispute and discomfort. Now, as was only natural, he felt himself to be cheated of his rights.

'But you *know* my niece!' he cried, in some impatience.

Delay always turned him red.

'It is true, sir,' Palethorpe admitted, 'the young lady is known to me. By acquaintance, though, not by scientific study.'

No one could take exception to Palethorpe, with the result that he had got so far and no farther. He was above ambition. The colonial air had not destroyed his willingness to serve a master; both he and his discreet wife were of the doormat class, although of that superior quality which some impeccable doormats have. Sometimes the couple would discuss the feet that used them, or would lay evidence before each other, it might be more correct to say, for discussion implies criticism, and the Palethorpes did not criticize.

For instance, Mrs Palethorpe would begin:

'I do believe the paisley shawl suits me better than I would have thought. Do you not consider, Mr Palethorpe, the shawl suits me, after all?'

'Yes, yes. Very well. Very well,' her husband answered steamily.

For, on this, as on almost every occasion, they were sipping tea. They were both near and far. In each other's company, the Palethorpes always were.

'The pattern suits me. I can carry it off. Being rather slim. Now stout ladies, I do not intend to criticize, it is not my habit, as you know, but Mrs Bonner cannot resist a large pattern.'

'Mrs Bonner is of a generous, one might even say an *embarrassingly* generous nature. It was kindness itself to hand on the shawl.'

'Oh, I appreciate it, Mr Palethorpe. It was the height of generosity. Mrs Bonner is of that character which is definitely sustained by generous giving. She is for ever pressing presents.'

'And after so little wear. The paisley shawl is of the July consignment. I can remember well. Some ladies did consider the patterns a little florid for their tastes.'

'But tastes do differ.'

'Even perfect tastes. We cannot deny, Edith, that Mrs Bonner is in perfect taste.'

'Oh, Mr Palethorpe, do not mortify me! If I was to harbour such a thought. Not in perfect taste!'

'And Miss Belle.'

'And we must not forget poor Miss Trevelyan.'

'No.'

'Although she is an intellectual young lady, and sometimes rather quiet.'

The Palethorpes sipped their tea.

'The little girl is grown a pretty child. But serious, one would say,' Mr Palethorpe resumed.

'Altogether like, pardon me, like Miss Trevelyan. Which is pure coincidence, of course, for the little girl is not hers.'

The Palethorpes did grow steamy over tea in that climate.

Then Mrs Palethorpe asked:

'How long is it, would you say, since the expedition left?'

'I did make a note of it, as of all events of importance, but without consulting my journal, I could not speak with certainty.'

'I would not inconvenience you,' Mrs Palethorpe said.

351

She stirred her tea.

'That Mr Voss, Mr Palethorpe, I have never asked, but did he not impress you as, to say the least, well, I do not wish to be vulgar, but, a funny sort of man?'

'He is a German.'

Then Mrs Palethorpe asked with inordinate courage:

'Do you consider this German is acceptable to Mr Bonner?'

Her husband changed position.

'I do not know,' he said, 'and am too discreet to ask.'

Then, when his wife was crushed, he added:

'But I do know, from long association with my employer, that Mr Bonner will not see what he does not wish to see, and all Sydney waiting for him to remove the blinkers.'

Mr Palethorpe gave a high, thin laugh, which was full of feeling, therefore quite unlike him.

'All Sydney? Well, now! Is not that a slight exaggeration?'

'My dear Edith,' said Mr Palethorpe, 'if a person is not allowed some occasional latitude, where will he find his recreation?'

His wife sighed agreement. She did invariably agree, because she was so pleased with him.

Then the Palethorpes continued to sip their tea, themselves a superior milky white, like the cups they had brought out from Home. No coarse stuff. They sat and listened to the rather melancholy accompaniment of their stomachs, and were soon walking in the rain in the neighbourhood of Fulham, their spiritual environment.

No one could take exception to the Palethorpes, which made them the more exasperating, as Mr Bonner realized upon that occasion when he had been hoping for advice. Palethorpe sensed this, he always did, and accordingly was quick to soothe.

Palethorpe said:

'I do trust the young lady's health will benefit by a short course of salt-water baths.'

'It is not her health, Palethorpe,' answered the merchant. 'That is, it is, and it is not.'

'Ah?' hinted his inferior, with that inflection which derives from superior knowledge.

'Altogether, I do not know what to make of it.'

Then the merchant went away, disappointed, and leaving disappointment behind.

Mr Bonner took the brougham, which was waiting for him, as always at that hour. After composing his legs for the journey, he unfolded them, and asked to stop at Todmans', where they robbed him over three pears, beautifully nesting in their own leaves, in a little box. So he sat in the gloom of the enclosed brougham, holding the box of expensive pears, surrounded by their generous scent, gradually even by their golden light, and hoped that the material offering he intended making to his niece would express that affection which might be absent from his voice and looks. He was rather lonely in the brougham.

When they were entering the stone gateway of the house at Potts Point, which was no longer so very agreeable to him, he would have stopped the vehicle, and walked up the drive to postpone his arrival, but his attempts to attract attention were muffled by the upholstery; his voice fell back upon him, and he had not the will to raise the little lid through which he might have communicated with the driver. So he was carried on, unhappily, until there they were, clopping under the portico.

The door was already open.

'Oh, sir,' said Betty, the most recent of the girls who had replaced the dead Rose, 'Miss Laura is taken proper sick.'

The merchant, to whom the effort of extricating himself from the brougham had given a congested look, was still holding his pears. It was a grey, gritty afternoon.

He did not consider it desirable to stimulate the flow of intelligence from this girl, a thin thing in her inherited dress, so he confined himself to uttering a few sounds that could not possibly have been construed as human.

'Ah, Mr Bonner,' said his wife, upon the stairs, and less avoidable, 'I was on the point of sending. It is Laura. She is desperately ill. I brought Dr Bass. He left but a moment ago, most unsatisfactory. That young man, I will have it known amongst *all* our acquaintance, turned the pages of a book in my presence, to *diagnose*, if you please. When anyone of experience, when even *I* know, it is a brain fever. Mr Bonner, I must confess I am distracted.'

Indeed, her rings were scratching him unpleasantly.

Mr Bonner mounted higher on the spongy stairs. The ripe fruit had become dislodged inside the little box, and for all its sensuous perfection, was jumping and jostling as if it had been cheap and woody. He no longer cared for this house; it was since Belle had gone, Belle the golden, who would smell of ripe pears – or was he confused? – on those untroubled days between hateful summer and vicious winter.

'Well, then, we will send for Dr Kilwinning,' Mr Bonner heard his strange voice.

'Oh, dear, you are so good, we have always known.' His wife was mopping her eyes with a shred of cambric and a handful of rings.

No one of all Mrs Bonner's acquaintance was ignorant of what Dr Kilwinning would dare to charge, and that he was become accordingly the best physician in town.

But the Bonners were not a great comfort to each other as they went towards their niece's door. Life was exceeding their capacities.

Laura was lying in her handsome bed, looking at nothing and at everything. During the crisis, which no one had explained very well to the perplexed merchant, the aunt had unbraided her niece's hair. Now, the dark, hot hair appeared disagreeable to the uncle, who disliked anything that suggested irregularity. Nor could he remember when he had last entered his niece's room, which gave him the impression of being littered with fragile secrets, so that he was forced to walk delicately, his every step an apology, and his thick, fleshy body looked quite grotesque.

Laura had to turn her head. She said:

'I am sorry to be such an inconvenience to you.'

It was difficult, but her rather thin lips had managed that ridiculous sentence.

Mr Bonner sucked his teeth, and was moving even more delicately to atone for his deficiencies.

'You must lie still,' he whispered, imitating somebody he had once heard in a sick-room.

'It is really nothing,' said Laura. 'But one of those stupid indispositions. That are difficult to explain.'

How gravely her jaws contended with speech. Her stiff and

354

feverish form, inside which she could move about quite freely, was by now of little importance; it was, truthfully, nothing. Yet, between bouts of fever, she was idiotically comfortable, and could even enjoy the fumbling sympathies of her uncle and aunt.

'Oh, dear, dear, dear Laura,' Aunt Emmy was crying, 'that we should suffer this. I cannot bear not knowing whatever it may be, but your uncle will bring the good doctor, who will explain everything.'

In times of stress Mrs Bonner transferred her own simplicity to those about her, and would address them as if they were, in fact, little children.

'You will see,' she added.

She was touching, and touching her young niece. To cover her up. Or to discover a reason for their suffering.

Looking at those two children from her tragic distance, Laura Trevelyan felt intolerably old. If she could have done something for them, but she could not. Even restored to full health, there would be nothing she could do, she realized, for her uncle and aunt.

Then Mr Bonner cleared his throat. Rescued by his wife's words, he said in a young man's voice:

'Yes. The doctor. I will send Jim round. He will be here in two shakes. Yes. I will write a note.'

'And if he should be at his dinner?' remembered his wife.

'I will make it worth his while to leave any dinner,' said the merchant.

Given favourable circumstances, he was a man of power and influence.

Now he went about this business, after abandoning on a console table in the shadows of the room the unfortunate pears. These soft, innocent fruit seemed to proclaim a weakness that he would have liked to keep secret.

There the pears were, however, even if they remained temporarily unnoticed by Laura Trevelyan and Mrs Bonner. The latter continued desperately to tend her niece, bringing in succession a little toast-water, a good, strong broth that had slopped over while being conveyed from the kitchen, and a milk jelly in a pretty shape. When all these had been refused the aunt cried out passionately:

355

'What more can I do? My dear, tell me, and I will do it.'

As if there had been a grudge between them.

'I do not ask you to do anything,' said Laura Trevelyan.

She had closed her eyes, and was smiling a smile that Mrs Bonner would have liked to interpret, but the girl was, in fact, so suffused with fire and weakness that she could not have borne her aunt even an imaginary grudge.

Notwithstanding, her niece's defenceless eyelids exposed Mrs Bonner to fresh attacks of remorse.

'It is always easier,' she complained, 'for those who are ill. They may lie there, while we who have our health must suffer. We are the weak, helpless ones.'

In the last resort of that helplessness, she held to her niece's forehead a handkerchief soaked far too liberally in eau de Cologne, while continuing to disinter her own buried sins.

So the evening passed in activity and frustration. Dr Kilwinning came, and Dr Bass returned. Men's boots commanded the stairs, and much masculine self-importance was expended. If the ignorance of young Dr Bass could at least be blamed, it had yet to be discovered what purpose the knowledge and experience of Dr Kilwinning would serve, although the eminent physician himself did drop several hints, together with many ornamental smiles, that he kept saved up for the consolation of ladies. Mrs Bonner had, in addition, great confidence in his beautiful cuffs, linked by lozenges of solid gold, in which were set rubies, though in most tasteful proportion.

'And the very lightest diet,' said the important doctor. 'Soups.'

He smiled, and it became a mystic word, dimly steaming upon his tongue.

Mrs Bonner was compelled to smile back.

'So nourishing,' she sighed, herself by now nourished.

But her husband would not respond to such treatment. He began to look cunning. He was making his eyes small. As Dr Kilwinning remarked in confidence afterwards to a lady of his acquaintance, the merchant spoke with a directness that one would only expect from a very *ordinary* man. Mr Bonner said:

'Yes, Doctor. But what is this sickness my niece has got?'

His wife feared at first that his want of delicacy might give offence.

'It is still too early, Mr Bonner,' the doctor said, 'to diagnose the illness with anything like certainty. It could be one of several fevers. We must observe. And care for the patient.' Here he smiled at Mrs Bonner, who returned his smile devotedly.

'Hm,' said the merchant.

'I still declare it is a brain fever,' ventured Mrs Bonner.

'It could well be,' sighed the doctor.

'I would like to know the reason for this fever,' said the merchant. 'A reason can be found for everything.'

Then the doctor gave one of those jolly, indulgent laughs, and patted Mr Bonner on the elbow, and went away, followed by Dr Dass, whose shamefully honest ignorance Mrs Bonner had by this time forgotten.

That night Laura Trevelyan was racked by her fever, and called out repeatedly that the hair was cutting her hands. Her own hair was certainly very hot and heavy. But soft. Mrs Bonner made several attempts to arrange it in some way that might lessen the patient's discomfort.

'Oh, mum, it is terrible,' said Betty, the new girl, 'it is terrible to think they may take it off. Such lovely hair. There was Miss Hanrahan had the whole of her hair taken from her for the scarlet fever. But sold it to a lady who wanted to make pads for her own. So it was not quite lost. And Miss Hanrahan growing another lovely head.'

'Go to bed, Betty,' said Mrs Bonner.

'I will sit up with Miss Trevelyan, if I may, mum,' the girl proposed.

But Mrs Bonner was determined to bear her own cross.

'I would never forgive myself,' she cried, 'if anything were to happen. And to my own niece.'

When the girl was gone, she prepared herself as if for a journey, with shawls, and plaids, and a book of sermons that she always held in an emergency, and presently her husband came, who could no longer sit alone in the desert that the house had become. Not suddenly, not tonight, not to Mr Bonner alone. These two people, looking at each other at intervals, in hope of rescue, had begun to realize that their whole lives had been a process of erosion. Oases of affection had made the desert endurable, until now the fierce heat of unreason threatened to wither any such refuge.

So the Bonners rambled helplessly, thinking of that transparent child whom nature had so heartlessly removed from them, and of this darker, opaque one, who had never really been theirs.

Once in the night, Laura Trevelyan, who was struggling to control the sheets, pulled herself up and forward, leaning over too far, with the natural result that she was struck in the face when the horse threw up his head. She did not think she could bear the pain.

'The martingale!' she cried out, willing herself not to flinch. 'We have left the martingale at the place where we rested.'

When she was more controlled, she said very quietly:

'You need not fear. I shall not fail you. Even if there are times when you wish me to, I shall not fail you.'

And again, with evident happiness:

'It is your dog. She is licking your hand. How dry your skin is, though. Oh, blessed moisture!'

Whereupon, she was moving her head against the pillow in grateful ecstasy.

Such evidence would have delighted the Palethorpes, and mystified the Bonners, but the former were not present, and the latter were drooping and swaying in their own sleep on their mahogany chairs.

*

So the party rode down the terrible basalt stairs of the Bonners' deserted house, and onward. Sometimes the horses' hooves would strike sparks from the outcrops of jagged rock.

Since the expedition had split in two, the division led by Voss seemed to move with greater ease. It was perhaps obvious that it should. Those under his command, including the aboriginal boy, were struck by the incandescence of the man who was leading them. They were in love with that rather gaunt, bearded head, and would compel themselves to ignore the fact that it was a skull with a candle expiring inside.

In the prevailing harmony of souls, anything that could detract from human dignity – the incident of the raft, for instance, or that of the missing compass – was forgotten. All the members of the party, even the unhappy Harry Robarts, who was being torn intermittently in two directions, were as emanations of the one man, their leader. The blackfellow was a doubtful quantity, but there was nobody, except perhaps the leader himself, who did not expect to discard him. In fact, the others longed to be one less, so that they might enjoy their trinity.

It was the mules and few surviving horses that deserved pity, for these were without the benefit of illusion. They endured their fate, the former sullenly, the latter with a tired patience, no longer looking for a vegetation that did not exist. If they were to be allowed to die, they would. But from time to time they were thrown small handfuls of hope: once it was a patch of grey grass upon a hummock of red sand; once they devoured the thatch from some old native huts, swallowing and groaning, and afterwards stood still, the long, unnatural hairs quivering upon their withered lips. Temporarily, their bellies were filled, but not the days.

Nights were, by contrast, short and exquisite both to animals and men, for desires and intentions, no longer burning, were abandoned in favour of comradeship, dreaming, and astronomy, in the case of men, or pure being, in that of horses. Nobody, except Voss, was concerned whether his bones would rise again from the earth, when his green flesh, watered by the dew, was shooting nightly in celestial crops.

Relinquishing the pretence of tents, which in any event they would have been too weak and exhausted to erect, the three white men huddled close together at the fire. So, too, the wrecks of horses appeared to derive comfort from closeness, and would lie with the ridges of their backbones exposed to the darkness, not far from their irrational masters. All were united then, in the scent of sweat and the tentative warmth of bodies.

Voss said once :

'Are you not sorry, Harry, that you did not return with your friend?'

'What friend?' asked the lad dreamily.

'Judd, of course.'

'Was he my friend?'

'How am I to tell, if you cannot?'

The German was half angry, half pleased.

Presently the boy said, looking in the fire:

'No, sir. If I had gone, I would not a known what to do when I got there. Not any more.'

'You would have learnt again very quickly.'

'I could have learnt to black your boots, if you had a been there, sir. But you would not a been. And it would not be worth it. Not since you learnt me other things.'

'What things?' asked Voss quietly, whose mind shouted.

The boy was quiet then, and shy.

'I do not know,' he said at last, shyly. 'I cannot say it. But know. Why, sir, to live, I suppose.'

He blushed in the darkness for the blundering inadequacy of his own words, but in his weak, feverish condition, was vibrating and fluctuating, like any star – living, in fact.

'Living?' laughed the German.

He was shouting with laughter to hide his joy.

'Then I have taught you something shameful. How they would accuse me!'

'I am happy,' said Harry Robarts.

The German was shivering with the cold that blew in from the immense darkness, and which was palpitating with little points of light. So, in the light of his own conquest, he expanded, until he possessed the whole firmament. Then it was true; all his doubts were dissolved.

'And what about you, Frank?' he said, or shouted again, so recklessly that one old mare pricked up her drowsing ears.

'Have I not taught you anything?' he asked.

'To expect damnation,' said Le Mesurier, without considering long.

In the uncompromising desert in which they were seated, this answer should have sounded logical enough, just as objects were the quintessence of themselves, and the few remaining possessions of the explorers were all that was necessary in that life.

But Voss was often infuriated by rational answers. Now the veins were swollen in his scraggy neck.

'That is men all over,' he cried. 'They will aim too low. And achieve what they expect. Is that your greatest desire?'

Either Le Mesurier did not hear, or else one of his selves did not accept the duties of familiar. It was the lad who replied to the question in the terms of his own needs.

'I would like to eat a dish of fat chops,' he said. 'And fresh figs, the purple ones. Though apples is good enough. I like apples, and could put up with them instead.'

'That is your answer,' said Le Mesurier to Voss. 'From a man going to his execution.'

'Well, if I was asked what I would take for me last dinner,' said the boy. 'And who would not eat? What would you choose?'

'Nothing,' said Le Mesurier. 'I would not eat for fear that I might miss something of what was happening to me. I would want to feel the last fly crawling on my skin, and listen to my conscience in case it should give up a secret. Out of that experience I might even create something.'

'That would not be of much good,' said Harry Robarts, 'not if you was to die.'

'Dying is creation. The body creates fresh forms, the soul inspires by its manner of leaving the body, and passes into other souls.'

'Even the souls of the damned?' asked Voss.

'In the process of burning it is the black that gives up the gold.'

'Then *he* will give up the purest,' said Voss.

He pointed to the body of the aboriginal boy, whom they had forgotten, but who was lying within the light of the fire, curled in sleep, like some animal.

Of the three souls that were dedicated to him, Voss most loved that of the black boy. Such unimpaired innocence could only be the most devoted. Whereas, the simplicity of Harry Robarts was not entirely confident – it did at times expect doom – and the sophistications of Frank Le Mesurier could have been startling echoes of the master's own mind.

So that Voss was staring with inordinate affection at the black-gold body of the aboriginal.

'He will be my footstool,' he said, and fell asleep, exalted by the humility of the black's perfect devotion and the contrast of heavenly perfection. Sleep did, in fact, crown man's sweaty head with stars.

But in the morning Jackie could not be found.

'He will have gone to look for a strayed horse,' said Voss at first, with the bland simplicity that the situation demanded.

'Horses!' cried Harry Robarts. 'No horse of ours has the strength to stray.'

'Or to find water,' Voss persisted.

'The waterholes are dry in hell,' remarked Le Mesurier.

'Then, he will come,' said Voss. 'Eventually.'

There was still some brown muck left in their canvas water-bags, and this they held carefully in their mouths. They did delay a little, although it began to appear to all that it was immaterial whether the native returned or not.

One of the horses, it was seen, would not get up again. The hair of its mane was spread out upon the ground, its bones barely supported the shabby tent of its hide, and the gases were rising in the belly, in one last protest, as the party pushed on.

By the time the sun had mounted the sky, their own veins had begun to run with fire. Their heads were exact copies of that same golden mirror. They could not look into one another for fear of recognizing their own torments.

Until the head of Harry Robarts was rendered finally opaque by the intense heat of the sun. He had acquired the shape and substance of a great reverberating, bronze gong.

'I do not want to complain,' he mumbled and throbbed. 'But it is going on and on.'

Then he was struck.

'I am beaten!' he shouted, and the bronze doom echoed out through many circles of silence.

'Listen,' said Voss. 'Did you not hear some sounds at a distance?'

His lips would just permit words.

'It is my own thoughts,' said Le Mesurier. 'I have been listening to them now for some way.'

Nor would he look up from the desolate ground to which his eyes had grown accustomed. He would not have asked for more than this.

'It is the devils,' shrieked Harry Robarts, who was rolling upon a steed of solid fire.

It was often the simple boy who first saw things, whether material or otherwise. Now the German himself noticed through that haze of heat, the deeper haze, then the solid evidence, it appeared, of black forms. But still at a considerable distance. And always moving. Like corporeal shadows.

Voss dared to smile.

As the expedition advanced, it was escorted by a column at either side.

'When we run together,' said Le Mesurier, whose attention had been drawn, 'that will be the centre of the fire.'

For the present, however, there was no sign that any fusion of the three columns might occur.

While the white men, with their little trickle of surviving pack-animals and excoriated old horses, stumbled on through the full heat of day, the blacks padded very firmly. Sometimes the bodies of the latter were solid as wood, sometimes they would crumble into a haze of black dust, but, whether formless or intact, they expressed the inexorability of confidence. By this time, each party was taking the other for granted. Women had come up, too, and were trailing behind the men. There were several dogs, with long, glistening tongues, from which diamonds fell.

Feeling his horse quiver beneath him, Voss looked down at the thin withers, at the sore which had crept out from under the pommel of the saddle. Then he did begin to falter, and was at last openly wearing his own sores than he had kept hidden. Vermin were eating him. The shrivelled worms of his entrails were deriding him. So he rode on through hell, until he felt her touch him.

'I shall not fail you,' said Laura Trevelyan. 'Even if there are times when you wish me to, I shall not fail you.'

Laying upon his sores ointment of words.

He would not look at her, however, for he was not yet ready.

In spite of his resistance, their stirrup-irons grappled together as they rode. Salt drops of burning sweat were falling upon the raw withers of the horse, making the animal writhe even in its weakness.

So they rode through hell, that was scented with the *Tannen-baum,* or hair blowing. His mouth was filled with the greenish-black tips of hair, and a most exquisite bitterness.

'You are not in possession of your faculties,' he said to her at last.

'What are my faculties?' she asked.

Then they were drifting together. They were sharing the same hell, in their common flesh, which he had attempted so often to repudiate. She was fitting him with a sheath of tender white.

'Do you see now?' she asked. 'Man is God decapitated. That is why you are bleeding.'

It was falling on their hands in hot, opaque drops. But he would not look at her face yet.

They had come to a broad plain of small stones, round in shape, of which at least some were apparently quartz, for where the swords of the sun penetrated the skin of the stone a blinding light would burst forth. These flashes of pure light, although rare, brought cries to the mouths of the three white men. The light was of such physical intensity. Laura Trevelyan, who had experienced sharper daggers, was silent, though. She rode apart, and waited.

When the men had recovered from their surprise, it was seen that the two columns of natives had come upon their rear, and were standing ranged behind them in an arc of concentrated silence. Voss dismounted, and was waiting. For ages everybody stood, and it seemed that nothing would ever happen beyond this commingling of silences, when there was a commotion in the ranks of the blacks, and an individual was pushed forward. He came, looking to the bare ground for inspiration, and when he had approached, Voss addressed him.

'Well, Jackie, I do not blame you,' he said. 'I knew that this would have to happen. What next?'

But Jackie would not lift his head. Subtle thoughts that he had learnt to think, thoughts that were other men's, had made it too heavy. His body, though, shone with a refreshed innocence.

Then he said:

'No me. Jackie do nothun. These blackfeller want Jackie. I go. Blackfeller no good along white men. This my people.' The renegade waved his arm, angrily, it seemed, at the ranks behind him. 'Jackie belong here.'

Voss listened, touching his beard. He was smiling, or that was the shape his face had taken.

'Where do I belong, if not here?' he asked. 'Tell your people we are necessary to one another. Blackfellow white man friend together.'

'Friend?' asked Jackie.

The word was twanging in the air. He had forgotten its usage.

Now the tribe began to murmur. Whether asking, urging, or advising, it was not clear.

Jackie had grown sulkier. His throat was full of knots.

'Blackfeller dead by white man,' he was prompted to say at last.

'Do they wish to kill me?' asked Voss.

Jackie stood.

'They cannot kill me,' said Voss. 'It is not possible.'

Although his cheek was twitching, like a man's.

'Tell them I will not die. But if it is to deprive them of a pleasure, I offer them friendship as a substitute. I am a friend of the blackfellow. Do you understand? This is the sign of friendship.'

The white man took the boy's hot, black, right hand in both his, and was pressing. A wave of sad, warm magic, and yearning for things past, broke over the blackfellow, but because the withered hands of the white man were physically feeble, even if warm and spiritually potent, the boy wrenched his hand away.

He began gabbling. Two men, two elders, and a younger powerful native now came forward, and were talking with Jackie, in words, and where these failed, with signs. That of which they spoke was of great importance and, even if deferred by difficulties, would, it appeared, take place.

Then Jackie, whose position was obviously intolerable, raised his eyes, and said:

'No good, Mr Voss.

'These blackfeller say you come along us,' he added, for he was still possessed by the white man's magic.

Voss bowed his head very low. Because he was not accustomed to the gestures of humility, he tried to think how Palfreyman might have acted in similar circumstances, but in that landscape, in that light, not even memory provided a refuge.

The eyes of the black men were upon him. How the veins of their bodies stood out, and the nipples.

As they watched.

The white man was stirring like a handful of dry grass. He was remounting his horse.

In his feebleness, or the dream that he was living, as he was hauling himself up by the pommel he felt the toe of his boot slither from the stirrup-iron. He felt some metal, undoubtedly a buckle, score his chin for a very brief moment of pain, before he was back standing on the ground. It was an incident which, in the past, might have made him look ridiculous.

But the black men did not laugh.

Then Voss, behaving more deliberately, succeeded in seating himself in the saddle, swaying, and smiling. The blood which had begun to run out of his chin was already stanched by the dry atmosphere, and the flies sitting on the crust of blood.

Even so, the woman had ridden closer to him, and was about to make some attempt to clean the wound.

'*Lass mich los*,' he said, abruptly, even rudely, although the rudeness was intended, rather, for himself.

Now the party had begun to move forward over the plain of quartz, in which, it was seen, a path must have been cleared in former times by blacks pushing the stones aside. The going was quite tolerable upon this pale, dusty track. Some of the natives went ahead, but most walked along behind. Now there was little distinction between skins, between men and horses even. Space had blurred the details.

'Good Lord, sir, what will happen?' asked Harry Robarts, rising to the surface of his eyes.

'*They* will know, presumably,' replied the German.

'Lord, sir, will you let them?' cried the distracted boy. 'Lord, will you not save us?'

'I am no longer your Lord, Harry,' said Voss.

'I would not know of no other,' said the boy.

Again the man was grateful for the simple boy's devotion. But could he, in the state to which he had come, allow himself the luxury of accepting it?

As he was debating this, Laura Trevelyan rode alongside, although there was barely room for two horses abreast on that narrow path.

'You will not leave me then?' he asked.

'Not for a moment,' she said. 'Never, never.'

'If your teaching has forced me to renounce my strength, I imagine the time will come very soon when there will be no question of our remaining together.'

'Perhaps we shall be separated for a little. But we have experienced that already.'

They rode along.

'I will think of a way to convince you,' she said, after a time, 'to convince you that all is possible. If I can make the sacrifice.'

Then he looked at her, and saw that they had cut off her hair, and below the surprising stubble that remained, they had pared the flesh from her face. She was now quite naked. And beautiful. Her eyes were drenching him.

So they rode on above the dust, in which they were writing their own legend.

*

The girl, Betty, was in tears the evening they took the hair from Miss Trevelyan by order of Dr Kilwinning. It was that lovely, she said, she would keep it always, and stuff a little cushion with it.

'That is morbid, Betty,' said Mrs Bonner.

But the mistress allowed the girl to keep the hair, because she was touched, and because it no longer confirmed her strength to deny other people the fulfilment of their wishes.

When they had put away the dressmaking scissors, Laura Trevelyan's desecrated head lolled against the pillows. She was lying with her eyes closed, as she did frequently now, and Dr Kilwinning was taking her pulse, an occupation which filled a gap and prevented the ignorant from talking.

Of all those people who witnessed the removal of the hair, Mr Bonner was most stunned, who had never before seen a woman without her hair. It made him walk softly, and, shortly after the operation, he went out of his niece's room, calculating that nobody would notice his absence.

When, finally, his wife came down with Dr Kilwinning, there he was, loitering at the foot of the stairs, near the stair cupboard, to be exact, as if he had been an intruder in his own house.

The doctor was for leaving with all speed of his patent-leather boots.

But these fleshy old people, who had wizened in a few days, were hanging upon him. The rather common old woman would have seized him by the cuffs. Alas, his status as fashionable physician failed to protect him from a great many unpleasantnesses. If anything, the fees he charged seemed, rather, to make some individuals aspire to get their money's worth.

'But tell me, Doctor, do you consider it to be infectious?' Mrs Bonner was asking.

'In a court of law, Mrs Bonner, I would not swear to it, but it would be as well to guard against the possibility of infection, shall we say?'

Dr Kilwinning, whose elastic calves had brought him mercifully to the bottom of the stairs, there encountered Mr Bonner, and they nodded at each other, as if they had only just met.

Mr Bonner hated Dr Kilwinning. He could have punched him on the nose.

'Oh, dear, then if it is *infectious*,' Mrs Bonner was crying, 'there is the danger of the little girl.'

'I did not *say* it was infectious. Indeed, it should not be.' Dr Kilwinning laughed. 'But the will of God, you know, has a habit of overruling the opinions of physicians.'

'Then,' said Mr Bonner, who could not stand it any longer, 'there is something wrong somewhere. If the physician receives the fee that some physicians do receive, he should form an opinion that the Almighty would respect. If that is blasphemy, Dr Kilwinning, I cannot help it. You have forced me to it.'

Mrs Bonner was aghast. Dr Kilwinning moistened his rather full lips, that were so fascinating to some women. Then he showed his fine, white teeth.

He said:

'Please do not blame me for your own nature, Mr Bonner.'

And the front door was rattling.

'He is gone, at least,' said the merchant.

'And very likely will not return. Oh, dear, Mr Bonner, look what you have done. The little girl upon my mind, too. Though I do declare still, it is a simple brain fever, if that can be called simple which people die of. Regularly.'

So that Mrs Bonner remained uncomforted.

She was continually washing her hands, but could not cleanse herself of all her sins. She had Betty walk about the house with a red-hot shovel, on which to burn a compound of saltpetre and vitriol, that was most efficacious, somebody had claimed, although Mrs Bonner had forgotten who. Then, when the fumes rose from Betty's shovel, the mystery deepened, and everyone in the house was unhappier than before.

Except possibly Mercy, the little girl. Her world was still substantial, when it was not melting into dreams. Particularly she loved Betty's game of smoke. She would try to catch the smoke. She loved doves. She loved the marbles from the game of solitaire. If she loved her mother less than all these, it was because she had not seen her lately.

But her grandmother did come instead.

In the beginning, Mrs Bonner had taken charge of Laura's child perhaps as an act of expiation, but soon became enthusiastic. Before going about her duties, she would disinfect herself most rigorously, of course. She would lay aside her rings, trembling all the while, until her impatient skirts hastened through the passages, and she was free at last to snuff up the sweet smell of cleanliness from the nape of the childish neck. This elderly woman would grow quite drunk on kisses, although it was but a mixed happiness that her secret vice brought her, for she would be reminded of her own child, living, but married, and of the several others she had buried in their babyhood.

'Who am I? Who am I, then?' she would ask, tickling the child's stomach, while looking over her shoulder to make certain that nobody had seen or heard. 'I am your Gran. Your *Grand*-mother.'

The child knew.

So Mrs Bonner was appeased.

In the first stages of her illness Laura Trevelyan had seemed to forget Mercy, but on the night when they cut off her hair, she roused herself, and said:

'I would like to see her.'

'Whom?' they asked.

'My little girl.'

'But it would not be wise, dear,' said the aunt, 'on account of the possibility of infection. Dr Kilwinning would bear me out.'

The sick woman was thinking of something. Her face was giving it painful shape.

'But if it were to be for the last time?' she asked.

'That is morbid talk,' said Aunt Emmy, 'when Dr Kilwinning is so particularly pleased with your progress.'

Then Laura Trevelyan began to laugh, except that she could not bring it out.

'Oh, I shall not die,' she did just manage. 'Or you will not bury me.'

'Laura, Laura!' cried the aunt, horrified by the suffocated words that had struggled out of the scorched lips.

'Because, you see, I am the only survivor of you all.'

'Will you take a little cold broth if I bring it?' asked Mrs Bonner, in self-defence.

Although her niece did not reply, she brought the soup, and was less troubled than usual when it was refused, as if the drinking of it had been but of secondary importance.

Presently Laura said:

'Let us return to the subject of Mercy. Do you remember those people, those Asbolds?'

'Only now that you have reminded me,' Aunt Emmy said, but coughed a little wheezy cough.

Laura was silent again for quite an appreciable space, until Mrs Bonner began to suspect the presence of some terrible danger. There was, moreover, a heavy, cloying smell that had begun to irritate and worry her, inasmuch as she was unable to trace its origin. Her niece's silence and the musty smell did fill the room with foreboding.

Laura opened her eyes. The aunt had never seen them so fine, nor so revealing. It was just for this reason that Mrs Bonner would not allow herself to look at them. She began to arrange the hairbrushes.

'If I were to make some big sacrifice,' Laura was saying. 'I cannot *enough*, that is obvious, but something of a personal nature that will convince a wavering mind. If it is only human sacrifice that will convince man that he is not God.'

She began to cough. Mrs Bonner was frightened.

'Oh, dear, it is my throat. It is the terrible Sun that he is imitating. That is what I must believe. It is a play. For anything else would be blasphemy.'

When her aunt had held water to her lips, again Laura opened her eyes very wide in her molten head.

She said:

'So we must make this sacrifice, if necessary, over and over, till we are raw and bleeding. When can she go?'

'Who?'

Mrs Bonner trembled.

'Mercy.'

Laura Trevelyan moistened her lips.

'To the Asbolds, as we have arranged. She is such a kind woman. She has such cool cheeks. And plum trees, were they? You see, I am willing to give up so much to prove that human truths are also divine. This is the true meaning of Christ. As Mrs Asbold will tell you. Won't she? It is the secret we have had between us, all this time, since she would not look at me, and I saw that it was only a question of who should make the sacrifice.'

Mrs Bonner was distraught.

'When will she go?' Laura asked.

'We shall talk about it some other time,' gasped Mrs Bonner.

'Tomorrow at the latest,' Laura replied. 'I shall make a point of gathering all my strength, all the night.'

'Yes, yes. Rest.'

'So that I shall be strong enough.'

Mrs Bonner was almost suffocated by unhappiness and the mysterious smell.

Laura appeared to be sleeping. Only once she opened her eyes, and in a voice of great agony, cried out:

'Oh, my darling little girl.'

When, later, Mr Bonner came into the room, he found his wife in a state of some agitation.

'Such a scene!' Mrs Bonner whispered. 'She has decided, for some reason, that she ought to give up Mercy, as a kind of sacrifice, to send her to the Asbolds after all.'

'Then would it not be best to act upon her wishes?' suggested the unhappy merchant. 'Particularly as they coincide with your own.'

'Oh, but she is out of her wits at present,' said Mrs Bonner. 'It would not be right.'

Mr Bonner seldom attempted to unravel the moral principles of his wife.

'Besides,' she added.

But she did not elaborate. On the contrary, she assumed an expression of cunning, to mask that secret life which she had begun to share with Laura's child.

Mr Bonner would have been content to preserve the silence.

'Oh, but there is a most intolerable smell! Do you not smell it?' the good woman burst out.

'Yes,' said Mr Bonner. 'I expect it is the pears.'

'Which pears?'

'The pears that I brought home for Laura, oh, on that night, the first night of her illness, and put down. Yes, here they are, my dear. In the confusion they have escaped your notice.'

'*My* notice!' cried Mrs Bonner.

There, indeed, were the black pears, somewhat viscid, in their nest of withered leaves.

'Disgusting! Do, please, remove them, Mr Bonner.'

He was quite relieved to do so, this powerful man who had lost his power.

When she had dispatched the odious pears, and was alone except for her sleeping niece, Mrs Bonner was the better disposed for thought. I will think, she used to say, but in all her life had never discovered the secret of that process. It was a source of great exasperation to her, although most people did not guess.

Now, all night she was ready in fits of waking to welcome thought, which did not come. Then I am an empty thing, she admitted helplessly. Yet, she had been pretty as a girl.

By ashy morning, all joy or consolation seemed to have left the old woman, except their child, who was to go too.

So she rose quickly when the sun was up, and bundling the rich sleeves back along her arms, blundered into that room where Mercy had woken in a sound of doves.

'There,' said the woman. 'We are together now.'

The child seemed to agree. How she fitted herself to the body. Beyond the window, all was now a drooling and consolation of

372

doves. In the sunrise which was flooding the cool garden Mrs Bonner forgot those incidents of the past that she chose to forget, and was holding the flesh of the child against the present. All dark and dreadful things, all that she herself could not understand, might be waved away, if she could but keep the child.

'How you do dribble,' she said, almost with approval. 'Dirty little thing!'

So she would address her secret child.

And Mercy clearly saw through the crumpled skin to those greater blemishes, which, in her presence, there was no necessity to hide.

That morning, when she was again decently concealed beneath a clean cap, Mrs Bonner went in to her niece, and was very brisk.

'I declare you have slept beautifully, Laura,' she said, arranging the pillows with her competent hands.

Laura did not contradict, but let things happen, for innerly she was inviolable.

And soon her aunt was trembling.

'Will you not let me brush your hair?' she asked.

'But I have none,' Laura replied.

Sometimes Mrs Bonner developed palpitations, which she would admit to her husband when it suited. Now, however, she realized that he had already left; the morning was hers, to arrange as she wished.

Laura turned her eyes, in that face which there was no escaping since the hair was cut, and said:

'You will see that everything is packed neatly, Aunt, because I would not like to create a bad impression. You will find almost everything in the small cedar chest. Excepting those six night-dresses – you will remember we had too many – and the gauffered cap which Una Pringle gave. They are on the top shelf of the tallboy on the landing.'

Mrs Bonner's face, that had been pretty in girlhood, was visibly swelling.

'I do not know,' she answered. 'You must speak to your uncle. He would not allow it. One cannot dispose of a soul as if it were a parcel.'

Again, in the afternoon, Laura said:

'I expect they will hire a carriage, or some kind of sprung conveyance. They would not carry a little child in a dray. All the way to Penrith.'

Mrs Bonner occupied herself with a piece of tatting.

Towards evening Laura raised herself on the pillows, and said:

'Do you not see that I shall suffer by it? I could die by it? But I must. Then he will understand.'

'Who?' cried Mrs Bonner, her breath rank from her own suffering. 'Who?'

And, laying down her work, she looked at her niece's black eyelids.

Laura Trevelyan, by this time at the height of her illness, was almost dried up.

'O Jesus,' she begged, 'have mercy. Oh, save us, or if we are not to be saved, then let us die. My love is too hard to bear. I am weak, after all.'

That evening, when Mr Bonner came in, unwillingly, he inquired:

'Is there any improvement?'

His wife replied:

'Do not ask me.'

There was some little consolation in the unexpected return of Dr Kilwinning. He was smelling of a glass of port wine that he had been invited to taste at a previous house, but which the Bonners forgave him in the circumstances.

Dr Kilwinning controlled his rich breath, and announced that he proposed to bleed Miss Trevelyan the following day. As he left the room, an ill-fitting door of a wardrobe was jumping, and flouting the silence. It was not a very good piece of furniture, but Mrs Bonner did truly love her niece, in whose room she had put it.

All the evening the old people were flapping like palm leaves.

The sick woman conducted herself at times with such rational gravity that her hallucinations were doubly awful whenever she felt compelled to share them.

'I think it better,' she announced, 'if I do not see Mercy again. After all. In the morning, that is, before she goes. You will be sure that she has only a light breakfast, Aunt, because of the jolting of the cart. And she must wear something warm that can be taken off in the heat of the day.'

Then:

'You will attend to it, Aunt? Won't you?'

'Yes, yes,' said Mrs Bonner, who was wrestling with her conscience as never before.

In search of air or distraction, she went and drew back the curtains. Such was her preoccupation with earthly matters, she did not often notice the sky, but there it was now, most palpable, of solid, dark, enamelled blue. Or black. It was black like well-water, so cold her body could not bear it. But the great gaudy jumble of stars did please the child in her. And a curious phenomenon. As she followed its broad path of light, she almost dared hope it might lead her out of the state of mortal confusion.

'Look, Laura,' she called, holding back the curtains, her eyes moist. 'A most unusual and wonderful thing.'

She stood, flattening herself ingratiatingly against the sash, in hopes that the patient might be able to see merely by turning her head.

'Do you not want to look at it, Laura?' she begged.

But Laura Trevelyan, who was again with her eyes closed, barely answered:

'I have seen it.'

'Silly girl,' said Aunt Emmy, 'I have but just drawn the curtains!'

'It is the Comet,' said Laura. 'It cannot save us. Except for a breathing space. That is the terrible part: nothing can be halted once it is started.'

When Mr Bonner returned, his wife was still holding the helpless curtain.

'Ah,' he said, and his eyes showed that he too had hoped to escape along the path of celestial light, 'you have seen the Comet, about which they are all talking. It is expected to be visible for several days.'

'I was drawing Laura's attention to it,' Mrs Bonner said.

'In the absence of an official astronomer, Mr Winslow is recording his observations,' the merchant revealed, 'and will send a report Home by the first packet to leave.'

Then the two old people stood rather humbly watching an historic event. In that blaze, they were dwindling to mere black points, and as the light poured, and increased, and invaded the room, even Laura Trevelyan, beneath the dry shells of her eyelids, was bathed at least temporarily in the cool flood of stars.

*

Towards the end of the afternoon, when the rim of the horizon had again grown distinct, and forms were emerging from the dust, they seemed to have arrived at the farther edge of the plain, from which rose an escarpment. Slowly approaching its folds of grey earth, the party was at length swallowed by a cleft, furnished with three or four grey, miserable, but living trees, and, most hospitable sight of all, what appeared to be an irregular cloth, of faded green patchy plush.

All the animals became at once observant. Moisture even showed in the dry nostrils of the dragging horses, whose dull eyes had recovered something of their natural lustre. Little velvet sounds began to issue out of their throats.

Here, miraculously, was water.

In the scrimmage, and lunging, and groaning that followed, the riders were almost knocked off, but did, by luck and instinct, keep their seats. The blackfellows, who were laughing generously out of their large mouths, ran whooshing amongst the animals to restrain them, but soon desisted, and just laughed, or scratched themselves. After the exertions of the journey and emotion of their meeting with the whites, they themselves did not much care what happened.

It was their ant-women who were engrossed by the continuance of life, who wove into the dust the threads of paths, who were dedicated to the rituals of fire and water, who shook snake and lizard out of their disgusting reticules, and who hung golloping children upon their long and dusty dugs. For the moment, at least, it appeared that men were created only for the hours of darkness.

As for the white men, dazed by so much activity, they accepted to be set apart, while hands, or swift, black birds made a roof of twigs over them. Soon they were completely encased in twigs, beyond which voices crackled. It seemed that an argument of procedure was taking place. Some of the blackfellows would, some would not. Some were tired. Others shone with a light of inspiration and yearning.

Presently, Jackie came and sat down amongst the white men, whose ways he knew, but it soon became apparent, from his sullen manner, that he was but obeying orders.

'What will they do to us, Jackie?' Le Mesurier asked. 'What ever it is, let it be quick.'

Jackie, however, did not intend to understand.

And Le Mesurier continued to sit, staring indifferently at the fragile, yellow-looking bones of his own hands.

Various blacks came and went. A young girl, of pretty, barely nubile breasts, and an older, very ugly woman, seated themselves behind Jackie, suggesting a relationship recently formed. The boy, though obviously possessive, was insolent to the two women. They, in their turn, were rather shy.

Some men came, who had painted their bodies, and who filled the twig shelter with the smell of drying clay. There was, in addition, the wholly natural, drugging smell of their bodies, and of ants. As the singing began, somewhere in the rear, in that cleft of the escarpment where they were encamped, round the trampled mud of the waterhole, under the quenched blue of the sky, the two women in the twig cage were playing nervously with the long hairs of their armpits; their eyes were snapping in the shadows.

The singing, as monotonous as grey earth, as grey wood, rose in sudden spasms of passion, to die down, down, as the charcoal lying. The voices of dust would die right away. To rise and sing. One voice, alone, would put on the feathers of parakeets in gay tufts of song. The big, lumbering pelican voices would spread slower wings. There was laughter, too, of young voices, and the giggling of black women.

'At least I intend to observe this ceremony,' the German announced, remembering a vaguely scientific mission.

He began to unfold his difficult legs.

'No,' said Jackie, in an unusually high, recovered voice. 'No, no. Not now.'

So they continued to sit. Through the chinks in the very black twigs, blue was poured into blue, until there was no measuring its depths. Sparks were flying, or stars. There was the smell of hot wood-ash, and cold stars.

Before the end came.

There was a definite end.

'Do you hear, the heathen blacks have stopped?' said Harry Robarts, the clumsy white boy.

Jackie had gone from there, followed by his two women, now as cold as dead lizards.

The silence seeming to allow their freedom to the trinity of whites, Voss went to the door, and was looking out.

'Look, Frank, Harry,' he called, 'at this unearthly phenomenon. Whatever may happen, it is too beautiful to ignore.'

His voice trembled from the effort of breaking the bonds of language. His woodenness was falling from him, and he was launching out into the fathoms of light.

'Lord, sir, what is it, then?' asked Harry Robarts.

'It is evidently a comet,' said Le Mesurier.

Harry was ashamed to ask for further explanation, but bathed in his reverent ignorance. It was beautiful. He was hollow with it.

Now the darkness was full of doubt and almost extinguished voices. The branches of trees, or black arms, were twitching, as Voss continued to observe the quick wanderer, almost transfixed by distance in that immeasurable sky. His mouth, thirsty for so long, was drinking down the dark blue.

'Yes. A comet, evidently,' he was gulping.

Then Jackie was standing in the silence.

'Why are you afraid?' Voss asked.

The blackfellow was quite cold.

But, with his dark body and few words, he began to enact the story of the Great Snake, the grandfather of all men, that had come down from the north in anger.

'And what are we to expect?' asked Voss humorously. 'This angry snake will do what?'

'Snake eat, eat,' cried the black boy, snapping at the darkness with his white teeth.

Voss was roaring with pleasure.

'Then the blacks will not kill us?' asked Harry Robarts. 'We are saved?'

'If we are not devoured by blacks,' Voss replied, 'or the Great Snake, then we shall be eaten by somebody eventually. By a friend, perhaps. Man is a tempting morsel.'

Harry, who could not understand, was comforted, rather, by his more immediate prospects.

Voss addressed the aboriginal.

'You want for white man save blackfellow from this snake?'

The explorer, however, was still laughing. He was so light.

'Snake too much magic, no good of Mr Voss,' Jackie replied.

'Then you do not believe in me,' said the German, suddenly sober, and as if he had really expected to find someone to replace himself in his own estimation.

The night was quiet as the blacks lay against their fires, under the walls of the golden snake. They would look up sometimes, but preferred that the old men should translate this experience into terms they could understand. Only, the old men were every bit as unhappy. All their lives haunted by spirits, these had been of a colourless, invisible, and comparatively amiable variety. Even the freakish spirits of darkness behaved within the bounds of a certain convention. Now this great fiery one came, and threatened the small souls of men, or coiled achingly in the bellies of the more responsible.

During the night, after Voss had crawled forward to put some sticks upon the fire that had been lit at the mouth of the twig hut, Le Mesurier asked softly:

'What is your plan, then?'

'I have no plan,' replied Voss, 'but will trust to God.'

He spoke wryly, for the words had been put into his mouth.

Le Mesurier was blasted by their leader's admission, although he had known it, of course, always in his heart and dreams, and had confessed it even in those rather poor, but bleeding poems that he had torn out and put on paper.

Now he sat, looking in the direction of the man who was not God, and, incidentally, considering his own prospects.

'That is a nice look-out for us,' spluttered the abject disciple.

'I am to blame,' said Voss, 'if that confession will make some amends.'

He sat humbly holding a little leaf.

'If you withdraw,' Le Mesurier began.

'I do not withdraw,' Voss answered. 'I am withdrawn.'

'And can give us no hope?'

'I suggest you wring it out for yourself, which, in the end, is all that is possible for any man.'

And he crumpled up the dry leaf, Le Mesurier heard.

The latter had expected too much of hands which were, after all, only bones. As it grew light, he found himself looking at his own transparent palms.

Meanwhile, what had become of the fiery snake? As they engaged in their various daylight pursuits, of hunting, digging for yams, mending nets, and paying visits, the general opinion of the sobered tribe was that the Great One had burrowed into the soft sky and was sleeping off the first stages of his journey to the earth. The whites were now ignored, as being of comparative unimportance. All men were, in fact, as wichetty grubs in the fingers of children. So the tribe remained entranced. Their voices spoke softer than the dust, their shoulders were bowed down with the round, heavy sun, as they continued to wait.

The white men in their twig hut were offered no alternative. In the silence and the course of the day they listened to the earth crack deeper open, as their own skulls were splitting in the heat.

Frank Le Mesurier began to go through his possessions, flint and tinder, needle and thread, a button, the shreds of stinking shirts, the ends of things, the crumbs, the dust, all the time looking for something he had mislaid, and did eventually find.

This book no longer bore looking at, although his life was contained in its few pages: in lovely, opalescent intaglios, buckets of vomit, vistas of stillest marble, the livers and lights of beliefs and intentions. There was the crowned King, such as he had worshipped before his always anticipated abdication. There was Man deposed in the very beginning. Gold, gold, gold, tarnishing into baser metals.

During the afternoon, this wreck of an ageless man hobbled out through the crackling heat, out and away from the edge of the camp, as if called upon to ease nature. There was a skeleton of a tree, he saw, in white, bleached wood. He could see the distinct grains of dust. After he had sat a while, unoccupied, at the foot of the tree, he began to tear up the book, by handfuls of

flesh, but dry, dry. His lips were flaking off. The blood must dry very quickly, he imagined.

And that is exactly what it did.

Bracing himself against the tree, Frank Le Mesurier began to open his throat with a knife he had. Such blood as he still possessed forgot itself so far as to gush in the beginning. It was his last attempt at poetry. Then, with his remaining strength, he was opening the hole wider, until he was able to climb out into the immense fields of silence.

The body of Le Mesurier glugged and blubbered a little longer before lying still. Even then, one of the ankles was twitching, that had come out of the large boot. Everything was too large that had not shrunk.

So Harry Robarts, who had been attracted by the paper blowing about, eventually found him, and was running, and stumbling, himself scattered, and crying:

'I told yer! I told yer!'

He was blowing about, but must, somehow, return to his leader.

When he got in, Voss said, without raising his eyes:

'It is poor Frank.'

The boy was shaking like a paper.

'And the blood running out!' he cried. 'Oh, sir, he has slit his throat!'

It had not occurred to him that a gentleman might lie in real blood, like an animal.

'We must see if we cannot go presently and bury him,' Voss said.

But both knew that they would not have the strength. So they did not mention it again. They were pleased to huddle together, and derive some comfort from an exchange of humanity.

That night the boy crawled as far as the doorway and announced that the Comet had slid a little farther across the sky.

'I am glad to have seen it,' he said. 'It was a fine sight. And soft as dandelions.'

Voss suggested that he should return into the depths of the hut, for the night air in the small hours could be injurious to him.

'I will not feel it,' said Harry. 'I will pull it up to my chin. Besides, I can protect you better from here.'

Voss laughed.

'There is little enough of me left to protect, and of such poor stuff, I doubt anyone would show an interest.'

'I had a newt in a jar, did I tell you?' Harry Robarts asked. 'And a bird in a cage. It did not sing as it was supposed to do, but I grew fond of it. Until they opened the door. This thing, sir, in the sky, has it come to stay?'

'No,' said Voss. 'It will pass.'

'A pity,' said the boy. 'I could get used to it.'

'Go to sleep,' murmured Voss, who was irritated.

'I cannot. There are some nights when everything I have ever seen passes through my head. Do you remember that box of yours, that I carried to the shipside, on London River?'

The man would not answer.

'Do you remember the flying fishes?'

'Yes!'

The man was maddened finally.

'Are you not going to sleep?'

'Oh, there is time for sleep. Sleep will not pass. Unless the dogs dig. And then they only scatter the bones.'

'You are the dog,' said the man.

'Do you really think so?' sighed the drowsy boy.

'And a mad one.'

'Licking the hands.'

'No. Tearing at one's thoughts.'

As the two fell into sleep, or such a numb physical state as approximated to it, Voss believed that he loved this boy, and with him all men, even those he had hated, which is the most difficult act of love to accomplish, because of one's own fault.

Then sleep prevailed, and the occasional grumbling of the blacks, still at the mercy of the fiery snake, and the stirring of those earthly fires against which they lay, and the breaking of sticks, which break in darkness, just as they lie, from weight of time, it appears.

While they were asleep, an old man had come and, stepping across the body of Harry Robarts, sat down inside the hut to watch or guard Voss. Whenever the latter awoke and became aware of the man's presence, he was not surprised to see him, and would have expected anyone. In the altering firelight of the camp, the thin old man was a single, upright, black stroke, becoming in the cold light of morning, which is the colour of ashes, a patient, grey blur.

Voss was dozing and waking. The grey light upon which he floated was marvellously soft, and flaking like ashes, with the consequence that he was most grateful to all concerned, and looked up once in an effort to convey his appreciation, when the old man, or woman, bent over him. For in the grey light, it transpired that the figure was that of a woman, whose breasts hung like bags of empty skin above the white man's face.

Realizing his mistake, the prisoner mumbled an apology as the ashy figure resumed its vigil. It was unnecessary, however, for their understanding of each other had begun to grow. While the woman sat looking down at her knees, the greyish skin was slowly revived, until her full, white, immaculate body became the shining source of all light.

By its radiance, he did finally recognize her face, and would have gone to her, if it had been possible, but it was not; his body was worn out.

Instead, she came to him, and at once he was flooded with light and memory. As she lay beside him, his boyhood slipped from him in a rustling of water and a rough towel. A steady summer had possessed them. Leaves were in her lips, that he bit off, and from her breasts the full, silky, milky buds. They were holding each other's heads and looking into them, as remorselessly as children looking at secrets, and seeing all too clearly. But, unlike children, they were confronted to recognize their own faults.

So they were growing together, and loving. No sore was so scrofulous on his body that she would not touch it with her kindness. He would kiss her wounds, even the deepest ones, that he had inflicted himself and left to suppurate.

Given time, the man and woman might have healed each other. That time is not given was their one sadness. But time itself is a wound that will not heal up.

'What is this, Laura?' he asked, touching the roots of her hair, at the temples. 'The blood is still running.'

But her reply was slipping from him.

And he fell back into the morning.

An old, thin blackfellow, seated on the floor of the twig hut, watching the white man, and swatting the early flies, creaked to his feet soon after this. Stepping over the form of the boy, who was still stretched across the entrance, he went outside.

*

After a fearful night, Mrs Bonner insisted that Jim Prentice go and fetch Dr Kilwinning.

'For such good as it may do.'

Her husband said:

'We would have done better to stick to the simple young fellow we had in the beginning, rather than waste our money upon this nincompoop in cuffs.'

Each wondered who was to blame, but it could not be laid at anybody's door at that early hour.

'He is very highly spoken of,' sighed Mrs Bonner, who was wearing all her rings, as ladies do at a shipwreck or a fire, for this was the disaster of her orderly and uneventful life.

'Silly women will speak highly of a doctor if they like the cut of his coat,' complained the merchant. 'There is nothing so fetching to some, as a tight, black, bull's back.'

'Mr Bonner!' his wife protested, although she could enjoy an indelicacy.

His shanks were very white and thin by that light, but his calves were still imperious, and the festoons of the nightshirt, between his legs as he sat, were of an early, pearly grey, and the very best quality material.

Because he had been her husband, the old woman felt sadly moved.

'There are times,' she said, 'when you say the unkindest things.'

Some of his strength was restored with her words, and he cleared his thick, thonged throat, and declared:

'I will tell Jim to bring the doctor over in the brougham, so that there need be no fuss about harnessing other horses at this hour. Some people can make difficulties. And fetching the doctor's man out. It is a different matter if the horse is not required, nor the man.'

Mrs Bonner was blowing her nose, of which the pores had been somewhat enlarged by the hour and emotion.

Now also, she glanced towards her niece's sick-bed. If she did this less frequently, it was because her courage failed her. She had become intimidated by the mysteries with which her house was filled.

However, by the time the groom had fetched Dr Kilwinning, and driven him through the shiny shrubs, and deposited him under the solid sandstone portico, the master and mistress were neatly dressed, and appeared to be in full possession.

The doctor himself was remarkably neat, and particularly about his full, well-cut, black back, which Mrs Bonner determined in future not to notice.

He was carrying a little cardboard box.

'I propose to let some blood,' he explained. 'Now. Although I had intended waiting until this evening.'

The old couple drew in their breath.

Nor would Mrs Bonner consent to look at those naked leeches, lolling upon the moist grass, in their little box.

As the day promised scorching heat, they had already drawn the curtains over the sun, so that the young woman's face was sculptured by shadow as well as suffering. But for a painful breathing, she might not have been present in her greenish flesh, for she did not appear directly aware of anything that was taking place. She allowed the doctor to arrange the leeches as if it were one of the more usual acts of daily life, and only when it was done did she seem concerned for the ash, which, she said, the wind was blowing into their faces from off the almost extinguished fires.

Once she roused herself, and asked:

'Shall I be weakened, Doctor, by losing blood?'

The doctor pursed his mouth, and answered to humour her:

'On the contrary, you should be strengthened.'

'If that is the truth,' she said. 'Because I need all my strength. But people have a habit of making truth suit the occasion.'

And later on:

'I think I love truth best of all.' Pausing. 'That is not strictly true, you know. We can never be quite truthful.'

All the time the leeches were filling, until they could no longer twitch their tails. Mrs Bonner was petrified, both by words that she did not understand, and by the medusa-head that uttered them.

Laura Trevelyan said:

'Dear Christ, now at last I understand your suffering.'

The doctor frowned, not because his patient's conclusion approached close to blasphemy, but because he was of a worldly nature. Although he attended Church, both for professional reasons and to please his rather fashionable wife, the expression of faith outside its frame of organized devotion, scandalized, even frightened this established man.

'You see,' he whispered to Mrs Bonner, 'how the leeches have filled?'

'I prefer not to look,' she replied, and had to shudder.

Laura's head – for all that remained of her seemed to have become concentrated in the head – was struggling with the simplicity of a great idea.

When she opened her eyes and said:

'How important it is to understand the three stages. Of God into man. Man. And man returning into God. Do you find, Doctor, there are certain beliefs a clergyman may explain to one from childhood onward, without one's understanding, except in theory, until suddenly, almost in spite of reason, they are made clear. Here, suddenly, in this room, of which I imagined I knew all the corners, I understand!'

The doctor was prepared to speak firmly, but saw, to his relief, that she did not require an answer.

'Dear God,' she cried, gasping for breath, 'it is so easy.'

Beyond the curtains the day was now blazing, and the woman in the bed was burning with a similar light.

'Except,' she said, distorting her mouth with an irony which intensified the compassion that she felt, and was now compelled to express, 'except that man is so shoddy, so contemptible, greedy, jealous, stubborn, ignorant. Who will love him when I am gone? I only pray that God will.

'O Lord, yes,' she begged. 'Now that he is humble.'

Dr Kilwinning had to tear at the leeches with his plump, strong hands to bring them away, so greedily were they clinging to the blue veins of the sick woman.

'That is clear, Doctor?' she asked.

'What?' he mumbled.

The situation had made him clumsy.

'When man is truly humbled, when he has learnt that he is not God, then he is nearest to becoming so. In the end, he may ascend.'

By this time Dr Kilwinning's cuffs had acquired a crumpled look. The coat had wrinkled up his back. Upon departure, he said quite sincerely:

'This would appear to be a case where medicine is of little assistance. I suggest that Miss Trevelyan might care to talk to a clergyman.'

But when the eventuality was broached, Laura laughed.

'Dear Aunt,' she said, 'you were always bringing me soups, and now it is a clergyman.'

'We only thought,' said Aunt Emmy; and: 'All we do is intended for the best.'

It was most unfair. Everybody jumped upon her, even for those ideas which were not her own.

But Laura Trevelyan was temporarily comforted by some illusion. Or by the action of the leeches, hoped her uncle, against his natural scepticism. At all events, she did rest a little in the course of the afternoon, and when the breeze came, as it usually did towards four o'clock, a salt air mingled with the scent of cooling roses, she remarked in a languid voice:

'Mercy will be there. They are taking her down out of the cart. I hope there are no wasps, for she will be playing a good deal, naturally, under the fruit trees. How I wish I might lay my head, if only for a little, in that long, cool grass.'

Suddenly she looked at her aunt, with those eyes which saw more than others.

'Mercy went?' she asked.

'That was your wish,' said Aunt Emmy, moistening her lips, and forced her handkerchief into a tighter ball.

'I am glad,' said Laura. 'My mind is at rest.'

Mrs Bonner wondered whether she were not, after all, stronger than her niece.

*

Voss attempted to count the days, but the simplest sums would swell into a calculation of universal time, so vast that it filled his mouth with one whole mealy potato, cold certainly, but of unmanageable proportions.

Once he asked:

'Harry? *Wie lang sind wir schon hier?* How many days? We must catch the horses, or we will rot as we lie in this one place.'

As if to rot were avoidable. By moving. But it was not.

'We rot by living,' he sighed.

Grace lay only in the varying speeds at which the process of decomposition took place, and the lovely colours of putrescence that some souls were allowed to wear. For, in the end, everything was of flesh, the soul elliptical in shape.

During those days many people entered the hut. They would step across the form of the white boy, and stand, and observe the man.

Once, in the presence of a congregation, the old blackfellow, the guardian, or familiar, put into the white man's mouth a whole wichetty grub.

The solemnity of his act was immense.

The white man was conscious of that pinch of soft, white flesh, but rather more of its flavour, not unlike that of the almond, which also is elliptical. He mumbled it on his tongue for a while before attempting to swallow it, and at once the soft thing became the struggling wafer of his boyhood, that absorbed the unworthiness in his hot mouth, and would not go down. As then, his fear was that his sinful wafer might be discovered, lying before him, half-digested, upon the floor.

He did, however, swallow the grub in time.

The grave blackfellows became used to the presence of the white man. He who had appeared with the snake was perhaps also of supernatural origin, and must be respected, even loved. Safety is bought with love, for a little. So they even fetched their children to look at the white man, who lay with his eyes closed, and whose eyelids were a pale golden like the belly skin of the heavenly snake.

In the sweet, Gothic gloom in which the man himself walked at times, by effort, over cold tiles, beneath gold-leaf, and grey-blue mould of the sky, the scents were ascending, of thick incense, probably, and lilies doing obeisance. It would also be the bones of the saints, he reasoned, that were exuding a perfume of sanctity. One, however, was a stinking lily, or suspect saint.

It began to overpower.

One burning afternoon the blacks dragged away the profane body of the white boy, which was rising where it lay. They let out yells, and kicked the offending corpse rather a lot. It was swelling. It had become a green woman, that they took and threw into the gully with the body of the other white man, who had let his own spirit out.

The plump body and the dried one lay together in the gully.

There let them breed maggots together, white maggots, cried one blackfellow, who was a poet.

Everybody laughed.

Then they were singing, though in soft, reverential voices, for it was still the season of the snake that could devour them; they were singing:

> 'White maggots are drying up,
> White maggots are drying up. . . .'

Voss, who heard them, saw that the palm of his otherwise yellow hand was still astonishingly white.

'Harry,' he called out in his loneliness, 'come and read to me.' And then:

'*Ein guter Junge.*'

And again, still fascinated by his own surprising hand:

'*Ach*, Harry is, naturally, dead.'

Only he was left, only he could endure it, and that because at last he was truly humbled.

So saints acquire sanctity who are only bones.

He laughed.

It was both easy and difficult. For he was still a man, bound by the threads of his fate. A whole knot of it.

At night he lay and looked through the thin twigs, at the stars, but more especially at the Comet, which appeared to have glided almost the length of its appointed course. It was fading, or else his eyes were.

'That, Harry,' he said, 'is the Southern Cross, I believe, to the south of the mainmast. That is where, doubtless, their snake will burrow in and we shall not see him again.

'Are you frightened?' he asked.

He himself, he realized, had always been most abominably frightened, even at the height of his divine power, a frail god upon a rickety throne, afraid of opening letters, of making decisions, afraid of the instinctive knowledge in the eyes of mules, of the innocent eyes of good men, of the elastic nature of the passions, even of the devotion he had received from some men, and one woman, and dogs.

Now, at least, reduced to the bones of manhood, he could admit to all this and listen to his teeth rattling in the darkness.

'O Jesus,' he cried, '*rette mich nur! Du lieber!*'

Of this too, mortally frightened, of the arms, or sticks, reaching down from the eternal tree, and tears of blood, and candle-wax. Of the great legend becoming truth.

Towards evening the old man who sat with the explorer cut into the latter's forearm, experimentally, cautiously, to see whether the blood would flow. It did, if feebly. The old man rubbed a finger in the dark, poor blood. He smelled it, too. Then he spat upon his finger, to wash off the stain.

The following day, which could also prove to be the last, was a burning one. The blacks, who had watched the sky most of the night in anticipation of the Great Snake's disappearance, were particularly sullen. They had suffered a fraud, it seemed. Only the women were indifferent. Having risen from the dust and the demands of their husbands, they were engaged in their usual pursuit of digging for yams. All except one young woman, who was exhausted by celestial visions. Almost inverted, she had dreamt dizzily of yellow stars falling, and of the suave, golden flesh, full of kindness for her, that she had touched with her own hands.

Consequently, this young person, to whom a mystery had been revealed, as if she were an old man, increased in importance in the eyes of the others. Her companions were diffident of sharing their chatter. They talked round, rather than to the young initiate, who had been, until recently, the little girl they had given to Jackie, the boy from a tribe to the eastward.

That day the men returned earlier than usual from the hunt,

and were questioning the unfortunate Jackie, who suffered the miseries of language. They could not hew the answers out of his silence. He remained an unhappy, lumpish youth.

Then the old fellow who had let the blood of the white man came into their midst showing his finger. This member was examined by everyone of responsible age, although there was no longer any trace of blood. By sundown, all were angry and sullen.

So the explorer waited. He did not fear tortures of the body, for little enough of that remained. It was some final torment of the spirit that he might not have the strength to endure. For a long time that night he did not dare raise his eyes towards the sky. When he did, at last, there were the nails of the Cross still eating into it, but the Comet, he saw, was gone.

There was almost continuous tramping and stamping on earth. It had become obvious to the blacks that they were saved, which should have been the signal to express simple joy, if, during all those days, they had not been deceived, both by the Snake and by the white man. So the blacks were very angry indeed, if also glad that one of the agents responsible for their deception still remained to them.

Voss listened.

Their feet were thumping the ground. The men had painted their bodies with the warm colours of the earth they knew totem by totem, and which had prevailed at last over the cold, nebulous country of the stars. The homely spirits were dancing, who had vanquished the dreadful ones of darkness. The animals had come out again, in soft, musky fur and feather. They were dancing their contribution to life. And the dust was hot beneath their feet.

Voss could hear them. As it was no longer possible for him to turn his neck more than an inch or two, he did not see, but could smell the stench of their armpits. The black bodies were sweating at every pore.

Then he heard the first scream; he heard the rattle of chains, and knew.

In the night the blackfellows were killing the horses and mules of the white men, as it was now their right. The emaciated animals could not rear up, but made an attempt with their hobbled forelegs. Some, ridiculously, fell over sideways. Their eyes were glittering with fear in the firelight. Their nostrils were stiff. Blood ran. Those animals that smelled the blood, and were not yet touched, screamed more frightfully than those which were already dying. Tongues were lolling out. If the mules were silenter, they were also perhaps more desperate, like big, caught fish leaping and squirming upon the bank of a river. But their eyes glazed finally.

None of this was seen by Voss, but at one stage the spear seemed to enter his own hide, and he screamed through his thin throat with his little, leathery strip of remaining tongue. For all suffering he screamed.

Ah, Lord, let him bear it.

Soon the bowels of the dying animals were filling the night. The glistening, greenish caverns of their bellies were open. Drunk with the foetid smells, the blacks were running amongst the carcasses, tearing out the varnished livers, and hacking off the rough tongues.

Almost before the blood was dry on their hands, they had fallen to gorging themselves, and in a very short time, or so it seemed, were sucking the charred bones, and some were coughing for a final square of singed hide that had stuck in going down. It was, on the whole, a poor feast, but the bellies of all had swelled out. If they were beyond pardon, it was their lean lives that had damned them.

Voss heard the sucking of fingers beside the fires, as the blacks drowsed off into silence, deeper, closer, their own skins almost singed upon the coals.

As for himself, a cool wind of dreaming began about this time to blow upon his face, and it seemed as if he might even escape from that pocket of purgatory in which he had been caught. His cheeks, above his exhausted beard, were supple and unfamiliar. The sleek, kind gelding stood, and was rubbing its muzzle against its foreleg, to gentle music of metal, which persisted after he had mounted. Once he had ridden away, he did not look back at the past, so great was his confidence in the future.

Thus hopeful, it was obvious she must be at his side, and, in fact, he heard a second horse blowing out its nostrils, the sound so pitched he would have known it to be morning without the other infallible sign of a prevailing pearliness. As they rode, the valleys became startling in their sonorous reds, their crenellations broken by tenuous Rhenish turrets of great subtlety and beauty. Once, upon the banks of a transparent river, the waters of which were not needed to quench thirst, so persuasive was the air which flowed into and over their bodies, they dismounted to pick the lilies that were growing there. They were the prayers, she said, which she had let fall during the outward journey to his coronation, and which, on the cancellation of that ceremony, had sprung up as food to tide them over the long journey back in search of human status. She advised him to sample these nourishing blooms. So they stood there munching awhile. The lilies tasted floury, but wholesome. Moreover, he suspected that the juices present in the stalks would enable them to be rendered down easily into a gelatinous, sustaining soup. But of greater importance were his own words of love that he was able at last to put into her mouth. So great was her faith, she received these white wafers without surprise.

After lingering some time with their discoveries, the two figures, unaffected by the interminable nature of the journey, and by their own smallness in the immense landscape, remounted their stout horses and rode on. They were for ever examining objects of wonder: the wounds in the side of a brigalow palm, that they remembered having seen somewhere before; stones that sweated a wild honey; and upon one memorable occasion, a species of soul, elliptical in shape, of a substance similar to human flesh, from which fresh knives were continually growing in place of those that were wrenched out.

All these objects of scientific interest the husband was constantly explaining to his wife, and it was quite touching to observe the interest the latter professed even when most bored.

From this luminous state Voss returned for a moment in the early morning. His faculties promised support, and he felt that he was ready to meet the supreme emergency with strength and resignation.

All that night, the blacks, although stupefied by gorging, had been turning in their sleep beside the fires, as if they were full but not yet fulfilled. About the grey hour several old men and warriors arose. Almost at once their bodies became purposeful, and they were joined by the guardian of the white man, who went and roused the boy Jackie.

Now, Jackie, whether sleeping or not, immediately went through all the appearance of waking, and himself gave an imitation of purposefulness, while shuddering like black water. He was still terribly supple and young. His left cheek bore the imprint of a bone-handled clasp-knife given him by Mr Voss, and upon which he had been lying. It was perhaps this sad possession, certainly his most precious, which had begun to fill him with sullenness. He was ready, however, to expiate his innocence.

All moved quickly towards the twig shelter, an ominous humpy in that light. Jackie went in, crowded upon by several members of his adoptive tribe still doubtful of his honesty. But the spirits of the place were kind to Jackie: they held him up by the armpits as he knelt at the side of Mr Voss.

He could just see that the pale eyes of the white man were looking, whether at him or through him, he did not attempt to discover, but quickly stabbed with his knife and his breath between the windpipe and the muscular part of the throat.

His audience was hissing.

The boy was stabbing, and sawing, and cutting, and breaking, with all of his increasing, but confused manhood, above all, breaking. He must break the terrible magic that bound him remorselessly, endlessly, to the white men.

When Jackie had got the head off, he ran outside followed by the witnesses, and flung the thing at the feet of the elders, who had been clever enough to see to it that they should not do the deed themselves.

The boy stood for a moment beneath the morning star. The whole air was trembling on his skin. As for the head-thing, it knocked against a few stones, and lay like any melon. How much was left of the man it no longer represented? His dreams fled into the air, his blood ran out upon the dry earth, which drank it up immediately. Whether dreams breed, or the earth responds to a pint of blood, the instant of death does not tell.

*

Also early in the morning, Mrs Bonner started up from the chair in her niece's room in which she had been, not exactly sleeping, but wrestling with horrid tangible thoughts. She jumped up, out of the depths, and saw that it was Laura who had rescued her. The young woman was moving feebly on her sick-bed, while calling out with what remained of her strength after the bleedings to which she had been subjected on several occasions.

The aunt looked at her niece and hoped that she herself would know how to act.

'What is it, my dear?' begged the frightened woman. 'I know that I am foolish, but pray that I may rise above my foolishness. Just this once. If only you will tell.'

Realizing that there were cupboards which she would never be allowed to arrange had stamped an expression of confusion, even of resentment, on Mrs Bonner's good face. She stood looking at her niece, who was trying to disburden herself, it was at once clear, for veins stood out in her throat, and she was streaming with moisture and a peculiar grey light. This latter effect was caused, doubtless, by the morning, as it came in at the window, and was reflected by the panes, the mirrors, and various objects in ornamental glass.

'O God,' cried the girl, at last, tearing it out. 'It is over. It is over.'

As she spoke, she shivered, and glistened.

The aunt put her hand on the niece's skin. It was quite wet.

'It has broken,' said Aunt Emmy. 'The fever has broken!'

She herself had dissolved into a hopeful perspiration.

Laura Trevelyan was now crying. She could not stop. Mrs Bonner had never heard anything quite so animal, nor so convulsive, but as she was no longer frightened, she did not pause to feel shocked.

'Oh, dear,' relief had made the old thing whimper, 'the fever is broken. We must praise God.

'Eternally,' she added, and heard it sound exceptionally solemn.

But Laura Trevelyan cried.

Presently, when she was calmer, she said:

'At least I shall look forward to seeing my little girl before very long.'

'Then you know that I disobeyed your wishes?' Aunt Emmy gulped.

'I know that my will wavered, for which I hope I may be forgiven,' her niece replied. '*He* will forgive, for at that distance, I believe, failures are accepted in the light of intentions.'

'Who will forgive, who condemn, I cannot say, only that nobody has ever taken into consideration my powers of judgement,' Mrs Bonner complained. 'No, I am a muddler, it has been decided, and not even my own family will allow that I sometimes muddle right.'

Laura, by this time too exhausted to submit to more, was falling into a sleep that appeared peaceful enough, at least, to listen to, and watch.

When she had wiped her smeary face with an Irish handkerchief that could have been a dish-clout, Mrs Bonner's first impulse was to wake her husband, such was her relief, and tell him there was now some possibility that their niece might recover from her terrible illness. She did go a little way along the passage, before thinking better of it. For Mr Bonner, a man of reticence in moments of emotion, might not have done justice to the situation. So she hugged her joy selfishly, in the grey house in the still morning, and let her husband sleep on.

14

THREE little girls, three friends, were tossing their braided heads in the privacy of some laurels, a nest of confidences and place of pacts, to which they almost always repaired with the varnished buns that the younger Miss Linsley distributed to the children at eleven o'clock.

'I like potatoes,' Mary Hebden said.

'Mmmm?' Mary Cox replied, in doubt.

'I like pumpkin best,' said Mary Hayley.

'Oh, well, *best*!' Mary Hebden protested. 'Who was talking of *best*?'

They were all three skipping and jumping, as they licked the few grains of sugar off the insipid, glossy buns. It was their custom to do several things at once, for freedom is regrettably brief.

'I like strawberries *best*.' Mary Hebden jumped and panted.

'Strawberries!' shrieked Mary Cox. 'Who will get strawberries?'

'I will,' said Mary Hebden. 'Although I am not supposed to tell.'

'That is one of the things you expect us to believe,' Mary Hayley said. 'As if we was silly.'

'Simple dimple had a pimple,' chanted Mary Cox.

'Syllables of sillicles,' sang Mary Hayley, in her rather pure voice.

'Very well, then,' said Mary Hebden. 'I had begun to tell. But will not now. Thanks to you, they will not be able to say I cannot keep promises.'

Mary Hebden had stopped. She shook her braids with mysterious importance, and began to suck her inkstains.

'Old ink-drinker!' accused Mary Cox.

'I will drink sherbet this afternoon,' said Mary Hebden.

She held her finger up to the light, and the sucked ink shone.

'Like anything, you will,' said Mary Hayley. 'Between sewing and prayers.'

'Very well, then,' cried Mary Hebden, who could not bear it. 'I will tell you.'

All the braids were still.

'I am going to a party at Waverley, for grown-up people, at the home of Mrs de Courcy, who is a kind of cousin of my father's.'

'A party in term time?' doubted Mary Cox.

'And if it is for grown-ups, why should a child be going?' asked Mary Hayley. 'I do not believe it.'

'It is a special occasion. It is quite true, I tell you.'

'You have told us so many things,' said Mary Cox.

'But this is true. I swear it upon my double honour. It is a party for my uncle, who has come back from searching for that explorer who got lost. That German.'

'Uggh!' said Mary Hayley. 'Germans!'

'Do you know any?' asked Mary Cox.

'No,' Mary Hayley replied. 'And I do not want to. Because I would not like them.'

'You are the silly one,' Mary Hebden decided.

'My father says that if you cannot be English, it is all right to be Scotch. But the Irish and everyone else is awful,' said Mary Hayley. 'Although the Dutch are very clean.'

'But we are not English, not properly, not any more.'

'Oh, that is different,' said Mary Hayley. 'Yourself is always different.'

'Any way,' said Mary Hebden, 'if that German had not got lost, and my uncle had not gone to look, there would not be a party.'

'But if your uncle did not find the German,' said the doubting Mary Cox.

'It was still a brave thing to do,' Mary Hebden replied.

'My father says,' said Mary Hayley, 'the German was eaten by blacks, and a good thing, too, if he was going to find land for a lot of other Germans.'

'Listen, Mary,' said Mary Cox, 'could you make us a parcel with some little cakes and things? If you are really going.'

'That would be stealing,' Mary Hebden replied.

'But you can steal from your cousin,' said Mary Hayley. 'Just a few cakes. And us living on boiled mutton.'

'I will see, then.'

'How will you go?' asked Mary Cox.

'In a hired carriage, with Miss Trevelyan.'

'Oooohhh!' moaned those who were less fortunate.

'You awful thing!' cried Mary Cox.

'I will tell *you* something,' said Mary Hayley.

'What?'

'Miss Trevelyan let me brush her hair.'

'I do not believe it. When?'

'The night I was so bilious, because I was nervous, because Mamma had left for Home.'

'It was the treacle toffee that Maud Sinclair made.'

'Any *way*,' continued Mary Hayley, 'Miss Trevelyan took me into her room, and let me brush her hair. It was so lovely. It was all cut off once, but grew again, thicker than before.'

'I heard my aunts talking, and there is something funny about Miss Trevelyan.'

'Oh, that! It is all nonsense. I thought: if only I could snip a little bit of hair. Her back was turned, of course. But I did not have the courage.'

'Look, there she is!' Mary Hebden pointed.

'Where?'

They were turning and burning in the secret laurels. Then they shook out their week-day pinafores, and raced.

'I will beat you,' Mary Hayley squealed.

'Gels!' called the elder Miss Linsley, who was chafing her cold hands upon the hot veranda. 'It is never too early to practise self-control.'

Older girls, or more practised young ladies, were walking and talking, and frowning at the dust that the three Marys had kicked up. Anything more graceful than the older girls could only have broken; the laws of nature would have seen to it. Their porcelain necks were perfect, and their long, cool hands always smelled of soap. Deftly they carried large, clean books in the crooks of their arms, against their brittle waists, albums of pieces for piano and harp, histories of England, botanies, sheaves of porous drawing-paper. On Friday evenings they studied deportment.

'Who will control Mary Hayley?' Lizzie Ebsworth frowned.

'I was under the impression,' Nelly Hookham began, lowering her voice on account of the seriousness of what she was about to communicate, 'I was always under the impression that the Hayleys were Roman Catholics.'

And she looked over her shoulder.

'Oh, dear, no,' said Maud Sinclair, who was plain and kind. 'My aunts know them. The Hayleys are all right.'

'This one, of course, is encouraged by Miss Trevelyan,' said Nelly Hookham.

'Yes,' said Lizzie. 'There she is.'

The three girls stood watching, their necks turned beautifully.

'Poor thing,' said Maud Sinclair.

'Why?'

'Well, you *know*,' said Nelly Hookham.

'But do we know?' asked Lizzie Ebsworth.

'She has had a hard time,' Maud Sinclair said.

'She is horrid,' said Lizzie. 'She is sarcastic in mathematics.'

'She is certainly rather peculiar,' sighed Nelly.

'She is a dear, really,' said Maud.

'I would not dare speak to her about anything of interest,' said

Nelly. 'I would be terrified, in fact, to speak to her about any-thing that was not strictly necessary.'

'Certainly she is sometimes severe,' Maud allowed. 'But, poor thing, I expect it is because she is disappointed.'

Lizzie Ebsworth was embarrassed. She laughed.

'How old do you suppose she is?'

'Twenty-six.'

'At least.'

Silence fell.

'Do you know,' said Lizzie, 'I have received a letter from Mary Hebden's eldest brother, whom I met at the Pringles' last winter.'

'Oh, Lizzie, you did not tell us!'

'What colour is he?'

Lizzie was carefully breaking a twig.

'I do not think one would say he is any particular colour,' she replied, after some consideration.

'I like reddish men,' Nelly Hookham confessed too quickly, and blushed.

'Oh, *no*.'

'Well, I mean, not so much red,' she protested, 'as a kind of *warm* chestnut.'

She blushed even deeper.

'I know what Nelly means,' Maud said, thoughtfully. 'I can think of several reddish men. Poor Ralph Angus, for instance.'

'He was my cousin,' said Nelly, and rearranged her books.

The others were sympathetically shocked.

'So tragic,' said Lizzie, who was used to accompany her mother on morning calls. 'And such a valuable property.'

'My father is of the opinion that they have discovered a para-dise somewhere in the middle of the Continent, and cannot bear to return. But that is only a theory, of course,' said Maud.

'I do not think that Ralph would be so lacking in human instincts,' Nelly blurted.

'But the German.'

The leaves of the laurels were shaking and quaking. Then the bushes erupted, and a little girl staggered out, dressed in a ser-viceable stuff, of the same colour as the foliage. It was not what one would have chosen for a child.

'Why, it is Mercy,' they said.

Maud put down her books, and prepared to eat her up.

Mercy screamed.

'Have you no kisses for me?' Maud asked.

'No,' Mercy screamed.

'Then what will you give me?'

'Nothing.' Mercy laughed.

'If you are so unkind, I shall take this,' Maud teased, touching a marble that the little girl was carrying. This also was green.

'No.'

She would guard what she had.

'At least you must talk to us nicely,' Nelly coaxed the silence.

'Who is your mamma?' Lizzie asked.

The big girls waited. It was their favourite game.

'Laura.'

'Laura? Who is Laura?'

'Miss Trevelyan.'

'Miss?' Lizzie asked.

'Oh, Lizzie!' Maud cried.

Mercy laughed.

'And your father?' asked Nelly.

'I have no father,' said Mercy.

'Oh, dear!'

The big girls were giggling. Their white necks were strewn with the strawberries of their pleasure and shame.

'What is this?' Maud asked.

'That is a marble that my granny gave me.'

It was, in fact, a marble from Mrs Bonner's solitaire board.

'You have a granny, then,' said Maud.

'She is almost fully equipped, you see,' Lizzie giggled.

It was killing. If they had not loved the little girl, it would have been different, of course. Any further expression of their love was prevented, however, by Miss Trevelyan herself, who had begun to shake the hand-bell.

Then the big girls gathered their spotless books, touched their sleek hair, looked down their immaculate fronts, and resumed their rehearsal for life in the walk towards the house. How important their hips were, and their long necks, and their rather pale wrists.

Miss Trevelyan returned the bell to the place where it always stood.

At the Misses Linsleys' Academy for Young Ladies, at which she had been employed as a resident mistress for almost two years, Miss Trevelyan was held in universal respect. If she was too diffident to distribute her affections prodigally, especially amongst the cold and proud, those affections did exist, and were constantly being discovered by some blundering innocent. So she was loved in certain quarters. When she was disliked, it was almost always by those to whom justice appeared unjust, and there were the ones, besides, who feared and hated whatever they did not understand.

Nobody misunderstood Laura Trevelyan better than Mrs Bonner, and her niece's decision to accept employment as a school mistress, after her miraculous recovery from that strange illness, might have caused the aunt endless concern, even bitter resentment, if she had thought more deeply about it, but Mrs Bonner was most fortunate in that she was able to banish thought almost completely from her head.

Upon Laura's first announcing her decision, it must be admitted she sustained a shock.

'People will laugh at us,' she declared.

There is no more grievous prospect for persons of distinction; but upon investigating the nature of the Misses Linsleys' venture, and discovering that its aim was to provide for a mere *handful* of girls, of the *best* landed class, the refinements of a home in a scholastic atmosphere, Mrs Bonner's resistance virtually collapsed, and if she continued to grumble, it was only on principle.

'It is the kind of step a distressed gentlewoman is forced into taking,' she felt compelled to say, 'or some poor immigrant girl without connexions in the Colony.'

'It is surprising to me,' said the merchant, starting on a high note, because sometimes in conversation with his niece the breath would begin to flutter in his chest, 'it is surprising that you have never contemplated matrimony, Laura. There is many a young fellow in the country would jump at the opportunity of union with such a respectable firm.'

'I do not doubt it,' said Laura, 'but I would not care to be the reason for anybody's marrying a store.'

'It would be in the nature of a double investment,' the uncle answered gallantly.

'Mr Bonner,' protested his wife, 'I am prepared to believe bluntness a virtue in business, but in the family circle it is not nice.'

Laura laughed, and said:

'If its motive is kindness, then it is indeed a virtue. My dear, good Uncle, I shall remember that virtue whenever I am entangled in arithmetic with a dozen inky little girls.'

'Arithmetic!' Mrs Bonner exclaimed. 'Although I was born with a head for figures, I always hold that no lady can honestly profess mathematics. It is a man's subject, and Miss Linsley would do well to call in some gentlemanly man. A thorough grounding is all important in arithmetic.'

'It is one of the subjects Miss Linsley informs me I shall be expected to teach,' Laura said, and added: 'Why should I not exercise my wits? They are all I brought into the country when I came here a poor immigrant. Yes, Uncle, your kindness apart, that is all I was. And now it is my hope to give the country something in return.'

'My dear,' Mrs Bonner laughed, and she was still a pretty girl, 'you were always so earnest.'

'The country,' Mr Bonner began, 'I am always the first to do my duty by the country.'

'Indeed,' said Mrs Bonner, 'we are all a sacrifice to that, what with the servant question, and the climate, which is so ruinous to anyone's complexion.'

'I am inclined to be sallow,' Laura admitted, and stood up.

'And what of your duty to your family?' Mr Bonner asked.

'I was never yours,' Laura told the unhappy truth, 'except at moments, and by accident.'

'I do sometimes wonder what is not by moments and accident,' Mrs Bonner said, and sighed.

'Oh, let us not talk of matters that are beyond our powers of control,' Laura begged, and went out into the garden.

There her sensibilities were whipped by such a gritty wind that they became partly numbed.

Yet, there were many smiling days, including that on which

403

she left her uncle's house, with a few books, and such clothes as were suitable and necessary, packed in two trunks. If her possessions were meagre, so she had chosen.

'Like some foolish nun,' were Mrs Bonner's last words.

But Laura was, and continued, content. The vows were rigorous that she imposed upon herself, to the exclusion of all personal life, certainly of introspection, however great her longing for those delights of hell. The gaunt man, her husband, would not tempt her in. If he still possessed her in her sleep, those who were most refreshed by the fruits of that passion were, with herself, unconscious of the source.

Miss Linsley did once stir, and remark to her younger sister, Hester:

'I am sensible of the enthusiasm this young woman has breathed into the life of the school, and grateful for the devotion which inspires her efforts, but do you consider it desirable that she should single out individual girls and read poetry with them in her bedroom?'

'I do not know, Alice,' said Miss Hester, who was dependent on her sister for opinions and initiative. 'Which poets do you suppose they read?'

'I must ask,' said Miss Linsley.

But she did not.

Dedicated to culture, this immortelle recoiled from poetry, almost as if it had been contrived as part of an elaborate practical joke, and might shoot out without warning, to smack her in the middle of her withered soul. She was happier with established prose, but since the arts had to be practised, if only to increase the mystery of woman in the minds of dreadful colonial males, her preference was for the study of music, discreeter than the spoken word, sketching and water-colour, if confined to flowers, fruit, or a pretty landscape, and that hardy stand-by, leatherwork, for which an elderly gentleman's services were obtained.

Such were her standards and ideals, in spite of which her girls, or young ladies of the best landed class, had begun to breathe poetry. They were even writing it, under the vines, on fragrant scraps of paper, and inside the covers of books.

Once when Miss Linsley had called Miss Trevelyan into her

study, as was her frequent habit, to ask for anything but advice, she did just happen to remark:

'Miss Trevelyan, Maud Sinclair must be reminded not to leave her belongings in the hall. Here is her Botany, for instance, with verses written on the fly-leaf. Original verses, I take them to be.'

Miss Trevelyan read.

'A love poem,' was her grave judgement.

'Do you not find it disturbing that young girls should be writing love poems on the fly-leaves of their lesson books?'

'It is usual at that age,' Miss Trevelyan said. 'Particularly amongst girls who read. They are in love with what others have experienced. Until the same experience is theirs, the best they can do is write a poem. Did you never compose an indifferent love poem at Maud Sinclair's age?'

'I most certainly do not remember,' Miss Linsley replied.

From yellow she was becoming pink. Her annoyance teetered on the verge of giggles, as she rode her disapproval with determination.

'But do you not consider it a most unhealthy state of affairs?'

'I would call it a fortunate indisposition,' Miss Trevelyan suggested. 'Probably poor Maud will suffer from excellent health for the rest of her life.'

Miss Trevelyan was really rather queer but, secretly, Miss Linsley was longing to admire.

So, briskly, she changed the subject.

'I have received a letter,' which she produced as evidence, 'from a Mrs de Courcy, who is known to your aunt, it appears. It is an invitation to little Mary Hebden for Thursday week. As you know, I do not approve of parties during term, but as this is a particular occasion, in honour of Mary's uncle, Colonel Hebden, who has returned from an expedition into the bush, I propose to accept.'

'Oh,' said Miss Trevelyan. 'Yes.'

'Now, it is suggested that you should accompany Mary,' Miss Linsley continued.

'I?'

'Colonel Hebden has expressed a wish to make your acquaintance, as a friend of Mr Voss, the lost explorer, for whom he has been searching.'

'I?' repeated Miss Trevelyan. 'But I fail to see how I can be of use or interest. It is all done with. I knew the person in question very slightly. He dined once at my uncle's house.'

'It is the Colonel's wish,' Miss Linsley said. 'And I cannot disappoint Mrs de Courcy, who, I am told, is the widow of a judge.'

'I,' said Miss Trevelyan, 'I am confused.'

As she went to her room, to revive herself for morning school with thought and cold water, several little girls who greeted her were frightened by the wind of her skirts, as well as surprised at her appearance, for her skin had turned a dark brown. But in her room, the mistress realized how little she knew herself, for she did wish to be questioned by the Colonel, though trembling already for the consequences, whatever they might prove to be.

Very quickly the day was upon them. As she waited in the hall for Miss Trevelyan and the hired carriage, Mary Hebden, in a pretty gauffered hat, thought she might be sick upon the sweating stones. She sat very formally, however, the starch of her best petticoat cutting cruelly into her knee, in every way a worthy sacrifice to Mrs de Courcy's gathering.

Mrs de Courcy, a lady in comfortable circumstances, was herself excited, though not at the prospect of her party, for she entertained a good deal. She was moved, rather, by the presence of her cousin, Colonel Hebden, a tall, copper-coloured gentleman of a distinguished ugliness, who had done such a brave thing in going off into the bush after the lost explorer, not at all a desirable individual, she understood, and a foreigner as well.

'You are singularly uncommunicative on the subject of your expedition,' she now complained to the Colonel, whom she had bidden early, so that she might enjoy looking at him, and hearing things that other people would not. 'Did you find *nothing*?'

'A button under a tree,' said the Colonel, who could not take delightful women seriously.

Moreover, he had at one time allowed himself to be persuaded that his cousin was the most delightful of all.

'A button? If I am such an idiot!' protested Mrs de Courcy. 'You are an exasperating wretch, Hugo. But I shall stop pestering, since I am not a person to be trusted with information of significance.'

'You cannot expect a man returned from the bush to be obsessed by information of significance when faced with whipped cream,' Colonel Hebden replied.

'Yet, you *are* obsessed,' said Mrs de Courcy, whom he had intended to please.

A woman of some intelligence, she had set to work early in life to disguise her share of intellect, out of regard for the exigencies of Society, and a liking for the company of men. Such ruthlessness was almost justified by her triumphs as a hostess, the success of her late husband's career, to which she had devoted herself unceasingly, and the continued admiration of all gentlemen. If most ladies were guarded, if not actually cold in their relationships with Mrs de Courcy, it suited her, for ladies did not enter into her scheme, except to keep the ball rolling through the hoops of social intercourse.

'Obsessed,' she repeated, patting a bow of the dress which she could no longer feel suited her.

'I have lost the habit of civilized life,' explained the Colonel.

'You are in love with the country!' cried Mrs de Courcy, with deliberate raucousness, making it sound like a lesson a parrot had learnt.

Today, however, he was not pleased by a display of mere skill.

'If you had been a man, Effie, you might have become an explorer. You are sufficiently tenacious. Your thirst for conquest would have carried you over the worst of actual thirst.'

'Though my character may be nasty enough, as you suggest, I would have become an explorer out of sheer boredom,' Mrs de Courcy broke in.

'Voss appears to have been inspired.'

'Oh, Voss, Voss, Voss! And noble You? Do not tell me that you are not inspired also!'

'I am a tentative explorer,' said the Colonel, quite humbly for an imposing man, 'or less than that, even – one who follows in the tracks of another, not so much to find him alive at the end, as to satisfy curiosity.'

'You are honest,' cried his companion, 'and that is why I love you.'

That you no longer love me, and I am not honest enough to admit, was what she did not add.

Instead, she said, extending her throat, until it reached the point where youth returns:

'I have a surprise for you.'

The Colonel expressed gratitude, even though he did not hope to experience surprise.

'Strawberries,' he said, dutifully.

'Strawberries, certainly. But also a bitter draught. At least, I am told it is bitter by those who know. A young woman who was acquainted with your German. How intimately, those who are close to her refuse to admit. But it is common knowledge that they were conducting a correspondence.'

'This is capital, Effie!' shouted the Colonel, at last forgetful of the furniture.

'Oh, yes,' said Effie. 'Capital. Then I shall claim my reward.'
And did.

Just then, one of the three old servants who had waited on Mrs de Courcy for years came to announce the arrival of the first guests. The mistress was unperturbed, since old Margery, although still able to function so admirably at her duties, was almost deaf and blind, as well as unsurprised.

'Let us go down, then,' said the hostess to Colonel Hebden, not without glancing moist-eyed at herself in a convenient glass, 'let us go down and allow the worthy people to demolish what remains.

'The young woman, by the way,' she thought to add, 'is under the impression that it is you who have sent for her.'

'If it were I, not you, the situation could be embarrassing.'

'I do not doubt that, in either event.'

As he followed his cousin, the Colonel was busily lowering his head to avoid cracking it upon the lintels, and in consequence did not attempt to prolong the conversation.

Guests were arriving all the time. The more established among them stood about between the flower-beds, on the springy lawns, and examined with an exaggerated interest the magnificent shrubs for which Mrs de Courcy's garden was famed, while others pretended not to eye the tea-tables, which had been set up beneath the natural canopy of a weeping elm. Except for an enormous silver urn, ornamented with shells, wreaths, and mythical figures in a variety of positions, the load of these tables was protected from flies and eyes by nets, so weighted with festoons of little crystal beads that the valleys were green with mystery and the snowy peaks thrillingly exposed. While some of her guests were indulging in the ecstasies of soul that such a garden usually provokes, and others wondered whether they were correctly buttoned or whether to recognize the Joneses, Mrs de Courcy regarded everything as inevitably humorous, weaving in and out, in her expensive dress, refusing to countenance a segregation of the sexes, ladies who would talk bonnets and preserves, or gentlemen who must discuss wool and weather. Such was the skill of the hostess, everyone was soon daringly mixed, and in no time had she organized a game of croquet for the completely inarticulate.

'I cannot bear it if we are a mallet short. Perhaps Mr Rankin will look in the little summer house behind the tea trees. I see that he is the *practical* one.'

Young girls fell to neighing.

With her experience behind her, and a cool southerly breeze, the hostess could not help but succeed. Simple people, worthy tradesmen and their wives, and sheep-and-bullocky gentlemen from the country, were prevented by their very simplicity from wondering whether Mrs de Courcy might be considered fast, whereas those others who were of the same worldly category as herself were always far too busily engaged to notice. She was accepted, then, through ignorance and by collusion, and should have been satisfied. Yet she would sometimes halt within the frame of the conventions, like some imperious lily and, while eyes admired her for her beads and spangles, know that she would have preferred the summer's *coup de grâce*.

'Almost everybody as obedient as one would wish.' She frowned at the Colonel.

'My dear Effie,' he laughed, 'if I am a disappointment to you, it is because I am in some way deficient. You must learn to accept the deficiencies of human beings.'

'There, at least, is your surprise,' his cousin revealed, giving the most exquisitely tragic inflexions to flat words.

'Why, Mary!' boomed the Colonel, and had to embrace the vision of his niece.

The latter had forgotten that agreeable smell peculiar to her uncles, her father, and all acceptable men, and was, in consequence, taken aback. In her embarrassment and pleasure, she was warning him about her good hat.

'What! Grown so old?' protested Colonel Hebden.

'And Miss Trevelyan, who has so kindly accompanied Mary from her school.'

Now he did notice the person in the grey dress, whom Mrs de Courcy had summed up – wrongly – at a glance. The Colonel, who was accustomed to walk carefully on approaching nests and waterholes, so as not to break sticks and cause alarm, proceeded to question his niece quite professionally on her scholastic achievements. He would ignore the schoolmistress for the time being.

Laura Trevelyan was perfectly at home in the environment to which she was no longer expected to belong. There were few by now who recognized her. New arrivals in the Colony, of whom invariably there seemed to be a preponderance, were unaware of her origins, and those who were safely established had too little thought for anything but their own success to point to an insignificant failure. This judgement of the world was received by Laura without shame. Indeed, she had discovered many compensations, for now that she was completely detached, she saw more deeply and more truthfully, and often loved what she saw, whether inanimate objects, such as a laborious plateful of pink meringues, or, in the case of human beings, a young wife striving with feverish elegance to disguise the presence of her unborn child.

This young woman, arranging stole, gloves, and a little, fringed parasol, did approach the schoolmistress with some defiance, and remark:

'Why, Laura, fancy meeting you. Mamma understood from Mrs Bonner that you had renounced the world.'

'Why, Una,' Laura replied, 'if Mrs Pringle understood that I had entered an enclosed order, that was misunderstanding indeed.'

Then the two friends stood and laughed together. If Mrs McAllister laughed too long, it was because she had always disliked Laura, and Laura had lost in the game of life. Now was the moment for Una to produce her husband, which Una did, as further evidence of her triumph; whereupon Laura recognized the eligible grazier of the picnic at Point Piper. So what more remained for Una Pringle to achieve? Unless the days upon days upon days.

'How happy you must be at Camden,' Laura said.

'Oh, yes,' Una was forced to admit. 'Although there are still a great many alterations to be made. It is one of those houses. And the white ant, I do believe, is in every sash.'

Una's orange giant stood with his fists upon his hips, and grinned. His teeth were broad, and wide-set, which fascinated Laura.

'And lonely,' continued Una McAllister, closely examining Laura Trevelyan. 'You would not believe it could be lonely at Camden.'

Una's husband almost split his excellent coat.

'You will soon have the baby,' Laura consoled.

Una flushed, and mentioned strawberries.

So her husband followed, with the patience of a man accustomed to coax a mob of sheep through a gateway.

After that, Laura Trevelyan remained standing, in her grey dress, in the midst of the company, and it appeared as though, for once, Mrs de Courcy had failed, it could have been deliberately, until Colonel Hebden approached, on his long and rather proppy legs, and announced without preamble:

'Miss Trevelyan, I would be most interested to have a few words with you on a certain subject, if you would spare me ten minutes.'

Knowing that he was to be her torturer, Laura Trevelyan had not looked at Colonel Hebden until now. His face was kind, although its remaining so would perhaps depend on whether he attained his object.

'I do not imagine I shall be able to satisfy your curiosity,' Miss Trevelyan answered at once, clasping her hands together as they walked away. 'I had heard that you wished to question me. It would give me great pleasure. But —'

They were marching rather than walking, and regimented words filled her mouth.

'I do not want to open old wounds, nor intrude upon your private feelings,' the equally stilted Colonel pursued.

Although wooden, he continued, nevertheless, to walk firmly towards a little summer-house that he had spied out beforehand, behind some tea trees. The schoolmistress, through necessity, was trying to match his gait, almost like a man. She was rather dark, but pleasant.

'I am grateful for your concern in the matter,' she was saying. 'But I assure you your delicacy is misplaced. Mr Voss was an acquaintance of a few days, indeed, no more than a few hours, if one stops to consider.'

'Quite,' said the Colonel, putting his hand in the small of her back to guide her into the summer-house. 'It is natural, Miss Trevelyan, to form impressions even in a few hours. But, if you are unwilling to share those impressions, who am I to force you?'

They continued to stand, although there were some benches and a small, rustic table. The furniture moved grittily as the man and woman jostled it.

'But I know so very little,' Miss Trevelyan protested.

If that little is not everything, the Colonel felt.

They were sitting down. They were putting their hands in front of them on the table.

'And besides,' she said, 'if my memories are partly of an unpleasant nature, I do not care to tell them of somebody who is, or, rather, who could be, dead. I do know, however, that Mr Voss had some very undesirable, even horrible qualities.'

'That is of the greatest interest,' said the Colonel.

'Otherwise,' she said, 'I do not believe that he would have been a man.'

If it had been Mrs de Courcy who had spoken, the Colonel would have understood that this was the point at which to make a joke.

But the schoolmistress was moistening her lips.

'Such horrible qualities,' she added, 'one wonders whether one has not interpreted them according to what one knows of oneself. Oh, I do not mean what one *knows*. What one suspects!'

She was very agitated. Although still a young woman, and beautiful, she had aged, he realized, and recently. Her dark eyes were filling the little summer-house. They were brimming and swimming.

'Do you consider the unfortunate qualities of which you speak might have grated on the men under his command and weakened his hold as a leader?'

She was looking about her. Now she was caught. The little summer-house was most skilfully constructed, of closely plaited twigs. It had a deserted smell.

She could not answer him, nor look, not even at his bony hands. The silence was stretching. Then, when it had almost broken, she shuddered, and cried out:

'You would cut my head off, if letting my blood run would do you any good.'

'It is not for my sake. It is for Mr Voss.'

'Mr Voss is already history.'

'But history is not acceptable until it is sifted for the truth. Sometimes this can never be reached.'

She was hanging her head. She was horribly twisted.

'No, never,' she agreed. 'It is all lies. While there are men, there will always be lies. I do not know the truth about myself, unless I sometimes dream it.'

'Shall I tell you what I know?' asked the Colonel keenly. 'About Voss? Or are you not sufficiently interested in the fate of a mere acquaintance?'

'For all your kindness, you are the cruellest,' she said, looking at the table.

'On my travels I spent several nights at Jildra Station, the property on the Darling Downs from which the expedition started out. Mr Boyle, the owner, was helpful, but unreliable, owing to his inordinate liking for rum. Two blackfellows from Jildra accompanied Voss to the west. One, an old man, returned soon after setting out. The second reached the station, how long afterwards I am unable to calculate owing to Boyle's vagueness, but certainly a considerable time. The old man, Dugald, talked to this boy, who seemed to be in a state of perpetual mental distress, even unhinged, in Boyle's opinion. Boyle questioned Dugald, who professed to have learnt from the lad that a mutiny had taken place. Then the boy – Jackie, I think his name was. . . .'

'Jackie,' said Laura Trevelyan.

The Colonel frowned at his audience for the interruption, and continued.

'Jackie wandered away from Jildra. He returns on and off, but his movements and behaviour are incalculable. I would have questioned Dugald personally, but was informed that the old native had died a few weeks before my arrival at the station.'

Colonel Hebden, who was accustomed to tearful women, had become conscious of a dry, burning misery. He did not look at Miss Trevelyan, however.

'Another fact of interest. Some time after the apparent disappearance of the expedition, a tribe of aboriginals, driven eastward by drought, put in at Jildra, were entertained by the station natives, and fed by the owner. On one occasion, it appears, the visitors held a corroboree, in the course of which they enacted a massacre of horses. Again, Boyle, who was almost continually in his cups, could not provide me with satisfying details.'

In the silence the two people listened to the pricking of the tea-tree walls.

'What of Jackie?' Laura Trevelyan said.

She did not ask. She was too heavy. Her intonation was one of statement, rather.

'You know,' said the Colonel, 'that is where I have failed. I will go back. You have convinced me, Miss Trevelyan, that I should. Thank you.'

'Oh, no,' she begged. 'Do not go back. They are dead. It is over. Let them be. We suffered enough, all of us.'

'Of all those men, some could have survived. Jackie did. And we must not forget the mutineers. However blameworthy their behaviour, we cannot abandon them, poor devils.'

Miss Trevelyan bit her mouth.

'Voss could have been the Devil,' she seemed to remember, 'if at the same time he had not resembled a most unfortunate human being.'

How unfortunate, the Colonel saw, now that the pride of this young woman had crumbled into a distorted pity. For a man, he was extraordinarily interested in women. He had always been interested rather than in love, except in the case of his wife, and there his love was, perhaps, more a mingling of appeased convention and affectionate respect.

But he could not continue to look at the schoolmistress, waiting for her to resume her shell, nor would words of comfort have been other than clumsy, so he simply said:

'I am sorry. Perhaps you would rather I left you.'

She refused his offer, however, saying:

'One must resist the impulse to hide in corners.'

Then she got up, smoothing her rather suitable dress of plain grey.

As they walked between the trees towards the guests, she continued to tremble, and Mrs de Courcy, who had been expecting them, came forward looking anxious.

'Is there anything I can do for you?' she asked of Miss Trevelyan, in accents that expressed sympathy, while her face was searching for some clue.

'No, thank you,' Laura replied, but gratefully

Nobody could be ungrateful to anyone as beautiful and condescending as Mrs de Courcy.

There was soon no reason to remain at the party. The luxurious tea-tables had begun to look derelict, and little Mary Hebden, running hot and sticky amongst the guests, had become, regrettably, a nuisance.

At one old gentleman, who had been entertaining her by knotting his handkerchief into a variety of clever shapes, she shouted at last:

'I could push you over if I liked. I am stronger than you.'

So that her governess decided to remove her. In doing so, and in thanking Mrs de Courcy for the pleasure her charge had experienced, Miss Trevelyan omitted to take leave of Colonel Hebden.

'Did you like my uncle?' asked Mary, almost as soon as they were seated in the carriage.

'Yes,' said Miss Trevelyan. 'He was extremely agreeable. And kind.'

Mary Hebden sighed, for all the men she knew, or it could have been that she was feeling sick from over-eating. Then the two passengers huddled against each other, in the stuffy atmosphere of oats and chaff that distinguished all vehicles from a livery stable.

'And what are your plans?' asked Mrs de Courcy of Colonel Hebden under the weeping elm.

'I intend to return to Bathurst tomorrow,' the Colonel volunteered.

'I am happy to think Amelia and the children will benefit from your consideration,' Mrs de Courcy said.

'But shall leave shortly for Brisbane and Jildra. I realize that I did not fulfil my undertakings in those parts.'

'You realized today. Thanks to Miss Trevelyan. I am jealous.'

'You have no cause to be. I do not doubt that Miss Trevelyan is a young woman of considerable attainments. Quite beautiful, too. But beauty of an intellectual cast.'

'Do not tell me!' cried Mrs de Courcy in mock rage.

In fact, all emotions must now be simulated, she knew from experience. If their relationship was to endure at all, it must do so on the frail thread of irony.

'You devil,' she added.

'I have heard that word before,' he laughed, opening his rather craggy face. 'But, in this instance, its use is unjustified. Truly it is.'

It would have taken a far more serious accusation to quench the high spirits that the prospect of his journey had aroused. The attempts of the schoolmistress to discourage him had acted as a spur, and he had remained in a state of elation ever since. A man of less developed vanity might have inquired more deeply into Miss Trevelyan's fears. But Colonel Hebden did not. In fact, he would give little further thought to one who could be of no more use to him.

15

FORCED to spend several months on his property at Bathurst in the company of his amiable wife, whose unselfishness tended to make her dull, and his children, who did not notice him at all, Colonel Hebden passed the time, somewhat irritably, in attending to his own affairs, and in dispatching letters to a number of acquaintances who shared his vice, the insatiable desire for perpetual motion through the unpleasanter portions of Australia.

Finally, when all arrangements were made, the Colonel began to move north, gathering his party as he went. The company, however, was not fully assembled until they reached Jildra.

Brendan Boyle, who had been informed by Hebden of his intention to continue the search for Voss and who had responded with his usual rather flamboyant generosity, promising a mob of sheep, two native stockmen, and various articles of tackle that he personally would not have been without on such a journey, was waiting on the veranda, bursting out of his trousers, the shirt straining on his hairy navel, when the expedition arrived. The leader and the host had barely exchanged civilities, the members of the exploratory party had scarcely begun to ease their limbs, and the station blacks to enjoy an examination of the strangers' goods, when Hebden asked anxiously :

'Tell me, Boyle, did you have any luck?'

This referred to a passage in his letter of several months earlier, in which the Colonel had written :

With reference to the boy Jackie, it is most important that you detain him if he camps down with you before my arrival. If you should hear of his whereabouts even, from other natives, I would ask you to send word to him that his assistance is needed in locating the remains of Voss and his party, as well as those of the mutineers, or, if God should grant that any of these men be still alive, their unfortunate persons.

Now the Colonel could not wait to hear.

Boyle laughed. Out of respect for his stained whiskers, he formed his full lips into a delicate funnel, and spat.

'Jackie,' said the grazier, 'did pass through Jildra a couple of weeks ago.'

'And you did not apprehend him?'

The Colonel was quite taut.

'Apprehend Jackie!' said Boyle. 'A man would as well attempt to put a willy-willy in a bag.'

'Did you at least question him?'

'Useless,' sighed Boyle.

The Colonel would cheerfully have put under arrest this subordinate who had failed in his duties, but, in the circumstances, had to content himself with a show of blazing heartiness.

417

'My dear fellow,' he exclaimed, 'do you know what you have done? You have only thrown the needle back into the haystack.'

Boyle waved a puffy hand.

'Jackie,' he said, 'is mad.'

'Madness will sometimes make sense,' replied the Colonel piercingly.

'I do not doubt you would have drawn the teeth out of the patient. Everybody always would have, except myself,' said Boyle, who was still cheerful. 'But come inside, Hebden, and let us sit down to a friendly drink. I can offer you some genuine Jamaica. None of this local stuff.'

So Jackie was not apprehended, just then.

*

What of Jackie?

On the most fateful day of his life, this boy, who had experienced too much too early, had run from the camp of his adoptive tribe. He ran a good deal at first, while the red light rose higher in the empty morning, but when the yellow sun took full possession of the sky the fugitive figure began to walk, though even then he was forced intermittently to run, as flashes of the grey soles of his feet would indicate.

The boy, whose isolation in the colourless landscape was not made less terrible by his black skin, carried with him his empty hands. He wore a girdle of bark cloth, and round his neck, upon a string that he had begged one evening from Mr Judd, the bone-handled pocket-knife, a present from their leader. So that, as well as being alone, he was almost quite naked. In normal circumstances, the isolation would gradually have been reduced by the many little measures that made life agreeable and possible: by following the tracks of animals, by looking into scrub or logs, by looking for water or honey, by looking, always by looking. Temporarily, however, his eyes would not see clearly, and the loneliness was increased by his thoughts. Terrible knives of thought, sharpened upon the knives of the sun, were cutting into him. At night his thoughts, less defined, became, or were interchangeable with those spirits that haunted the places where he chose to sleep.

So Jackie continued on his way. Whether he made fire or not, he was not saved from darkness. When it was necessary he did dig for yams, or stone a lizard, or suck the liquid roots of certain trees, or even the leaves of trees while the dew was still upon them, because to quench thirst and satisfy hunger were habits that he had learnt. Once he stalked some emu chicks, and eventually clutched a straggler and was feeling for his little knife, but suddenly preferred to wring the bird's neck.

How, finally, he came to lose the knife he could not tell, but threw off the broken, greasy string, glad for what was a disaster of some practical significance.

The absence of the knife's physical weight did not relieve his spirit, however. Because he was without obligations and there was nobody to observe, he would certainly play at times as if he had been still a child, but these short lived games did not really interest him, for duties were allocated to children at a very early age.

At least he knew the comfort of motion. He was always travelling. Once at dusk, in an outcrop of rock, he came upon the hip-bone of a horse still wearing its grey hide and, next to it, a snaffle ring that rust was eating. The boy could not help but recall the immaculate, the superhuman perfection that the splendour of all such harness could suggest. In his mind it glittered, as in the country of its origin. He touched the ring, but became more cautious, even afraid, as he approached the fusty clothes that contained the few remains of a man. Then, he kicked the bundle, and rummaged in it. It was, he saw, the last of the one they called Turner, whom he had avoided whenever possible on account of his smell, which was the particular smell of all dirty white men.

The boy lingered in that darkening desert of broken windmills and old umbrellas. Beyond the rocks, with their cutting edges of glass, he found a handful of hair. He pulled the tuft as if it had been a plant – at least it was growing out of the sand – and as he shook it free, he shivered for the sensation of white man's hair, that he was touching for the second time. This was fine, frizzy stuff, a smouldering red in the last light. This, the blackfellow realized, would be the hair of Mr Angus. He remembered the thighs of the young man gripping the withers of a horse, and his pink skin shining through a wet shirt.

419

In that desert place the light continued to deepen.

Whatever else there might have been, Jackie knew there was no time left to discover it. So he ran from the dead men. When overtaken by darkness, about a mile off, he had reached a patch of brigalow scrub, and there he lay down.

Moonlight was of doubtful benefit when it came, because all night the spirits of the dead were with him. The thin soul of Turner was hanging like a possum, by its tail, from a tree. There was a cracking of sticks and whips by Mr Angus, who would rise up very close in a huge, white, blunt pillar of furry light. The boy thought he would not be able to endure it, and was pouring sand upon his head. When daylight came, his eyes were turned up and the rims of his eyelids staring outward, in a kind of fit. But he soon recovered in the heat of the morning and continued eastward, talking to himself of what he had seen.

As he left the country of the dead behind him, he realized that he had not found the remains of Mr Judd. Journeying along, through the glare of the sun and the haze of memory, the form of the big white man was riding with him on and off, the veins in the back of his broad hand like the branches of a tree, his face a second copper sun. This link between the flesh and the sullen substance of nature was in itself an assertion of life, and the boy would hang his head in relief and shame.

Jackie promised himself great happiness in talking to old Dugald. As he approached Jildra, he began to sing. To his disappointment, however, he discovered that Dugald had become so old he was again young, and he, Jackie, was weighed down with the wisdom of age. So he did not tell Dugald much beyond some uninteresting facts concerning the mutiny of the white men. All else he kept to himself.

For it is not possible to communicate lucidly with men after the communion of souls, and the fur of the white souls had brushed the moist skin of the aboriginal boy as he shuddered in the brigalow scrub. He was slowly becoming possessed of the secrets of the country, even of the spirits of distant tribal grounds. The children of Jildra ran screaming from him and hid in the gunyahs, and when he went from there, whole tribes of strange natives would beat the trees as he approached, or sit in

no longer truly in command. His party continued to follow at his heels, because they feared to stop.

Judd was mumbling some of the time, and would look up from under floury eyebrows, like an old, deceived dog. Ah, if he could have thrown off that body which had always been a trial to him, whether hewing stone, receiving the cat, streaming through forests of tropical grass, bearing chains, crossing deserts, but to part company was not permitted till the very last. In the desert of earthly experience he must watch his hopes drying up, past and present, flesh and memory, his own clumsily reliable hand, the little suet dumplings his wife was heaping on his full plate, the innocent vein in a horse's ear, the twin fountains of his wife's love rearing high in trustfulness. Sleep was stirring on her dusty bed, and when he had bitten the nipple of her left breast, she cried out in anguish that the years had been deceiving her. He had to laugh, though. In the end, he laughed, all of us is bit. It was the kind of joke he could enjoy.

Again he was the old, baggy man, and would ride on because it had become a habit. The flies were filling the red rims of his eyes. Only a faint future was visible through the dust.

'Albert,' called Turner, who was the weakest, and who, for that very reason, still admired his illusion of the strong, resourceful friend. 'Do you see it?'

'Do I see what?'

'The water.'

'Do I see the water!'

'We must come to it.'

They rode in silence, listening to one another's snuffling of dust and mucus.

Angus hated Turner now. Always a decent, passionless young fellow, endlessness had taught him to hate. So he hated Turner. He hated Judd also, but expressed that hatred differently. Since he had been forced by circumstances to put himself in the convict's hands, open dislike could have reflected on his own judgement. Yet, he would continue to hate Judd, whether standing with him in the pits of hell, or recognizing the man from his phaeton as he drove down George Street after dinner.

'Arr, Gawd,' cried Turner, 'I cannot go on! I cannot!'

'Keep it to yourself, then,' Angus advised. 'We are all in the same condition.'

Turner's nose began to whimper. He coughed and coughed, but emptily, and was retching dry.

Judd no longer paid much attention to his companions, since he was fortunate enough to be riding in advance of them.

So that the silence and isolation began to eat at Ralph Angus, until he wondered how he might ingratiate himself with his hateful leader, Judd. That the latter was also admirable made their relationship even more unfortunate. Already in childhood, the young man saw, he had been repelled by what he most admired. He remembered playing in his little frock in his godmother's conservatory. Mists were descending, the fur of soft leaves was mingling with his cheeks, when he tripped and fell over a gardener's wrinkled boots. The man at once bent down, and lifted him up, into the world of animal flowers. How frightened he was, and in love with the strong colours of the hairy throats. Suffocating scents drove against him, and the different smell of the gardener. The man's hands were different, too, that could perform the strangest miracles. Then he had buried his own blenching, ineffectual nails in the different skin, and fought the man's laughter. The heads of spotted flowers were reeling.

Yet, the servant had remained superior in his strength and easy temper, and when the child had been returned to the ground, and run away upon his fastest wheels, he had wondered which of his possessions to bring and put in the man's hands.

So, now, the young grazier knew that he must ingratiate himself also with the hateful, the unfeeling, worst of all, the superior Judd, whose back it was ahead.

'Judd!' he called, lifting up his voice from the depths where it lay. 'Judd, I have a suggestion to make.'

Judd neither answered, nor turned, although it was evident that he was waiting to receive.

Angus rode, or forced his horse almost level with the man who had become his leader.

'Let us open the veins of one of these horses that are almost done. And wet our lips. Would it not be an idea?'

Judd did not answer.

Angus felt relieved that he was not quite level with the con-

wife, though even more with his own perspicacity in choosing her.

She, who all her life had reflected the sun, was the colour of moonlight on this occasion. Thanks to various devices of an ingenious dressmaker, including the judicious use of mother o' pearl, she was shimmering like blue water. The moon itself could have rained upon her hair, in a brief shower of recognition, and as she floated through the altered room, a big, conquered, white rose dropped its tribute of petals at her feet.

Night had indeed, taken possession. The solid scents of jasmine and pittosporum that were pressing through the open window had drugged the youngest children to the extent that they were clutching drowsily at their mother's hoops to stay their inevitable fall.

'You must leave us now,' she said softly, loosening the tight grip of their hands.

Then she kissed them, in order, before they were carried out. Very small children, she had decided, would only have lain about in heaps and run the risk of being trodden on.

Soon after this, the guests began to arrive.

There was no lack of rank and fashion, it appeared, and all were vociferous in their admiration of Mrs Radclyffe's candid beauty, while hastening to detect its blemishes. For instance, her throat, of which other mothers had always predicted the worst, had thickened undeniably. If the world of fashion overlooked the generosity of her glance, it was because such virtues embarrassed it, even destroyed the illusion of its power. Belle, in her simplicity, secretly admired those who were light and meretricious, imagining they had found the key to some freedom she had never yet experienced, nor would, because she did not dare. This diffidence, far from diminishing her beauty, enhanced it in the eyes of the elegant by restoring the strength they had been in danger of losing. They would declare:

'My dear, there is none lovelier than Belle Radclyffe, although she is not what she was as a bride. Do you remember?'

Here would follow noises suggestive of severe colic.

'Yet, one might say she is improved, in a certain sense. Such *spirituality*!'

More noises, less physical, but more mysterious.

433

'Many a hard outline would be softened if its owner possessed but *half* of Belle's charm.'

Here someone was demolished.

'But would you describe Mrs Radclyffe as an entertaining companion?'

'Entertaining? It rather depends upon what you wish the word to imply. I do know others who might be described as *more entertaining than Mrs Radclyffe*. But no woman, of course, is endowed with *all* the qualities. And Belle is so sweet.'

'And dresses so beautifully. If not after the highest fashion.'

'More of an individual style.'

'I must say it does require considerable courage to appear with such an ornament in the hair.'

'The moonstones.'

'The moonstones? Effie! The Moon!'

'Sshhh!'

'Effie, do you not realize that Belle Radclyffe has come as the Moon?'

A thin laughter continued to uncoil.

Guests were circling and wondering which others they should avoid. Only their iridescence mingled. The men, in black, were clinging together for protection.

'Mrs de Courcy, it was so kind of you to come,' Mrs Radclyffe said, advancing.

Learning phrases from the more accomplished, she did not learn them well enough and spoke them with a hesitation, which did charm momentarily even the crueller women.

'You know that I would die for you, Belle. I would die for you alone,' said old Effie de Courcy, who was doing something to her chignon and looking round.

It was doubtful to which of the gentlemen that lady would offer the cold remains of her looks, but to one she must, out of habit.

Now the insignificant figures of several poor or grotesque individuals, known to most of the company, began unaccountably to make their appearance. There was a Dr Bass. Nobody would have guessed that the worthy physician had any other function beyond the prescription of pills. There was Topp, the music-master, who had been coming to everybody's house for years, to the exasperation of everybody's girls, and naturally Topp had always been allowed a slice of madeira cake and a glass of port, but in isolation, of course. There was that old Miss Hollier, a fright in pink net, who could recite pedigrees by the yard, and from whom one escaped only by buying a lotion for removing freckles. The presence of such persons provided the first unmistakable evidence that something was amiss. A Member of the Legislative Assembly was frowning, and several ladies were looking at their long kid gloves and giving them a tweak. Then it was noticed that children also were present, both of the house, and other young people, lumpy girls, and youths at the age of down and pimples. Strangest of all, Willie Pringle had arrived. Certainly Willie had grown up, which nobody had ever expected. That he had remained ridiculous, nobody was surprised. On returning from France, where he had lived for some years in a state of obscure morality, he had painted, and was still painting, a collection of what no one could describe as pictures; it was a relief to be able to admire the gold frames.

Immediately on entering the Radclyffes' drawing-room, Willie Pringle kissed his hostess because he loved her. This drew a gasp of horror from the guests.

'What kind of entertainment can Mrs Radclyffe be preparing for us?' the Member wondered to his immediate circle.

Mr Radclyffe would have remonstrated with Pringle if he had not held him in the highest contempt. He was also uneasy at the prospect of his own approaching nakedness, which would coincide with the arrival of his wife's cousin. He still hated Laura Trevelyan.

Belle Radclyffe moved amongst her guests, and now, surprisingly, said to some, who were most resentful of it:

'I have asked you all toinght because I value each of you for some particular quality. Is it not possible for each to discover, and appreciate, that same quality in his fellow-guests, so that we may be happy together in this lovely house?'

It was most singular.

The doors and windows were standing open, and the blue night was pouring in. Two little boys, with scrubbed, party faces, had fallen asleep upon an upright sofa, but their dreams were obviously filled with an especial bliss.

Several kinder guests were murmuring how entertaining, how sweet, following upon the speech by their hostess, but most took refuge immediately in their own chatter and the destruction of their friends.

Amongst the gentlemen, the talk was principally of the discovery of the wild white man, said to be a survivor from the expedition led by that mad German twenty years before. The man, who professed to have been living all those years with a tribe of aboriginals, had been brought to Sydney since his rescue, and had attended the unveiling of a memorial to his leader that same day in the Domain.

Now everyone was pushing in their attempt to approach old Mr Sanderson of Rhine Towers, and Colonel Hebden, both of whom had been present at the ceremony.

'Is it a fraud?' voices were heard to ask.

'It is something trumped up to discredit the Government for its slowness in developing the country,' others maintained.

Mr Sanderson would only smile, however, and repeat that the man was a genuine survivor from the expedition, known to him personally. The assurances of the old grazier, who was rather confused by his own goodness and the size of the gathering, were a source of irritation to the guests. Colonel Hebden could have been a statue, in stone or metal, he was so detached, hence impregnable, but the people might have vented their spite on old Sanderson if something had not happened.

Just then, rather late, for she had been detained at her school by a problem of administration, Miss Trevelyan, the headmistress, arrived. Her black dress, of a kind worn by some women merely as a covering, in no way detracted from the expression of her face, which at once caused the guests to differ sharply in opinion. As she advanced into the room, some of the ladies, glittering and rustling with precious stones, abandoned their gauzy conversations and greeted her with an exaggerated sweetness or girlishness. Then, resentful of all the solecisms of which they had ever been guilty, and it appeared their memories were full of them, they seized upon the looks of this woman after she had passed, asking one another for confirmation of their own disgust:

'Is she not plain? Is not poor Laura positively ugly? And such

436

a freakish thing to do. As if it were not enough to have become a schoolmistress, to arrive late at Belle's party in that truly hideous dress!'

In the meantime Miss Trevelyan was receiving the greetings of those she recognized. Her face was rather white. Holding her head on one side, she murmured, with a slight, tremulous smile, that could have disguised a migraine, or strength:

'Una, Chattie, Lizzie. Quite recovered, Elinor, I hope.'

'Who is this person to whom all the ladies are curtseying?' asked Mr Ludlow, an English visitor, recommended to the Radclyffes by a friend.

'That is Miss Trevelyan I must attempt to explain her,' volunteered the Englishman's neighbour.

The latter immediately turned away, for the object of their interest was passing them. It happened that the speaker was Dr Kilwinning. Even more richly caparisoned than in the past, the physician had continued to resent Miss Trevelyan as one of the few stumbling blocks he had had the misfortune to encounter in his eminently successful career.

'I will tell you more presently,' he said, or whispered loudly into the wall. 'Something to do with the German explorer, of whom they have just been speaking.'

'What a bore!' guffawed Mr Ludlow, to whom every aspect of the colonial existence was incredible. 'And the young girl?'

'The girl is the daughter,' whispered Dr Kilwinning, still to the wall.

'Capital,' laughed the Englishman, who had already visited the supper room. 'A green girl. A strapping, sonsy girl. But the mother!'

People who recognized Miss Trevelyan, on account of her connexions and the material glories of the past, did not feel obliged to accept Mercy. They received her with flat smiles, but ignored her with their eyes. Accustomed to this, she advanced with her chin gravely lowered, and an expression of some tolerance. Her glance was fixed on that point in her mother's vertebrae at which enemies might aim the blow.

Then Laura met Belle, and they were sisters. At once they erected an umbrella in the middle of the desert.

'Dearest Laura, I would have been here to receive you, but had gone up to Archie, who is starting a cold.'

'I could not allow you to *receive* me in our own house.'

'Do you really like the gas? I loved the lamps.'

'To sit reading beside the lamps!'

'After the tea had been brought in. You are tired, Laura.'

'I am rather tired,' the schoolmistress admitted.

It was the result of her experience of that afternoon, for Mr Sanderson had been so kind as to send Miss Trevelyan a card for the unveiling of the memorial.

'You should have come, too, Belle.'

'I could not,' Belle replied, and blushed.

Small lies are the most difficult to tell.

The cousins had arrived at a stiff and ugly chair. It was one of those pieces of furniture that become cast up out of an even life upon the unknown, and probably perilous shores of a party, there to stay, marooned for ever, it would seem.

'I shall sit here,' said Laura.

No one else would have dared, so evident was it that the stern chair belonged to its absent owners.

'Now you can see,' people were saying.

'Is she not a crow?'

'A scarecrow, rather!'

'Do not bring me anyone,' Laura Trevelyan enjoined. 'I would not care to be an inconvenience. And I have never succeeded in learning the language. I shall sit and watch them wearing their dresses.'

This woman, of the mysterious, the middle age, in her black clothes, was now commanding the room that she had practically repudiated. One young girl in a dream of white tarlatan, who was passing close enough to look, did so, right into the woman's eyes and, although never afterwards was she able to remember exactly what she saw, had been so affected at the time that she had altered her course immediately and gone out into the garden. There she was swept into a conspiracy of movement, between leaf and star, wind and shadow, even her own dress. Of all this, her body was the struggling core. She would have danced, but her heels were still rooted, her arms had but reached the point of twitching. In her frustration the young person attempted, but failed, to remember the message of the strange woman's eyes, so that it appeared as though she were intended to remain, at least a little longer, the victim of her own inadequacy.

Laura Trevelyan continued to sit in the company of Mercy, who did not care to leave her mother. Bronze or marble could not have taken more inevitable and lasting shapes than the stuff of their relationship. The affection she received from one being, together with her detachment from all others, had implanted in the daughter a respectful love for the forms of all simple objects, the secrets of which she was trying perpetually to understand. Eventually, she must attempt to express her great preoccupation, but in what manner, it was not yet clear. That its expression would be true was obvious, only from looking at her neat brown hair, her strong hands, and completely pleasing, square face.

In the meantime, seated upon a little stool at the feet of her mother, she was discussing with the latter the war between Roman Catholic and Protestant maids that was disturbing the otherwise tranquil tenor of life at their school.

'I did not tell you,' Mercy informed, 'Bridget has blackened Gertrude's eye, and told her it will match the colour of her soul.'

'To decide the colour of truth! If I but had Bridget's conviction!'

The two women were grateful for this humble version of the everlasting attempt. Laura was smiling at Mercy. It was as though they were seated in their own room, or at the side of a road, part of which they had made theirs.

Strangers came and went, of course. Young people, moved by curiosity. An Englishman, a little drunk, who wished to look closely at the schoolmistress and her bastard daughter. A young man with a slight talent for exhibiting himself had sat down at the piano and was reeling off dreamy waltzes, whereupon Mrs de Courcy persuaded the Member of the Legislative Assembly to take a turn, and several youths were daring to drift with several breathless girls.

At one stage, the headmistress began to knead the bridge of her nose. She had, indeed, been made very tired by the episode in the Domain.

The platform had groaned with officials and their wives, to say nothing of other substantial citizens – old Mr Sanderson, who was largely responsible for the public enthusiasm that had subscribed to the fine memorial statue, Colonel Hebden, the schoolmistress who had been a friend of the lost explorer, and, of course, the man they had lately found. All of these had sat listening to the speeches, in the pleasant, thick shade.

Johann Ulrich Voss was by now quite safe, it appeared. He was hung with garlands of rarest newspaper prose. They would write about him in the history books. The wrinkles of his solid, bronze trousers could afford to ignore the passage of time. Even Miss Trevelyan confessed: it is agreeable to be safely dead. The way the seats had been fixed to the platform, tilted back ever so slightly, made everybody look more official; hands folded themselves upon the stomach, and chins sank in, as if intended for repose. The schoolmistress was glad of some assistance towards the illusion of complacency. Thus, she had never thirsted, never, nor felt her flesh shrivel in crossing the deserts of conscience. No official personage has experienced the inferno of love.

So that she, too, had accepted the myth by the time the Premier, still shaky from the oratory prescribed for an historic occasion, pulled the cord, and revealed the bronze figure. Then the woman on the platform did lower her eyes. Whether she had seen or not, she would always remain uncertain, but applause informed her that here was a work of irreproachable civic art.

Soon after this everyone regained solid ground. Clothes were eased, civilities exchanged, and Miss Trevelyan, smiling and receptive, observed the approach of Colonel Hebden.

'You are satisfied, then?' he asked, as they were walking a little apart from the others.

'Oh, yes,' she sighed. 'I am satisfied.' She had to arrange the pair of little silken acorns that hung from the handle of her parasol. 'Though I do wish you had not asked it.'

'Our relationship is ruined by interrogation,' laughed the Colonel, rather pleased with his command of words.

Each recalled the afternoon in Mrs de Courcy's summer-house.

'Years ago I was impressed by your respect for truthfulness,' he could not resist saying, although he made of it a very tentative suggestion.

'If I am less truthful now, it is owing to my age and position,' she cried with surprising cynicism, almost baring her teeth at him.

'No.' She recovered herself. 'I am not dishonest, I hope, except that I am a human being.'

Had he made her tremble?

To disguise the possibility, she had begun speaking quickly, in an even, kind voice, referring not so much to the immediate case as to the universal one:

'Let none of us pass final judgement.'

'Unless the fellow who has returned from the grave is qualified to judge. Have you not spoken to him?'

As her appearance suggested that she might not have heard, the Colonel added:

'He appears to share the opinion you offered me at our first meeting; that Voss was, indeed, the Devil.'

Now, Miss Trevelyan had not met the survivor, although old Sanderson, all vague benevolence since time had cast a kinder light upon the whole unhappy affair, had gone so far as to promise him to her. Seated on the platform, listening to the official speeches, she had even been aware of the nape of a neck, somewhere in the foreground, but, deliberately, she had omitted to claim her right.

'I do not wish to meet the man,' she said, and was settling her shawl against a cold wind that was springing up.

'But you must!' cried Hebden, taking her firmly by the elbow.

Of dreadful metal, he towered above her, with his rather matted, grizzled hair, and burning desire for truth. Her mouth was dry. Was he, then, the avenging angel? So it appeared, as they struggled together.

If anybody had noticed, they would have made an ugly group, and he, of course, the stronger.

'Leave me,' she strained, out of her white mouth, 'I beg of you, Colonel Hebden!'

At that moment, however, old Sanderson, whom no one of any compassion would willingly have hurt, emerged from the group still gathered round the statue, bringing with him a man.

'Miss Trevelyan,' said the grazier, smiling with genuine pleasure, 'I do believe that, after all, I have failed to bring the two of you together, and you the most important.'

So it was come to pass.

Mr Sanderson smiled, and continued:

'I would like you to meet my friend Judd.'

The leaves of the trees were clapping.

She was faced with an elderly, or old-looking man, of once powerful frame, in the clothes they had provided for him, good clothes, fashionable even, to which he had not accustomed himself. His large hands, in the absence of their former strength, moved in almost perpetual search for some reassuring object or position, just as the expressions were shifting on his face, like water over sand, and his mouth would close with a smile, attempt briefly to hold it, and fail.

'So this is Judd, the convict,' said Miss Trevelyan, less harshly than stating a fact, since she must stand on trial with him.

Judd nodded.

'I earned my ticket-of-leave two years, no, it would be four years before the expedition left.'

All the old wounds had healed. He could talk about them now. He could talk about anything.

His lips parted, Colonel Hebden watched quite greedily. Old Sanderson was bathed in a golden glow of age. Such warmth he had not experienced since the lifetime of his dear wife.

'Yes, yes,' he contributed. 'Judd was a neighbour of mine in the Forties. He joined the expedition when it passed through. In fact, I was responsible for that.'

Miss Trevelyan, whose attention had been engaged by the ferrule of her parasol, realized that she was expected to speak. Judd waited, with his hands hanging and moving. Since his return, he had become accustomed to interrogation by ladies.

'And were you able to resume your property?' Miss Trevelyan asked, through her constricted throat.

There was something that she would avoid. She would avoid it to the end. So she looked gravely at the ferrule of the parasol, and continued to interrogate a man who had suffered.

'Resume?' asked Judd, managing his tongue, which was round like that of a parrot. 'No. It was gone. I was considered dead, you know.'

'And your family?' the kind woman asked.

'All dead. My wife, she went first. It was the heart, I think they told me. My eldest boy died of a snakebite. The youngest got some sickness, I forget what.' He shook his head, which was

442

bald and humble above the fringe of white hair. 'Anyways, he is passed on.'

The survivor's companions expressed appropriate sympathy.

But Judd had lived beyond grief. He was impressed, rather, by the great simplicity with which everything had happened.

Then Colonel Hebden took a hand. He could still have been holding the lady by an elbow. He said:

'You know, Judd, Miss Trevelyan was a friend of Mr Voss.'

'Ah,' smiled the aged, gummy man. 'Voss.'

He looked at the ground, but presently spoke again.

'Voss left his mark on the country,' he said.

'How?' asked Miss Trevelyan, cautiously.

'Well, the trees, of course. He was cutting his initials in the trees. He was a queer beggar, Voss. The blacks talk about him to this day. He is still there – that is the honest opinion of many of them – he is there in the country, and always will be.'

'How?' repeated Miss Trevelyan. Her voice was that of a man. She dared anyone.

Judd was feeling his way with his hands.

'Well, you see, if you live and suffer long enough in a place, you do not leave it altogether. Your spirit is still there.'

'Like a god, in fact,' said Colonel Hebden, but laughed to show his scepticism.

Judd looked up, out of the distance.

'Voss? No. He was never God, though he liked to think that he was. Sometimes, when he forgot, he was a man.'

He hesitated, and fumbled.

'He was more than a man,' Judd continued, with the gratified air of one who had found that for which he had been looking. 'He was a Christian, such as I understand it.'

Miss Trevelyan was holding a handkerchief to her lips, as though her life-blood might gush out.

'Not according to my interpretation of the word,' the Colonel interrupted, remorselessly, 'not by what I have heard.'

'Poor fellow,' sighed old Sanderson, again unhappy. 'He was somewhat twisted. But is dead and gone.'

Now that he was launched, Judd was determined to pursue his wavering way.

'He would wash the sores of the men. He would sit all night

443

with them when they were sick, and clean up their filth with his own hands. I cried, I tell you, after he was dead. There was none of us could believe it when we saw the spear, hanging from his side, and shaking.'

'The spear?'

Colonel Hebden behaved almost as though he himself were mortally wounded.

'But this is an addition to the story,' protested old Mr Sanderson, who also was greatly perturbed. 'You did not mention the spear, Judd. You never suggested you were present at the death of Voss, simply that you mutinied, and moved off with those who chose to follow you. If we understood you rightly.'

'It was me who closed his eyes,' said Judd.

In the same instant that the Colonel and Mr Sanderson looked across at each other, Miss Trevelyan succeeded in drawing a shroud about herself.

Finally, the old grazier put an arm round the convict's shoulders, and said:

'I think you are tired and confused, eh, Judd? Let me take you back to your lodgings.'

'I am tired,' echoed Judd.

Mr Sanderson was glad to get him away, and into a hired brougham that was waiting.

Colonel Hebden became aware that the woman was still standing at his side, and that he must recognize the fact. So he turned to her awkwardly at last, and said:

'Your saint is canonized.'

'I am content.'

'On the evidence of a poor madman?'

'I am content.'

'Do not tell me any longer that you respect the truth.'

She was digging at the tough roots of grass with the ferrule of her parasol.

'All truths are particoloured. Except the greatest truth of all.'

'Your Voss was particoloured. I grant you that. A perfect magpie!'

Looking at the monstrous ants at the roots of the grass, Miss Trevelyan replied:

'Whether Judd is an impostor, or a madman, or simply a poor

creature who has suffered too much, I am convinced that Voss had in him a little of Christ, like other men. If he was composed of evil along with the good, he struggled with that evil. And failed.'

Then she was going away, heavily, a middle-aged woman, over the grass.

Now, as they sat in the crowded room, full of the deceptive drifts of music and brutal explosions of conversation, Mercy Trevelyan alone realized the extent to which her mother had been tried by some experience of the afternoon. If the daughter did not inquire into the origin of the mother's distress, it was because she had learnt that rational answers seldom do explain. She was herself, moreover, of unexplained origin.

In the circumstances, she leaned towards her mother from where she sat upon her stool, the whole of her strong young throat swelling with the love she wished to convey, and whispered:

'Shall we not go into another room? Or let us, even, go away. It is simple. No one will miss us.'

Then Laura Trevelyan released the bridge of her nose, which her fingers had pinched quite white.

'No,' she said, and smiled. 'I will not go. I am here. I will stay.'

Thus she made her covenant.

Other individuals, of great longing but little daring, suspecting that the knowledge and strength of the headmistress might be accessible to them, began to approach by degrees. Even her beauty was translated for them into terms they could understand. As the night poured in through the windows and the open doors, her eyes were overflowing with a love that might have appeared supernatural, if it had not been for the evidence of her earthly body: the slightly chapped skin of her neck, and the small hole in the finger of one glove, which, in her distraction and haste, she had forgotten to mend.

Amongst the first to join Miss Trevelyan was the invertebrate Willie Pringle, who, it transpired, had become a genius. Then there was Topp, the music-master. Out of his hatred for the sour colonial soil upon which he had been deposited many years before had developed a perverse love, that he had never yet succeeded in expressing and which, for that reason, nobody had suspected. He was a grumpy little man, a failure, who would continue to pulse, none the less, though the body politic ignore his purpose. To these two were added several diffident persons who had burst from the labyrinth of youth on that night, and were tremblingly eager to learn how best to employ their freedom.

The young person in the gown of white tarlatan, for instance, came close to the group and spread her skirts upon the edge of a chair. She balanced her chin upon her hand and blushed. Although nobody knew her, nobody asked her name, since it was her intention that mattered.

Conversation was the wooden raft by which their party hoped eventually to reach the promised shore.

'I am uncomfortably aware of the very little I have seen and experienced of things in general, and of our country in particular,' Miss Trevelyan had just confessed, 'but the little I have seen is less, I like to feel, than what I know. Knowledge was never a matter of geography. Quite the reverse, it overflows all maps that exist. Perhaps true knowledge only comes of death by torture in the country of the mind.'

She laughed somewhat painfully.

'*You* will understand that. Some of you, at least, are the discoverers,' she said, and looked at them.

That some of them did understand was the more marvellous for their realization of it.

'Some of you,' she continued, 'will express what we others have experienced by living. Some will learn to interpret the ideas embodied in the less communicative forms of matter, such as rock, wood, metal, and water. I must include water, because, of all matter it is the most musical.'

Yes, yes. Topp, the bristling, unpleasant little thing, was sitting forward. In the headmistress's wooden words, he could hear the stubborn music that was waiting for release. Of rock and scrub. Of winds curled invisibly in wombs of air. Of thin rivers struggling towards seas of eternity. All flowing and uniting. Over a bed of upturned faces.

The little Topp was distracted by the possibility of many such harmonies. He began to fidget and snatch at his trouser leg. He said :

'If we do not come to grief on our mediocrity as a people. If

446

we are not locked for ever in our own bodies. Then, too, there is the possibility that our hates and our carnivorous habits will unite in a logical conclusion: we may destroy one another.'

Topp himself was sweating. His face was broken up into little pinpoints of grey light under the globes of blue gas.

It fascinated Willie Pringle.

'The grey of mediocrity, the blue of frustration,' he suggested, less to inform an audience than to commit it to his memory. He added at once, louder and brisker than before: 'Topp has dared to raise a subject that has often occupied my mind: our inherent mediocrity as a people. I am confident that the mediocrity of which he speaks is not a final and irrevocable state; rather is it a creative source of endless variety and subtlety. The blowfly on its bed of offal is but a variation of the rainbow. Common forms are continually breaking into brilliant shapes. If we will explore them.'

So they talked, while through the doorway, in the garden, the fine seed of moonlight continued to fall and the moist soil to suck it up.

Attracted by needs of their own, several other gentlemen had joined the gathering at the farther end of the large room. Old Sanderson, arrived at the very finish of his simple life, was still in search of tangible goodness. Colonel Hebden, who had not dared approach the headmistress since the episode at the unveiling, did now stalk up, still hungry for the truth, and assert:

'I will not rest, you know.'

'I would not expect it,' said Miss Trevelyan, giving him her hand, since they were agreed that the diamonds with which they cut were equal both in aim and worth.

'How your cousin is holding court,' remarked Mrs de Courcy, consoling herself with a strawberry ice.

'Court? A class, rather!' said and laughed Belle Radclyffe.

Knowing that she was not, and never would be of her cousin's class, she claimed the rights of love to resent a little.

At one stage, under pressure, Mrs Radclyffe forgot her promise and brought the headmistress Mr Ludlow. Though fairly drunk with brandy punch, the latter had remained an Englishman and, it was whispered by several ladies in imported poult-de-soie, the younger brother of a baronet.

447

Mr Ludlow said:

'I must apologize for imposing on you, madam, but having heard so much in your favour, I expressed a wish to make your acquaintance and form an opinion of my own.'

The visitor laughed for his own wit, but Miss Trevelyan looked sad.

'I have been travelling through your country, forming opinions of all and sundry,' confessed Mr Ludlow to his audience, 'and am distressed to find the sundry does prevail.'

'We, the sundry, are only too aware of it,' Miss Trevelyan answered, 'but will humbly attempt to rise in your opinion if you will stay long enough.'

'How long? I cannot stay long,' protested Mr Ludlow.

'For those who anticipate perfection – and I would not suspect you of wishing for less – eternity is not too long.'

'Ohhhh dear!' tittered Mr Ludlow. 'I would be choked by pumpkin. Do you know that in one humpy I was even faced with a stewed crow!'

'Did you not also sample baked Irish?'

'The Irish, too? Ohhh dear!'

'So, you see, we are in every way provided for, by God and nature, and consequently, must survive.'

'Oh, yes, a country with a future. But when does the future become present? That is what always puzzles me.'

'Now.'

'How – *now*?' asked Mr Ludlow.

'Every moment that we live and breath, and love, and suffer, and die.'

'That reminds me, I had intended asking you about this – what shall we call him? – this familiar spirit, whose name is upon everybody's lips, the German fellow who died.'

'Voss did not die,' Miss Trevelyan replied. 'He is there still, it is said, in the country, and always will be. His legend will be written down, eventually, by those who have been troubled by it.'

'Come, come. If we are not certain of the facts, how is it possible to give the answers?'

'The air will tell us,' Miss Trevelyan said.

By which time she had grown hoarse, and fell to wondering aloud whether she had brought her lozenges.